Praise for
STARFIST I: FIRST TO FIGHT

"CAUTION! Any book written by Dan Cragg and David Sherman is bound to be addictive, and this is the first in what promises to be a great adventure series. *First to Fight* is rousing, rugged, and just plain fun. The authors have a deep firsthand knowledge of warfare, an enthralling vision of the future, and the skill of veteran writers. Fans of military fiction, science fiction, and suspense will all get their money's worth, and the novel is so well done it will appeal to general readers as well. It's fast, realistic, moral, and a general hoot. *First to Fight* is also vivid, convincing—and hard to put down. Sherman and Cragg are a great team! I can't wait for the next one!"

—RALPH PETERS
New York Times bestselling author
of *Red Army*

By David Sherman and Dan Cragg

Starfist
FIRST TO FIGHT
SCHOOL OF FIRE
STEEL GAUNTLET
BLOOD CONTACT
TECHNOKILL
HANGFIRE
KINGDOM'S SWORDS
KINGDOM'S FURY
LAZARUS RISING
A WORLD OF HURT
FLASHFIRE
FIRESTORM

Starfist: Force Recon
BACKSHOT
POINTBLANK
RECOIL

STAR WARS: JEDI TRIAL

By David Sherman

Fiction
The Night Fighters
KNIVES IN THE NIGHT
MAIN FORCE ASSAULT
OUT OF THE FIRE
A ROCK AND A HARD PLACE
A NGHU NIGHT FALLS
CHARLIE DON'T LIVE HERE ANYMORE

THERE I WAS: THE WAR OF CORPORAL HENRY J.
    MORRIS, USMC
THE SQUAD

Demontech
ONSLAUGHT
GULF RUN
RALLY POINT

By Dan Cragg

Fiction
THE SOLDIER'S PRIZE

Nonfiction
A DICTIONARY OF SOLDIER TALK
GENERALS IN MUDDY BOOTS
INSIDE THE VC AND THE NVA (with Michael Lee Lanning)
TOP SERGEANT (with William G. Bainbridge)

Books published by The Random House Publishing Group
are available at quantity discounts on bulk purchases for
premium, educational, fund-raising, and special sales use.
For details, please call 1-800-733-3000.

BLOOD CONTACT

Starfist
Book Four

David Sherman
and
Dan Cragg

A Del Rey® Book
BALLANTINE BOOKS • NEW YORK

Sale of this book without a front cover may be unauthorized. If this book is coverless, it may have been reported to the publisher as "unsold or destroyed" and neither the author nor the publisher may have received payment for it.

A Del Rey® Book
Published by The Random House Publishing Group
Copyright © 1999 by David Sherman and Dan Cragg

All rights reserved.

Published in the United States by Del Rey Books, an imprint of The Random House Publishing Group, a division of Random House, Inc., New York, and simultaneously in Canada by Random House of Canada Limited, Toronto.

Del Rey and colophon are registered trademarks of Random House, Inc.

www.delreybooks.com

Library of Congress Catalog Card Number: 99-90665

ISBN 0-345-42527-8

Manufactured in the United States of America

First Edition: December 1999

10   9

To the United States Marines
and the Royal Marines,
in whose footsteps the
Confederation Marines of Starfist
are proud to follow

PROLOGUE

Assilois apVain lounged in his workstation in the dimly lit control room, keeping an eye on the bank of screens that nearly surrounded him. His screens, and those at four other workstations, glowing with real-time images that ranged the spectrum from gamma to radio, provided the room's only illumination. A few of the screens showed pictures easily intelligible to any human eye. Most of them showed shifting schematics, writhing eddies, images in unreal colors, or moving graphs. A few showed rippling, particolored curtains.

Only two of the sites in the normally crowded control center were occupied. Everyone else, other than the few people needed to maintain the systems, was at the holiday gala hosted by Dr. Nikholas Morgan. As administrative chief of the exploratory mission to Society 437, Morgan was the de facto head of state. His word was law on Society 437—or so he believed. The 846 scientists and technicians at Central, the main scientific station on Waygone—which is what everybody but Morgan called the planet—had other ideas about who was in charge. The hundred-odd scientists and technicians of the off-site exploratory mission counted themselves lucky that they were posted to Aquarius or Frosty stations and didn't have to put up with Chief Morgan.

But two months had passed since Confederation Day, and there hadn't been any holidays or other excuses to break the tedium of work, so Morgan arbitrarily declared a "holiday," complete with mandatory attendance at the "gala." Division chiefs with field studies and experiments in progress grumbled or howled in agony at Morgan's fiat, but they brought all of their staffs back to Central. Dr. Morgan controlled mission resources; scientists who displeased him found their resources reallocated to someone else.

Suddenly apVain sat upright and stared intently at a corner of one of the screens he was monitoring.

"Do we have a supply run coming in?" he asked. When he didn't get an answer, he shot a glance at Suzrain Hirsute, the climatologist at the other workstation. He saw the shimmer of a privacy barrier around Hirsute and so activated the intercom inside Hirsute's workstation and repeated his question.

"Not that I know of," Hirsute replied absently. "Why?" He didn't look up from the atmospheric data he was monitoring.

"Someone just dropped into orbit, that's why." ApVain sounded annoyed. He peered quizzically at the blip on his radar scope. "When we set up here, I told Chief Morgan one of the satellites needed to be oriented outward. If we had an all-spectrum satellite looking outward, we would have seen this ship days ago." A surveillance technician, apVain was responsible for geological data via satellite gathering sensors.

Nearly all of the satellites in orbit around Society 437 were focused on a section of the planet's surface. Only one of the satellite-borne radars scanned from horizon to horizon, and just then it showed an unexpected blip in orbit.

"Hmm? What'd you say?" Hirsute asked as he continued to monitor the atmospheric data.

"Someone just dropped into orbit."

Hirsute looked at apVain and blinked rapidly. "No one's due for two months. Are you sure?"

"Of course I'm sure," apVain snapped. "Look." He pointed an accusing finger at the scope.

The climatologist levered himself out of his chair and joined apVain to look over his shoulder at the radar scope. Clearly visible just above the horizon was a blip against the black of space.

"Are you sure that's not one of the other satellites?" Hirsute asked.

ApVain tapped the screen. "It's at a higher altitude than our satellites. And it's too big. It's a starship, not a satellite."

"Who is it?"

ApVain shook his head and reached for his comm unit. He was going to give Morgan a piece of his mind for not alerting him to the arrival of an unscheduled ship.

"What was that?" Hirsute asked.

"What was what?" ApVain looked back at the scope.

"There was a blip, right here." Hirsute touched the screen. Numbers were vanishing from the screen where he pointed. "It suddenly appeared, moved a short distance, then vanished."

"Impossible," apVain said. Hirsute was pointing well below the altitude of the satellites. But as apVain looked, a blip appeared and vanished in a different spot, much closer to Central Station. "What the—" ApVain leaned forward, as though getting closer to the screen would give him more data. He made quick mental calculations from the numbers that had flashed next to the blip. "If that continues on the same course, it'll land near here in half an hour." He shook his head. "But it can't be. There's nothing that appears and vanishes on radar like that."

"Could it be the thing I saw?"

ApVain shook his head. "Too far away—nothing moves that fast in atmosphere." His fingers started tapping out Chief Morgan's code on his comm unit, then apVain stopped and stared at the scope again. A smaller blip dropped out of and curved away from the orbiting starship. He put the comm unit down and tapped keys on the radar control board. New numbers scrolled across the screen.

"That starship just dropped a shuttle on course to land at Aquarius Station. Why would a starship drop someone on Aquarius instead of coming to Central first?"

Hirsute thought about it for a moment. He swallowed and croaked, "Pirates. Only pirates would go to an outstation instead of landing at the main settlement."

"Oh hell." ApVain snatched up his comm unit and frantically tapped out Chief Morgan's code.

Before he finished, another blip appeared, far too close to be the same object headed for Aquarius Station.

"It's landing here!"

"But they haven't signaled us."

ApVain scrabbled at his console controls. He brought up the visual from the surveillance camera outside the control center just as something struck it and the picture dissolved into static. Frantic, he fumbled with his comm unit and tapped in the numbers again. "Chief," he said when his call was answered, "I think we've got trouble. Looks like there's a starship in orbit; a shuttle is headed toward Aquarius and someone just landed here." His jaw clenched as he listened to Morgan's reply. "I'm not playing some kind of practical joke," he snapped. "They just came in out of nowhere. No signals, no nothing. Someone is here. They might be pirates."

Suddenly the starship in orbit just disappeared from the screen and the satellites registered a huge explosion.

As apVain was explaining that the starship appeared to have been destroyed, the door to the control center slammed open and the two men jerked their attention to it. Hirsute's scream was cut short, becoming a gurgle as he collapsed.

CHAPTER
ONE

"Owen, old pal, what are we going to do with ourselves tonight?" Lance Corporal Joseph "Shadow" Dean asked his woo, back in the first fire team cubicle after Retreat formation the day of the big fight. Owen glowed a happy pink at the sound of Dean's voice and wobbled precariously on the back of the chair where it had hopped when the Marine came into the room. Its big, staring eyes regarded Dean affectionately; at least Dean sometimes thought they did. "Wooo, wooo," Dean said softly as he shrugged out of his utilities.

The creature glowed a brighter pink and responded, "Woooo, wooo." Shortly before he went on home leave, Lance Corporal Dave "Hammer" Schultz, Dean's teammate, had said, "I do believe Owen thinks you're his daddy!"

"Impossible!" Corporal Leach, the first fire team leader had interjected, "goddamn Dean-o is just too damn ugly to be anybody's daddy."

Dean had grown very fond of the woo since he'd brought it back from Diamunde. In fact, Owen had become Company L's mascot. Even Top Myer was deferring to Owen when he met him on his daily barracks walk-throughs.

"I know how Marines like to start menageries of pets and call them mascots," the old first sergeant had remarked to Captain Conorado one day shortly after the company had returned from Diamunde, "but I've always been against it. Jesu, Skipper," he added, "first thing you know, the company area begins to look like a goddamn zoo! Marines get ahold of all these damn things and then they're underfoot and shitting all over everything. Why, First Sergeant Tacitus, over in Kilo Company, he caught one of his corporals, brought back a clutch of raptor eggs from Wanderjahr and was hatching them in a homemade incubator behind his wall locker! You know, those things they call wolves on Wanderjahr. Corps oughta issue a general order forbidding pets in the damn barracks, instead of leaving the decision up to unit commanders, beggin' your pardon, sir," he added quickly.

"I know, I know, Top," the company commander replied, "but in this case we're going to make an exception." And so Owen stayed with the company. Almost as if the woo understood Top Myer's opposition to his presence in the company area, whenever it saw the first sergeant it jumped up where it was plainly visible and began to glow a bright pink, something woos were said to do when content. To the Marines of Company L it meant Owen was offering the first sergeant a friendly greeting.

"He likes you, Top, he really does," Gunnery Sergeant Bass whispered into the first sergeant's ear. "He doesn't do that for anyone else but Dean. Damnedest thing I ever saw."

Gradually Top Myer was won over, and before long he casually acknowledged Owen's presence whenever the two met. Since woos disposed of their body waste through respiration, like plants, Owen never left a mess behind, and that counted heavily in his favor with the first sergeant.

Owen was thriving on Thorsfinni's World. The rocks there, from which the woo's digestive system extracted necessary trace elements, suited him superbly. All the Marines had to do to keep Owen glowing a satisfied pink was to provide him every morning with chunks of rock they gathered off the parade ground.

Woos were said to be intelligent, but to what degree was open to debate. They were the highest life-form yet found on the planet Diamunde, and people who'd had long contact with them swore they were more intelligent than the terrestrial canine, but that evidence was purely anecdotal and had not been verified in the laboratory.

After his experience with the woos on Diamunde, however, Dean knew there was much more to the creatures than the little bit science had been able to deduce. He had accepted Owen as a companion, not a pet, and named him in honor of a writer, A. Block Owen, whose adventure stories he'd read as a boy. Dean's first actual combat operation cured him forever of reading war fiction, but he'd enjoyed Mr. Owen's stories, and besides, the woo somewhat resembled the writer, with his bulbous head and saucerlike eyes. Since most Marines had read Mr. Owen's swashbuckling adolescent novels as boys themselves, the woo's new name was instantly recognized by the men of Company L.

But despite Owen's company, something was definitely missing from Lance Corporal Joseph Dean's life. With so many of the other Marines of third platoon on leave, winding down after the hell of Diamunde was proving much more difficult than it had been after 34th Fleet Initial Strike Team's operations on Elneal and Wanderjahr. Schultz and Leach had gone on leave, but as much as Dean dreamed of having a room to himself, as do all men who live in barracks, he was lonely in the cubicle without the other two Marines. His two closest buddies, MacIlargie in the first squad's third fire team and Claypoole over in second squad, were also on leave. Dean had become very close to "Wolfman" MacIlargie on the deployment to Diamunde—where Dean earned the nickname "Shadow," because he'd stuck close enough to the Confederation's ambassador to save her life. He itched to go to town with Wolfman and reminisce, or sit around the barracks with the other men of the third platoon, reliving the details of that experience with the other Marines.

Gunnery Sergeant Charlie Bass, third platoon's commander since the kidnapping and murder of the previous commander, had taken a month's leave in New Oslo, where he was staying with his squeeze. He'd invited Dean and the other men of the platoon who'd stayed behind to visit him there, but Dean had declined because he thought his presence would be an imposition. Captain Conorado, Company L's commander, had offered to put Dean up for a weekend with his family in New Oslo—officers were allowed to marry and bring their families to their FIST bases—but Dean politely declined that offer too. Although the generosity of the offer pleased him enormously, he would have felt too awkward in the Skipper's home to be comfortable there.

Dean had decided against going on leave himself, despite the fact that he was eligible and Top Myer had encouraged him to go.

"Dean," the first sergeant had told him, "you're at the top of the list for home leave, with your mother dying and all. And I thought you said you wanted to go back to Wanderjahr—for whatever reason, I'll never know." Of course, by then everyone in the 34th knew that Dean had had an affair with Hway Kuetgens, the oligarch's daughter.

"I know, First Sergeant, but, well, my mom's been gone quite a while now and I have nobody else back on Old Earth I'd care to see. Maybe when I ship over I'll go back there—or somewhere."

Top Myer had been delighted that Dean was thinking about reenlisting, but all he said was, "Well, can't force you to take leave, son. But if you stay at Camp Ellis, I'll have you on shit details from dawn to dusk, until the guys get back and we go on our next deployment."

In fact, Dean had no place he wanted to go, and after thinking it over, he realized that returning to Wanderjahr, where he'd met the first love of his life, just would not work. As a new oligarch, filling her mother's place as ruler of Morgenluft Staat, Hway would not be free to spend much time with him. But with so many familiar faces missing, hanging around Camp Ellis was no fun either. And at night he had recurring dreams of combat on Diamunde that did not leave his mind when he was awake.

Brigadier Sturgeon understood very well what Lance Corporal Dean was going through. He knew that readjusting from combat to garrison duty was not an easy transition for young men—and by no means was Dean the only Marine in

34th FIST who was having that problem, although most would never mention it. The brigadier had never put much faith in psychiatry or so-called "grief counseling," but that kind of help was available—professional consultation and treatment with various drugs—for those who wanted it. As far as he was concerned, that was for sailors and soldiers, not Marines. The FIST commander knew from personal experience that long-term healing was best assured through close association with other men who had shared the same experiences. As long as the Marines of the 34th hung together, they could get through anything. But with so many of the old hands away, it was proving difficult for the younger men like Dean.

So Brigadier Sturgeon ordered the days filled with the Marines' age-old prescription for depression and distraction: hard physical labor. The days started with vigorous calisthenics on the grinder, followed by training sessions on weapons and tactics, interspersed with cross-country marches and close-order drill, where the platoons in each company competed with each other to see which could march faster, longer, and harder; on the parade ground the corporals and sergeants had their men shouting the age-old cadences marching men rely on to make the miles go by more quickly:

I don't know, but I've been told
'Finni pussy is mighty cold!

And there were the endless company details that ranged from repeated cleaning of weapons and equipment—and the attendant in-ranks inspections to make sure the gear was *really* clean!—to whitewashing the rocks along the walkways outside the barracks. And Dean spent many hours working with Sergeant Souavi in the company supply room, conducting interminable inventories.

Camp Major Pete Ellis, 34th FIST's home base, was located on Thorsfinni's World, one of the most distant human-settled worlds, and was considered a hardship post. Even so, it was not without places where healthy young Marines might find innocent diversions. The night of the big fight, Captain Conorado had dismissed Company L early, so Dean found himself at loose ends. He really didn't want to go into Bronnoysund, the liberty town just outside the main gate of Camp Ellis, but the more he thought about what lay before him that weekend, the more a cold beer and a thick reindeer steak seemed appealing. Besides, there was Erika—a slim dark-haired girl at Big Barb's who spoke such flawless English—and she was available. Thinking of her caused a pleasant tingling in Dean's loins.

"So let's go to Big Barb's," he said to Owen. Big Barb's was the ship's chandlers, bar, and whorehouse in Bronnoysund that served as Company L's unofficial command post whenever the men were in town. The woo wobbled and glowed pleasantly at the words. Sometimes Dean thought Owen actually did understand English. Dean had met an old prospector on Diamunde who swore that woos could read human thoughts.

Owen fascinated the 'Finnis. They had never seen such a creature before, and the woo enjoyed their good-natured attention. Dean certainly did: He could never pay for any beer when the 'Finnis were admiring Owen. And on those nights when Dean drank too much beer, Owen perched happily on his shoulder, lighting the way as the young Marine staggered to the parking lot for the bus back to Camp Ellis.

At first that night, Big Barb's was not crowded. The few 'Finnis who were there, mostly men off the fishing ships that anchored in the harbor, bought Dean a round of beer and played with Owen, but after a few pleasantries, returned to their endless card games.

"Where's Erika?" Dean asked a waitress as he seated himself at a vacant table. She nodded upstairs, and Dean felt his heart sink, thinking she was with another man. Owen, who'd been glowing bright pink when they entered the bar, turned a dull orange, almost matching Dean's mood.

It was only then that Dean noticed Corporal Pasquin sitting by himself in a far corner, nursing a beer. Since they were in the same platoon, Dean knew he should have at least acknowledged the corporal's presence. But since he was off duty, miffed at Erika, and the corporal didn't like him anyway, Dean just ignored him. Pasquin glared at him but kept to himself.

"Owen!" Erika shrieked as she came running down the broad staircase that led to the second floor, where the girls had their rooms. She ran to Dean's table and placed a large kiss on Owen's bulbous forehead.

"What about me?" Dean asked sourly. There were times when he felt ambiguous about Owen being around.

"Ach, my darling Joe!" Erika put one hand behind Dean's head and kissed him full on the lips, her long dark hair enfolding them both in its rich tresses. She smelled fresh and clean, and her teeth scraped pleasantly against his. Momentarily, Dean forgot about his ego. She sat down and put a soft hand on his thigh. The waitress brought another schooner of ale, from which Erika enthusiastically poured herself a glass. She raised it, toasted Owen, and drank thirstily. Dean laughed and did the same. Together they finished the schooner and ordered a second one.

"I bought myself some nice thinks today, Joe," Erika said, making circles with her finger on the wet tabletop.

"Yeah?"

"That's why I was a little late coming down," she added.

Dean brightened immediately. "Oh," he responded.

"Would you like to see dem?" she asked quietly.

Upstairs, Dean put Owen on the mantel, then undressed and crawled under the covers with Erika. "Where's your new 'thinks'?" he asked as he snuggled down beside her.

"You see dem, Joe! Dere on the back of the chair!"

They both laughed. Dean rolled over on top of Erika. Then he froze.

"Vat is it? Vat's wrong?" she asked.

Dean shook his head. "That goddamned Owen!"

"Oh, Joe, you shouldn't talk like dat!"

"No, I can't do it while he's sitting up there. It's—It's like somebody's watching!"

Indeed, Owen *was* watching, his luminous eyes staring unblinking down on the pair. Dean leaped naked out of the bed, opened the closet and thrust Owen inside. "You take it easy in there, old buddy. I got some heavy work to do out here," Dean said, and closed the door. For the next hour pink light seeped out from beneath the closet door, dimly illuminating the two figures as they enjoyed themselves on the bed.

Things had picked up at the bar by the time the pair descended the big staircase. Several crewmen from a fishing vessel that had just come into port were standing there, drinking and talking loudly. A big man with a full beard slammed his mug down hard as the couple crossed the floor to an empty table and shouted, "Erika!" then something in Norse Dean didn't catch, but his gesture was clear enough.

"Never mind him." Erika shrugged as she guided Dean toward a table with one arm. "He tinks he's got a claim on me. He doesn't. Dat odder one too." She nodded at Pasquin, who was glaring sullenly at them from his corner. "He haf dirty mind." She shook her head disgustedly. She squeezed Dean's arm in hers. Owen perched comfortably on an unoccupied chair at their table.

The big, bearded man shouted again, louder this time, and in English, "You goddamn Marine, leaf my Erika alone!"

"Uh-oh," Dean muttered, his back to the bar. Owen jumped onto Dean's shoulder and emitted several quick bright flashes of white light. Dean whirled around. The man was already halfway to where he stood, a wicked fillet knife grasped in one hand. Owen's flashing had temporarily blinded the man, but he blinked rapidly several times and came on, his eyes tiny slits against the light. Owen leaped back toward Erika. The attacker carried the knife extended before him in his right hand and low, a foot or two from his right side.

Dean feinted toward the attacker's knife arm, stepped inside his reach and punched him solidly on the left ear as the man whirled past. The fisherman shook his head and pivoted toward Dean, who stepped in quickly again and smashed his fist onto the tip of the attacker's nose. Blood spurted everywhere and the man stepped back a pace but held firmly onto the knife, so Dean kicked him solidly in the groin. The man doubled over, gasping, and the knife clattered harmlessly onto the sawdust floor. Dean rammed his knee hard under the fisherman's chin, and the sound of his teeth slamming together could be heard all the way up on the second floor.

Breathing heavily, more from fear than exertion, Dean stood in a fighting stance over his opponent as the fisherman groped on the floor for the knife, muttering curses while the blood from his broken nose splattered the sawdust. Dean's legs felt rubbery under him, but at the same time he was wildly elated. Without even thinking, he'd done just what his instructors in unarmed combat had taught him—attacked relentlessly until his opponent was down. But the man wasn't out yet. Dean wound up to deliver the knockout blow to the back of his head.

Before he could, a tremendous weight smashed into Dean's right shoulder and bounced sickeningly off the side of his head. Big Barb herself had laid him low with a chair. The next thing he knew, he was being dragged and pulled through the sawdust as men threw punches all around him. With Erika's help, he got to his feet and they staggered out the door into the cold night. Back inside, pandemonium reigned as the patrons carried on the fight. Big Barb was among them, screaming for order and bashing heads with the best. She wasn't called "Big" Barb for nothing.

Dean was bleeding from the blow struck to the side of his head. Erika found a hankerchief and dabbed at the blood. She was laughing. "My wunnerful Marine!" she said. "You knock him silly!"

Dean began to laugh too. Owen, who'd stayed firmly attached to Erika's shoulder throughout, glowed a subdued pink.

They found a restaurant a few blocks up the street and

slipped inside. The place was warm and smoky, crowded with late evening diners. Heads turned when people noticed Owen sitting on Erika's shoulder, but evidently nobody had a second thought about the big bloody smear on the side of Dean's head, or the sawdust that still clung to his liberty utilities. The 'Finnis were brawlers, and no one in the settlement considered a black eye or a fat lip out of the ordinary on a man or a woman.

Dean and Erika ordered two huge reindeer steaks and large schooners of beer, and when they were done with the meal, Erika ordered Clintons and both lighted up.

"Who was that guy?" Dean eventually asked.

Erika shrugged. "Karl. He is nice enough man when not drinking, but nobody special. You goddamn Marines, going away all the time, what's a girl to do?"

Dean nodded and gingerly felt the side of his head. "That goddamned Barb, jeez."

"She keep order dat way." Erika laughed. "Besides, you pick up one of dem chairs, yah? You know, dey could be lots heavier? She make dem out of soft wood 'cause dey get broke so much, and besides, she don't want to kill her customers!"

"Couldn't prove it by me," Dean said ruefully. His fingers came away with crusted blood on them. Well, a hot shower would take care of that.

As if reading his thoughts, Erika said, "We take good, long, hot shower, we get back to my place, Joe." She winked and blew a cloud of cigar smoke into the air. Owen, who did not like tobacco smoke, sat glum and dull gray on Erika's shoulder.

Outside they walked arm in arm down the dark street, bodies close together. Impervious to the cold night air, Owen dozed on Erika's shoulder. Suddenly, a horrible face, nose twisted, bulbous, and red over a leering mouth full of broken teeth, popped up before them. It was Karl! He held one hand over his eyes before Owen could go into his flashing routine.

"You broken my nose," Karl said accusingly. "No, no," he said to Owen, "don't do dat! Is okay. Yah, everytink is okay."

Karl swayed drunkenly in front of them. "I loose my knife too," he added. "Ve haf dam good fight, yah, Marine?" Karl grinned. "Nex time I come back here, we fight, okay? Maybe nex time I wins." He stepped into the street to let them pass, waved good-naturedly at the pair, then staggered off into the dark.

Erika stared at Dean for a moment and then doubled over with laughter. "You know, Joe, I tink dat Owen, I tink he is very good friend for you Marines!"

A voice in the dark sounded throughout the barracks one night several days later:

"Prettiest girl I ever seen
Was smokin' thule in my latrine."

Dean shot bolt upright in his rack. "Sounded just like that fool, Wolfman!" he muttered. Footsteps came down the hallway, then the door to the third fire team's cubicle right next door burst open with a crash.

"Drop your cocks and grab your socks!" MacIlargie shouted, sliding his seabag noisily across the floor. "Thirty-fourth FIST is now combat ready!"

Well, not quite, but it was getting there. Its men were coming home.

CHAPTER
TWO

"Gunnery Sergeant Charlie Bass . . ." Brigadier Sturgeon began sternly.

The wall behind the desk he sat at, on which Bass's eyes were fixed, held 2-D pictures of Confederation President Cynthia Chang-Sturdevant, Confederation Minister of War Marcus Berentus, and Chairman of the Confederation Combined Chiefs of Staff Admiral Horatio Perry. Confederation Marine Corps Commandant Kinsky Butler was depicted in a hologram. The four images were flanked on one side by the Confederation flag and on the other by the gold-and-scarlet Marine Corps flag and 34th FIST's battle standard—the latter so thickly festooned with campaign and unit-citation streamers it was barely visible through the pennants. Four men sat in chairs along one side of the office: Colonel Ramadan, Sturgeon's chief of staff; FIST Sergeant Major Shiro; Commander Van Winkle, the FIST's infantry battalion commander; and Sergeant Major Parant, the infantry battalion sergeant major. Standing at attention in front of the brigadier's desk, Gunnery Sergeant Charlie Bass, acting platoon commander of third platoon, Company L, was flanked by his company commander and first sergeant, Captain Conorado and Top Myer.

"It has come to my attention," Sturgeon continued, "that a certain platoon in this FIST's infantry battalion has a tendency to run wild when it's on liberty." He fixed Bass with a steely eye and drummed his fingers on his desktop.

"Sir?" Bass said into the void.

16

"You know what I mean, Gunnery Sergeant," Sturgeon snapped. "I'm talking about the third platoon of Company L."

Bass's jaw clenched. His platoon didn't run wild. When his men were on duty, they were the most disciplined platoon in the entire FIST, and he'd bet the pension he didn't really expect to live to collect on that. So what if they were particularly high-spirited when they were on liberty?

"When your platoon pulls liberty in Bronnoysund, it makes more noise, damages more property, and gets into more fights than any other unit in this FIST. It's a wonder that every man jack among them hasn't been in front of Commander Van Winkle for nonjudicial punishment—or before me for a formal court-martial!"

"Sir, it's a good platoon. My men work hard and they play just as hard."

Sturgeon seemed to ignore Bass's defense of his platoon. "I think the matter could be properly resolved if third platoon, Company L, had a regular platoon commander instead of an acting commander."

There it is, Bass thought bitterly. I won't accept a commission, so they won't let me keep a platoon. Maybe they'll give me an ensign as good as the last one. The last officer of third platoon, Ensign vanden Hoyt, had died bravely during the fighting on Diamunde. Bass had served as acting platoon commander ever since.

"You always say you refused a commission because you can do more good for the Marine Corps by training and taking care of the Marines in one platoon or one company than by becoming an officer and losing touch." Sturgeon snorted at the implication that officers lost touch with the enlisted men they led, and exchanged glances with the other officers. "Therefore, I'm going to exercise a prerogative available to me as commander of a remote FIST. That is to assign senior noncommissioned officers to fill the billets of commissioned officers on a permanent basis. Commander Van Winkle concurs with me that you can probably do the job. Captain Conorado has said he can put up with you as long as I agree to bust you a grade or two if you screw up. So I'm assigning you to permanently fill the position of platoon commander."

The brigadier stood abruptly. A broad grin split his face and he extended his hand across the desk. "Charlie," he said when the stunned Gunnery Sergeant Bass took his hand, "just because you refuse to accept a commission doesn't mean I can't get an officer's work out of you."

Bass hardly heard Sturgeon's last words. Conorado was pumping his other hand, Myer was pounding on his back. Van Winkle and the two sergeants major were on their feet and crowding in to offer congratulations. Ramadan hovered behind them, trying to find space to squeeze in to add his own.

Charlie Bass had been with third platoon, Company L, 34th FIST for more than two years. On Diamunde he'd begun his third stint as acting platoon commander. Both of the previous times, he'd had to yield command to newly commissioned ensigns. The first one . . . well, he preferred not to think about Ensign Baccacio, who hadn't had enough enlisted experience before getting commissioned. The second, vanden Hoyt, had been a staff sergeant and a good platoon sergeant before being commissioned an officer. Most officers—all Marine officers—were commissioned from the ranks, and he didn't resent giving up command. But sometimes . . . And the constant changing of commanders couldn't help but be disruptive to the platoon. Now third platoon was his. He wouldn't have to give it up to the next junior officer, a man who'd probably come aboard with less experience than Bass had, who'd join the company on his first assignment as an officer.

Bass was overwhelmed. He mumbled his thanks to the men congratulating him, but later couldn't remember what any of them said or what he replied.

The campaign on Diamunde had nearly been a disaster. It was particularly tough on third platoon: it had not only lost its commander, it also lost a squad leader, three of six fire team leaders, and a gun team leader. A PFC had been killed in action as well. In a blaster platoon, seven men dead out of thirty was heavy casualties no matter what kind of operation they happened on, and Diamunde had been maybe the toughest campaign Bass had ever served on. Two other members of third platoon had been seriously wounded in the campaign and, even though they had returned to it, were still on light duty. Third platoon was in serious need of replacements. They got them. Well, they quickly got six, and six out of seven wasn't bad.

The Marines of Company L stood in formation on the parade ground behind their barracks. At first glance something seemed not quite right about the formation, even though the garrison-utility-clad Marines were in uniformly erect positions, and the lines they stood in might have been laid out by a surveyor. The woo squatting at attention in front of third platoon wasn't the oddity. Neither was it the fact that First Sergeant Myer, who rarely attended the company's morning formations, stood to the left of Captain Conorado. A second glance showed the problem—there were gaps in the ranks. Open spaces had been left for the men who were no longer with Company L. Captain Conorado's eyes, and First Sergeant Myer's, were held by the holes in the ranks. They'd lost some good Marines on Diamunde. Any losses were too many, but the gaps were far too many. Behind the Skipper and the Top, Company Gunnery Sergeant Thatcher stood in front of a smaller formation, twenty-one Marines drawn up in two ranks. The next time the company fell into formation, those Marines would be in it and there wouldn't be any gaps.

"We lost good Marines." Conorado was finishing up his eulogy to the men who died on Diamunde. "We lost good friends." He didn't shout, but his voice was loud and clear and no one in the formation had to strain to hear him. "But they aren't gone, not totally. They were Marines, and as Marines they will be remembered by the Corps for all time. You will carry them with you for the rest of your lives. Marines who follow along after you will carry you just the same.

"Centuries ago our progenitors, the United States Marines, had a saying: 'Marines don't die. They go to hell and re-group.' Those old Marines also said that Marines guard Heaven's gates.

"Our companions remain with us in our hearts. Someday, whether it's as battle casualties, as the result of the ravages of illness, or simply from old age, we will rejoin them. Now let us take a moment of silence to remember them."

Conorado bowed his head, as did the hundred Marines facing him. Behind him Thatcher lowered his head. Some of the twenty-one other Marines, the replacements, bowed theirs as well. Most of them had been through such cere-monies before. All of them felt uncomfortable; the ceremony reminded them of their own mortality, and starkly brought home to them the fact that they were replacing well-liked and respected men.

After a moment Conorado cleared his throat and everyone looked up again.

"Behind me," Conorado said, "are Marines newly assigned to Company L. They have already been assigned to platoons, you have already met some of them. When you are dismissed, you will go by platoons to areas that have previously been as-signed to you. The new men will go with you so that you can formally meet them all and your platoons can be reorganized. But before I release you, one other piece of company busi-ness remains."

He paused and looked from one end of the company to the other, then called out, "Gunnery Sergeant Charlie Bass, front and center!"

Bass stepped briskly from his platoon sergeant's position and marched to stop two paces in front of the company com-mander. He sharply saluted. Conorado returned the salute, then Bass faced left and took a few more paces to stand at Conorado's right side.

"Gunnery Sergeant Charlie Bass," Conorado said to the

company, "as you all know, has been serving as acting platoon commander of third platoon since Ensign vanden Hoyt was taken prisoner by the rebel forces on Diamunde. As of this morning, by direction of Brigadier Sturgeon, Commander, 34th FIST, Gunnery Sergeant Charlie Bass is no longer acting platoon commander, he *is* platoon commander." He pivoted to face Bass. "Gunnery Sergeant Bass, take your position as platoon commander."

Bass again saluted Conorado. "Aye aye, *sir*!" he said loudly. When the captain returned his salute, Bass pivoted and marched to the platoon commander's position in front of third platoon, which had been empty until then.

Conorado looked at his company again, it seemed to each Marine that his skipper looked him directly in the eye. Conorado filled his chest, then bellowed, "Platoon commanders, dismiss your platoons." He made an about-face, and he and Myer marched back into the barracks.

While the platoon commanders took their men to the assigned locations, the platoon sergeants joined Gunny Thatcher and took their incoming men from his control. Sergeant Hyakowa, first squad leader of third platoon, acted as platoon sergeant. He took six new men to the company classroom. Conorado and Myer were already there.

Hyakowa put the replacements in the front row of seats. In another moment the entire platoon was present, everyone seated and looking attentively at their company commander. Finally, Conorado spoke.

"I've already met with all the platoon commanders and platoon sergeants, so everybody knows what to do. I'm here with you, the men of the third platoon, because your loss of leaders on Diamunde was so much greater than anybody else's. Third platoon is going to have the greatest reorganization in the company. There is one leadership change that I want to tell you about myself. You are not getting a new platoon sergeant." He held up his hand to forestall questions. "By that I mean you aren't getting somebody new, someone you don't know. I'm sure that every one of you who's been here for any time at all will agree with Brigadier Sturgeon, Commander Van Winkle, Top Myer, Gunny Bass, and me that Sergeant Hyakowa richly deserves to be your new platoon sergeant."

Cheers and shouts of congratulations broke out. The Marines closest to him slapped Hyakowa on the shoulders or pounded his back. Hyakowa had acted as platoon sergeant on many occasions, so everyone knew that he would do a superb job. Even the woo seemed pleased. It hopped onto Hyakowa's shoulder, where it glowed a bright pink.

"As you were, people!" Top Myer bellowed. The pandemonium died out and the Marines looked back to Conorado.

"Gunny Bass and Sergeant Hyakowa have spent considerable time figuring out a reorganization of this platoon. Top Myer, Gunny Thatcher, and I agree with what they've come up with. So I'll let them tell you the rest of your reorganization." Abruptly, he stepped out, heading for the classroom entrance.

"Platoon, a-ten-*shun*!" Myer bellowed.

The Marines jumped to their feet and stood rigidly at attention as Conorado left, followed closely by Myer.

"Relax, sit down," Bass said as soon as they were gone. He strode to the front of the classroom, where Hyakowa joined him, facing the platoon. They waited a moment while the Marines resumed their seats. The six men in the front row, in a new situation, not knowing much if anything about their new leaders or fellow Marines, sat stiffly while the Marines behind them lounged. Some of the new men watched the woo as it returned to its usual perch on Dean's shoulder.

Bass studied the men in the front row for several seconds, then raised his eyes to look at the rest of the platoon. "We've got a lot of new Marines for you to meet. I'll call out their names." He looked back at the front row. "When I say your name, stand up and turn around so everyone can see you. Many of you have already met Corporal Pasquin." Pasquin stood and glowered at the platoon. "I've read his record and spent some time talking with him. He was on one campaign when he was with 25th FIST. He also served on a peace-keeping mission to Cross and Thorn, and a peacemaking deployment to Rodina when he was with the 18th, so he's been around a bit. He's on his second enlistment. I'm sure once he gets to know everybody and gets his feet wet here, he'll turn out to be a fine asset to this platoon." Pasquin sat and Bass went on to the other new men, none of whom had the rank or experience that Pasquin did.

"PFC Dobervich joins us from Arsenault. Right, he's a boot, this is his first duty. The same goes for PFC Hruska. PFC Yi just graduated from gun course. PFC Quick," he shook his head, "is an oh-one," infantry military occupational specialty, "just like the rest of us, but he spent his first four years in the Corps on embassy duty. This is his first assignment as a real Marine." He raised his voice and continued talking over the breakout of laughs and jeers that greeted Quick as he stood, red-faced. "PFC Rowe joins us from 11th FIST. He's got a couple of campaign ribbons, one for a peace-keeping mission and one for an indigenous-forces training operation—and most of you know what they can be like. Now he's going to find out what it's like to be a Marine in the active Corps." This time Bass allowed the laughter to go on for a moment while he stood slightly bowed, looking at the floor to hide his eyes.

"All right, here's the deal," Bass said, standing erect, arms akimbo. "We've got two squad leader positions to fill." He paused to clear the lump that suddenly filled his throat. "I don't think anybody will have any problem with Ratliff and Bladon moving up. Knock it off!" he snapped as his men began congratulating the new squad leaders. "I'm sure a day will come when they're busting your asses to get you ready for an inspection, or to take an objective with more people shooting at you than you think you can face, when you won't be so happy with them." He paused and glared at his men in mock menace. A couple of the new men swallowed and wondered what kind of hardass they had for a platoon commander.

"Sergeant Kelly," he nodded toward the gun squad leader, "is now the senior squad leader and will be acting platoon sergeant when either Sergeant Hyakowa or I are gone. Now, we've got four fire team leader slots to fill. The first one's easy—we've got a new corporal, Corporal Pasquin. Rabbit, if I give you Dornhofer as your first fire team leader, can you handle Pasquin for second fire team?"

"No problem, boss," Ratliff replied.

"Fine." He looked at another Marine. "Juice, think you're ready to be a fire team leader?"

Lance Corporal Justice "Juice" Goudanis jumped in his seat and gawked at Bass. After a few seconds he closed his mouth and swallowed, then said, "I do believe so, Gunny."

"He okay with you for third fire team, Rabbit?"

"If he can't do the job, I'll kick his ass around the barracks until he can," Ratliff said, straight-faced.

"Fine. Sergeant Hyakowa and I will spell you if it takes that long. Also, you get Schultz, Dean, Van Impe, and Godenov. Your new men are Dobervich and Quick. Divvy them up however you want, then let Sergeant Hyakowa and me know what you did.

"Tam, your fire team leaders are Rat and Chan. Okay with you?"

"Chan did real good as shift leader with the feldpolizei on Wanderjahr," Bladon answered. "Yeah, he's fine with me. And I know the Rat's going to continue to do the outstanding job he's always done."

Corporal "Rat" Linsman lifted his chin and tried to look superior. Lance Corporal Chan's heart raced and his eyes glowed. He was sure he could do the job, he hoped he could.

"Good. You also get Watson, Claypoole, Nolet, and MacIlargie." He shook his head. "Think you can handle MacIlargie?"

Bladon laughed. "No problem. He's still learning chapter one of the book I wrote when I was a PFC. I know all of the stunts he'll try to pull better than he does."

"All right. You also get Hruska and Rowe. Get 'em organized and let me know what you did."

"Hound, Stevenson gets your second gun team. Yi's your new man."

Sergeant Kelly simply nodded. The gun squad was lucky, it had only lost one man on Diamunde.

"That's it, then. Unless anybody has any questions, squad leaders . . . Yes?" He nodded to MacIlargie, who raised his hand.

"Uh, Gunny? I was paying close attention to what you were saying, but I only heard two fire team leaders named for second squad. Did I miss something?"

"No-o-o," Bass drew the word out, "but I imagine you'll wind up wishing you were in first squad. Squad leaders, do it. Tam, see me and Wang in the passageway for a moment."

The three squads broke up into groups in different parts of the company classroom as Bass, Hyakowa, and Bladon left.

Ratliff had one new man to put in each fire team. Since Pasquin was a corporal, he had to be a fire team leader. Ratliff gave him two men who'd been on operations with the company, Dean and Godenov. He pretended not to notice the glances Pasquin and Dean exchanged when he made the assignments. Dean bristled at the look Pasquin gave the woo.

Why me? Dean wondered, stifling a groan. Rabbit should have given him Schultz—Hammer would straighten this guy out in a hurry.

Dornhofer was his most experienced fire team leader—he got first fire team and the least experienced man, Dobervich, along with the toughest man in the company, Lance Corporal Schultz. Goudanis, the least experienced fire team leader, was third fire team leader, with Lance Corporal Van Impe, who might have gotten the promotion if he wasn't still on light duty from the wounds he received on Diamunde, and PFC Quick, who at least had some experience, even if it wasn't in the infantry.

Bladon returned in a couple of minutes. He was grinning

widely, but wouldn't tell anyone what Bass had wanted to see him about.

After Bladon made his assignments, MacIlargie, looking confused, asked, "Corporal Bladon, you put me and Rock in the same fire team."

Bladon nodded. "That's right. You and Claypoole. All of my troublemakers together, right where I can keep an eye on you."

"Who's our fire team leader?"

Bladon laughed. "You'll find out soon enough," he said with a smile. "Then you'll probably wish you were in a different company."

MacIlargie turned to Claypoole, a pained expression on his face. "What'd I do, Rock?" he asked. "What'd I do wrong? I haven't done anything wrong yet."

"I'm not sure that's the problem," Claypoole answered softly. He looked a bit queasy himself.

Bladon was still laughing as he left the classroom to tell Bass and Hyakowa about the assignments.

CHAPTER
THREE

In nearly two years, Company L only had two promotion ceremonies. During the previous year, on board the amphibious battle cruiser *Tripoli* en route to Diamunde, Charlie Bass was promoted from staff sergeant to gunnery sergeant. Almost a year before that, on the Confederation ship HM3 *Gordon* bound for Elneal, there was a promotion ceremony for the company's squad and fire team leaders, whose ranks were lower than called for in the table of organization.

The infrequency of promotion ceremonies wasn't unusual—promotions came slowly in the Confederation Marine Corps. When there weren't many casualties, promotions were very slow. Thirty-fourth FIST had suffered very few casualties on Elneal, none on Wanderjahr. But the war on Diamunde had opened up a lot of slots for promotion, especially in the FIST's infantry battalion. The sharp end of the stick always gets chipped and dented and the infantry battalion was the point of the sharp end.

The entire battalion, resplendent in dress reds—high, stock-collared scarlet tunics over blue trousers for the enlisted men, scarlet tunics over gold trousers for the officers—formed up on the pebble-strewn parade ground flanked by the barracks. Nearly all of the Marines, except for the most junior men who had just arrived on Thorsfinni's World with the 34th FIST as their first duty assignment, had at least one medal sparkling on their chests, usually the Marine Expeditionary Medal. Most had one or more silver comets glinting on the medal's ribbon, indicating multiple awards. Many wore ribbons indicating unit citations. A few wore personal decorations for heroism. Some of the Marines in the battalion had so many medals, they clumped together and projected far out from their chests.

Usually, for sergeants and below, company commanders presided over promotion ceremonies held in the individual company areas, but on this occasion Commander Van Winkle was going to handle the ceremony himself. Too many Marines had been lost on Diamunde, and he felt it necessary to give these promotions with his own hand: partly to honor the men who had died or were wounded too badly to return; partly to emphasize to everyone the importance of the promotions, and the value of the ranks the newly promoted men would have. Van Winkle believed it would also make an impression on the replacements. The new men should know that their battalion commander cared, that his Marines were important to him.

There was another point Van Winkle took into consideration. The Diamunde campaign, the third major war on that world, rated more than just another comet on the Marine Expeditionary Medal, and a new campaign medal had been struck for it. Along with distributing promotion warrants, Van Winkle would pin these medals on the new lance corporals, corporals, sergeants, and staff sergeants. He'd been briefly annoyed when Brigadier Sturgeon said he wanted to preside over an awards ceremony for decorations for heroism, but quickly let that annoyance go. The ceremony was going to be long enough as it was, without making the men stand for the additional time involved in making the personal awards, so perhaps it was better to have two ceremonies on different days.

Commander Van Winkle completed his brief and, he hoped, inspirational remarks, and then, in a voice that carried without amplification to everyone on the parade ground, commanded, "Sergeant Major, call the roll!"

Battalion Sergeant Major Parant cried out in an even louder voice, "The following Marines, front and center!" He lifted a sheet of parchment, holding it at the top with his left hand and the bottom with his right, and began reading off names in company order, alphabetically within platoons. Each name was preceded by the rank the Marine was being promoted to. Eleven men were called from K Company. Nine names were called from the first and second platoons of Company L, which had been in the thickest of the fighting in the Diamunde campaign. Company L's third platoon by itself had five.

"Sergeant Bladon!" Sergeant Major Parant called, and the new second squad leader broke ranks and marched forward to join the growing rank in front of the reviewing stand. "Corporal Goudanis! Staff Sergeant Hyakowa! Sergeant Ratliff! Corporal Stevenson!" Altogether, sixteen Marines from Company L were called forward to be promoted. Mike Company had the second largest number of promotions, fourteen. Headquarters Company had six.

Finally, the forty-seven Marines were standing in one long line in front of the reviewing stand. Parant turned to face Commander Van Winkle and announced, "Sir, all present and accounted for!"

"Thank you, Sergeant Major," Van Winkle said, then held up another sheet of parchment and read, "Know ye all men, that placing special trust and confidence in . . ." The commander recited the names in the same order they had been called forward, using the words of the archaic Marine promotion warrant, which hadn't been changed in centuries, to announce the promotion of the forty-seven Marines. When the reading was over, he rolled up the parchment and handed it to the ensign who was his aide. He descended the three steps from the reviewing stand to the parade ground and was followed by the battalion sergeant major and the aide. Parant carried the individual promotion warrants, and the aide bore a case with forty-seven Third Diamundean Campaign medals.

Moving from one man to another, Van Winkle handed over a promotion warrant and then shook the Marine's hand while saying a few words of congratulations. Then he took a medal from the case and pinned it onto the man's tunic.

"You're getting pretty impressive there, Staff Sergeant," he said when he pinned the medal on Hyakowa's tunic. Hyakowa already had eight campaign medals and several comets on his Marine Expeditionary Medal, to compliment his Good Conduct Medal and the Silver Nebula and Bronze Star medals for bravery he had earned on earlier campaigns.

"Thank you, sir," Hyakowa said. "It happens after time."

"I always thought there was a wise guy hiding under that calm and collected surface of yours," Sergeant Major Parant said. "Maybe we should assign you to a different company—you've been hanging out with Charlie Bass too long."

Hyakowa snorted discreetly.

"Congratulations, Staff Sergeant, you deserve it." Parant gave Hyakowa's shoulder a stiff, short-swing left as he shook hands with him. "I owe you three more."

Hyakowa managed not to react to the sharp punch. "You have to catch me first, Sergeant Major," he said. The enlisted men of the Confederation Marine Corps practiced a time-honored ritual—pinning on the stripes. Every enlisted Marine of equal or higher rank was allowed, during the day or two following a promotion, to punch a newly promoted Marine on the shoulder one time for each chevron and rocker of his new rank. A staff sergeant's insignia was three chevrons over one rocker.

Parant laughed lightly and moved on with his commander to Sergeant Ratliff.

It took three-quarters of an hour for Van Winkle to pass out all the warrants and pin on the campaign medals. The battalion had been standing at attention for close to an hour and a half by then. It was time to release the men—but not until after a few closing remarks.

"We are Marines," Van Winkle said, resuming his position on the reviewing stand and taking a moment to look over his battalion. "More than that, we are the epitome of Marines—the infantry. From time immemorial, Marines have been the tip of the spear, the sharp end of the stick. Wherever and whenever there have been Marines, Marines have been the first to go into conflict, the first to make contact with the enemy. It is Marines who have guarded the most important installations at home and abroad, on-world and off. It is Marines who went ashore to secure ports, Marines who guarded shipping and fought off and defeated pirates and other raiders. It is Marines who, simply by appearing on the scene and making known their willingness to do battle, have prevented wars—only the foolish are willing to fight against Marines.

"We are the few, we are the proud. We are an undying band of brothers. We are the guardians of all we hold true and dear. We the Marines stand ever vigilant, ready at a moment's notice to step into harm's way. When we do, we know we will defeat that harm. We know that because we know our leaders are the finest leaders there are, as are the Marines who were promoted today, and as are the lance corporal fire team leaders and corporal squad leaders who have yet to be promoted. We know we will take care of our own. And we know we are the best. We are Marines."

He paused and looked out over his battalion again, 467 men and officers strong. "This one battalion," he announced, "could have faced and defeated a fifteen or twenty thousand man division of the twentieth century. You could have defeated Napoleon at Waterloo without assistance. You could have stemmed the tide of Ghengis Khan's Golden Hoard. Caesar's Legions would have shattered against you. Alexander's army would have died at your feet. This single battalion could have taken Troy in an hour or two. I am awed by the power you represent." He had to stop to clear the lump that grew in his throat. "And this is only half the strength of 34th FIST! Marines, I salute you." He sharply raised his right hand in salute.

" 'Tal-lion, present—arms!" Sergeant Major Parant bellowed.

As one, the men and officers arrayed before him returned Van Winkle's salute.

The commander was almost overcome with emotion. He got control of himself, swallowed the lump that welled up again, and filled his chest with air. *"Company commanders,"* he shouted, *"take your companies!"* He turned about and left the reviewing stand from the steps in its rear. His staff followed.

Across the parade ground, company commanders about-faced and cried out orders. Each of their companies turned its facing from ranks to columns, and on command the companies stepped out, marching sharply to the cadence called by their commanders.

When Captain Conorado dismissed Company L back at the company area, PFC Godenov approached Sergeant Ratliff.

"Co—Sergeant Ratliff?" Getting used to all the new ranks in the platoon would take some doing. "What Commander Van Winkle said at the end . . . is all that really true about Marines?"

"Mostly," Ratliff replied. He didn't give the answer his full attention. His mind was too full of the promotion he'd just received. "The commander exaggerated a bit. Marines haven't always been the first ones in. There have been major wars that Marines almost didn't get into at all. But yeah, Marines are the point, we're usually the first." It sunk in then, who asked the question, and Ratliff took Godenov by the shoulder and looked into the younger Marine's eyes. "Izzy," he said seriously, "we are the best, and we know it. So do most other people. Anybody who doesn't know it and thinks they can beat us usually winds up sorry they met us. Now get into the barracks and change into your garrison utilities."

"Right, Sergeant Ratliff. Thanks."

When Ratliff let go of his shoulder, Godenov raced to the barracks. He didn't even notice that he wasn't bothered by being called "Izzy." All his life he'd been tormented by the questioning play on his name, "Is he good enough?" Usually, no matter what he did, other people answered, "No." But on Wanderjahr he had demonstrated that he was good enough. On Diamunde he confirmed that demonstration. Now he was coming to understand and believe that the proper answer to the question "Izzy Godenov" was an unequivocal "Yes."

CHAPTER
FOUR

Cameron stared disconsolately into the small fire. Things had not been going well for him, not at all, since the group's arrival on Society 437 six months ago. Opposite the fire, snuggled against the cave wall, Minerva stirred in her sleep. Her blond hair, once so beautiful, was matted and dirty, as shaggy as the men's. She stank too. They all did. None of them had spent much time on personal hygiene for months. But she was the only one of the surviving pirates Cameron could trust.

The cave they were hiding in extended for uncounted kilometers under the mountains. They only used the first hundred meters or so of the tunnel system that led into the caverns, but they had explored extensively behind the entrance and were satisfied that the place might provide refuge if . . . Cameron didn't want to think about "what if." He was sure their puny defensive measures would amount to nothing if those things did come after them in there. But he'd been careful not to share his thoughts with the others, for fear the tenuous grip he had on them would snap.

He stirred the embers of the dying fire and it flared up brightly. The fernlike trees they were using for fuel burned slowly and gave off adequate heat and hardly any smoke. That was good, because there was no smoke to bother them inside the damn cave and none to seep to the surface and give away their hiding place. At least something on that godforsaken lump was in their favor.

From the shadows farther inside the cave someone was

pissing. Cameron could just make out Rhys Apbac, leaning against the wall back there. "Rhys!" he shouted. "We have to live in here!"

"I'm not going outside at night, Georgie boy," Rhys answered, shaking himself off. "Not with them things out there. No-siree." Rhys rearranged his clothes. "Thanks to you, Georgie boy," he added sourly.

"You'd have been dead six months ago with the others if it hadn't been for me," Cameron replied in a tired voice. He was referring to Captain Scanlon and the hundred other members of the Red 35 Crew, as the pirate gang had called itself. The surviving pirates blamed him for everything. True enough, it had been Cameron's idea to raid Society 437, but who could've imagined that those things . . .

Cameron shook his head and got to his feet. Carefully, he negotiated his way up the steep tunnel through the sleeping figures littered around tiny fires. At the cave entrance two men armed with the group's last functional plasma weapons—ancient relics even when Cameron was born—kept fitful watch. They crouched behind a barricade of small boulders, scanning the rock-strewn slope below. In the pale moonlight the larger rocks cast weird shadows across the open spaces. If a man stared at them long enough, the shadows took on a menacing life of their own, but nevertheless, the things hadn't bothered them in months.

"Lowboy, I'm going outside," Cameron whispered to one of the watching men.

Lowboy stared at Cameron's back as he clambered over the chest-high barricade of rocks that blocked the cave's entrance—too high and steep, they hoped, for one of those things to get over, but just negotiable enough for a man. Lowboy wanted very much to burn a hole through Cameron. Sure, he was the "leader," but only by default. No. They had to conserve the energy packs, and besides, those . . . things might sense the energy release and come to investigate.

Lowboy sincerely hated Cameron, if that was his real name—nobody in the Red 35 Crew ever went by his real name. He'd showed up at their headquarters a year ago, breathing hatred and vowing damnation upon the entire Confederation of Worlds, saying he wanted to join their band, offer them his "services." Educated fop, that's what he was, Lowboy reflected, not real pirate material. But Scanlon had accepted him into the crew. Now look what that's got us, Lowboy thought bitterly. A knife for Cameron, that's it, Lowboy told himself. He'd kill Cameron when the time was ripe. Him and that bitch of his. Hell with it, he thought, none of us is getting off this planet alive anyway, may as well have some satisfaction before those things get me.

Outside, Cameron stood bathed in the moonlight as he urinated down the slope. They were nearly a thousand meters above the swamp, and the mountains rose another thousand meters behind them. Those things didn't like the elevations. And they liked to stay near water. The only problem, living up there, was fuel and food. There was food at Aquarius Station, about thirty kilometers to the north of the mountain range, and the indigenous amphibians that inhabited the swamps were edible when they could be caught and killed. But leaving the mountains was very dangerous. The others were frightened; they would be content just to remain in the cave until they starved. Cameron knew that only his incessant goading had forced them to forage. The last expedition had been almost two months ago, and they would need to resupply soon.

What the hell, he thought, maybe I'll just give in and we can all stay here and starve. We'll never get off this goddamn planet anyway. No wonder everyone referred to it as Waygone. It was way gone all right. Oh, someone'll come, sooner or later, he told himself, but the question is, will we be around later? He suspected those things had left them alone for a while because they were busy with something else. Once they turned their attention back to the pirates . . . Well, no profit thinking about that eventuality.

Cameron put himself back into the rags that passed for his

trousers. He cinched the belt at his waist as tightly as he could. He'd lost at least thirty pounds since they came here, and he was conscious now of wearing the same clothes he'd worn when they landed at Aquarius. Well, who brings a change of clothes on a pirate raid? he thought. They were only supposed to stay a few hours anyway. There would be fresh clothes at Aquarius if he could get the others to go there with him. They'd fled the place in such a panic six months earlier that nobody thought to grab anything useful, much less replacement garments. In their wild desperation to get as far away from those things as they could, none of them thought he'd live six months anyway.

If I can't convince these bastards to go back to Aquarius Station with me, Cameron thought, Minerva and I will go by ourselves. Anything was better than crouching in the caves like frightened troglodytes, even taking a chance they'd run into those things again. Jesus, how come nobody knew those things were here in the first place? he wondered for the nth time.

Over the months in the mountains, Cameron had changed in ways that surprised even him. He'd taken charge of the survivors, imposed his will on them and made the correct decisions to keep them alive. At times he wished he'd just let them fend for themselves, but deep inside he knew he was responsible for them as much as for himself. He didn't much care for the survivors of Scanlon's band: Rhys Apbac and Lowboy were scum, and sooner or later he knew he'd have to deal with them. Minerva was a different case. He cared what happened to her, the first time in his life he'd felt that way about another person.

And he'd forgotten how much he'd hated the Confederation. Just then, as he stood looking down the slope, he'd have given anything to be on board a starship, leaving Waygone, even if it meant spending the rest of his life in prison. Even if it meant again facing up to who he really was.

But the most important change he'd undergone was that in the face of terrible danger, the man who called himself

Cameron was the only one who had not given in to panic. Not like the last time . . .

The sun was coming up. The first rays were already illuminating the peaks above him. Watching the sun rise was just about the only pleasure he could get out of life in the mountains—that and Minerva, of course.

She'd lost weight too. Her pelvic bones and ribs had begun to show prominently when the two of them lay together. Cameron rather liked that, except that her slenderness was due to malnutrition. Thinking of her, he hitched up his trousers and walked back into the cave.

The Red 35 Crew pirate band called itself that because their leader, Finnegard Scanlon, considered red his favorite color and the number 35 a lucky one for him. In real life Scanlon ran a legitimate import business from a remote mining and prospecting world called New Genesee, "Jenny" to locals. Jenny was the oldest settlement in its sector of Human Space, and had the largest population, but it was still a distant backwater compared even to Thorsfinni's World. And, as with any frontier world, the law had not yet reached Jenny in any force, so fortunes could be made there if a man was quick and ruthless.

Scanlon made a living furnishing the colonists and surveyors of neighboring worlds with the necessities. That was the facade he lived behind anyway, with the hundred or so men and women he employed. But whenever a little smuggling operation was afoot or a raid was conducted, they all happily made the transition from employees to outlaws—to Red 35 Crew—and when the operation was over, they quietly returned to being hardworking citizens.

Scanlon planned the forays with the utmost care. For one thing, he never combined piracy with legitimate business. His public affairs were always in perfect order and his accounts open for audit by anyone who wished to see them. And he kept no records on his illegal and highly profitable enterprises. No illegal goods were ever allowed into his warehouses on Jenny, and they stayed in the holds of his star-faring vessels only long enough to be offloaded on an uncharted asteroid or one of the small moons scattered throughout various systems where he kept his stashes.

Other pirate bands, operating along more traditional lines—roving and marauding—also preyed on commerce between the pioneer worlds, and Scanlon made a public show of cooperating with the authorities to wipe them out. But when Scanlon himself "hoisted the Jolly Roger"—he liked that ancient term for raiding—he could be more vicious than any of his competitors. They were aboveboard about what they were and what they did, but Scanlon lived a double life. Piracy was merely business for Scanlon, and to protect his identity he did not leave behind many witnesses. He raided only when the chances of success were assured and the potential profits very high, and he was very good at foisting the blame on other bands for his depredations. Before Cameron came along, Scanlon had been enjoying a string of very profitable heists.

When Cameron showed up looking for a job at Scanlon's offices at Sodus Bay, the capital city of New Genesee, he was turned down at first. Lowboy, Scanlon's "personnel director," had advised his boss that Cameron was too chancy, and Scanlon agreed. It was dangerous to let someone you didn't know into an operation like his, so Cameron was told to go back to his hotel and look for other work. Meanwhile, Lowboy put a tail on the stranger. If he turned out to be a spy for a competitor or working for the Confederation, Lowboy would take care of him.

Cameron knew a lot about the military and he drank a lot. And he hated the Confederation Marine Corps. "Probably an ex-Marine," Lowboy advised Scanlon. "Probably got kicked out."

Scanlon thought about that. "We could use someone with a bit of military experience," he mused. "Think he really means it? I mean this hard-on for the Marines?"

Lowboy shrugged. "Sounds like he does. The guy drinks a

lot. I mean a *lot*. No undercover agent would ever make that mistake. Still . . . He says his name is George Cameron. I checked him out in the Blue Book"—the register of commissioned Marines—"and there's nobody by that name in there, and never has been."

Scanlon laughed. "Hell, nobody uses his real name around here! Ex-enlisted?"

Lowboy shrugged again. "He claims to have been an officer."

"Ask him to come back for an interview," Scanlon said.

"I don't know, Cap'n—"

"Ask him."

Finnegard Scanlon was a good judge of character. He saw several valuable qualities in the young man who called himself George Cameron. For one thing, Cameron appeared as much disgusted with himself as with the Confederation Marine Corps, upon which he blamed all his difficulties with some vehemence. When Scanlon asked him what had happened, Cameron became evasive. Scanlon smiled to himself. Clearly, the guy had screwed up badly. That was very good; Cameron would be malleable. They talked about infantry weapons and tactics. Yes, Cameron knew them well; maybe he *had* been an officer. Certainly an NCO. He was intelligent, knew weapons, tactics, communications, could handle administrative details.

That Cameron had showed up for the interview with alcohol on his breath was actually in his favor, to Scanlon's way of thinking. It tended to support his conclusion that Cameron really was an outcast looking to hide himself and get back at society at the same time.

"How would you like to work for me, George?" Scanlon eventually asked.

Cameron accepted the offer immediately.

In the following months, Cameron showed he could supervise the loading of a cargo hold, draw up an accurate shipping manifest, and carry his own weight on a raid.

The raid had been a small affair, just a brief touchdown on a nearly uninhabited world to heist construction robotics, but Cameron neutralized the tiny work force at the site quickly and effectively and established a defensive perimeter immediately afterward, from which he held off the security force until the snatch was completed. Everyone in the Red 35 Crew had gotten off safely, and no witnesses were left behind. Even Lowboy had been impressed, although the new man had demonstrated some reluctance when ordered to kill the survivors. But a man could learn to do that sort of thing.

About a month after he'd joined them, Minerva attached herself to Cameron. A clerk in one of Jenny's mining camps, she'd been recruited on Old Earth under false pretenses. The company actually wanted someone to service the men in its operation on Jenny, and not by keeping their pay records straight. She soon became very unpopular with her bosses, but she did keep the men's pay records straight. When her contract ran out, she decided to find other work. After pushing drinks in the dives around Sodus Bay for a while, she wound up a shipping clerk in Scanlon's business. She was pretty and, just coincidentally, had guts and brains.

The other men in Scanlon's crew respected her. Scanlon's inflexible rule on women in his organization was that no man could force himself on one who was a member of the crew. Minerva and Cameron met because he knew unarmed combat and had volunteered to teach his skills to the others. During a demonstration, while thinking of someone else whom he wanted to hurt, he'd applied too much pressure to Minerva's left arm, which had snapped. Cameron was genuinely sorry, and she liked the awkward way he tried to make up for it. After her experiences in the mining camps and the bars on Jenny, it was refreshing to have a man pay attention to her not because he wanted something from her, but just to be nice. And with Minerva, Cameron really tried to be nice; when he was with her, the burning hatred and disgrace that had driven him to the fringe world of New Genesee subsided.

* * *

The raid on Society 437 had been Cameron's idea.

"They have scads of stuff we can use," he pointed out during one of Scanlon's strategy sessions. "They have three stations operating down there. We take the one called Aquarius, in the tropics. There's forty or fifty technicians there, tops. We'll outnumber them two to one, and we can shut them down in no time flat, heist their hardware and be gone before the big station, Central, knows what's happened."

"Hell, George," Lowboy said, "that's a goddamn scientific survey team down there! The Confederation's invested trillions in that expedition. You don't think they'd sit by and let us strip the joint!"

"Who's to stop us? They have no—repeat, no—military security. If the survey team has followed the standard TO and E, the only weapons they have are to protect against unfriendly animals. Shit, they're all scientists and eggheads! I bet most of them don't even know how to use the few weapons they have. Besides, they're so spread out, they couldn't possibly reinforce Aquarius."

"Why not, Cap'n?" Rhys Apbac chimed in enthusiastically. Rhys was always ready to go on a raid. He grinned fiercely at the others and recited the only piece of poetry he knew, an ancient highwayman's ditty he'd managed to memorize after years of practice:

"Come tighten your girth and slacken your rein,
Buckle your holster and blanket again;
Try the click of your trigger and balance your blade,
For he must ride sure who goes riding a raid."

Scanlon ignored Rhys, who sat there grinning triumphantly at the others after finishing his recitation. He said to Cameron, "The Confederation might get pissed enough to send a really significant naval force out here if we mess with 437, George."

"Count on it," Cameron replied. "They'll send Marines, bet you money. But so what? Before that can be done, the Bureau of Human Habitability, or whatever they call it, will have to request a military force be dispatched there. That can take six months. By then the stuff we get will all be sold. There are a dozen wildcat mining and construction teams working throughout five or six systems who'll buy the sophisticated gear we can get on 437, no questions asked, cash on delivery. What's the Confederation going to do then? Investigate everybody in the whole damned quadrant?"

Indeed, Scanlon owned two starship freighters that could go anywhere in Human Space. There was no limit to where they could go to conduct a raid, or where they could go to sell whatever they got.

Scanlon thought a bit. Lowboy watched. He was beginning to dislike Cameron, who had just come into the Red 35 Crew, and was already worming his way into Scanlon's confidence. And he had that bitch Minerva too, Lowboy thought. Goddamn whore. Lowboy had tried to score on her once himself, and she'd rejected him. He detested her after that, and he'd grown to resent Cameron's relationship with her.

"George, can you plan this raid and pull it off?" Scanlon asked.

"You bet, Captain! Right down to the microns. Leave it to me."

"Okay," Scanlon said with finality. Lowboy mentally kicked himself for not having thought of the raid first. Well, he reflected, maybe Pretty Boy Georgie would have an accident on Society 437.

And the raid would have worked perfectly, just as Cameron had planned it, except for one horribly unforeseen circumstance.

Back at the fire, Cameron nudged Minerva with the toe of his boot. She sat up sleepily. "What's for breakfast, Georgie?"

"Raw beef, Minnie," Cameron answered. He grabbed a glowing brand from the fire to light his way. It seemed they were back in the Stone Age. That's another thing we need, he reflected: energy packs.

Grinning, Minerva got up and followed him far back into the cave, away from where the others were just beginning to stir. "Georgie," she whispered, her breath hot in his ear, "are we going to make it?" meaning, Would they survive this ordeal?

"You bet, honey," Cameron answered, by which he meant what they were about to do in the near darkness of the cave's recesses. What the hell, he thought, the future would still be there when they were done.

CHAPTER
FIVE

Ulf Thorsfinni's Saga

Ulf Thorsfinni was the last of his breed. Tall, muscular, athletic, blond, and cursed with an irresistible urge to see what lay beyond the horizon, plunder whatever was there, and bring the booty home.

Tall, muscular, athletic, and blond were just as desirable physical characteristics in the mid-23rd century as they had been throughout all the history—and prehistory—of Northern Europe. But the irresistible urge to see what lay beyond the horizon was a curse, as all the horizons of Earth had long since been gone past and nothing new was left to see. Even if there had been, society in general frowned on plundering whatever was there. And the civilized people at home didn't even want the booty brought back.

Had he lived in an earlier age, Ulf Thorsfinni's exploratory exploits might still be commemorated in sagas to rival those of Eric the Red, Lief Ericsson, or Ragnar Hairy-Breeks. Or he might have been a king, cast in the mold of Harold, Olaf, Haakon, or Magnus. Instead, it was his fate to be the scion of a family of commerce—and not merely *a* family of commerce, but *the* Family of Commerce.

The Thorsfinnis had started small, back in the early 22nd century, when Great-Grandpapa Thorsfinni sold the family fishing trawler and used the proceeds to purchase a pine tree strand, which he clear-cut and then replanted with hickory, oak, and other hardwoods. For some years Thorsfinniwold, as Great-Grandpapa Thorsfinni named his wood strand, served as a nursery, providing saplings to architects and landscapers. When the trees that weren't sold as saplings grew large enough, some of them were culled and sold to wood-carvers and cabinetmakers at what would have been exorbitant prices had hardwoods not been so rare and difficult to come by. That provided the kroners (an archaic term even then) for Great-Grandpapa Thorsfinni's grand plan.

The profits of the nursery and hardwoods, and they were substantial, were used to buy a partnership in a fledgling venture capital bank. Unlike his partners, who used their income from the bank to live very rich lives, Great-Grandpapa Thorsfinni used his share of the profits to quietly buy up portions of the shares of his partners, each of whom thought he was merely selling a few shares to the juniormost partner so he could increase his earnings and begin to live as richly as they were. Needless to say, the partners were quite surprised when one day Great-Grandpapa Thorsfinni announced that, as majority partner, he was taking full control of the bank and they could either sell the remainder of their shares to him or accept whatever dividends he deigned to declare. Few of them took him seriously enough to sell immediately. They all took him seriously when they discovered how small were the dividends that the majority owner doled out. Thorsfinnibank, as the business was quickly renamed, thereafter became the richest and most prestigious venture-capital bank in Scandinavia.

Great-Grandpapa Thorsfinni didn't merely lend to entrepreneurs who came to him for the financial backing they needed to make their—and Thorsfinnibank's—fortunes. He invested money in his many childrens' projects as well.

Great-Uncle Leif went into mining in a big way with Thorsfinnimineral. Great-Aunt Emily built an amazingly successful tropical jungle theme park on the Arctic Circle, which she called Thorsfinniworld. With his Thorsfinniherring, Great-Uncle Haakon became one of the greatest fishing farmers in the North Atlantic. Great-Aunt Gertrude bought a failing spaceshipyard and converted it to Thorsfinniship, the world's first shipyard devoted entirely to starship construction. Great-Uncle Olaf and his Thorsfinnientrepreneurship went through a series of endeavors, each of which he sold at a humongous profit. Great-Aunt Mildred borrowed money from Thorsfinnibank to buy her way into the tiny remnant of European royalty and became Empress Mildred I. Not that she had an empire to be empress of, but the entire world quickly came to know her as Empress Mildred, and wherever she went, which was just about everywhere, even the powerful bowed and scraped.

Grandpapa Magnus Thorsfinni was the only failure of the lot. Everything he tried his hand at crumbled, went under, failed. As much out of pity as out of a feeling of family equity, Great-Grandpapa Thorsfinni left two shares of his holdings to each of Grandpapa Thorsfinni's children for each single share he left to his other grandchildren. There were no business failures among Great-Grandpapa Thorsfinni's grandchildren. By the time Ulf reached his majority, it seemed to the great-grandchildren of Great-Grandpapa Thorsfinni that the Thorsfinnis owned all of Norway, most of the rest of Scandinavia, half of the rest of Europe, and significant chunks of Asia, Africa, the Americas, and Australia, not to mention substantial holdings on other worlds. They didn't own quite that much, but it certainly felt to the great-grandchildren that they did.

Young Ulf looked around and felt despair. He saw no horizons left to go beyond. There was no major endeavor, other than the arts, in which the Thorsfinnis were not already a power—and Ulf was unable to draw a straight line even with a ruler and could not write a coherent sentence. He was tone deaf too. Moreover, he couldn't stand artists of any sort, so being an impresario was out of the question.

What Young Ulf really wanted to do was build a dragonship and go a-Viking. But, as noted above, that was impractical. So he did the next best thing. He went to Uncle

Herrman, who now owned and ran Thorsfinniship, Great-Aunt Gertrude's starshipyard, and bought a starship—at a family discount, of course.

The *Glittertenden* was a magnificent ship, a Ragnarok-class cruiser, a civilian design based on the Confederation Navy's Crowe-class amphibious assault battle cruiser. In its appropriate military configuration, it carried a navy warship crew of three thousand plus an assault force of two full Marine FISTs, each two thousand men strong, and was powerful enough that, with a handful of destroyers in escort, it could single-handedly defeat any of the secondary worlds in the Confederation, or nearly any of the nonconfederated worlds in all of Human Space. In its civilian configuration, the Ragnarok-class cruiser could carry a crew of four hundred along with some ten thousand colonists, or an eight hundred member crew and six thousand vacationers.

To please Young Ulf, Uncle Herrman had a dragon-head prow constructed on the part of the ship arbitrarily designated the bow. The dragon-head was totally nonfunctional, of course, but it made Young Ulf's chest swell with pride.

Ulf then set about finding like-minded spirits who wanted to go a-Viking, and to find a suitable world on which they could do it.

Finding a world was easy. About the time Great-Grandpapa Thorsfinni had bought into what became Thorsfinnibank, a deep-space probe discovered a planetary system 150 light-years from Sol. One planet of the system was within the liquid-water range of its primary. It had gravity within five percent of Earth and a breathable, though aromatic, atmosphere.

There were, quite naturally, life-forms native to the planet. Some of the fauna was rather large and voraciously carnivorous. None were venomous to humans, however. Some of the flora was edible after a fashion. Which is to say a human being could eat it without being poisoned, and it would take months of a purely native diet before any nutrition-deficiency symptoms became apparent. The animals could be eaten as well, and with the same considerations.

The planet in question had no name, just some meaningless, bureaucratic alphanumeric designation. It had no landmass of continental size. It did, however, have a proliferation of islands. The most desirable, in Ulf's eyes, was an oblong running roughly north to south, about the size of Scandinavia, and closer to one of the poles than to the equator. More, this large island was mountainous, craggy, rocky, and rent with coastal fissures that could accurately be called fjords. The island was cold in the winter and balmy in the summer, and surrounded by a gray, crashing ocean reminiscent of the North Atlantic.

An attempt was made early on to colonize the planet. The attempt didn't take. The first problem was its distance from Earth. In the early days of interstellar colonization, few people were willing to go so far from home, so there weren't enough colonists to assure a sufficiently varied gene pool. The small number of willing colonists wasn't the only problem caused by distance. It was too expensive to ship everything needed for the colony, and would take generations with the then-existing technology to develop local resources to the point where the colony could sustain itself. Then there was the aromatic atmosphere—it was rank with the odor of fish. After less than a generation the bedraggled survivors managed to importune the Confederation to resettle them on a more hospitable world.

But it was just the kind of home from which a proper Norseman would want to go a-Viking, and Ulf industriously went about lining up colonists.

Eventually, the passenger manifest for the maiden voyage of the *Glittertenden* had eight thousand names on it, to go along with a crew of nine hundred. The Viking-colonists were of all ages, from suckling babes to oldsters—every stedding, Ulf believed, needed an elder. Alas, from Ulf's point of view, not all of them were Norwegian. There simply weren't that many Norwegians who wanted badly to go a-Viking—especially not once they learned the details of the world they were to populate. So Ulf had to fill out the ranks with non-Norwegians. He made every one of the foreigners adopt a Norwegian name, however, so Thorsfinni's World is populated in large measure by dark-haired, swarthy Neilsons, kinky-haired Knutsons, and sallow-skinned Sturulsons.

Thorsfinniworld was the name of Great-Aunt Emily's tropical jungle theme park, so Young Ulf had to go against family tradition in naming his world. He called it, instead, Thorsfinni's World. He named the large island Niflheim. He married a woman he insisted adopt the name—and be called—Frigg. They had two sons, whom he named Balder and Thor. He built a proper dragon-head ship and sailed the seas—and took his sons with him as soon as they were old enough to scramble about the deck without falling overboard. Ulf Thorsfinni had a grand time.

Until one day the Confederation Navy came knocking at his door and told him they needed to establish a base in that sector of Human Space and they were going to do it on his world.

It was immediately evident to everyone that ten thousand 23rd century Vikings—the population had grown some in the twenty-five years since Ulf first went a-Viking—dressed in furs and chain mail and swinging broad swords were no match for the reinforced company of Confederation Marines backing up the admiral who made the announcement. So Ulf Thorsfinni grudgingly agreed to the base, even though few if any of the navy and Marine personnel assigned to his world would bear Norwegian names.

He did, however, manage some concessions. The base was located on a remote section of Niflheim, well removed from the "major" centers of population. Only local building materials could be used in construction, which limited the navy and Marines to wood and stone. All construction had to be done by local contractors, which meant everything was made from wood, as there were too few stone masons to do as much construction as the base required.

The construction concessions gave a slight boost to the economy, what with all those contractors getting the work and all those local suppliers supplying the materials. The contractors got more work when they built Bronnoysund, the liberty town that sprang up outside the main gate of Camp Major Pete Ellis, which became the home of 34th FIST, Confederation Marine Corps.

In time, the citizens of Thorsfinni's World came to like the military presence on their world. The navy, based near New Oslo, gave them strange and exotic people to laugh at. And the Marines at Camp Ellis were more than happy to oblige the citizens of Bronnoysund in their favorite occupations of eating, drinking, brawling, and cuddling for warmth in the cold and dank.

CHAPTER
SIX

Freya Banak, a.k.a. "Big Barb"—a sobriquet she liked, incidentally, and had trademarked for her personal use—was deservedly famed for her evil disposition. A big woman in later middle age—around seventy-five—she weighed three hundred pounds and was six-foot-four in her wooden clogs. Big Barb had broken up more fights in her establishment than 34th FIST's battle standard had campaign streamers. And she ran a tight ship: No patron of hers was ever cheated by a waitress or a whore, and when one patron tried to abuse another at her bar, he could count on summary and violent ejection into the street. But Freya Banak had one weakness: Gunnery Sergeant Charlie Bass.

"Charlie-e-e," Big Barb crooned after they were seated in her private office at the rear of the bar, "vat brinks you here dis afternoon? Coffee?" She poured a big mug full of the strong, steaming coffee the citizens of Bronnoysund liked so much. It couldn't, as Marine tradition had it, burn the camouflage paint off a Dragon, but Gunny Bass felt his nervous system tightening just at the smell of the stuff. Still, he took the proffered cup with thanks and sipped at it cautiously, feigning great pleasure.

Barb sat hugely behind her antique desk, hands clasped under her capacious breasts, fingers as big as sausages entwined, enormous thumbs twiddling nervously. Her gaptooth smile, reminiscent of an idiot's leer, was anything but, Bass knew. She was just enormously pleased to be alone in the back office with her favorite Marine. Despite himself,

Bass was flattered. Oh, he could take Barb if he wanted to, but Mohammed's hairy balls, she was so damned fat! And yet the two of them had a lot in common. Both were used to having their way, and both knew instinctively when to act decisively, and when either made a decision—whether to toss out a bum or to attack a fortified position—it was done with rapid calculation and no second thoughts, just hi diddle diddle, straight up the middle.

Bass carefully placed his nearly full cup on a corner of Barb's desk. He thought: She does have magnificent hair. It was done in long platinum braids that hung down on either side of her chest. Fat, yes, but her complexion was perfectly clear and lustrous. Bass sometimes thought if only she'd lose 150 pounds . . .

"Barb, Diamunde was hard on the 34th—"

"Yah, you lose some men. I hear all about it. Eagle's Cry, he vas killed and some odders. I am sorry, Charlie."

Bass nodded. "I've had five men in my platoon promoted, Barb, and we need a place to throw a party. Can you rent me your big back room, next Saturday sundown through Sunday noon? We'll need beer, steaks, all that for let's say sixty people, the thirty men in my platoon plus guests. I expect the brigadier and Sergeant Major Shiro'll make an appearance, as well as Commander Van Winkle, Sergeant Major Parant, Captain Conorado, Top Myer, some buddies from other platoons the men might bring as guests. You know, the usual lineup for a platoon bash."

Barb smiled broadly. "Sure, Charlie!" She made a note on a pad by her side. "Hey, I hear you now are platoon commander. Got you up to officer's slot, yah? But you still a gunny. How come you never go for an officer, Charlie?"

Bass shrugged. "No time, Barb. Besides, the Corps already has a commandant, and like I've always said, if I can't be Pope, I don't wanna be a Catholic." Barb laughed and her whole body shook. Her laugh sounded from way down inside her belly, and the harder she laughed, the redder her cheeks glowed. When Barb was laughing, men forgot her foul mouth and hamlike fists. Her laugh was infectious. Bass grinned, and that made her laugh even harder. "What'll all that cost me, Barb?"

Still chuckling, Barb made some calculations and named a figure. Bass's eyebrows shot up. The figure was quite reasonable but he still wanted a better deal. He leaned back in his chair before replying. "Okay, but the five guys promoted, if they want to, they get a free all-nighter with the girl of their choice."

Now it was Barb's turn to lean back. She put her hands behind her head. Bass marveled again at the vast expanse of her breasts, which were as big as pillows. She looked back at him through narrowed, calculating eyes, but there was a twinkle in them. "Okay," she said at last, and thrust out her hand. Bass took it. For such a huge hand, it wasn't that bad-looking; soft and warm, big but feminine.

After the perfunctory shake, Barb held on for a long moment. "I alvays like you, Charlie," she murmured as she stood up. Bass stood too as she came around the desk. She walked lightly for such a big person. Barb was packed solid, like a huge, firm sausage, no unhealthy folds of skin hanging about her face and neck or arms. She jiggled like a bowl of gelatin, not a mound of suet. She reached out and grabbed Bass by one arm. It took all his strength to stand his ground. She placed the other arm in the small of his back and drew him to her capacious breasts. "Charlie, I haf alvays liked you," she whispered. Her breath was sweet and warm in his ear. A man could do worse, Bass reflected.

When they were done, Big Barb liked Charlie Bass even better than before.

"I'm going to keep these remarks short," Brigadier Sturgeon said. The men of third platoon, Company L, stood in a circle about the FIST commander in Big Barb's private party room. As the guest of honor, he was required to make some remarks. "I have several other promotion parties to attend this evening, and at every one of them I'll be obliged to have two or three beers."

His remark was greeted by polite laughter.

"In the recent past I've developed a rather close relationship with some of the men of third platoon here. Claypoole and Dean over there earned their stripes on Wanderjahr, and I took them with me through some mighty tense times on that deployment, let me tell you. And they never let me down. The men of this platoon, this company, this battalion, the men of 34th FIST, have never let anybody down and they never will."

This remark was greeted by a roar from the men of third platoon.

"What's a promotion mean?" the brigadier continued after the shouting died down. "Well, for one thing, it's a bit more beer money in your pocket." Another roar of approval from the Marines. "It means a bit more authority too, maybe a new job, another digit to your specialty code. And yes, your new stripes will look great when you wear your dress reds on liberty somewhere. But what a promotion really means is that the military professionals who have been placed over you recognize your ability to share the burden of leadership. And leadership is a burden. It's not fun, it's not easy, and if you do it right, you won't win any popularity contests. But remember this always: if you are a good leader, your men will live to hate your guts. So those chevrons are the marks that show the whole world just where you stand in the ranks of the professionals."

The Marines shouted, clapped, and stamped their feet until the floor under them shook. Commander Van Winkle, Sergeant Major Shiro, and Sergeant Major Parant, also guests of honor, were right in there with the rest of them, shouting and whistling and stamping their feet. The brigadier raised his arms for silence. "I know there are some of you who don't want to be promoted. Lance Corporal Schultz over there is one of them. That's his privilege. He's proved his worth on many a battlefield. At least I know he's not looking for my job." Again much laughter. Those nearest Schultz clapped him heartily on the back.

Dean, who was standing closest, hammered him hardest. He would sorely miss the taciturn lance corporal now that he'd been transferred to first squad's second fire team. Bass had said it was to train him to back up the new fire team leader, Corporal Pasquin, and Dean understood it meant he'd someday be in line for a corporal's stripes. But when they went into combat again, Dean knew he would miss the steadying presence of Lance Corporal "Hammer" Schultz. And besides that, there was Pasquin. Goddamnit, Dean thought, why did Hammer have to be so stubborn? He'd have made a fine corporal to lead second fire team. Now he would be stuck between PFC Izzy Godenov, who always seemed unsure of himself, and the new corporal, who for some reason had taken an almost instant dislike to Lance Corporal Joe Dean.

"Okay, men, enough speechifying. Just let it be known how proud I am of the officers and men of the 34th FIST." Sturgeon glanced at Van Winkle to see whether the infantry commander wanted to say anything. When Van Winkle shook his head, Sturgeon turned to the Company L commander. "Now, Captain Conorado?"

Conorado stepped into the spot vacated by the brigadier and said, "Let the games begin!" Gunnery Sergeant Bass and Sergeant "Hound" Kelly, gun squad leader, emerged from the crowd. They were to "officiate." Someone brought a small table and set it in the center of the circle. Five of Big Barb's best-looking girls marched in at a signal from Bass and placed five two-liter schooners of beer on the table. Into each schooner Kelly dropped the chevrons of each promoted man's new rank: Hyakowa to staff sergeant; Bladon and Ratliff to sergeant; and Goudanis and Stevenson to corporal. The five promoted men were shoved and pushed into the circle.

"By the authority vested in me and all that bullshit," Bass bellowed, "we will now vest our beloved comrades into the sacrosanct strata of their recent elevations in rank." That was the "wetting down" of the new stripes. In order of rank, each man would be called in turn, and be required to drink the schooner dry. It was not necessary that every drop be consumed, but deliberately pouring the beer on the floor was not permitted; it could only be spilled on the drinker. After each man was done, Bass and Kelly would then pin the dripping chevrons.

Staff Sergeant Hyakowa stepped boldly to the table and seized the schooner. "Goddamn, I'm dry!" he shouted. "I haven't had a beer since—since—an hour ago!" With that, he began to gulp the beer down. With each gulp the assembled Marines shouted "A-ruh-ha!" until the schooner was empty. Hyakowa banged the empty glass loudly on the table and belched with enormous satisfaction. He had not spilled a drop! Bass handed the dripping chevrons to Kelly, who pinned them to the new staff sergeant's sleeve—with a stapler.

Bladon went next.

The ceremony over, the brigadier excused himself, and everyone dispersed to the wooden tables set up in the center of the large room. Girls came in carrying steaming platters of reindeer steak and schooners of beer. The laughter and talking echoed off the walls and men had to shout to be heard. The NCOs, less the five recently promoted, were on their honor to remain reasonably sober for the night, to break up any fights that might start, and also to help guide the drunks safely back to Camp Ellis when the party was over the following morning.

Dean had tried to find himself a place next to Schultz but instead wound up sitting between Corporal Pasquin and Izzy Godenov. After a few minutes Erika came in and squeezed between Godenov and Dean. Corporal Pasquin cast an angry glance at Dean when she sat down, but he said nothing. She draped an arm around Dean's and Godenov's shoulders. "How goes it, my happy Marine?" she whispered in Dean's ear, and kissed him. Her breath smelled of beer and her cheeks were flushed. Dean couldn't resist a smile. She ate bits of steak from his and Godenov's platters, drank half a schooner of beer with them, then excused herself. "I see you later," she whispered in Dean's ear.

Across the table MacIlargie was beerily describing how he and Dean had fought their way out of the cell Marston St. Cyr had put them into when he'd kidnapped the Confederation's ambassador on Diamunde. During the telling, Pasquin cast sour glances sideways at Dean, who tried to ignore him.

" 'A rather close relationship,' " Pasquin sneered at last, mimicking Brigadier Sturgeon's words.

"Huh?" Dean said. Beside him Godenov looked at Pasquin with a troubled expression on his face.

"I know guys like you, Dean. The officers ever stop suddenly, you'll break your nose."

Dean could only stare at the corporal in disbelief. He'd probably had more to drink that he should have, Dean reasoned. He took a big gulp out of his own glass, because he didn't know what else to do.

"You don't like what I jus' said? Shove it!" Pasquin said.

Again Dean did not know how to respond. He could not understand why the new man disliked him so much.

"We'll have to issue you an extra ration of toilet paper—" Pasquin began, but Dean had had enough.

"Look, Corporal Pasquin, you won't find any ass kissers in this outfit," he said hotly, "and until you prove you ain't one yourself, better you just shut the fuck up!" Dean instantly regretted the words, but there they were nonetheless.

Pasquin grabbed Dean's sleeve. "Look here, sonny—"

Someone laid a big hand on Pasquin's shoulder then, and he looked up. "Hammer . . . ?"

"It's 'Lance Corporal Schultz' to you, Corporal Pasquin. Nobody calls me Hammer until they earn the right to call me Hammer. And you ain't earned that right yet. Who you callin' 'sonny' anyway, Corporal? I've seen your ribbons. You ain't been in half the shit old Dean-o here's been in."

"I'm an NCO, Schultz—" Pasquin began.

"Yeah," Schultz answered, "and that's all you are for now.

Just remember, you fuck with old Dean-o here and you fuck with me." With that Schultz left.

"Sheez," Pasquin said, shaking himself, "that guy's had too much to drink. I'll talk to the gunny about him."

"Won't do any good," Godenov said. "He and Bass are tight. Why, on Elneal—"

"Oh, shut up, 'Not Good Enough'!" Pasquin almost shouted. "I don't need advice from a PFC! Man, how'd I ever get stuck with you two birds? I never seen such a collection of asshole buddies—"

"Corporal," Dean said, "you ever make a remark like that again about any man in this outfit and they'll have to feed you through your asshole from then on, 'cause that's how far down your throat I'm gonna shove your teeth."

Pasquin blanched. "Dean, threatening a noncommissioned officer is a court-martial offense!"

"I don't give a damn. Corporal, you've been on my case from the first day you got here, and I don't know why. But I am getting sick of you and your smart mouth. Just lay off me, okay?" Calmly, Dean picked up his beer glass and drained it. Pasquin stared at Dean. Godenov meanwhile stared at Pasquin, a huge grin on his face. Without another word, Pasquin got up and left the table.

"Jeez," Godenov sighed, "you're off to a good start with our new fire team leader!"

Dean considered that for a moment. He was frankly surprised at himself; it was the first time he had ever mouthed off to a superior in the Corps. Pasquin was a corporal and his fire team leader, but Pasquin had been way out of line with his remarks. Godenov was witness to that if it came to a captain's mast. Dean doubted it would, but he didn't know Pasquin well enough yet.

And Hammer! Dean had always felt a bit wary of Schultz, the no-nonsense combat veteran. But Schultz had told Pasquin, "You fuck with old Dean-o and you fuck with me," and, "You ain't been in half the shit old Dean-o here's been in." Those remarks did for Dean's self-respect what no medal given by the commandant himself could ever do.

"Izzy, why the hell is that guy on my ass?" Dean asked. "I can't figure it."

"Simple, Joe, he's jealous."

Dean looked sharply at Godenov. "Jealous?"

"Yeah. You're only a lance corporal but you got it through a meritorious promotion given by the brigadier himself, and you got a hero medal and he doesn't, and you been in a real war and he hasn't. Also," he leaned close and whispered, "he wants Erika real bad, an' she won't have a thing to do with the bastard."

Dean started. He remembered the night he'd had the fight with the sailor and what Erika had told him about Pasquin at the time. But he could not understand how anybody could be jealous of medals and promotions.

"Well, he'll just have to remain jealous," Dean replied, and that settled the matter—for the time being.

Corporal Raoul Pasquin sauntered disconsolately down the street. That he'd left the platoon party early would be noted, but he didn't care. He hadn't volunteered for duty with the 34th and he didn't want to be on Thorsfinni's World. Mentally he kicked himself. He should never have let that wiseass Dean get the better of him. But he had been out of line, Pasquin admitted at least that to himself. And that damn Schultz! A "professional PFC," not afraid of anybody because he wasn't going anywhere in the Corps except maybe back to private, and that didn't bother a guy like him.

Now he'd gone and violated etiquette by stomping out of the party early. Bass would have him in his office first thing Monday morning. I better get my pussy layin' on my back from now on because I can only screw up! he thought wryly. He stopped. That was a thought. There was a place on the other side of town—and that would give him the excuse he needed to deflect the platoon commander's wrath. Anybody'd understand a man's need to get laid. No, no, he told himself.

Not with Charlie Bass. He'd see through it. Better just tell the truth—that he'd been sent to the 34th because his previous commander wanted to get rid of him.

"It was a goddamn accident!" he shouted aloud to the empty street. "An accident!" he said to the frigid night. There was no response. There never was. He shook his head sadly and walked on. Eventually he caught a ride back to Camp Ellis.

Maybe it had been an accident, but nobody else saw it that way.

PFC Orest Kindrachuck of the gun squad was known as a man who'd eat anything. PFC Nick Rowe of the second squad's third fire team claimed to be a man who'd bet on anything. It was inevitable the two would clash. At around 04 hours the following morning—for months afterward Marines argued over the precise time of the challenge—Rowe bet Kindrachuck a large sum of money—the witnesses argued about how much afterward, and with every telling the sum grew—that he couldn't drink a schoonerful of urine. Kindrachuck took him up on it. One of Big Barb's girls—and not the prettiest—obligingly filled a schooner halfway. "Not enough!" Rowe insisted, and he filled it to the rim. While a crowd of inebriated Marines stood watching with bated breath, Kindrachuck lifted the schooner to his lips and began to chugalug the vile concoction. His Adam's apple bobbed up and down as steadily he drank the schooner dry. A small golden rivulet coursed slowly down one side of his mouth but otherwise he did not spill a drop of the liquid.

"He drank it all!" someone whispered in awe. The entire room had fallen into a deep and amazed silence. After that night Kindrachuck was known as "Chugalug Kindrachuck," but now he stood there, swaying slightly, a sickish expression on his face. Suddenly he doubled over and vomited copiously on the floor. Men shouted and staggered away from the spray.

"You—You—didn't—say," Kindrachuck gasped when he

was done, "that I had to keep it down! Pay up!" He wiped yellowish slime from the sides of his mouth with one hand.

Rowe stared at the mess on the floor, chunks of half-digested steak and vegetables mixed in a beige-colored broth of urine and beer. "Okay!" he shouted, holding up his arms for silence. "Okay, Orie. Here's the deal. I bet you twice as much that you won't, that you can't, eat that slop with a spoon!" The room plunged again into a dead silence. Eat . . . ? Everyone was totally horrified at the dimensions of the new bet. "Double or nothing!" Rowe shouted, breaking the spell. In hushed tones, as befitted deals made in the presence of such an awesome wager, Marines laid side bets.

Kindrachuck hesitated only briefly. "Gimme a goddamn spoon!" he shouted.

For the next month PFC Orest "Chugalug" Kindrachuck had more loose cash in his pockets than ever before in his life, and everyone in third platoon remembered that night as one of the finest they'd ever had.

CHAPTER
SEVEN

The morning after the promotion party, a tall corporal in dress reds came out of the Company L office and walked past the company's campaign streamer staff—it may have been only his imagination, but it looked fuller than the last time he'd seen it. Had to be his imagination, the FIST had only been on two operations since he was last on Thorsfinni's World. The corporal's left chest was adorned with nearly a dozen medals, and a wound stripe decorated the lower part of his left sleeve. His expression could have been described as blank, but it had traces of an almost superhuman calmness and a touch of grimness. There was an unsettled quality to his eyes that could have been interpreted as suppressed fear, but was maybe just a bit of nervousness.

The corporal walked slowly down the mirror-polished floor of the corridor, past the 2-D portraits of the chain of command on its institutional-ochre walls, and mounted the stairs to the barracks' second deck. He paused at the head of the stairs and looked to the right into the company classroom, which off-duty Marines were using in its alternate capacity as the company recreation room. Then he looked to his left, where a series of doors lined the corridor. He took a deep breath, turned that way, and slowly, with growing confidence, began walking. Halfway along the corridor he stopped and turned to an open door. He crossed his arms and leaned against the jamb, looking into the room.

It was a fire team room, living quarters for three men. The room was a mess, as was to be expected on an off day, even more on the day following a big party. Only one man was visible, though sounds coming through the door to the head alerted the corporal that someone else was probably at home.

The Marine in the room was sitting in his skivvies on his unmade rack, looking the worse for wear. He was staring blankly at the screen of a personal vid.

Must have been one hell of party, the corporal thought. I'm sorry I missed it. He cleared his throat.

Bleary-eyed, the young Marine looked up. He struggled to focus on the man in the doorway and finally decided the Marine with two chevrons on his dress reds sleeves and a lot of medals on his chest was someone he didn't know. "Can I help you with something, Corporal?" he asked as politely as his condition allowed.

"You're MacIlargie," the corporal said. It didn't quite come out as an accusation.

MacIlargie blinked rapidly. He started to shake his head but thought better of it. The way his head felt, shaking it would probably make it fall off, and then he'd really be in trouble.

"I'm Mac," he confirmed. It slowly got through to him that this stranger knew who he was, but he didn't know who the corporal was. "Who're you?" he blurted, then groaned and clutched his throbbing head for speaking so suddenly.

"I remember you!" came an excited voice from the adjoining door. "You're—"

"I remember you too," the corporal interrupted. "You're Claypoole."

"You're Corporal Kerr! Damn, I'm glad to see you back again." Claypoole stood, fresh from the shower, one hand holding around his waist the too-small towel the military has issued for as long as military organizations have issued towels. The shower had partly cleared his hangover.

MacIlargie pivoted his head toward Claypoole. Corporal Kerr? Was he supposed to know him?

"Hey," Claypoole said, hit with sudden inspiration, "are you back with third platoon? The platoon's been reorganized.

Except, Mac and me, we don't have a fire team leader yet. We're supposed to be getting some hardass coming to be second fire team leader. If you're back with third platoon, you can be our fire team leader, how about it?"

MacIlargie turned his head, more quickly than he should have, to stare ar Kerr. The moan that escaped his open mouth was partly from the increased throbbing in his brain case, partly because he caught on more quickly than Claypoole had. "You're our new fire team leader," he croaked. "You're the one. Sergeant Bladon said you'd make me wish I was in a different company."

Kerr looked at him levelly. "You aren't as badly hungover as you put on, are you? Glad to hear that. Get dressed and go down to see Corporal Doyle. He'll show you my gear. Bring it up." He looked up at Claypoole. "You don't really expect me to live in a sty like this, do you? Get started on a field day. I expect to find this room at least halfway fit for human habitation by the time I get back." He shook his head and turned away. "That's what I get for doing something dumb and nearly getting myself killed," he said as though talking to himself, but loudly enough for Claypoole and MacIlargie to clearly hear him. "I come back and they stick me with the platoon's goddamn problem children as a test to see if I'm still good enough to be a Marine corporal."

Kerr walked to the end of the corridor, to the room shared by third platoon's squad leaders, to see if any of them was awake.

Claypoole and MacIlargie stared at each other, horrified. That wasn't the Corporal Kerr who Claypoole remembered. The wound Kerr got on Elneal should have killed him. Maybe it had, and when the doctors pieced the body back together a different person occupied it. MacIlargie didn't know anything about Kerr; he hadn't joined the company until after the campaign on Elneal. All he knew was, so far, the corporal was living up to every fear he had of a hardcase NCO.

* * *

The squad leaders were awake, even if Ratliff and Bladon didn't look particularly alive. Sergeant Kelly, who as one of those designated to make sure the others made it back to base hadn't done nearly as much drinking as the other two, was the first to see and recognize Kerr. He jumped to his feet and crossed to the door in two long steps.

"Kerr!" he said as he grasped Kerr's hand and pulled him far enough into the room to wrap an arm across his shoulders. "Damn, it's good to see you. Man, we thought you were just about dead. Welcome back."

"I *was* just about dead," Kerr said leadenly. "It's good to be anywhere."

Ratliff and Bladon managed to rouse themselves from their funereal state. Ratliff stopped moving once his feet were on the floor and let his body slump over his lap. "Welcome back, Kerr," he croaked.

Bladon struggled all the way to his feet. He extended his hand to Kerr, overbalanced, jerked his hand back, and almost toppled backward before gaining a wobbly balance. He worked his mouth for a moment to find enough saliva to speak. "Kerr, I am so glad to see you." Overwhelmed by the effort required to talk while standing, Bladon plopped backward onto his rack, where he mimicked Ratliff's posture.

"I am really sorry I missed that party," Kerr said. He shook his head at the two new sergeants.

"You think they're bad?" Kelly said. "You should see Juice and Stevenson. I don't think they're going to come to until tomorrow." He snorted. "Hell, they might not even be sobered up in time for morning formation the day after that."

Bladon ratcheted his head up and tried to focus on Kerr. It took too much effort; he closed one bloodshot eye and found he could fix the other on Kerr. "You're in my squad." His breath was heavy with the effort of speaking. "Second fire team leader. You got Claypoole and MacIlargie."

An expression that might have been pain, might have been dismay, washed quickly across Kerr's face. "My squad leader," he said in the same dull voice he'd spoken in before. "Last

time I saw you, you were a corporal and I was senior to you."
He shrugged. "Things like that happen when you almost get
killed." He shook off the momentary moroseness and continued in a more lively voice, "Yeah, I already know about
Claypoole and MacIlargie. I saw Sta—*Gunny* Bass, and—"
He paused half a beat to make sure he got it right the first
time. "—*Staff Sergeant* Hyakowa in the company office.
They told me." He shook his head. There had been a lot of
changes in third platoon since Elneal. They were going to
take some getting used to.

"How'd Hyakowa look?" Ratliff asked, not really believing
that the platoon sergeant could already be up and about.

"Not too bad," Kerr said. "Gunny Bass forced the detoxi-
fier down him a little while ago."

Ratliff and Bladon turned bleary eyes toward each other.
Detoxifiers, that sounded good. Each wondered if the other
had the strength to get up and go get some, because he didn't.

A memory flashed through Kerr's mind, and he staggered
and had to put a hand on the wall to balance himself. The
others were too unsteady themselves to notice.

Again, in little longer than the blink of an eye, he saw that
scene. Third platoon was in the village of Turlak Yar on Elneal. Suddenly, two old Raptors, the ground-support aircraft,
swooped down and fired plasma guns on the village, mur-
dering people and setting their houses ablaze. The Marines
raced madly for their defensive positions around the village.
The Raptors made three passes before they turned and flew
away. As they did, a horde of horsemen boiled over the bluff
and charged into the burning village. Horsemen! Wielding
projectile rifles with fixed bayonets, like something out of a
historical vid!

Horsemen with rifles and fixed bayonets were so archaic,
the Marines had never given serious consideration to the possibility of anyone attacking them that way. And no one had
any idea the Siad rebels had Raptors.

Hundreds of horsemen were milling about, others racing
randomly from spot to spot, firing their rifles with deadly

accuracy, stabbing with their fixed bayonets. The Marines fought furiously and were killing large numbers of the horsemen, but there were so many of them. Then Kerr and McNeal were mobbed by a mass of snorting, stomping horses.

The next thing Kerr knew, he was in postsurgical intensive care in a hospital. When he recovered enough for the doctors to carry on a conversation with him, they told him they were surprised he'd lived through his injuries. And they expressed admiration for the enlisted medical personnel who served with the Marines. "I know the corpsmen the navy medical corps assigns to Marine FISTs are top-notch," said the head physician on Kerr's case. "You're proof that they're even better than I thought. You owe your life to the corpsman who stabilized you on the scene." The doctors expected him to regain full use of all his limbs and faculties. They expected him to be as good as new once his therapy was complete.

Physically, he was. Mentally . . . Every now and again, though, that memory flashed through his mind and for a moment nearly incapacitated him. He was usually able to shake it off before anyone noticed. Secretly, he wondered if he'd ever be able to fight again, and he wondered if he'd always be able to recover from the memory so quickly. He also secretly wondered if he was still fit to be a Marine corporal; he wondered if he could still lead men at all, much less lead them in combat. He'd come so close to death, he wasn't sure he could go in harm's way again without cracking.

Quickly, as always, Kerr recovered.

"So, Tam," he said in a steady enough voice, "my squad leader, what's our training schedule look like?"

Bladon fixed one bloodshot eye on Kerr and gingerly searched through his mind for an answer that would be intelligible to both of them.

CHAPTER
EIGHT

Dr. Blossom Enderle, Chief of the Confederation Bureau of Human Habitability Exploration and Investigation (BHHEI), was worried. For nearly a century, starting out as a field scientist, Dr. Enderle had devoted her life to the exploration and investigation of new worlds for the ever-expanding populations and entrepreneurs of the Confederation of Worlds. For the last twenty years she had been chief of BHHEI, or "Behind," to its scientists and technicians, because the bureau's communications with its field teams, due to the distances involved, always lagged months behind.

Dr. Enderle had weathered many crises during all those years. Hundreds of lives had been lost; entire teams and their vessels had simply disappeared in deep space without a trace. Other teams had met with disaster on the new worlds. In each of those many incidents, BHHEI had investigated and organized mostly successful rescue efforts of teams in distress.

The criterion for authorizing a rescue operation was simple. Exploratory teams were required to maintain constant communication with BHHEI via Beamspace drones launched according to a rigid schedule. Whenever a scheduled drone was missed, the bureaucratic wheels began to turn. Most often the drones failed for mechanical reasons, but the BHHEI had no choice—when a drone was not received on time, the worst was assumed and the navy was asked to investigate.

Society 437 was now overdue on its six-month report, and Society 437 was different. One of the biggest—hence most expensive—teams had been sent to that world, almost a thousand of the best scientists and technicians the bureau could gather. The scale of resources devoted to Society 437 was important because BHHEI's budget was always threatened by Confederation politicians anxious to divert money to their pet projects, and if some disaster had befallen that mission in particular, serious cuts would be called for—and probably effected.

But most important of all was that the leader of this expedition, Dr. Nikholas Morgan, was a scientist of preeminent standing in the Confederation of Worlds. He was also the brother of Henri Morgan, the most powerful member of the Space and Exploration Committee of the Confederation Congress, the man who could single-handedly cut BHHEI's purse strings. And he would, because he despised deep-space exploration as a waste of money. He argued there were plenty of ways to spend money on the populated worlds of Human Space without spending trillions to find new planets for colonization. But basically, Senator Henri Morgan hated scientists. Technicians were fine; they fixed things. Scientists were arrogant intellectuals who considered themselves superior to the majority of mankind because they "understood" things the common man could never comprehend. Scientists were the "priests" of an esoteric religion whose arcane body of knowledge gave them "insight" into how the universe worked. To Henri Morgan it was all bogus mumbo-jumbo perpetrated by people who'd avoided real work all their lives.

Dr. Nikholas Morgan did not quite fit that profile. No retiring intellectual, Nikholas was an assertive and outspoken crusader who had little patience with people who disagreed with him. His acerbic tongue had earned him countless enemies, but also countless admirers, people who worshiped him because he disdained and discomfited the rich and powerful, who were helpless when confronted by his wit and intelligence. Henri was very happy his brother had not gone into politics.

* * *

Dr. Enderle now had two visits to make, both unpleasant, in ascending order. The first was to Admiral Horatio Perry, Chairman of the Combined Chiefs of Staff. In cases of emergency, the Chief of BHHEI was authorized to communicate directly with the Chiefs, to expedite a response by cutting through the normal bureaucratic chain. On matters of routine liaison, Dr. Enderle would go through the Minister for Colonization who in turn would take the matter to the Confederation Council on which Admiral Perry sat as an adviser to Madame Chang-Sturdevant, Council President.

For his part, Admiral Perry considered BHHEI a pain in the behind. Since he had been chairman, the Confederation Navy had launched no fewer than twenty-five rescue missions to bail out egghead scientists who for one reason or another had neglected proper drone maintenance or otherwise stumbled into predicaments any well-organized military man would have anticipated and avoided. He considered the operations an unnecessary drain on his resources, already spread thin throughout Human Space on legitimate military tasks.

Dr. Enderle had decided to visit each man personally. That would take time out of her busy schedule, and she regretted that. Many details still had to be worked out regarding the rescue mission, the public relations angles being most important. Approval of the mission was assured, regardless of how she opted to contact Admiral Perry or Senator Morgan. But because of the seriousness of the situation, she felt it necessary to meet with the men face-to-face. It was especially important to meet with Senator Morgan, who, while often at odds with his brother, was still Nikholas Morgan's closest living kin. He deserved to hear the news in person instead of over a vidscreen from some bureaucrat sitting in an office miles away. And he controlled funding for BHHEI. Dr. Enderle was honest enough to admit to herself that it was the funding that motivated her. Personally, she considered Senator Morgan an odious demagogue, living proof that democracy doesn't work.

Dr. Enderle called for her car. It would take twenty minutes' surface travel to reach Admiral Perry's office on the other side of town. She wanted to see the sun and breathe fresh air on the way to the meetings. It was springtime in North America, and the city of Fargo, in what had once been the state of North Dakota, was particularly attractive in that season.

The Confederation Council, in effect the government of the Confederation of Worlds, had established itself in Fargo at the request of the United States government. A generation after the city of Washington had been obliterated, during the Second American Civil War, the government abandoned the new metropolis that had risen from its ruins and reestablished the federal enclave in the far western reaches of its territory. Fargo was selected as the new seat of government because it offered plenty of room for expansion. Years later, when the Confederation of Worlds was established, the U.S. government, which had led the way in the exploration and colonization of space and was a charter member of the Confederation, invited the Council to establish itself in Fargo as well. By the beginning of the 25th century the seat of the Confederation government had grown from a small city of 100,000 into a megalopolis of more than ten million people occupying the entire 1,200 square miles of what had been Cass County, North Dakota.

Now, on a fine spring morning, Dr. Blossom Enderle was on her way to the office of the Chairman of the Combined Chiefs to formally solicit his aid, as required by law, to find out what had happened on Society 437. She wondered idly as her landcar sped along the immaculate streets what the ancient peoples who had once inhabited that land would think could they see it. As far advanced as civilization had become, she often reminded herself, human nature had not changed one iota from the way it must have been in the Stone Age. She understood that scientists like Nikholas Morgan occasionally forgot that.

The Marine guards on duty at the main entrance to the Combined Chiefs' office complex snapped to attention when Dr. Enderle presented herself at the guard desk. She had called ahead, and, as ever, the military establishment was ready for any important visitor. A lance corporal, stunningly handsome in his immaculate dress red uniform, politely conducted her through a maze of corridors to Admiral Perry's office. Once turned over to one of his aides, an army major, she was asked to have a seat. The major bustled about officiously and offered her refreshments. Dr. Enderle noted that his uniform did not fit him well. The man was at least forty pounds overweight. She noted again that the enlisted personnel around the headquarters always looked so sharp, while the officers got away with a less than perfect military appearance. An admiral had once told her the reason: "Enlisted people have adult leadership; noncoms and chief petty officers are responsible for the enlisted people, but the officers are on their own."

"A cup of coffee, Major?" she replied to the offer of refreshments.

"Immediately, Doctor," the major replied, and pressed a button on the console beside his desk. An autosteward rolled from its closet and served the beverage. It was strong, sweet and hot, just the way she liked it. Before she was half finished, Admiral Perry came into the reception area.

"Good afternoon, Doctor," the admiral said, bowing slightly and gesturing toward his office. She followed him in and took the seat he offered. "How's everything at Behind these days?" Admiral Perry smiled. He knew what was coming and wanted to get in a dig before, as the law required, he was forced to do what Dr. Enderle would request of him.

"We have a Priority One," Enderle said tightly. The major followed her into the admiral's office and quietly set the coffee cup beside her chair before withdrawing. Briefly she outlined the situation.

"Are you sure Dr. Morgan just didn't, uh, forget to dispatch his drone on time," Admiral Perry said. "You know how wrapped up these guys get in what they're doing out there."

"I know Morgan, Admiral. You know him too. He would never let something as important as that slip. He knows what a stink a false alarm would cause in the, uh, community." Admiral Perry winced at the word "community," which to him meant the closed and very select society of scientists and intellectuals who usually considered the military an unnecessary nuisance and expense. At a recent Council meeting Enderle had argued strongly, and ill-advisedly in the admiral's opinion, for cutting fleet construction in favor of more funding for exploration and colonization. It was an old argument from her that fell flat on Madame Chang-Sturdevant, a staunchly promilitary President. The political climate could easily change one day; Blossom Enderle never would.

Admiral Perry studied Dr. Enderle as he considered just how to respond. She was showing her years, he thought. Her sharp, narrow face was a mass of wrinkles and her hair was thinning, but her black eyes were as bright as ever. People like her, he reflected, disdain people like us. Until they need us, and then it's like in the old poem, "A thin red line of heroes." Admiral Perry's anger surged. Against his will he found himself thinking, If something has happened to Morgan, at least it might shut the sonofabitch up for a while. Then he said, "I'll have my Operations deputy contact your staff in a few minutes, Doctor." He bit off the words. "Fortunately, we have the ships and the men to send on these—forays—no thanks to, uh," he was about to say "people like you" but said instead, "budgetary constraints."

Dr. Enderle knew exactly what the admiral had been about to say. She rose. "Thank you, Admiral Perry," she said. "You offer an excellent cup of coffee."

Back in her car, Dr. Enderle sighed. Well, that was done. Now to the really unpleasant task of the day, informing Senator Morgan that something might have happened to his brother.

The chambers of the Confederation Senate were housed in a sprawling complex in the Red River Valley. A guard at the entrance passed her perfunctorily into the main building, where she was on her own to find Senator Morgan's offices. She had to consult the building directory to do that.

"The senator is in a caucus now," a snotty receptionist told her and then went back to examining her nails. Dr. Enderle, head of a government agency that spent billions in appropriations, was left to sit in the reception area until the senator arrived—an hour later. With her long experience in government, Dr. Enderle knew full well that to the Confederation's elected representatives, who considered themselves gods, she was just another civil servant. She took her personal vid out of a coat pocket and activated it. She had time to read about a hundred pages of a historical novel titled *Knives in the Night*, when Senator Morgan finally came through the door.

The senator's swollen, florid face jiggled as he walked. "Ah, yes, Blossom. Been waiting long?" His voice sounded like boulders rolling down a mountainside. He breezed by her and straight into his office without asking her in. She winced at the way he used her first name, the master speaking down to his servant. Well, as a government official she was a "servant" of sorts, she reflected again, so she swallowed her pride.

Fifteen minutes later the snotty receptionist languidly informed her, "The senator will see you now."

Inside his vast office, Morgan sat behind an enormous desk. He waved her into a chair. The chairs about Senator Morgan's desk were specially designed so that even the tallest visitor was forced to look up at him. The diminutive Dr. Enderle cut a ridiculous figure sitting there, as if she were a small child again, sitting, against the rules, in Daddy's favorite lounger. It was just the effect Senator Henri Morgan desired.

"Sir, I may have some bad news about your brother."

Senator Morgan hated his brother. He was a scientist, after all. They had never agreed on anything all their lives. Nikholas, the younger of the two, considered Henri nothing more than a political opportunist, which he was, and a very good one at that. Nikholas never missed a chance to tell everyone that Henri merely cut back-room deals with other pork-barrel toadies to redistribute the Confederation's wealth, never equitably and never in the sacred cause of the advancement of science. In Nikholas's view, Henri feared ideas and the men who shared them because thinking men have always been the bane of politicians.

"Yes?" the senator replied. The question was neutral, as if someone had just called his name from the Congress floor for a comment on an issue under discussion. Enderle knew the Morgans hated each other. If Nikholas was dead, Henri wouldn't shed a single tear. But if his expedition had ended in disaster, Henri would use that as ammunition to sink BHHEI's funding the next time its budget came up for approval. That would really please the senator—a chance to savage BHHEI and be rid of his arrogantly self-righteous brother at the same time.

Briefly, Enderle explained the situation. Senator Morgan listened impassively.

"How long will it take to find out what's happened?" Morgan asked.

"Several months, sir, if the navy launches a ship immediately. First they'll have to designate a vessel, then assign the mission to some unit—"

"Keep me informed, Blossom."

The interview was over. Dr. Enderle got out of the oversize chair and walked rapidly out of the senator's sanctum. As she passed the receptionist's desk she paused, bent over her, and said, "You *are* looking fine today! Who's your undertaker?"

Dr. Enderle knew Admiral Perry despised her, and she knew that Senator Morgan was already happily arranging to torpedo her bureau. But those small animosities aside, Dr. Blossom Enderle was really concerned about the lives of the thousand scientists and technicians in Morgan's team, and she was afraid that something had gone terribly wrong on Society 437.

Preliminary surveys of the planet had revealed no life-forms inimical to human beings, but those surveys often failed to discover serious environmental threats. Morgan's earlier reports had come through with perfect regularity. She knew outsiders thought that her scientists got so wrapped up in their work that they sometimes forgot the basics, even on occasion forgetting to eat, but Morgan was a superb organizer and manager, and he had all the technical expertise needed to maintain his equipment. Even so, she worried.

"The people at Behind are really antsy about this Society 437 business," General Aldie Middleburg said. "Strange, sir, but I've worked with them on plenty of other incidents like this one and they've never before shown so much concern." As Operations Deputy for the Combined Chiefs, he and his staff had been in close contact with BHHEI's people for the last two days. "We'd have to launch anyway, but those folks think something nasty's happened out there."

"I know that," Admiral Perry answered, referring to the necessity of launching a rescue operation; the law required that. "They're 'concerned,' General, because with Nikholas Morgan's precious ass on the line, his brother's going to cut off their allowance," he added.

Normally, General Middleburg would have agreed with this assessment. "I don't know, sir," he ventured. Admiral Perry's eyebrows shot up at this. He nodded for General Middleburg to continue. "Project Golem has developed some activity out there."

Admiral Perry started. He saw the Golem reports on a regular basis, but personally he did not put much faith in them. He couldn't recall offhand any specific mention of activity anywhere in the general direction of Society 437, but then he was exposed to so much information, who could retain it all? "Golem. Society 437," he said to his computer monitor. Instantly, a top secret report appeared on his screen, the Society 437 portion highlighted, just two lines. The intelligence analyst who'd prepared the report rated the information fairly reliable. It had not been shared with BHHEI or anyone else outside the Combined Chiefs, and access to the information was strictly need-to-know for them as well—neither the Commandant of the Confederation Marine Corps, a full member of the Combined Chiefs, nor the Chief of Staff of the Army was cleared for this information.

Admiral Perry rubbed his chin thoughtfully. Now if Golem was on the money . . . "Who do we have who can deploy to that sector in the fastest time?" he asked his monitor. General Middleburg's staff had already compiled a list of available vessels, and it flashed onto his screen immediately. It was very short. "We probably don't need a capital ship for this mission," he mused. He reviewed the list of available units. If this was a Golem hit, a combat unit would be needed; a ship's landing party might not be able to handle what could come up on Society 437 if, in fact, anybody was still there. Marines.

"General, I see your staff recommends the CNSS *Fairfax County* and a contingent of Marines from the 34th FIST?" Admiral Perry thought about that for a moment. "Send the order," he sighed, and leaned back in his chair. "But, General Middleburg," he added, "specify in that order I don't want them to send more than a platoon of Marines. I'd send a corporal and two privates if I could get away with it. Damned if I'll waste the time of any more than a platoon on those people. We need to keep our deployable strength at as high a level as we can, to deal with really important things. I'm no gravel grinder, but I know even in the best of times infantry units are lucky to deploy with sixty percent of their authorized strength." He sighed again. "But 34th FIST can operate minus one platoon for whatever time it takes them to get to this place, straighten things out, and get back. Goddamn eggheads have probably all gone native or got wrapped up in their experiments. Nothing out there a platoon of Marines can't handle."

CHAPTER
NINE

Marine FISTs were dispatched to tend to the business of the Confederation of Worlds when force or the threat of force was called for. As a unit assigned to a remote outpost, the 34th Fleet Initial Strike Team often went to places nobody had ever heard of. Sometimes the simple arrival on the scene of a naval flotilla with an embarked FIST was sufficient to quell whatever disturbance had attracted the attention of the Confederation. Usually, the Marines had to make planetfall and deal with it directly, and they often had to fight. So they trained, constantly. No one knew what kind of operation the FIST would next be dispatched on, so they trained for every contingency their commanders could dream up—and from time to time the commanders dreamed up some doozies.

For now, nobody dreamed up doozies. Thirty-fourth FIST had taken the brunt of the heaviest fighting on Diamunde and had too many new men to integrate into its infantry battalion, air squadron, Dragon company, artillery battery, and head-quarters units, so training was fairly basic. Even so, the Marines trained as hard as Brigadier Sturgeon and his subordinate commanders could train them, to make sure they'd be ready when they were sent in harm's way again. When Marines go in harm's way, people die, and the Marines were determined that it was the other guys who would do the dying.

When they came in out of the field, off the live-fire range, out of the virtual-reality training chambers, and pulled liberty in Bronnoysund, they played as hard as they trained. Not much of the playing was at the level the promotion parties had reached, but enough of the Marines returned to Camp Ellis after liberty with split knuckles, blackened eyes, broken bones, and monumental hangovers to keep them satisfied and out of *serious* trouble.

Then there were the inspections. It seemed to the junior men and junior NCOs that inspections were thrown into the schedule whenever the commanders were too tired to maintain the pace of training. They didn't understand why the commanders held inspections instead of simply giving extended liberty, or even on-planet leave, which they thought would have made a great deal of sense and boosted morale tremendously. After all, the inspections seemed to be more about how pretty the gear and uniforms and barracks were than about how functional anything was. Few of the Marines were concerned with how pretty their gear and uniforms were—except for their dress reds; they wanted *those* uniforms to sparkle when they wore them. The men were concerned with how well everything worked; their lives depended on it. And so they wondered what happened to a man when he became an officer that made him suddenly so concerned with "pretty." Many of them had known a corporal or a staff sergeant who had been as rough and tumble as any enlisted Marine, then got commissioned and suddenly was taken by the very same "pretty" he'd complained so bitterly about before. Maybe, they told each other, it had something to do with the shiny precious metal of the officers' insignia, and the fancier uniforms they wore. If they glittered so much, so should everything else.

So life went; training, inspections, and liberty, as the component units of 34th FIST integrated their new men and prepared for the unknown.

One morning, after several months of garrison routine, Captain Conorado was a few minutes late arriving at morning inspection. So were Gunny Bass and Staff Sergeant

Hyakowa. Lieutenant Giordano, the company executive officer, had company Gunnery Sergeant Thatcher stand the men at ease while they waited for the company commander. Even though Owen the woo technically belonged to Lance Corporal Dean, it also served as the company mascot. Now, it sat in its formation location a few meters in front of third platoon, facing the command group. Owen's bright expression and cocked head made it look like it was wondering what was going on.

Captain Conorado came out of the barracks accompanied not only by Bass and Hyakowa, but by Top Myer, the company's first sergeant, and that was unusual. Top Myer almost never attended morning formation. Conorado looked displeased about something, and Bass and Hyakowa didn't look happy either. Myer was glowering, but that didn't mean anything—Top Myer usually glowered.

Gunny Thatcher didn't wait for Giordano's instructions— he called the company to attention as soon as he saw Conorado. The men waited expectantly while the captain took the company from Giordano and quickly went through the short list of business items he had for everyone. Then Conorado studied his company, looking more searchingly at third platoon than any of the others. Sharp-eyed Marines saw that the captain was nibbling on his lower lip.

"You all know that 34th FIST is one of the most active in the Marine Corps," Conorado began. "This FIST and its subordinate elements have been on more operations, expeditions, and other missions than almost any other unit in the entire history of the Confederation Marine Corps."

He paused a moment, then continued. "As you may know, the Bureau of Human Habitability Exploration and Investigation has research and exploration stations on numerous uninhabited planets throughout Human Space—and even beyond its fringes. One of those stations missed a reporting cycle. The bureau has asked the Marine Corps to dispatch a platoon to investigate. Thirty-fourth FIST is the closest to this world, Society 437, so the job falls to us. In particular, third platoon gets the call, and will mount out on a special mission in two days.

"Some of you have gone on investigations such as this before, so you know there's probably no emergency. Usually when a Behind mission fails to report as required, it's because the scientists got so wrapped up in what they were doing that they forgot to report. Either that or there was a malfunction in the courier drone." He stifled a shrug. "Sometimes pirates or some natural disaster wiped out the scientific mission. In the first case, the scientists and technicians don't need any help, just a reminder. In the other case . . ." This time Conorado did shrug. "By the time third platoon reaches Society 437, nearly a year will have passed since the courier drone should have been dispatched, and it will be too late to fight off any dangers."

The captain abruptly stopped talking and pursed his lips. It seemed to him that sending Marines to investigate the situation was a waste of valuable manpower. And he knew if 34th FIST mounted out during the three or four months third platoon was gone, his company would be dangerously shorthanded. But there were things he couldn't say. "That is all." He pivoted to face Gunny Thatcher. "Company Gunnery Sergeant, the company is yours."

"Sir," Thatcher said, pivoting to face Conorado, "the company is mine." He saluted and held the salute until Conorado began marching back to the barracks. Then he watched as the other officers and the first sergeant followed, and only then turned to face the company and dismiss it from formation.

The woo felt the mood in the platoon behind it and broke from its position to join the Marines. "Woo?" Owen seemed to ask a question as it jumped onto Dean's shoulder. It rippled through several colors, not at all sure what its emotional state should be.

Bass went to the company office while Hyakowa instructed the squad leaders to get their men packed and ready to go. As soon as the squad leaders had the men moving,

Hyakowa went to the company supply room to make arrangements with Sergeant Souavi for the storage of personal gear the Marines of third platoon would leave behind and the issuing of gear they'd need where they were going. Then he went to the company office looking for Bass.

"He's not here, Staff Sergeant," Corporal Doyle, the company's senior clerk, told him. Doyle was a bit surly; having one platoon detach for a mount-out meant more work for the two clerks. "He wanted to see the Skipper, but the Skipper was busy with the Top and couldn't see him."

Top Myer wasn't at his desk, and the door to the company commander's office was closed. Thatcher wasn't there either.

"Where'd he go?"

"I think he went to his quarters to pack."

Hyakowa grunted, and headed toward the wing of the barracks where the officers and senior noncommissioned officers had their private rooms. Bass's door was open.

"Why us?" Hyakowa demanded as soon as he entered the room. "Why are they sending third platoon? We've got more new men than any other platoon in the battalion, more new fire team leaders and squad leaders learning their new jobs. Hell, *I'm* a long way from fully knowing my job. We need the training time! We're the last platoon that should be sent out on something like this."

Bass was sitting on a chair in front of a chest of drawers, sorting through its contents, separating the items he was taking from those he was leaving behind. He didn't look up; a head shake was his only reply.

"Gunny, we need to talk to somebody, get some other platoon sent on this mickey mouse errand. Our Marines need to be spending their time on training exercises, not lounging around on a troop ship."

Bass looked up and snapped, "You think I don't know that, Wang? We have our orders, even though we disagree with them. We'll set up the best training program we can manage on board ship, that's all. This trip doesn't have to be a complete waste."

" 'We have our orders.' We follow them 'even though we disagree with them.' Gunny, do you have any idea how strange that sounds coming from you?"

Bass nodded. "I speak up when I disagree, yes. But when Mother Corps tells me to go someplace, I go. Doyle tell you about that?" He indicated a sheet of paper on top of the chest of drawers.

"No, what is it?"

"Read it."

Hyakowa stepped closer and picked up the page. It was orders from the battalion headquarters, signed by Commander Van Winkle himself, instructing Captain Conorado to detach third platoon under the command of Gunnery Sergeant Charlie Bass for an investigative mission to Society 437. At the bottom was an endorsement:

Heartily concur
(signed)
Theodosius Sturgeon
Brigadier, Commanding 34th FIST

"Doyle gave it to me when I went to see the Skipper," Bass said.

"Do you think Van Winkle asked the Skipper what platoon he wanted to send?"

"Didn't you notice how mad the Skipper seemed when he told us before formation? I don't think he was consulted. I think he was given orders just as we were given orders."

"But why us?"

Bass finished with the chest of drawers and stood to face his closet. "Maybe it's a test. Maybe someone wants to see if they promoted the right people. Then again," he turned to Hyakowa, "maybe somebody just thinks we're the best platoon in the FIST and they trust us to do the job right without having a higher ranking officer along to supervise."

Hyakowa looked at him oddly. That didn't sound right; it made too much sense.

* * *

When orders came down for a mount-out, they were always drop-everything, hurry-up-and-do-it-right-now. It didn't matter that third platoon had two days to get ready—the men had to pack and store, right now, whatever they weren't taking. So what if getting ready only took an hour? People higher up the chain of command had things to do and wanted to make sure the men were ready first.

"So now what do we do, Corporal Kerr?" MacIlargie asked an hour after morning formation.

Kerr glanced around the fire team room. Everything they were taking was packed, other than a few last minute items they'd need over the next couple of days, and was either stowed in the company supply room or secured in the fire team room.

"Field day. When I get back I want this room so clean you'd be willing to let Top Myer eat off the deck." He left Claypoole and MacIlargie alone and went in search of Sergeant Bladon. Kerr knew MacIlargie was right. What *were* they supposed to do for the next two days?

Claypoole glared at MacIlargie. "You had to ask, didn't you." It took a struggle, but he managed not to shout too loudly. "You couldn't keep your mouth shut—you had to ask. Now we have to clean this room again."

"What's he talking about?" MacIlargie said, giving the room a puzzled look. "This room *is* clean. Since he got here it's been cleaner that it's ever been! What do we have to clean?"

"Since it was your big mouth that caused this field day, I'm going to stand here and supervise, make sure you do it right."

"There's nothing to clean, I mean look at this." MacIlargie bent over to brush his fingers across the floor. Then Claypoole's words hit him. Still bent over, he looked up. "What'd you say?"

"I said, 'Since it was your big mouth that caused this field day, I'm going to stand here and supervise, make sure you do it right.' "

"What do you mean, you're going to supervise and I'm going to do it?"

Claypoole leaned forward aggressively and tapped the insignia on his collar with his thumb. "See that? I'm a lance corporal. You're a PFC. I rank you. In the absence of the fire team leader, I'm in charge. Get to work."

MacIlargie stood and gaped at Claypoole. Maybe he really should put in for a transfer, he thought.

Two days after getting their mount-out orders, third platoon assembled at the Camp Ellis landing field, which sometimes doubled as an orbital-craft terminal. Again, it was hurry-up-and-wait. They were on time, but the shuttle that would ferry them to the orbiting ship was an hour late. When they first saw the *Essay*, the navy's surface-to-orbit shuttle craft, it was a speck descending in a speed-eating spiral. When the *Essay* was still a thousand meters up, its coxswain pulled it out of its spiral and popped the drogue chute, slowing its speed further. At two hundred meters, forward-facing jets fired downward until nearly all forward motion was canceled and the *Essay* touched down with a slight bounce.

"It can't be," Charlie Bass murmured when he read the stenciled name on the side of the *Essay*.

"Can't be what?" Hyakowa asked.

"The *Fairfax County*. That ship was due for decommissioning the first time I mounted out on her." He shook his head. "That was more than twenty years ago."

"It's got to be another ship with the same name."

Bass looked beyond the stenciled name. "Nope. It's the AV-271. That was the *Fairfax*'s number."

Hyakowa shrugged. "I guess they refurbished her, made a new ship in the same hull."

"I hope so. The old *Fairfax* was a real scow." But Bass didn't believe it; the *Essay* needed to be scraped and painted. That wasn't a good sign.

The ramp dropped and two Dragons from the ship's compliment scooted out on their air cushions. They needed scraping and painting too. Bass groaned. Hyakowa swallowed.

"Let's do it," Bass said softly.

"Aye aye, boss." Hyakowa shouted orders to the squad leaders to have their men board the Dragons. Owen the woo perched on Lance Corporal Dean's shoulder and restrained its eagerness to examine the interior of the Essay. It had ridden on Dragons, though, and simply hopped into a niche in Dean's webbing for the trip to orbit.

The smudges on the null-g vacuum suits of the sailors who affixed the tunnel to the Essay so the Marines could exit the shuttle through the well deck into the ship proper did nothing to inspire Bass's confidence in the ship. Neither did the chief petty officer who oversaw the actual transfer—he needed a shave, and the cuffs of his uniform shirt were frayed.

The thrumming of motors and the whining of heavy equipment, noises that always assaulted the Marines' ears when they boarded ships in orbit, sounded a bit off—as if they were missing an occasional beat. The bulkheads of the passageways needed scraping and painting, and the decks were embedded with deeply ground-in crud. At one point, as the sailors towed the weightless Marines along the passageways to their compartment, Bass noticed that the gasket on a safety hatch was corroded badly enough to prevent it from making an airtight seal. He closed his eyes and forced himself to relax.

"It's a hold!" Hyakowa exclaimed when the Marines reached their destination. "This isn't a troop compartment, it's some kind of hold."

The large room the Marines were deposited in had rows of metal pipes going from the deck to the overhead three meters above. Horizontal metal frames, two-thirds of a meter wide and little more than two meters long, were supported by the pipes. The frames were half a meter apart. Each had a sheet of polymer stretched across it. Cots. Passages less than a meter wide ran between the rows of cots. A quick calculation showed two hundred cots.

Bass shook his head. "It's a compartment all right. This is what they used to look like. The *Fairfax* was built for use in the Third Sivistrian War. The Confederation had to move a lot of Marines and soldiers in a hurry, so the troops got packed into compartments like this." He sighed. "But they used to be in better condition."

The compartment's deck was as filthy as the passageways had been. The lighting was uneven, since some fixtures weren't working and hadn't been fixed or replaced. There were no personal lockers for the troops. Even the woo looked dismayed at the living conditions.

"All right, listen up!" Bass called out. His men turned to look at him from whatever perch or handhold they were anchoring themselves to. From their expressions, he knew they were more put out than he was by the compartment and the ship.

"You heard the Skipper when he gave us our marching orders—this isn't an emergency operation. As you can tell by our luxury accommodations, the navy doesn't put a high priority on it either. We'll be getting underway soon. Once we have gravity again, we'll rearrange this compartment to make it more livable. Now stand by, I'm going topside to see—"

He was interrupted by static from the ship's PA system. "Now hear this, now hear this," a slightly annoyed voice said through the static. "All hands not at duty stations, secure yourselves for getting underway. Gravity will go on in thirty seconds. That goes for the Marines too."

The static clicked off.

"You heard the man," Bass said. "Secure your gear in a lower rack and get into a higher one. Do it now."

There was a brief bustle as the Marines shoved their packs into lower rack spaces, then clambered into higher ones. They made it just in time.

A loud *clang* reverberated through the ship, followed by a steady vibration. Gravity returned, not in the smooth transition from zero to one the Marines were accustomed to on navy ships, but in chunks that jerked and bounced them on the polymer sheets.

"Oh, my aching back," MacIlargie grumbled when normal gravity was finally restored. "That thing is hard."

"Now you know why it's called a rack," Kerr said.

The *Fairfax County* was underway, headed for its first Beam jump point on its way to Society 437.

CHAPTER
TEN

Lieutenant Commander Lydios Bynum, in twenty years as a navy surgeon, had pulled "shore duty" only once: on a tour with the 127th FIST as a battalion medical officer. In charge of the battalion aid station during the Cathagenian Incursions on Wolozonowski's World, she had won a Gold Nova—the Confederation military's second highest decoration for heroism—when the station had come under intense infantry ground attack supported by artillery fire. Unmindful of the incoming fire, Dr. Bynum had found a lightly wounded NCO and ordered him to form a defensive perimeter around the medical complex.

The Marine sergeant had gathered a group of walking wounded who still had weapons, and with those men held off the advancing Cathagenian forces until reinforcements arrived. Meanwhile, Dr. Bynum calmly attended to her patients. Her anesthesiologist, a nurse, and a corpsman had all been killed while assisting her in the operating theater. She herself had suffered multiple puncture wounds caused by the mortar round that killed her surgical team. One small fragment had penetrated her larynx. She had continued her work as she spit up mouthfuls of blood to keep her lungs clear, giving her assistants orders in a whispering gurgle. Later, skilled surgeons replaced the larynx, but she never got back the clear soprano voice she'd been born with.

The Marine they were operating on at the time survived, due mostly to Dr. Bynum's skill and courage. But it had been a very close thing. Cathagenian grenadiers were already inside the aid station perimeter by the time a platoon of Marines arrived to drive them off.

That experience had taught Dr. Bynum two things: an appreciation for the abilities of Marine noncommissioned officers, and a profound contempt for military chickenshit. With that attitude she was guaranteed two things: never to be promoted beyond the rank of lieutenant commander, and consistently and distinctly unglamorous assignments—more than twenty years as a ship's surgeon, treating the injuries and diseases sailors sustained on shipboard and in a hundred ports throughout Human Space. One thing for sure: nobody ever messed with the ship's doctor on a starship.

When Dr. Bynum wore her uniform, the only decoration she displayed was the Gold Nova. Navy line officers who'd never been in combat, much less decorated for bravery, found themselves distinctly uncomfortable when she was around. Her assignment to the CNSS *Fairfax County* was to be her last. She'd been offered a pleasant and lucrative job as director of a civilian hospital in Brosigville on Wanderjahr, of all places, and when the current mission was over she would put in her retirement papers and settle down. Maybe she'd marry. Well, this last trip at least would be interesting, and besides, the *Fairfax* would be carrying a platoon of Marines, and she liked Marines.

Lydios Bynum's grandfather, Harry, had been an engineer on a deep-space merchantman, pursuing a profession that had been in his family for generations. Before that his people had sailed far from their West African homeland, earning their keep navigating Old Earth's oceans. Looking for a berth on an outgoing ship after completing a voyage to Kandaros, in the Joannides System, he'd met Lydios's grandmother. Alexandra Malakos had been a statuesque dark-haired beauty working in the shipping office owned by her father, Gregory Malakos. The Malakos family exported olive oil. Kandaros in the 25th century was famous for its olive oil production, an art its early settlers had brought with them from their Hellenic homeland on Old Earth.

Lydios remembered her grandparents vividly as a happy couple who enjoyed the pleasures of life, but of all things, they loved music most. Her grandparents could play various musical instruments and had reasonably good singing voices. Her mother, however, was a natural soprano, and though untrained, had sung professionally in her youth. Her fondest dream was to see her youngest daughter, Lydios, sing in an opera company.

The future navy surgeon loved music too, but as a child she endured the endless voice training sessions with a succession of tutors only because that was what her mother wanted. When asked by admiring adults if she would pursue a career in the opera, she would answer, "Yeah, maybe, kinda, sorta," which aggravated her mother, but instead of asking Lydios if she might have other goals in life, she pressed on with the interminable voice lessons. In later life that phrase, "maybe, kinda, sorta," became Lydios's stock response whenever asked a question she really did not want to answer.

Left to herself and among her friends, Lydios loved singing the ribald, humorous songs of the Kandaros folk tradition. By the age of eight she knew all the verses to "Clementine" and "Goober Peas." At her thirteenth birthday party she severely embarrassed her parents and voice teachers by substituting "Goober Peas" for "Il catalogo e questo," from Mozart's *Don Giovanni*:

> Sittin' by the roadside on a summer's day,
> Chattin' with my messmates, passin' time away.
> Layin' in the shadows, underneath the trees,
> Wearin' out our grinders, eatin' goober peas.

But Lydios was good, very good. By the time she graduated from conservatory, she'd developed a "lush" mezzo-soprano, as one critic described her voice. At her first public performance she sang Helmut D'Nunzio's arrangement of Virgil Thompson's Symphony on a Hymn. Her rendition of "Yes, Jesus Loves Me" so moved one critic that he wrote, "Her voice brims with warmth and a nuanced and imaginative interpretive gift that is utterly spontaneous and true to the languorous phonic poetry of late twentieth century American English."

Both her mother and father, but particularly her mother, almost had apoplexy when, shortly after her twenty-second birthday, the young woman solemnly announced she was going to become a doctor.

"Lidi!" her mother screamed, brown face almost turning white with fury, "You can't! You can't! Why, it'd mean—" She coughed and sputtered and staggered to a nearby settee where she labored to catch her breath.

"Honey," her father intervened, "you have trained for years to be a wonderful soprano, and you are—" He gestured, looking for the right word. "—you are a true artist. You have a great career ahead of you. Medical school now would mean years more of study. Why, you'd have to start all over again! You would never sing professionally! Think of what this means to your mother and me."

"And you will have to deal with—with dead things and blood!" her mother gasped from the settee. She groaned and put her head in her hands. "You will pull slimy things out of people's insides, Lidi!" Her mother almost fainted at the thought.

"I will save people's lives, Mother," Lydios responded quietly. "And I will make people feel better. Mama, Daddy, I love music too. But I will be a doctor."

When her youngest brother, whom Lydios loved dearly, was nearly killed in an accident, she had accompanied him to the hospital. She was so small and slight she was able to stand in a corner behind a partition and watch the proceedings without being noticed. When the surgeons had finished the ministrations that saved her brother's life, one of them spotted her standing there, her small brown face peering out at him. He said nothing, just pulled off his surgical mask and winked at her. From that moment forward Lydios Bynum knew she would be a doctor. But she had never dared mention it to her parents until now.

"And just how do you intend to pay for your medical schooling?" her father demanded, losing his patience at last. "I'll tell you this, young lady, you won't get anything from us! Not a thing! Come on, Lidi, how will you pay for this— this fantasy?"

Lydios had no answer to that, but Grandpa Harry did. "Lidi," he'd told her, "anybody can succeed with a Bynum behind them."

It took her thirteen years to complete undergraduate school, medical school, her internship and residency. Grandpa Harry left her enough money in his will so she could finish. Her parents passed on just before she graduated from medical school. They had left her nothing of the family fortune. And then she enlisted in the Confederation Navy. She knew that Grandpa Harry would've enjoyed living to see that, but it was just as well her parents were already gone because surely they would have died if they knew their intransigent daughter had opted to become a sailor.

Since a ship's surgeon was technically on call all the time, Dr. Bynum had learned to sleep whenever and wherever the opportunity arose, so often she would be awake when most of the crew were sleeping or standing watch. She frequented the wardroom during the mid-watch, or 04 hours standard, when she could have it mostly to herself. There, she would enjoy a quiet cup of coffee and a smoke. She usually avoided the place during the dog watches between 16 and 20 hours, when the dinner meal was served. Because of her irregular schedule, she could be in there when most of the other officers were at ship's stations or in their staterooms.

Lance Corporal Rachman Claypoole started and tried to jump to his feet when someone woke him up by thrusting a hot mug of coffee at him. He'd been dozing on the wardroom detail—nobody had come in for over an hour—and an officer had caught him sleeping. Damn! Court-martial offense. "Yessir! Right away sir," he mumbled, taking the mug to fill it before he realized it was already full. The officer stood there, grinning down at him. It was the dark-skinned female lieutenant commander, the doctor, the one with the Gold Nova. He'd seen her in the wardroom once or twice before, and she had always nodded at him in a friendly way. He wanted desperately to know how she'd won the Gold Nova, but Marine lance corporals, even one as bold as Claypoole, avoided familiarity with officers, even doctors, who were not quite the same as other officers. She never asked for anything when she came in, and served herself when she wanted something. Sometimes she just sat at a table for hours, smoking and reading on her personal vid, seldom talking to the other officers when they happened to wander in. Whenever Claypoole had managed to look over her shoulder at the stuff on her vidscreen, it'd been medical jargon, so he'd quickly lost interest.

"I thought you could use some coffee, Lance Corporal," she said, still smiling.

"Uh, yes si—ma'am." Claypoole took the mug, but from the expression on his face, he didn't seem to realize he was to drink it.

The doctor sat opposite him with her own mug and sipped from it. Her eyes twinkled as she watched Claypoole over the steaming coffee. She was a very small woman with closely cut black hair and fine features. Claypoole had often thought, in an idle, sexless way, like a man admiring a painting in a museum, that she was a pretty woman.

"You know, in eight hundred years the human species hasn't managed to invent anything that'll do it for you like coffee," she said, lifting her mug.

"Umm," Claypoole responded, raising his mug to his lips.

"I thought you could use a pick-me-up," she said.

"Thank you, ma'am. Uh, I better get back to work—"

"Relax. You're under the doctor's care now." This time she

smiled broadly, revealing perfect, pearly white teeth. "Besides," she said, looking around the wardroom, "this place is already too sanitary for the *Fairfax*. You'll give the rest of the ship a bad reputation."

Now it was Claypoole's turn to laugh. "Oh, well . . ." He shrugged and drank some more of the coffee. It was clear she wasn't going to report him for sleeping on duty. "I have to apologize, ma'am, but I just sat down for a minute, and next thing I knew . . ."

Dr. Bynum nodded. "Tell me about your Gunny," she said.

"You know something about Marines, don't you, ma'am? I mean you know our ranks and stuff." He hesitated, looking over his shoulder, but the wardroom was still empty except for the two of them. "Most navy officers, begging your pardon, ma'am, don't know a private from a sergeant major," he continued in a low voice.

She nodded again. "I was battalion surgeon with 127th FIST." Claypoole realized that must have been when she earned the Gold Nova, but still he did not ask about the medal.

Aside from talking about himself, Gunnery Sergeant Bass was Claypoole's favorite topic. The doctor listened, fascinated, as Claypoole told her about the knife fight with the Siad chieftain on Elneal. Another officer came into the wardroom during the telling but Claypoole was so wrapped up in the story he never noticed. Dr. Bynum glanced up briefly. It was that supercilious Lieutenant Snodgrass. Ignoring him, she turned her attention back to Claypoole's animated narrative.

Snodgrass seated himself on the other side of the wardroom. What the hell was the goddamned steward doing, he wondered, jawing with that officer? That was entirely unacceptable familiarity—fraternization. It was that doctor. Goddamn independent bitch. Count on a medic, especially a female, to destroy what little military discipline there was on a scow like the *Fairfax*, he reflected. He watched them, growing angrier by the minute. Well, she was a lieutenant commander, so she outranked him—in the wardroom anyway. A lieutenant commander and a doctor. He shook his head. And a goddamn woman.

Lieutenant Argal Snodgrass had graduated in the top five percent of his Confederation Naval Academy class, and in the five years since his commissioning—he'd been promoted to full lieutenant below the zone—he'd made no bones about his career plans. He would be an admiral. The lower classmen at the Academy—and every enlisted man afterward—who'd encountered Snodgrass when he was a midshipman wished he'd just get lost somewhere in space. He'd derived great pleasure from making the lives of those under him at the Academy as miserable as possible. As a junior officer with the Fleet, he had carried on the practice, to the extent his superiors would allow him, which never gave him the latitude he wanted. But one day . . .

Snodgrass learned about the *Fairfax County*'s mission to Society 437 from an uncle in the Ministry of Colonization. "Argie," the uncle had said, "this might be your chance! Dr. Morgan is one of the most highly regarded scientists in the Confederation. If you were a member of the expedition that rescued him . . ."

Immediately, Snodgrass's ambition fueled his imagination. "Dr. Morgan, I presume?" he could hear himself saying when his party rescued Nikholas Morgan from—from—whatever it was. He'd be famous! That line would be quoted forever! "Dr. Morgan, I presume?" Like that other guy a long time ago—what the hell was his name?—never mind, "Snodgrass" would be more famous than he. And all other things being equal, he fully expected a below-the-zone promotion to lieutenant commander as recognition for participating in the mission.

"Argie," another uncle, a captain in the Confederation Navy Bureau of Personnel, had exclaimed, "you are a line officer! You belong on a battle cruiser, not—not a goddamn scow like this troop carrier. You'll be gone almost a year! I can get you a job as aide to a Fleet admiral. Do you realize how valuable a fitness report signed by a Fleet admiral would look on your record? What the hell's gotten into you anyway?"

Eventually Snodgrass prevailed on his recalcitrant uncle and was assigned to the expedition as its special communications officer. "Uncle Jerry," he insisted, "you know they'll need a special communications officer on a mission like this. I'm qualified in deep-space communications, especially after my work with Project Golem. It'll only be temporary attached duty, after which I can get on with more important things. I really want this, Uncle Jerry." So at last the uncle, who really liked Argal and wanted him to succeed, was persuaded, but only after the ambitious lieutenant faithfully promised to accept as his next assignment a billet as a flag officer's aide.

What Snodgrass didn't tell his uncle was that he planned to write a book about the adventure when it was over. And when he discovered that the Marine element was to be commanded by a mere noncommissioned officer, he positively chortled. Everything was going his way! He'd somehow swing it to accompany the Marines planetside—the captain of the *Fairfax*, an odd old bird but an officer nevertheless, would never allow an enlisted man to be in charge of such an important detail. And naturally he would take over.

Commander Hank Tuit was captain of the CNSS *Fairfax County* because nobody else wanted the job and nobody else wanted Hank Tuit. He had been in command of the *Fairfax* for over a dozen years. Frankly, he hoped the navy had simply forgotten about him. A heavyset, gruff, but capable professional, Commander Tuit intended to spend the rest of his life commanding small vessels. He'd stick with the navy until they didn't want him anymore—which he thought would be any day now, once BUPERS remembered where he was—and then he'd happily get his master's certificate revalidated and command a merchant vessel. He'd continue his life on the bridge of a starship of some kind until he died there.

The *Fairfax County* was a superannuated scow. Commander Tuit knew that and was proud of it. He preferred "scows" to first-class ships of the line anyway, with all the spit and polish and naval folderol that made life with the Fleet such a pain in the ass. Nevertheless, Commander Tuit was a strict traditionalist when it came to the ancient customs spacefaring men had adopted from the seafaring navy. A ship's bell was struck on the bridge every thirty minutes to mark the passing segments of each watch, and at eight bells the next watch had damn well better be completely at stations.

And the *Fairfax* was a spaceworthy vessel—he'd made sure of that. As long as she got him where he was going and back again, he didn't give a damn if there was dirt on the bulkheads and cockroaches in the wardroom. Besides, the *Fairfax* was a troopship. Troops were the best cargo a captain could have. They never complained about anything, and they pulled all the nasty details on board that the sailors would otherwise have to attend to, which made for a happy crew. And Marines were the best cargo of all. They liked cockroaches.

Commander Hank Tuit didn't mind a cockroach or two himself. What he despised—in his view the perpetrators and perpetuators of the martinetism that made an otherwise exciting and worthwhile career mind-numbing drudgery—were Naval Academy graduates.

Rachman Claypoole despised wardroom duty, but when the shipboard details had been passed out, that's what he'd drawn. Well, there was always plenty to eat when the officers weren't around, and he had plenty of time off, and best of all, wardroom duty kept him off the really nasty details like waste ejection party.

Just dismissed from mid-watch duty, he was hurrying to get back to the troop compartment when he bumped into a sailor in the companionway.

"Excuse me," the sailor, a petty officer third class, said.

"No sweat," Claypoole answered, glancing up briefly. "Hey,

don't I know you from somewhere?" he said to the junior petty officer, a communications specialist, judging from the device above his rating. They looked each other over. "Yeah." Claypoole snapped his fingers. "Humpty! You're Humpty. You were on the *Denver* when we were deployed on Wanderjahr, and we had a few beers together in a joint in New Oslo, just before the FIST shipped out to Diamunde. Yeah. Humpty! I'm Rock Claypoole. Put 'er there." He stuck out his hand and they shook.

"It's Hummfree, actually," the petty officer said apologetically.

"Oh, yeah. Sorry, Hummfree. Er, what ya doin' here? On this—this—" Claypoole hesitated to insult the ship, since he knew sailors were ultra sensitive to jibes about their vessels, even a scow like the *Fairfax County*.

"Scow?" Hummfree volunteered.

"Yeah."

Hummfree leaned close to Claypoole, looking up and down the companionway before he spoke. "I'm with the special communications officer, Lieutenant Snodgrass." Claypoole made a face and nodded in sympathy. "I guess I can tell you about Project Golem now," Hummfree said.

"Yeah!" Claypoole answered. He remembered it now. Back at New Oslo, Hummfree had let it slip he was working on something called Project Golem, and then he'd clammed up right away and excused himself. Claypoole's attention was riveted on Hummfree.

"Project Golem," Hummfree whispered, "is a hush-hush signals-intelligence program designed to identify and track pirate vessels operating in deep space."

"Pirates!" Claypoole blurted out. With a hand, Hummfree signaled for silence.

"Pirates," Hummfree confirmed. "We get reports from merchant and navy vessels and police and military stations all over Human Space and we put them all into a huge data base. We have special units that do nothing but monitor message traffic between ships and their ports, and we have agents everywhere who watch what's going on. We're getting to where we can predict sometimes where the groups will hit next. Did you know there are over three hundred different pirate bands operating throughout Human Space?"

"Wow," Claypoole whispered. "Hey, Hummfree, do you think pirates—"

Hummfree leaned even closer. "Shhh. Maybe. That's why Lieutenant Snodgrass and I are along on this trip. Fleet intelligence and the Ministry of Justice think maybe an outfit called Red 35 might be involved . . ."

Claypoole sighed. Pirates! Now that was something new for the 34th! At least for him. "Hey, Hummfree, thanks, mate, thanks for the dump!" They shook hands again.

"Rock, promise me one thing."

"Sure."

"Keep all this under your hat, okay?"

"You bet! Hey, gotta go now. Gotta get in some rack time."

Claypoole continued out of sight down the companionway. Hummfree moved toward the crew's quarters, shaking his head. "Tell it to the Marines," he sighed. Maybe he shouldn't have exaggerated so much. What had gotten into him anyway? he wondered. Oh, well. Project Golem had proved a bust so far. He and his dipshit lieutenant were along to supplement the *Fairfax*'s communications department and maybe verify some Project Golem reports, but pirates on Society 437? He doubted it.

Back in the troop compartment, Claypoole couldn't wait to get MacIlargie aside. "Buddy," he whispered, "I was just talking to one of the sparkheads, and you won't believe what we're getting into!"

CHAPTER
ELEVEN

On the inside, Claypoole was swearing up a storm. On the outside, he was pleasant and smiling. Pleasant and smiling because he had to be that way around officers to keep out of trouble; he'd gone aft and seen the tiny, metal-sided, bare room designated as the brig aboard the *Fairfax County*, and didn't want to spend any time in it. Swearing up a storm because he thought it was flat wrong that a Marine should be assigned to steward duty in the officers' mess. He was an infantryman, damnit, a fighter, not a waiter! He should be training with the sensing and monitoring equipment the Marines would be using when they made planetfall or studying the scientific reports from Society 437. He'd pulled steward duty since the *Fairfax* reached Beamspace and he was tired of it. The only good thing about steward duty was that most of the officers ate at the same time so there wasn't much to do between meals—and his shift would end before the next mess call. The only "customer" he had at the moment was Lieutenant Snodgrass, who was drinking coffee and reading on a personal vid.

Probably some top secret communication that isn't supposed to leave the comm shack, Claypoole thought sourly. With the lieutenant in the wardroom, he couldn't go back to the game he'd been playing on his own vid; he had to look busy. So he was slowly wiping down all the tables and chairs with a static cloth. Maybe if he maneuvered right, he could get around behind the lieutenant and read over his shoulder, find out things before anyone else in the platoon knew them. That thought cheered him up.

Claypoole sped up his movement around the wardroom. He didn't move fast, which might attract the lieutenant's attention to what he was doing. He simply didn't move quite as languidly.

"Get me some more, Private," Lieutenant Snodgrass said, interrupting Claypoole's maneuvering. He held out his mug without looking up.

Startled, Claypoole glanced around to see who the navy officer was talking to. They were alone in the room.

"Didn't you hear me?" Snodgrass said sharply.

Claypoole looked at the lieutenant. Snodgrass was staring at him hard.

"Sorry, sir, you said 'private.' I'm a lance corporal. I didn't think you were talking to me."

"Who else would I be talking to?" Snodgrass shoved his mug at Claypoole.

"Dunno, sir. That's why I looked around, to see who you were talking to."

A corner of Snodgrass's mouth twisted in disgust. "More coffee." He held the mug out at arm's length.

"And it's 'lance corporal,' Mr. Snodgrass."

Snodgrass glared at him and motioned with his mug. "It'll be private if you don't get me more coffee right now."

"Aye aye, sir," Claypoole said, all pretense at cheerfulness dropped.

A moment later he had the mug refilled. He managed to resist the temptation to spill hot liquid on the officer as he handed it back. Snodgrass resumed his reading, and Claypoole took a step around behind the officer and feigned cleaning the table to his rear. Cautiously, he peered over Snodgrass's shoulder and read:

. . . *the Wombler war machine rolled slowly forward. Its organic treads rolled callously over the charred corpses of the Confederation marines who were killed in the brief, one-sided fight. The war machine's twin blaster cannons swiveled from side to side in search of a living target in the ruins of the deutrenium factory.*

Confederation Navy Lieutenant Horace Fairchild crouched behind a piece of laser-blasted machinery, watching the behemoth advance toward him. He hefted his hand blaster and wondered how he could disable the war machine with so flimsy a weapon. His eyes darted around the cavernous assembly room, seeking something more potent that he could use. There it was, a

Claypoole had begun reading from the top of the page and missed what Lieutenant Fairchild saw when Snodgrass hit the turn-page button.

The intrepid navy officer stood over the husk of the Wombler war machine and blew the tendril of smoke away from the muzzle of the assault blaster he'd used to kill it. Now to find the rest of the Wombler attack force and, Buddha's will be done, wipe it out.

Claypoole looked away from the vid and stood erect, a puzzled expression on his face. Wombler war machine? Tendril of smoke from the muzzle of an assault blaster? Buddha's will be done? One man—and a navy lieutenant at that— going up against an attack force to wipe it out? And every fool knew *Marine* was always spelled with a capital M when it meant Confederation Marine! He looked at the back of Snodgrass's head as though trying to see inside it. What on Earth was going on inside that man's head that he could read such drivel? He shook his head. There was no telling about officers. He sometimes thought that part of the commissioning process was the removal of several significant digits from the would-be officers' intelligence quotient. That was probably why Gunny Bass didn't want to get commissioned— he didn't want to get turned dumb.

"Are you through cleaning back there, Private?"

Claypoole jumped.

"It's 'lance corporal,' sir."

"Move around where I can see you. I don't like people

lurking behind me." He hit the turn-page button again as Claypoole moved to a different part of the wardroom.

Claypoole wondered how Snodgrass got his commission. Oh, sure, the big ring he wore attested to his graduation from New Annapolis, but how did he get into the Naval Academy? That insulting thing Marine drill instructors yelled at their recruits early in training came to his mind: "Are your mommies and daddies rich, did they promise to buy a commission for you?" Lieutenant Snodgrass certainly acted like he was from an I'm-better-than-you background.

Claypoole reached into his pocket and cleared his throat when he brought his hand back out. "Ah, Lieutenant Snodgrass, sir?"

Snodgrass looked up.

"Mind if I ask you a question, sir?" He accepted the lieutenant's curled lip as a yes. "What rank were you before you got commissioned?"

Snodgrass blinked and frowned. He was surprised by the question's impertinence. "Midshipman," he said coldly.

"Ah, yessir, I know that, sir." He nodded toward Snodgrass's ringed hand. "Your ring. You went to the Naval Academy, I know that. What I meant was, what was your enlisted rank?"

Snodgrass blinked again, then said in an even colder voice, "I was never a mere enlisted man."

It was Claypoole's turn to act surprised, then realization washed over his face. "Oh, yes, that's right. I'm sorry, Lieutenant Snodgrass, sir, I forgot. The navy lets people without experience get commissioned just because they've got an education."

"What are you implying?" Snodgrass half rose from his chair.

Claypoole's shrug was more casual than he felt. "Nothing, sir. No implication at all. It's just the old experience versus theory argument. The Marines believe that experience counts for more than theory, or at least that a man can understand the application of theory better once he has the experience to know what it means. All of our officers are commissioned from the ranks."

"What are you saying, Private?" Snodgrass stood all the way up and took a threatening step forward.

"I'm not saying anything, Lieutenant, merely observing a philosophical difference between the Marines and the navy."

"I don't believe you, Marine." Claypoole could almost hear a lower case m. "I think you're being insubordinate." Snodgrass now stood with his face inches away from Claypoole's.

"Oh, nossir! Nothing further from my mind. Just a simple observation."

Snodgrass sneered. "Commissioned from the ranks," he snorted. "Marine officers are little more than glorified sergeants. And this time, they didn't even see fit to send an officer, just a sergeant."

"Gunnery sergeant, sir," Claypoole said automatically.

Snodgrass turned red and glared.

"Uh, a sergeant is a squad leader, sir, a three striper. A gunnery sergeant outranks a sergeant pretty significantly."

"What's your name?"

"Lance Corporal Claypoole, sir."

"Well, 'Lance Corporal' Claypoole, I think I will have a little talk with the captain about your insubordination. You Marines need a little lesson in respect." He stormed out of the wardroom.

Claypoole looked at the hatch through which the navy officer disappeared and put his hand back into his pocket. He withdrew a small recorder and looked at it. It was running. He was glad he recorded that conversation. He was pretty sure he hadn't said anything insubordinate, and the recording could clear him if Snodgrass brought charges.

Later, in the troop compartment, he got the recorder out and replayed the conversation for some of the other men in the platoon.

"That Lieutenant Snodgrass sure is snotty," he said into the appalled silence that followed the recording. Thereafter, the men of third platoon referred to Lieutenant Snodgrass as "Snotty."

As they filed into the wardroom, the Marines of third platoon were cheerful in a way they hadn't been in weeks. They were back into Space-3 and only had to put up with the *Fairfax County* for a few more days before they reached orbit around Society 437 and made planetfall. Most of them were tired of studying the reports, and believed they could operate and maintain their sensing and monitoring equipment— motion, smell, and other detectors—in their sleep. It didn't matter to them what they'd find planetside, they'd be off the scow and using what they'd learned.

Gunnery Sergeant Charlie Bass was already in the room, one haunch resting on a table. A holoprojector squatted on the table next to him. He watched his Marines, heard their laughs, listened to their good-natured jibes. He didn't join in their high spirits. As routine as the investigation was likely to be, as likely as it was they'd find nothing more serious than an equipment malfunction at the research station, something ominous was tickling the back of his mind.

"Listen up, people," he said as soon as everyone found a place to sit. The Marines stopped their joking and looked at him. "We reach Waygone in three days. I don't know what we're going to find planetside, but it won't be a picnic."

Smiles vanished and all expressions suddenly became serious.

"Before I bring you up to date on what we've learned since the *Fairfax* arrived in this system, I have something I want you to see." He touched the control panel of the holoprojector and a quarter-size image of First Sergeant Myer popped into existence above the projector.

Someone snickered at the sight of the miniature, glowering first sergeant. Bass shot a glare at his men, and anyone else tempted to laugh decided against it.

As Top Myer's head moved side to side, the three-dimensional image gave the impression he looked each

Marine in the eye. Whatever the trick Myer used to create that illusion, it was effective. All the Marines gave the image their full attention. Even the woo seemed riveted by Myer's image and words.

"I know it's been a few weeks," Myer's recorded voice began. "But you heard what the Skipper said when he gave you this assignment. You most likely got the impression"—the image began pacing side to side, head down—"that this mission is a cakewalk that could be handled by two or three of the girls from Big Barb's. That might be so." Myer's voice was calm, almost uncharacteristically soft-spoken. "Most of the time when Marines are sent to find out why a Behind station missed a report, they find absentminded eggheads who forgot, broken equipment that prevented the report, or that some natural catastrophe wiped out the station's personnel." The image suddenly faced front and shouted loud enough to make many of the Marines jump, "But not always!" Even Bass moved away from the image.

"When you go planetside, you had damn well best be prepared for anything. Particularly for something unexpected and unpleasant! *Because those things happen!*

"Let me give you a few examples." The image resumed pacing, all the while glowering out at the Marines. "Society 408 missed a report and a company of Marines was sent to investigate. A week after they arrived they sent out an emergency drone. Eight months later, when a medical decontamination team arrived, three of those Marines were still alive. The rest of them had been killed by the same flesh-eating bacteria that wiped out the scientific mission.

"Society 299 missed a report. Marines went to find out why. You think you had a hard time fighting several armored divisions on Diamunde? The company that went to Society 299 had to fight a whole planet's worth of ambulatory, killer trees!

"The Marines who were sent to Society 74 found the survivors of that station reduced to slavery by semi-intelligent felinoids. The cat creatures who were using the remaining scientists to groom their hides, clean their living areas, and as occasional gourmet snacks outnumbered that Marine company thirty to one. Twenty Marines were killed in rescuing the seventeen surviving scientists and technicians.

"Camelot 499, the last of that series of human habitability explorations, was raided by pirates. Those pirates weren't content to take slaves and equipment, they wanted modern weapons. So they waited, about a thousand of them, for Marines to come. They were slick, they were. They sent their starship to an empty spot in space about two light-years away, where it wouldn't be noticed by an approaching Confederation Navy ship. Then they manned the control center. When the navy ship carrying a Marine company arrived, they sent a message identifying themselves as the mission. They said their drone launcher had been holed by a meteor. The Marines landed, expecting a warm welcome from a thousand scientists and technicians who hadn't seen anyone else in three years. What they got was a hot welcome from a thousand pirates who wanted to kill them! The pirates had a good ambush set up and killed fifteen Marines before any of the Marines got a shot off in return. That company lost another twelve before the surviving pirates surrendered."

Myer stopped pacing and faced front, hands clasped behind his back. "I could go on," he said mildly, "but I'm sure you've got the idea by now." He cocked his head. "Did you notice a common thread throughout that recitation? Something that happened in each of those incidents?" Myer's voice rose to a roar. *"In each case there was an entire company of Marines. You are just a platoon!*

"If a whole company could be that badly mauled by something it didn't expect, imagine what can happen to a platoon that isn't prepared. An unsettling thought, isn't it?"

He jammed his hands onto his hips, leaned forward and did the look-every-man-in-the-eye trick again. "The odds are either everything's all right or you'll arrive too late to do any good. But there have been too many incidents of Marines in one of these missions walking into something nobody

expected and getting seriously hurt. So when you go planetside, be prepared for anything." His voice roared out again,
"If any man jack in third platoon isn't prepared and gets himself or another Marine killed because of it, his ass is mine!

"One more detail you should know. The scientific mission
is called Society 437. But the scientists and technicians who
were assigned to it call the planet 'Waygone.' That's because
it is way the hell and gone out there. It's 'way gone' from the
inhabited worlds of the Confederation, and 'way gone' off
any and all shipping lanes. If you run into trouble, no one is
anywhere nearby who can give you any help. You're on your
own."

Myer stood erect, glowered out at the room again, and
snarled, "That is all." The image blinked out.

Bass touched the control panel again to turn off the projector. He gazed out at his men for a long moment. They all
looked serious. None of them seemed to have noticed that
Myer hadn't said anything about how frequently Marines
were sent to find out why a BHHEI mission missed a report,
or what percentage ran into an unexpected danger. That was
fine with Bass. He'd rather have the adrenaline pumping and
not be needed than for his platoon to walk into something and
not be ready to fight.

"You got the idea," he finally said. "We don't know what's
down there. It could be something or someone deadly. We go
in ready to fight if we have to.

"Now, what do we know today that we didn't know when
we got our orders? Not a lot. The *Fairfax*'s communications
center has been trying to make contact with the scientific
mission on Waygone since we came back into Space-3. What
they've found is most of the scientific satellites are working.
They're transmitting their data; atmospheric, topological,
geological, biota, etcetera. The kind of data the scientists and
technicians planetside need in their work. What the communications center hasn't been able to do is raise any people.
That could be a simple matter of the *Fairfax*'s communications gear not being good enough to communicate with the

planet at this distance, and that we'll get surface signals to-morrow or the day after. But that's not likely. It could mean the surface communications are down for some reason, but there are too many technicians on the surface for that to be likely. Most probably, something has gone seriously wrong down there.

"You heard what Top Myer said. When we make planetfall, we have to be ready for anything. The Top said everything about the situation on Waygone that I was going to say. I have nothing more to add." He turned to Hyakowa. "Platoon Sergeant, dismiss the men." Bass left the wardroom from the rear entrance.

CHAPTER
TWELVE

"Give me the blaster," Cameron said evenly, holding out his hand. Rhys Apbac continued to hold the weapon firmly across his chest with both hands. He said nothing, just glared down at Cameron. "Rhys," Cameron said patiently, carefully enunciating each word, "you will come with me and Lowboy will stay behind with the other blaster. Or you can stay here with Lowboy. But I am going and I am carrying the blaster. So hand it over. Now."

The debate about whether someone should try to reach Aquarius Station had been long and heated. The things had everyone so scared, most of the surviving pirates preferred to starve in the cave than take a chance on a foraging party to the abandoned station. They all feared that venturing forth from the safety—problematical as it was—of the cave would draw attention to themselves. Even Cameron admitted that was a possibility. But their clothes were in rags and they were starving. Their only chance of survival was to salvage something from the station. Privately, Cameron suspected those things knew precisely where they were hiding and hadn't finished them off for reasons of their own. Besides, someone would come eventually, and their best chance of rescue would be to leave some indication of their presence.

Rhys, Minerva, a pirate named Labaya, and his girl, Maya, had volunteered to accompany Cameron. But the whole thing had stalled over who would carry the weapon. Rhys still had it from his tour on guard the night before. Lowboy and the ones who would stay behind eagerly watched the confrontation. Lowboy hoped Rhys would finally put an end to Cameron's tenuous hold on the survivors. As weak as they all were after months of near starvation, Rhys was still an imposing physical presence, and even in good times he had been prone to violence for very little cause—a useful trait in a pirate, providing it could be controlled. He had volunteered to go along with Cameron not because he was a brave man, but because he was too stupid to be afraid, even after what they had all been through. That was also a valuable trait in a pirate, providing it could be channeled. Lowboy was afraid that Cameron might be the man to do that, ending his own chances to be somebody. They were so close to dying that a reasonable person would have asked what difference any of it made, but Lowboy was unreasonably ambitious.

"Rhys," Cameron repeated, "give me the blaster."

Rhys knocked Cameron's hand out of the way with the butt of the weapon. "Fuck you, Georgie," he replied. Cameron stepped forward swiftly and buried his knee in Rhys's crotch. He deftly snatched the blaster in midair as Rhys, a look of profound astonishment on his face, doubled over. Cameron slammed the weapon's butt twice into the side of Rhys's head as he collapsed in a heap at his feet. He did not move. "I guess he'll just have to stay behind," Cameron said matter-of-factly. The way he said it outraged Lowboy because it proved Cameron really was a tough sonofabitch, and now he had second thoughts about going up against the man. He'd hoped Rhys would've solved the problem for him.

"You might've killed him!" Lowboy shouted.

Cameron whirled on the others. "Yes," he grated, "and I'll kill you, Lowboy, if you don't get out of my way. You bastard, don't think I don't know you'd put a knife into me if you had the guts." He paused. "Okay. We're going. Remember this, Lowboy, the rest of you too." He was addressing those who were going to stay behind. "If we find anything useful and if we make it back here, we all share in it. The four of us are risking our asses to keep all of us alive, and if anybody forgets that, I will personally kill him." He slung the blaster and clambered up the barricade without looking back. The other three followed him.

"I guess he's right," a skinny pirate named Mouse said. Lowboy whirled and smashed his fist into the man's face.

Aquarius Station was situated about thirty kilometers north of the pirates' cave, on a large, lush island in the marsh that covered most of the land in equatorial Waygone. To get there they had to negotiate an extensive swamp that began at the base of the mountain and continued northward unbroken for hundreds of kilometers. When they had crossed the morass the year before, they'd been fleeing in terror from the things that had caught them at Aquarius Station. They'd been in better physical shape then; the trek would be far more difficult now. But Cameron knew land navigation, and he was sure he could guide them through the swamp to Aquarius. The whole time they were gone, from when they left the cave to their return, they would be vulnerable to those things. Crossing the swamp was the time of greatest danger, but they were desperate. Almost a full year had passed since their disastrous raid. They had to do something.

The first day's travel through the swamp was terrible, slogging through the mud and floating vegetation. Except for Cameron, none of them had experienced such physical exhaustion before. And they were constantly fearful that those things might suddenly appear and kill them all. After the first kilometer they were breathing in wheezing gasps and the air burned their lungs; every few meters they had to stop, to rest. Every step was contested by the clinging, viscous mud, and when they wrenched their legs out of the stuff to take the next step, noxious fumes assailed their noses and burned their throats. Soon their sense of smell became accustomed to the fetid swamp gas, but quicksand was a constant hazard, although by far not the worst. Unidentified creatures scraped and slithered against their legs as they waded through the slime, and at every moment they all expected the *real* terrors to lunge up at them from the mud. The heat and humidity were enervating, and in their weakened physical condition the four pirates succeeded in covering only a few kilometers after struggling all day long.

They remembered none of those things being quite so bad the first time through the swamp, but back then molten lava wouldn't have stopped them since they were all too terrified to take much notice of the stink, heat, and muck. Around dusk that first day they stumbled upon a hummock of grass big enough to hold all of them. It floated tranquilly in a large, shallow, scum-crusted lake, but they were too tired to object when Cameron declared it would be their campsite for the night. Exhausted, they climbed up onto it and collapsed. Fortunately, they had brought a lot of water with them from the caves—but little to eat.

The darkness soon grew impenetrable. All around them things thrashed and splashed in the shallow water, and the hissing and screeching of creatures hunting and dying in the forest on the fringes of the lake, not to mention flying creatures of all sizes that swooped upon them out of the darkness, constantly interrupted the fitful naps they were able to snatch. At dawn they were still exhausted.

Before it was fully light enough to see well, an elongated creature about a meter long and as big around as a man's thigh slithered out of the mud onto the hummock, evidently as surprised to find the humans there as they were to see it. Maya buried her knife in its head.

"Let's eat it," Labaya whispered, and they fell to the task with their knives. Inside the carcass they found soft white flesh, which they ate raw. It was somewhat slimy, but they felt refreshed by the meal.

"This ain't half bad," Minerva said. During their exile the pirates had eaten a wide variety of the local fauna with no ill effects, but until that morning they always had cooked the meat thoroughly.

Hunger sated, they watched the sun come up.

"This might be a right nice place," Maya said, resting her head against Labaya's chest, "if it wasn't for those . . . well, you know." She shuddered and nodded vaguely toward the sea, only a few kilometers from where they rested.

"Right now I don't give a damn," Labaya said. He had been a stocky, heavily muscled man before they were stranded, but Dugas Labaya had been reduced by starvation to a scarecrow. The women's hair was long and matted, and all of them were covered with bruises and lacerations. Minerva absently scratched an insect bite on her shin that had bled profusely before clotting but was bleeding again. She hardly noticed. Neither man had cut their hair or beard in weeks.

Cameron laughed. "Look at us," he said. "Don't we *really* look like pirates now!" The others did look and then started laughing. He stuck his nose under his armpit and sniffed. "Shit! We smell worse than this goddamn swamp!" he added, and they all laughed even harder.

"Shhh! Let's keep it down," Cameron cautioned suddenly, remembering. "Don't let's make any more noise than necessary."

"Well, so far, so good," Labaya said.

"Georgie, why don't we just stay here the rest of the day? Relax?" Minerva suggested.

Cameron thought about that briefly. He was feeling better after the meal, and would have welcomed a rest. But he rejected the idea. "Look, we'll hole up for a few days when we reach Aquarius, but staying here is dangerous. Besides, it'll get hotter than blazes once the sun's really up. We need to get across this damn swamp and into the Aquarius." He gestured up the waterway, deeper into the swamp. Automatically the others glanced in that direction, just in time to see something very big break the surface of the water, then submerge in a swirl of mud and green slime.

"Jesus God!" Minerva whispered. They all froze. The creature did not surface again, but a huge ripple marked its progress under the scum. Fortunately, it was heading away from them.

"Damn thing was fifteen meters long," Labaya whispered in awe, "and that was just the part I could see!"

Cameron swallowed. "Well, whatever it was, it wasn't one of them."

"Hell, George, we don't know what they are, so how do we know this thing ain't just a—a—a variety of some sort?"

"Look," Cameron answered, standing up, "it isn't one of them. We slogged through this soup all day yesterday and nothing came after us. We can't stay here. Let's get going again."

It took four more days to cross the swamp. At dusk on the fifth day Labaya, who had warily climbed a cycadlike tree to get their bearings—if he could see, he could be seen—spotted the large and badly overgrown island that had held the scientific colony known as Aquarius Station.

"It's no more than a klick dead ahead," he reported. He grinned at Cameron. "You guided us dead on, Georgie. How the hell'd you do it?"

"I had some experience, Duggy," he answered shortly. "Did you see any sign of life?" The four of them were crouched in a tight circle under the fronds in the diminishing daylight, heads close together, afraid to talk in a voice above a whisper. It was at Aquarius Station they'd been attacked, and none relished the thought that in a little while they would be walking among the remains of their late friends, if the encroaching vegetation and the swamp's animal life had left anything recognizably human behind after all this time. Cameron hoped the intervening year had given nature ample time to dispose of—what was left.

"We've got to be careful. I'll take the point," Cameron said. "The rest of you follow me at five-meter intervals. Walk slow and careful. Labaya, you take the rear. All of you keep your eyes on the person in front. If I stop, you all stop. I'll give you simple hand signals and you pass them on. We'll be on dry ground soon, no water swishing around, so let's do this in the proper military—uh, cautious manner. No talking until we get in there and establish a defensive perim—er, make sure there's no danger. Okay?" The others nodded. During the preceding days they had come to respect Cameron's judgment and guts. And he'd taken them that far without incident; they were confident they'd make it. They were also sure that nobody else in the band of survivors could have done it.

But they were not so confident Aquarius Station was unoccupied.

Carefully, Cameron parted the fronds in front of him. To his left was the main administration building. Behind that was the bungalow complex where the scientists had lived. Various outbuildings lay scattered randomly about the cleared space. None of the pirates knew what they housed, since their brief visit the year before had been unexpectedly interrupted. During that time plants and vines had reclaimed much of what the scientists had taken from the wild, but the place was not yet so overgrown they couldn't easily get around. Several swamp buggies and airfoils were rusting on a parking stand just beyond the forest fringe. About a hundred meters straight ahead was the landing pad for suborbital vehicles. Long dark shadows stretched across the compound. The sky opposite the setting sun was already aglitter with stars. They would have to move before total dark descended; their only source of light was the sun.

But they required food, clothing, and weapons immediately. If they could satisfy those needs, Cameron felt he could salvage the station's transmitter, maybe contact the rescue party. It'd been almost a year since the attack. The Confederation must have dispatched a rescue mission already! But food first. Then clothing. Then weapons. Those things could be killed with plasma weapons, spectacularly killed. There had to be weapons of some sort locked away in one of the buildings. He'd killed several of those things himself during the attack.

Cameron thought for a moment. He signaled for Minerva. "Bring the others," he whispered. She nodded and beckoned to Maya, who was almost hidden in the shadows; she in turn gestured Labaya to join them.

"I say we spend the night right here," Cameron whispered.

"I don't think I can make it another night," Maya almost sobbed. Cameron shivered. The clammy night dampness of the forest was already beginning to enfold them. It would be more comfortable inside one of the buildings. Cameron looked back across the compound. It was so dark now he could only just make out the administration building's outline. Well . . .

"Georgie, let's try to make it inside one of the buildings. It'll be a little warmer and drier inside. The place looks dead. At least maybe we can get some rest until morning."

Cameron did not think the things were around, and if they did come, the buildings would give them some protection. "Follow me," he said. "Put your hand on my shoulder," he told Minerva. "We'll keep contact that way, so nobody gets separated in the dark and makes a lot of noise stumbling around." When Minerva put her hand on Cameron's shoulder he felt that she was shaking.

They had quickly gathered the scientists and technicians together in the largest room in the admin building, those the pirates hadn't killed immediately.

"Why bother getting them together?" Rhys had asked. "We're just going to kill them anyway. What difference does it make if we kill them where we find them or kill them in a group?"

But Scanlon wanted to find out where the things they wanted were. If the pirates went around randomly killing the scientists, he wouldn't get that information and they'd have to spend more time in their pillaging.

"*Yi-i-i!*" someone screamed from outside. A man stumbled through the door. Cameron couldn't tell who it was because the flesh was bubbling off the bones beneath the right side of the man's face and down across his mouth, leaving his tongue flopping about in a lipless, cheekless maw, the white bones of his skull above the jawbone entirely exposed. As the pirates and scientists watched, transfixed, the flesh continued to dissolve off the man's head. The brain still lived, his heart and lungs still worked, but his features simply evaporated before their eyes! As he staggered blindly into the room, his eyeballs liquefied in their sockets. He was screaming, but as his tongue, larynx, and trachea liquefied, he could only emit a wheezing, blubbering gurgle. With each breath a hideous bubble of bright red blood spurted out his windpipe. Finally he crashed to the floor, where he lay wracked with spasms as his lungs and internal organs turned to sickly ooze. Blood spurted from his dissolving jugular as his heart labored to supply his brain, but that organ suddenly ran out of his skull as a putrid yellowish mess that mixed obscenely with the bodily fluids spreading out beneath him. With a final convulsive spasm, he was still.

The pirates stood there as if frozen by a violent arctic blast. But the spell was broken by a fusillade of blaster bolts being fired outside and more horrible screams. Scanlon took a step toward the door just as an inhuman giant rushed through. Scanlon fired automatically and the thing flashed into vapor. The brilliance of the flash blinded Cameron, and the wave of heat that washed over him made him briefly think he was going to be consumed by flames. But the heat passed as suddenly as it hit, and his vision cleared quickly.

"We have to get out of here!" Scanlon screamed, his voice breaking. They bolted for a door on the far side of the room. Cameron was saved because the panicky Scanlon went through without checking what was on the other side.

Cameron awoke with a start. It had been a dream. All was quiet save for the buzzing and hissing of fliers outside beginning the search for food. He blinked, then wiped the perspiration off his forehead. The others lay like heaps of rags, still sound asleep. It was morning, and outside, the black night had turned a dull gray. Silently he cursed himself. He'd been on guard the last hours of the night and had fallen asleep, like a damned boot.

Painfully, he got to his feet and stretched. Suddenly it

struck him: they were in the very room where the attack had happened. No wonder he dreamed about it. Yes, the door they came through a year ago was the same one they'd used last night to get into the building and—there—the skeleton of a man. Quietly, not to awaken the others, he stepped over to the body, by then just bones and rags. The bones were brittle and disintegrated at his touch. The man's skull had collapsed into dust and only his teeth remained intact. One glinted amid the whitish powder. It was solid gold. Johnny Lumberman! "Jolly Joking Johnny." It was he who'd come shrieking and stumbling through the door, his face dissolving like melting wax.

Now, as the light outside increased, Cameron could see the heaps and piles scattered about the room. Each had been the body of a scientist or technician who'd been slaughtered. Most of the pirates had gotten out of the building—and run straight into more of those things. That any of them survived was a miracle, and due to the fact that they'd all been armed and ready for a fight, even if the fight was far different from any they could have imagined.

He walked across the room and opened the door. The sun was up and it would be another clear, cloudless, hot day. Yes, right there, at his feet, was Scanlon's body. Minerva came out behind him. "Georgie . . . ?"

"Yeah," Cameron answered. Maya and Labaya came out. "Well," Cameron said, "at least we made it through the night."

The others stared down at Scanlon's remains. They recognized his body by the elaborate buckle that lay among the rotting clothing. Cameron bent down and picked it up. He tore off the fragments of belt that still clung to the device. Someone let out a small gasp.

"Georgie, do you think . . . ?" Labaya ventured.

"Think what, Labaya? Think we'll wind up like him? Think we'll make it?" He shrugged. "One thing for sure. There's no more Red 35 Crew, no more Finnegard Scanlon, but I'm still alive and I don't intend to give up while I got any fight left in me." He rubbed the buckle on his sleeve and stuck it in a pocket. "Now let's get to work."

They discovered two facts about Aquarius Station right away: All the scientific equipment had been removed, and there were no weapons in the place. The former did not quite register on the others, although they were quite disappointed by the latter fact. Cameron kept his fear about the missing equipment to himself. They did find food, plenty of it, pre-cooked and stored in highly transportable sealed packets, and clothing and soap and scissors and razors and mirrors and a reasonably potable water supply, a bit stale after a year in its huge tank, but welcome. They ate until they got sick, and then ate some more. They washed and washed and cut their hair and shaved and then washed all over again.

And they found boats, two of them, ultralight, durable sporting models with tiny but powerful energy packs that could propel them along at thirty kilometers per hour—if they could find a patch of clear water that ran straight long enough to reach that speed. Each could hold two persons with cargo.

"Well," Labaya said, "I'm not walking back through that swamp."

"You won't have to now," Cameron answered. Eagerly, they stowed food and clothing into the boats and then hefted them experimentally. When the loads reached the maximum weight two people, one man and one woman, could lift and carry comfortably, Cameron declared they were ready to head back.

"Shouldn't we leave a message, in case a rescue party comes here?" Maya asked.

"Good thinking," Cameron replied. They hunted about the station for a while until they found a suitable fragment of sheet metal and some paint in a repair shop.

"Georgie," Minerva asked, "if we're rescued and those—those things don't get us again, well, we're pirates, Georgie . . ."

She left the rest of her sentence unfinished. They all regarded her thoughtfully for a moment.

"I'll take a penal colony any day, to the way we've been living," Labaya muttered.

"That's right," Maya said. "Nothing could be worse than this goddamn place!"

"She's right," Cameron said. "Look at it this way: we didn't kill these people. We only came here to steal, and we never got a chance to do any of that. We must've broke some kind of law by landing here with larceny on our minds. But there's no evidence to link us to any of the real crimes we've pulled off. So we get maybe two to five for trespassing? Come on, let's leave a note. We won't mention anything about what we were doing here."

Carefully, Cameron spray-painted big letters on the metal as the others looked on anxiously. Done, he stood back to check his work.

"Looks good, Georgie. Now let's get going," Labaya said.

"Wait," Maya said. "Shouldn't we put a date?"

Cameron thought about that. "What the hell is the date?" he asked. "Anybody know exactly how long we've been here and when we came here, standard?" He scratched his head. Nobody said anything. "Okay," he said, and added something to the message. He looked at what he'd written and cursed. "How could I have misspelled that word?"

"That's good! That's good! It's been about a year," Maya said.

"Yeah, don't worry about your spelling, Georgie. They'll figure it out," Labaya said. "Let's get going."

They propped the sign up just inside the door to the main administration building, where it would be safe from the elements, and left.

The sign read: 14 SURVIVORS CAVE APPROX. 30 KM SW HERE GRATE DANGER, HURRY, HURRY, WRITTEN ONE YEAR AFTER ATTACK.

CHAPTER
THIRTEEN

"Nothing," Lieutenant Snodgrass said, thumping the display board with the flat of his hand. "The only transmissions from surface or orbit are automated signals."

Ensign Mulhoorn and Chief Petty Officer Kranston, the *Fairfax County* communications officer and chief of communications, exchanged a look. The special communications officer had found exactly what they had already reported to Captain Tuit. Neither of them understood Snodgrass's function on the mission, unless he was needed on the planetary surface, and they doubted that.

The CNSS *Fairfax County* had been in orbit around Society 437 for one standard day. It had deployed its string-of-pearls surveillance satellites on its first orbit and immediately put that necklace of geosynchronous satellites to work gathering all possible information of military interest: communications, weapons emissions, land traffic, air traffic, human congregations, weather. As far as the string-of-pearls could tell, there were no human beings on the surface of Society 437. No people, no land or air traffic, no large weapons in use or on standby, no kind of electromagnetic spectrum surveillance or tracking directed toward the ship. Most important, the only response to the transmissions from the *Fairfax* was an automated reply acknowledging communications received and recorded.

"I don't think anybody's there," Snodgrass said.

Gunnery Sergeant Charlie Bass stood in the center of the comm shack looking at all the displays, from time to time leaning forward to read a changing alphanumeric data display.

"What are those?" Bass asked, pointing over Snodgrass's shoulder at a concentration of dim splotches on a high-mag screen that showed the details of the land around the central station. The display was set to show heat signals that were congruent with life-forms. He winked at Mulhoorn and Kranston.

Snodgrass twitched one shoulder in a sort of shrug. "Those are too dim to be warm-blooded animals. The planet has large amphibians. That's a swampy area; those are probably amphibians sunning themselves."

"Probably, but not positively."

Kranston grinned and winked back at Bass. Snodgrass had entirely too high an opinion of himself and his abilities; he needed to have someone point out that he didn't know as much as he thought.

Snodgrass's lips curled as he thought something unkind about the intelligence of Marine sergeants. "There's nothing else they could be. That indicates a body temperature of about 29.5 degrees Celsius. That's close enough to the ambient air temperature to indicate cold-blooded animal forms."

Bass grunted and kept studying the display. "How big are they, can you tell?" he asked after a moment.

"I'm a communications officer, not a biologist," Snodgrass said, "so don't ask me. But I don't think a bunch of oversized newts is going to give us any trouble when we go planetside."

Bass made a neutral noise. Even if Snodgrass couldn't interpret the symbols that ran along the side of the display, Bass could. They indicated the life-forms were a little more than one and a half meters long on average. A few of them were more than two meters long. But some of them seemed to be moving about in a vertical orientation as though they were bipedal. He'd never heard of a bipedal amphibian. The *Fairfax County*'s data banks had the reports the scientific mission had filed with BHHEI. Bass had read all of those reports, most of them several times. None of them mentioned bipedal amphibians—or any other bipedal life-forms.

Bipedal or not, amphibians as big as those the display showed could pose a threat to the Marines.

Bass turned to Captain Tuit, who stood quietly watching the proceedings. "When do we go ashore, sir?"

Captain Tuit sighed. He feared that everyone on Society 437 was dead. It would be up to him and his own medical staff to find out what killed them.

"If your Marines are ready by the next time we pass over Central Station, you can launch then," he said. "My technical and medical people can drop on the next orbit and join you within a few hours after you make planetfall. That should give you enough time to secure the station."

"How much time do we have?"

The captain looked at a data display. "It looks like forty-three minutes."

"We'll be ready, sir. Have your people prepare the Essay for launch."

"Sir," Snodgrass said and stood, "that would leave the Marines alone on the ground for five or six hours. I think I should accompany them." The captain looked at Snodgrass. "Sir, I think a navy officer should be present from the beginning."

"Why?"

Snodgrass thought fast. He realized it wouldn't do to say that Marines under command of a mere sergeant weren't properly led. "Sir, I believe there is a navy regulation that requires a navy communications officer to be present when Marines are detached from a ship's complement to the surface of a possibly hostile planet."

Tuit nodded. "I'm familiar with the regulation. It calls for a 'communications officer or other appropriate communications specialist.' Which can be a seaman—or a Marine." He turned to Bass. "You do have a properly qualified communications man in your platoon, don't you?"

"Yessir, Lance Corporal DuPont is my comm man."

Snodgrass was grateful for the dim light in the comm shack; it hid the flush that spread across his face. "Sir, I am the special communications officer assigned to this mission. I believe going planetside is my proper function. Especially since it involves Project Golem."

Tuit hid his amusement and turned to Bass. "What do you think, Gunny?"

"Have you ever made planetfall with Marines, Mr. Snodgrass?" Bass asked, hiding his amusement as well as the captain had.

"I've made many planetfalls," Snodgrass replied with a curled lip.

"Yessir, I'm sure you have. But have you made any with Marines?"

"I've made just about every kind of planetfall the navy conducts." Snodgrass made no attempt to conceal the annoyance he felt at Bass's questions.

Bass raised an eyebrow at Captain Tuit. "I have no objection to Mr. Snodgrass accompanying us if he wants to."

The captain gave Snodgrass a searching look, then said, "All right, you can make planetfall with the Marines. Just remember one thing. Until we know what's going on planetside, and unless we find that conditions warrant otherwise, this mission is classified as an amphibious operation. That means that the instant the Essay touches down, operational command of all ground forces goes over to the ground force commander. Gunnery Sergeant Bass is the ground force commander."

"Yes, sir, I understand that." Of course, he thought, the first time any real decision needs to be made, I'll make it. A mere sergeant can't order a naval officer around.

As Bass walked toward the Marine compartment, he gave orders into his comm unit. By the time he reached the compartment, Staff Sergeant Hyakowa had third platoon's Marines in their chameleon uniforms and everything they were taking packed for landing.

"Assemble the platoon," Bass said.

"Aye aye," Hyakowa replied. Then, loudly, "Third platoon, on me."

In seconds twenty-eight faces seemed to hover in midair in front of Bass and Hyakowa.

"Here's the situation," Bass told his men. "We make planetfall in about forty minutes. So far the ship has not been able to raise anyone on the planet. So far, string-of-pearls surveillance has not shown anything that looks like people. It appears that the scientific mission isn't there anymore. We have no way of knowing what happened to them until we reach the surface and make an on-site investigation. Until we know otherwise for sure, we have to assume that something killed the scientists and technicians and if it's still there it will attempt to kill us as well. We go in hot.

"Any questions?"

There weren't any.

"All right, one more detail. Lieutenant Snodgrass requested permission to make planetfall with us. The captain and I agreed to allow him to."

"Ow-w-w!" Claypoole hooted. "Put him on my Dragon, I want to see this!"

"Right, put him with Claypoole," Corporal Goudanis called out. "I don't want him emptying his guts all over my squad."

"As you were, people," Bass said. "The man's an officer, even if he is a squid. Show some respect."

Bass's comment was greeted by a chorus of hoots and laughs.

"He's going to ride with me so I can make sure he doesn't choke to death," Bass said.

"Would anyone miss him if he did?"

"His mother probably would. Most mothers love their sons. Anyway, I'd have to explain how I lost a navy officer on a routine landing, and that wouldn't look good on my next fitness report. Now, if there are no other questions, finish getting ready and Staff Sergeant Hyakowa will take you to the well deck." He turned to Hyakowa. "Are you ready?"

"As ever," Hyakowa answered. "They'll be ready in a minute too. Do you want me to board them, or just get them there?"

"Just get them there. I'll be right behind you."

In another minute Hyakowa and Sergeant Kelly got the platoon lined up and headed toward the well deck. Most of them carried extra gear, the various sensors and detectors they'd need when they reached planetside.

Well deck. An ancient term, held over from the time when amphibious ships sailed seas of water instead of the void between the stars. The ancient well deck could be flooded and opened to the sea. It held water-going landing craft, which would ferry Marines, soldiers, or cargo from ship to shore. The modern well deck could be pumped dry of atmosphere and opened to interplanetary vacuum. It carried Essays, orbit-to-surface shuttle craft, clamped to its overhead. Each Essay could hold three Dragons, the light armored amphibious hovercraft used by the Marines for surface transport, though the Dragons carried by the *Fairfax County*'s Essays belonged to the navy.

The men of third platoon had just gotten into formation outside the Essay when Bass, chameleoned and carrying his pack, joined them. None of the Marines had on their helmets or gloves, so their heads and hands and the special equipment they carried were the only parts of them visible to the naked eye. The Essay's ramp was down, its three Dragons visible. The Dragons could each carry twenty combat-loaded Marines. Thirty Marines, two navy medical corpsmen, and one navy officer would board them momentarily, and then be flung out for what the Marines called "high speed on a bad road."

Bass murmured a question into his comm unit, listened to the reply, then told his men, "Lieutenant Snodgrass will join us in a few minutes. We'll begin boarding while we wait. First squad, Dragon One. Second squad, Dragon Two. Assault squad, Dragon Three. One corpsman in Dragon One, the other in Three. Staff Sergeant Hyakowa will ride with first squad. Mr. Snodgrass and I will ride with second squad." He looked directly at Claypoole. "And don't you say it."

Claypoole gave him his best innocent look.

"Squad leaders, board your men."

With hardly a word spoken, the Marines filed onto the Essay and into the Dragons, where they strapped themselves into the vehicles' webbing. As soon as each man was properly strapped in, the Dragons' automatic systems moved the webbing into acceleration couch attitude. Dragon Three raised its ramp as soon as the assault squad boarded. Hyakowa stopped on the ramp of Dragon One and looked back at Bass. Bass motioned him aboard, and the ramp closed behind him. Inside Dragon Two the men of second squad peered out at their platoon commander, watching him stand on the Essay's ramp as he waited patiently for Lieutenant Snodgrass.

Klaxons blared throughout the *Fairfax County*, then a voice came over the PA system in the well deck. "Commander Landing Force," it said, "is the landing force ready for launch?" The question was unnecessary; the Dragons' systems automatically informed the Essay whether or not all their passengers were properly strapped in, the Essay automatically notified the ship's launch system, which in turn automatically kept the bridge appraised of the current situation. But the navy had voice routines that must be followed, so the pro forma question was asked.

"Negative," Bass replied. "The landing force is waiting for its special navy attachment."

"Stand by, Landing Force. Special navy attachment is on its way."

Bass held back a grin. He knew the exchange was being heard all over the ship. Snodgrass would have a hard time living it down if the launch had to be delayed because he was late.

"Launch window opens in zero-two minutes, and will remain open for zero-three minutes," the PA voice announced.

"Landing Force will launch with or without special navy attachment."

"Landing Force understands," Bass said. This time he didn't hold back his grin. He waited another minute for Snodgrass, then boarded Dragon Two without him. Instead of going to his own station and strapping in, he stood with one foot inside the Dragon and the other on its ramp, looking out into the well deck. He ignored the voices of the Marines behind him joking about "Snotty" being late.

"The launch window is now open," the PA announced. "Landing Force, get secured so well-deck atmosphere can be pumped out."

Bass couldn't wait any longer. He stepped all the way into the Dragon and headed for his webbing to strap himself in.

"Wait for me! I'm here!" Snodgrass shouted.

Bass looked back. Beyond the Dragon's rising ramp he saw Snodgrass's head, bobbing with the rhythm of his pounding feet. The ramp stopped, then lowered.

Panting, Snodgrass jumped into the Dragon. "Where do I go?" he demanded, looking around wildly.

Bass pointed at the webbing next to his own.

Snodgrass went to the nearest webbing and began fumbling with it. It was obvious he wasn't familiar with the catches.

Bass stepped over to him and slapped his hands away from the webbing. "A rating always strap you in?" he asked as he fastened the webbing in place.

"What? I know what I'm doing."

Bass ignored him. He watched the webbing move the lieutenant into acceleration attitude, then quickly returned to his own station and strapped himself in as the ramp clanked shut.

Even through the combined hulls of the Dragon and the Essay, the Marines heard the air being pumped out of the well deck, followed by the opening of the well deck's drop hatch.

"Stand by for null-g," the ship's voice said. Everyone on board the ship prepared for the abrupt loss of gravity. "Three. Two. One. Null-g." The gravity generators, which were so much a part of the background noise on the *Fairfax County* that no one noticed them after being on board for a while, wound down with a short, sharp whine, and throughout the ship everything and everyone that wasn't secured to something suddenly started drifting. Everything and everyone that was secured began pulling gently against its holds.

"Land the landing force," the PA voice said, and the clamp that held the Essay to the well deck's overhead released. The magnet that had helped clamp the Essay to the overhead reversed polarity and slapped the top of the Essay, plunging it down, out of the well deck.

The Marines all shouted, screamed, or bellowed out to equalize the sudden pressure of the launch. One terrified scream on Dragon Two cut clearly through the yells of the Marines. No one wondered who it was. Even the newest, most junior of the Marines had made two previous assault landings and wasn't surprised by the force with which the Essay left the ship.

A couple of hundred meters below the ship, the Essay's engines cut in, first stabilizing the Essay and taking it clear of the ship, then sending it on a collision course toward the surface of the planet below. Five minutes after leaving orbit, the Essay reached an altitude of fifty thousand meters. Stubby wings deployed and front-facing breaking jets fired. Inside the Dragons it felt like they had run into a wall at full speed.

That's how it felt to Lieutenant Snodgrass. The officer, who had "made just about every kind of planetfall the navy conducts," had been screaming and tearing at his webbing ever since the Essay was ejected from the well deck. When the breaking jets fired, he lost the contents of his stomach.

"I heard that back there," shouted Dragon's crew chief, a petty officer third class, over the intercom. This was the first thing he'd said to his passengers. "You better use your suction tube to clean that up before it makes a mess, Marine." He didn't click off the intercom fast enough to completely cut off his gunner's laugh. The Marines laughed with the gunner.

They knew the sailors in the driver's compartment knew who had thrown up.

Fortunately, Snodgrass was in the position closest to the ramp, and his ejecta didn't spatter on anyone but himself. But some did get on the ramp and on the deck below his legs.

Bass leaned toward Snodgrass. "You heard the man, Mr. Snodgrass," he said. He reached above the webbing and pulled down the suction tube. "Protocol. Anyone who barfs cleans it up himself." He held the business end of the tube in front of Snodgrass's face. "Do it. Sir."

Snodgrass groaned and rolled his head from side to side, but didn't reach for the suction tube.

"Clean it up or continue to wear it."

The Essay's stubby wings shuddered as they bit into the thickening atmosphere. The coxswain cut off the braking rockets, turned on the atmosphere engines, and turned the Essay into a speed-eating spiral. Snodgrass dry-heaved.

"You aren't dying, Lieutenant, you just feel like it. You better clean that up before it decides to stick. We're about to start doing some serious jerking around."

Snodgrass turned a horrified expression to Bass. *"No-o-o?"* he moaned.

"Yes. You don't clean it up, you're going to slip and fall in it when you get out of your webbing."

Snodgrass turned even greener but took the suction tube and feebly waved it at the mess covering his front.

"The deck and ramp too."

The effort to bend himself toward the ramp proved to be too much, and Snodgrass collapsed backward into his webbing without doing the job.

Bass looked away from the lieutenant and to his men. "Don't say it," he mouthed at them. Most of them grinned back at him.

At a thousand meters the coxswain pulled out of the spiral and popped the drogue chute. The Dragons' webbing adjusted from acceleration posture to vertical.

"Stand by for touchdown," the Essay's coxswain announced.

The Dragon drivers cranked up their engines and the armored hovercraft lifted from the deck. A moment later the Essay splashed down on the surface of Society 437's ocean and dropped its ramp. The Dragons raced out and hummed over the water toward the shore two kilometers away. As soon as they were at a safe distance, the Essay lifted off for a suborbital altitude where it would circle until called back to the surface—or up to the orbiting ship.

Nine minutes after leaving the Essay that brought them from orbit, the three Dragons settled to the ground ten kilometers inland, just outside Central Station, and dropped their ramps. The Marines scrambled out of them and raced to form a defensive perimeter.

The *Fairfax County* wasn't visible in the morning sky from Central Station, but the flame from the engine of the Essay bringing the Marines to their planetfall was.

"They are coming," the large one said in a harsh, guttural tongue. He looked at the sky and, though his arms hung quietly at his sides, his hands twisted and flexed as though they gripped a weapon.

"We knew they would," the small one said. The slits on his sides opened and closed with his excited nose-and-lung breathing, and the useless fluttering of the gills inside them was visible.

"Do they come here?" the large one asked. He stood nearly two and a half meters tall and weighed about 170 kilograms. His gill slits also opened and closed needlessly.

"They would not start elsewhere," the small one replied. He stood little more than a meter and a half tall and weighed less than fifty kilos.

"We will attack them and kill them when they land," the large one said.

"No!" the small one barked.

The large one restrained a flinch.

"We do not know how many there are," the small one said. "See?" He pointed. A second flare was visible from another

Essay as it launched from the *Fairfax County*. "Look at it. The second shuttle is on a different landing trajectory. We will wait until they all come, when we are sure that all who are coming down are here and they are in one place. Then we will wait for them to join up with the others. Only when the Earth barbarians are all together will we attack, then will we kill them all. For now we will disperse into the swamps and move south. If their sensors detect us, they will see us as native creatures and not interpret us as a threat. We will not gather again until we gather to attack and kill them."

"Then we will wait for the next ones."

"Then we will wait for the next ones," the small creature agreed. "And we will kill all of them as well."

The large one bowed low to his leader. The leader bowed also, but his bow left his head higher than the head of his larger subordinate. They lowered their yellowish mud-colored bodies into the sluggish water of the swamp, spread their fingers and toes to stretch the webbing between them, and swam to where the others waited. In minutes the band gathered its weapons and other gear and, except for a few watchers left behind, spread in twos and threes deep into the swamp, heading away from Central Station.

CHAPTER
FOURTEEN

It was morning at Central Station on Society 437, "Way-gone." The sun was not far above the horizon, its rays filtered through the fronds of the ferns that were the dominant vegetation in the vicinity of the human station. As soon as the Marines cleared them, the three Dragons maneuvered into a wagon-spoke formation, fronts facing outward. If an attack came, at least one, probably two, of the Dragons would immediately be able to add its cannon fire to the blaster fire put out by the Marines. The Marines were belly down on rocky ground covered with something like lichen, peering through and over the low-lying, spiny bushes that grew between the fernlike trees. One man in each fire team looked at the landscape through his infra screen, the others used their eyes.

Insects with tubular bodies flitted about on multiple sets of wings that never stopped flapping, even when they lit on something. Some of the tube bodies were tiny, only as long as a fingernail was wide; some were longer than a man's forearm. Other insectoids wafted about on graceful, colorful, nearly translucent disk- or fanlike wings that seemed to move only enough to catch eddies of air. Insectoids of varying shapes and sizes crawled, skittered, or inched along the ground. Subsonic croaks that were almost felt rather than heard were the only indications of animals other than insects.

The forty or so buildings of Central Station squatted two hundred meters away, partly shielded from the elements by a tight loop of hills so low and regular that they looked like mounds or industrial slag heaps. The plans showed that the

136

ones on the outer rim of the settlement were apartment blocks. Closer in were the common buildings—mess hall, theater, shops. And the innermost buildings, closest to the arch of the hill loop, were the scientific and technical labs and shops. The control center, a domed circular building, sat just below the crest of the highest hill. Antennas of various types studded the hilltop. The buildings' exteriors were an earthy tan, like something one would expect to find in a desert environment. Most of them were trimmed in pastel hues, though a few had splashes of primary colors. Nothing was visible moving among the buildings other than some of the larger insects. There was not even the minor debris one might find on the streets of a human settlement.

"Raise the *Fairfax*," Bass said to third platoon's communications man, Lance Corporal Dupont, as soon as the squad leaders reported everyone in position and everything quiet. "Platoon Sergeant, deploy sensors."

Dupont held out the handset of his satellite radio as Hyakowa snapped the orders for the squads to deploy the various sensing devices they'd trained with on the trip to Waygone.

"Already got 'em," Dupont said. "The Skipper's on the horn himself." As soon as Bass took the radio handset, Dupont set up the control panel for the remote-piloted vehicle and launched it. For this mission the RPV was camouflaged to look like the granddaddy of the flying tube insects.

Bass said into the handset, "Skyhawk, this is Lander Six Actual. The objective is in clear sight. It doesn't look like anybody's at home. Over."

"Lander Six Actual, this is Skyhawk Actual," Captain Tuit replied. "Can you see any sign of what happened?"

"Negative, Skyhawk. From here it looks like they all went out on a picnic and didn't leave anybody behind to catch the phone. We're receiving data from our sensors now, and have launched the bug."

"Proceed with your investigation, Lander. We will monitor your transmissions. Med-sci is in its first orbit and will commence landing maneuvers as soon as you report LZ secure. Skyhawk out."

Bass gave the handset back to Dupont. He flicked on his helmet comm unit's all-hands circuit.

"Squad leaders and Dragons, receive on all-hands circuit, transmit on squad or command circuit. Everyone else, be on your squad circuit." That was the broadest level of communications the platoon could have without causing confusion from the babel of thirty-three voices trying to talk on one frequency. The squad leaders and Dragon chiefs acknowledged the order.

Bass turned his attention to the display board Dupont had just set up. The motion detectors showed nothing larger than an enormous insect within their one kilometer range. The infrared scanners found nothing warm-blooded anywhere in their line-of-sight range—which didn't mean there wasn't anyone or anything warm-blooded hiding out of sight in a hollow or behind foliage dense enough to block infrared rays. Or waiting in the buildings.

"Doesn't seem to be anybody around," Dupont said.

Bass grunted, then looked for Lieutenant Snodgrass. The navy officer was sitting against the stem of a tree fern ten meters away. Bass decided to leave him undisturbed for the time being and began issuing orders to his squads.

"First squad, shift left fifty meters, up fifty. Second squad shift right fifty meters, up fifty. Guns, keep together, assign one gun to give priority support to each squad. Dragons, hold position, keep alert. All hands, report anything suspicious or potentially hostile. Do it." He dropped his infra screen into place to watch the movement of the squads. The chameleoned Marines, virtually invisible to the naked eye, appeared in his view as man-shaped red blobs. The two blaster squads rushed, but didn't run. In little more than a minute they were both in their new positions, spread out and closer to the settlement.

"Second squad, assign a fire team to make a recon, then put

them on the command circuit so I can tell them what I want them to do."

"Roger," Sergeant Bladon replied. Bass heard him say, "Second fire team, you've got a recon. Stand by for instructions from the boss." There was a brief pause, then Bass heard an acknowledgment from Corporal Kerr over the command circuit. Bladon said, "Lander Six, recon is on command circuit. Over to you."

"Recon," Bass said, "we don't know who or what is in the settlement. Maybe nobody. Maybe somebody well-armed and equipped with infras and motion detectors. Get as close as you can while remaining unobserved. I want you to work your way around the right side of the settlement. Have all of your sensors up. Report everything you see, hear, or detect. Do not, I say again, do *not* enter the settlement. Maintain visual and audio contact with the platoon at all times. When you get as far around the right side as you can go without losing visual contact with the platoon, return. Understand?"

"Understood."

"Do it." Three red blobs detached themselves from second squad's area and withdrew back into the trees. Good beginning, Bass thought. Get totally out of sight before maneuvering closer. Kerr doesn't seem to have lost anything. He toggled on the circuit that allowed him to speak privately to the second squad leader.

"Good choice, Tam."

"Thought you'd like it, boss. Kerr needs the confidence builder."

He did need it. Bass suspected the big man's confidence was badly shaken. He needed some live action, not more training, to regain his self-confidence. The recon was low-risk, and Kerr was unlikely to run into anything that would severely test him; any mistakes he made probably wouldn't endanger his men. And it would give Claypoole and MacIlargie a chance to see their fire team leader in live action and gain confidence in his leadership. Unless there was someone or something in the settlement that neither the *Fairfax County* nor the Marines had been able to detect. If there was, the entire platoon might be in severe danger. Well, that was a major reason for sending a recon, to see if they could find some danger the ship and sensors missed. Bass put on the override circuit so he and the squad leaders could listen in on all transmissions from the recon.

Lieutenant Snodgrass suddenly appeared at Bass's side and demanded, "What are you doing, why are we just sitting here?"

Bass slowly turned his head toward the navy officer and raised his infra screen. "Mr. Snodgrass," he said in a deceptively slow and calm voice, "we are finding out what's here. Now go back to your tree and keep quiet." He didn't flinch from the vomitus stink wafting from the lieutenant's uniform.

"We know what's here," Snodgrass insisted. "Nothing. As senior officer present, I order you to move the platoon into the settlement to find out what happened."

"With all due respect, Mr. Snodgrass, as commander of the landing force, I order you to shut up and get down. I'll decide when to move the platoon into the settlement."

"There might be people in there who need our help. We have to get to them, we can't waste time out here."

Bass cocked an eyebrow at the sudden change in Snodgrass's assessment of what might be in the settlement but didn't comment on it. "If any people are in there, they're dead. Another half hour or so won't change that."

"Maybe they're hiding."

"If they're hiding, we better find out what they're hiding from before it gets to us, don't you think?"

Snodgrass raised his left hand, palm inward, to display the Naval Academy ring he wore, then tapped the gold orb on his collar. "I think I outrank you, Gunnery Sergeant. I think I'm taking command of this landing party."

Bass shook his head. A trace of annoyance sounded in his voice when he spoke. "Mr. Snodgrass, you're out of line. I wouldn't dream of taking command of anything from a sailor aboard ship. I don't know how things work on a ship. We're planetside now. This is my element, not yours. Now listen up, and listen up good. You embarrassed yourself during the drop from orbit. Shut up, sit down, and stay out of the way before you embarrass yourself again." He dropped the infra screen back into place and looked toward the ferns where Kerr's fire team had gone.

Kerr led Claypoole and MacIlargie far enough into the trees that the settlement was visible as only an occasional flash between the fronds. He dropped to one knee and signaled his men close.

"Mac," he said, using the comm unit even though the others were close enough for unaided voice, "everyone tells me you're good at evasive movement. That right?" On the command circuit he heard someone, probably Bladon or Ratliff, snicker. He ignored it.

MacIlargie grinned. "Yeah. Sergeant Bladon tells me I'm up to chapter two of the book he wrote when he was a PFC."

Kerr smiled wanly. Tam Bladon had been good, maybe the best he'd ever seen. He gave his head a sharp shake. Bladon probably still was that good. It was he himself who "used to be," Kerr thought. It remained to be seen if he still was.

"You heard Gunny Bass's instructions."

MacIlargie nodded.

"Remember the dorm building with the bright red and blue corners?"

"Yeah, I saw it."

"Do you know where we are relative to it?"

MacIlargie peered intently through the trees, as if he could spot the building if he looked hard enough. He nodded. "Approximately. If that's where you want to go, I can bring us out close to it."

"That's where I want us to go. Get as close as you can without anybody inside seeing us."

"Who's going to see us?"

"Probably no one. But if there is, I want to see him before he sees us."

"Right. We see him first. Good idea."

Claypoole, quiet until now, snorted. "Corporal Kerr, Mac's sort of slow on the uptake, but he catches on eventually."

"Let's go."

MacIlargie led off in a crouch. Kerr glanced at Claypoole, dropped his sleeve so he could see his gesture to stick close behind, and followed the red blob that was MacIlargie.

The fern trees weren't close together, they were spread out almost as much as the oaks and elms of a wooded park, but their fronds began spreading at or just above ground level, so they were more difficult to see through than similarly spaced deciduous trees. Spiny bushes, fern bushes, and fern-tree seedlings grew on the ground between the trees, making vision even more difficult. The rocky ground was covered with a lichenlike growth, so everywhere the eye looked was green. Even the sunlight that filtered down through the six-meter-high treetops was tinged green. The whole effect was almost like walking along the bottom of a kelp forest in a clear, green sea. Then, suddenly, vision cleared near the edge of the fern forest, and the hillocks of color-splashed buff buildings poked above the ground in front of them.

Momentarily, Kerr felt the way he had on his first combat operation. No, he realized, this isn't the way I felt then. Then, he'd been a new Marine, twenty-three years old, full of the training he'd undergone to earn the Eagle, Globe, and Starstream on his uniform emblems, cocky with the confidence the Marine Corps loaded him with. Then, he wasn't in charge, responsible for others—he was barely responsible for himself. Then, he'd never seen an enemy crumple, flamed by a bolt from the blaster he'd only fired at targets, things that didn't scream and die. Then, he'd never seen another Marine shed blood, become crippled or horribly dead. Then, he'd never nearly died himself. Then, he had no understanding of his own mortality.

Now he was experienced, with a dozen operations and campaigns behind him, well-aware of the hazards of going in harm's way. Now he was in charge, responsible for himself, his men, and his mission. Now he knew the meaning of combat; to kill men and keep killing them until the survivors gave up in terror. Now he'd lost count of the friends he'd lost, crippled or dead. Now he'd been wounded so severely he should have died himself. Now he was so acutely aware of his own mortality he didn't know why he was there or willing to go in harm's way once more.

In fact, part of him wasn't willing to go in harm's way. Part of him screamed out for release, for escape. Part of him gibbered in terror. Part of him wanted to run in panic back to the Dragons, to board one, to force the Essay to land and take him aboard, fly him back to orbit, so he could huddle in the safest place on the *Fairfax County* until it left that place of unknown, unimaginable danger. Part of him wanted to flee all the way back to Dominion, back to the farm where he was born and grew up. Part of him sent a torrent of fear surging up his spine to radiate outward to paralyze him. That part grew and threatened to take over.

No! Corporal Kerr was a Marine noncommissioned officer, a leader of men. He was a veteran of innumerable firefights, he knew how to handle himself and his men when fire rained. He'd been shot at and missed, he'd been shot at and nearly killed. He was alive! He was alive and wanted to stay that way. His men were alive and he wanted to keep them alive. He had a job to do. If he didn't want to do that job, if he was too afraid to do that job, he could have said so when he was in the hospital or undergoing therapy. He didn't have to be there, he could have chosen to get out of the Marine Corps, chosen to return to that farm on Dominion, to live out his life in peace. But he chose to return to active duty. He had requested a return to his old unit, knowing that 34th FIST was very active. He knew in advance he'd go once more, many times more, into harm's way.

If the gods of war wanted to kill Corporal Tim Kerr, well, they'd had their chance on Elneal. They gave him their best shot and he survived to come back for more. If he hadn't been killed on Elneal, if he could sustain those injuries, heal from them, and come back for more, no little operation on some minor backwater that didn't even have a permanent settlement was going to kill him!

With one powerful effort of will, Kerr got hold of the part of himself that wanted to run, wrestled it down, pinned it, and locked it into that compartment buried deep within his psyche where men in combat stick the terrors and horrors so they don't freeze them up, make them lay down and die.

He raised his infra screen. "Mac," he ordered in a voice that betrayed nothing of what he'd just felt, "use your infras, let me know if you see anything. Rock, run a cover-all pattern on the place with the sounder." With infrared and audio sensors in action, Kerr pointed his motion detector at the settlement and began sweeping it. He kept flicking his eyes back and forth between the motion detector's display and where he was pointing it. The detector picked up the largest insects as they flitted about, and a few withered fronds as gusts of wind rattled them, but that was all.

"Rock, Mac, anything?"

"Sounds just like a ghost town I saw in a trid," Claypoole replied, "you know the one, *Rim Station.*"

Kerr knew that trid, he'd seen it while he was convalescing. In the trid, a colonization ship arrived at a world that had been declared fit for human occupation, only to find the scientific station—a station not unlike the one here on Waygone— abandoned. It turned out that a space-faring alien species also had a research station on the world, which had somehow gone undetected. The aliens attacked the colonists and nearly wiped them out before a Marine FIST arrived to rescue the humans and kill all the aliens. Kerr shook his head. The trid hadn't been very realistic. It would have been impossible for an alien research station to remain undetected for three or more years of planetwide observation—and there was no way a message could have made its way back to Earth and a FIST dispatched in time to make the rescue. Nor was it realistic to assume that the first intelligent alien species humans encountered would be so automatically hostile.

But that was a trid, a fiction. This was a live reconnaissance patrol. He shook himself back to reality. *Rim Station* had nothing to do with the reality of where he was, what he and his men were doing. The part of him he'd just buried would have picked up on the vid and believed it, but he didn't.

"I don't see anything that doesn't look like a building or a bug," MacIlargie reported.

"Let's move. Back into the trees, circle another fifty meters, then close up again. Go." Kerr was feeling his old self again, a confident, capable Marine noncommissioned officer.

The three Marines melted back into the trees and approached the settlement at a different point. They repeated the maneuver three more times. Each time they neared the settlement they observed it with their sensors, but never detected any life bigger than the larger flying insects.

"Come on back," Bass finally ordered Kerr. The array of more powerful sensors the platoon deployed when it landed hadn't detected any nearby life-forms larger than the flying insects either. The meter-long amphibians they'd heard when they first landed had moved away, and none were closer than half a kilometer. The RPV had spotted a few of them before Bass redirected it to the swampy area southwest of Central Station, where the *Fairfax County*'s string-of-pearls had detected larger amphibians. But the RPV was flying over that area and its sensors weren't picking up anything as large as the ship's had.

Maybe they're migratory and they just moved away, Bass thought. He thought it, but he didn't necessarily believe it.

"Raise the ship," he said to Dupont.

Dupont handed him the radio handset. "Got 'em."

"Skyhawk, this is Lander Six Actual. Lima Zulu is secure. Land med-sci."

The Essay carrying the med-sci team was in a decaying orbit one-third of the way around the planet from Central Station when Bass put in the call. They were able to make their landing in another three-quarters of a standard hour. It wasn't a Marine assault landing, they didn't come in hard and fast and off the coast. The Essay made a slow, spiraling descent just like the one at Camp Ellis and touched down gently behind the Dragons.

Dr. Bynum was the first person off the Essay. Owen the woo leaped off right behind her. It held its head high to sniff the strange air, then playfully gamboled about, radiating a soft, contented pink as it examined everything it encountered until a voice called his name. It looked, saw Dean, galloped to him, screeched to a bumpy stop, and nuzzled its human.

As the woo romped, Dr. Bynum looked around and spotted Gunny Bass and Lieutenant Snodgrass approaching. Bass had his helmet off and his sleeves rolled up, so she could see him.

"Mr. Snodgrass," she said, acknowledging the officer's salute with a nod, then immediately looked at Bass. "What's the situation, Gunny?"

"No nearby life-forms bigger than the large amphibians the scientific team reported last year, and the nearest of them are half a klick away. Watch out for the bugs, though, some of them are big enough they just might carry you away if they gang up on you."

Bynum laughed lightly, then turned back to business. "No sign of survivors?"

Bass shook his head. "I've sent a squad through Central Station to the top of that hill"—he pointed at the rise with the antennas on its top—"but we haven't entered any of the buildings yet. No sign of people or remains on the streets."

"Lieutenant Commander," Snodgrass interrupted. "As senior officer present, I should give the report. Please direct your questions to me."

"Mr. Snodgrass, any communications report you think I should have, you can give me at the appropriate time," Bynum replied. "Right now, the commander of the landing force is briefing me on what I have to know before my med-sci team can proceed with its investigation."

"But Lieut—"

Bynum wrinkled her nose and looked at Bass. "Does everything smell like that around here? The air carries the distinct stench of something rotten, very much like stale vomitus." She had seen the stains on Snodgrass's uniform and knew quite well what the smell was.

"No, ma'am. The smell seems to be localized," Bass replied straight-faced. Snodgrass turned red.

Bynum looked toward Central Station. "If nobody's been in any of the buildings, we may as well begin in the admin center. Even if we don't find any signs of people, there should be some records that can tell us something."

"Exactly my thinking, ma'am."

"Gunnery Sergeant, I'm not, I think, older than you, at least not very much. But hearing 'ma'am' coming out of your mouth makes me feel that way. My name's Lydios, Lidi for short. If I may call you Charlie?"

Bass smiled warmly and gave the doctor a bow. "My friends do indeed call me Charlie. It'll be my pleasure, Lidi."

Snodgrass turned a deeper red as he struggled to stifle a protest. An enlisted man and a lieutenant commander on first name terms? This was an outrage! He knew if he reported this breech of military discipline to Commander Tuit, the ship's captain would just shrug it off. As soon as he had the chance, he would report it direct to the Admiralty. Even if he had to use the influence of one of his uncles to get his report into the proper hands.

Several hundred meters away a watcher huddled among the root pillars of a mangrovelike tree, one of the few woody species on Waygone. The watcher hunkered so low in the water that only her head from the bridge of her nose was above the almost stagnant surface. At so great a distance, even if an infrared receiver picked up her body heat emanations, it would read her small apparent size and low body temperature to be signs of a medium-size local amphibian. She wore the earpiece of a receiver that picked up burst transmissions from one of the eavesdropping devices the Master had ordered left around the Earth barbarian station. Though she was quite articulate in her own tongue, her xenolinguistic skills were poor, so she understood little of what the barbarians said. She understood enough, though, to know that all the barbarians who were coming to the surface were down and they were about to discover the surprises. She removed the receiver's headpiece, lowered herself beneath the water, and swam to where the large one in command of the watchers waited for her report. The large one, if he so chose, might have someone carry her report to the Master and the leaders, those who just came down and those who were hiding, where they waited for all the Earth barbarians to assemble. Perhaps the large one would choose her to deliver her report to the Master. That would be a rare honor, one she would cherish. But if the large one ordered her to return to observe, or to do anything or nothing else, she would obey unquestioningly.

CHAPTER
FIFTEEN

"Oh my God," Lieutenant Snodgrass gasped, "what happened in here?"

Dean glanced at the lieutenant. The navy officer was visibly shaken. Dean and the other Marines of first squad had seen dead men before, plenty of them, and besides, these appeared to have been dead a very long time. Sergeant Ratliff nudged one of the bodies with his foot. It was nothing more than a loose collection of clothing inhabited by bones. A gleaming white skull lay on the floor a few meters away but it was hard to tell which of the several bodies littering the floor it belonged to. Evidently animals had disturbed the remains and scattered body parts.

"Better inform Sergeant Bass," Snodgrass said to no one in particular. His voice quavered as he spoke.

"I've already told the Gunny, sir," Ratliff responded. The damn lieutenant was getting in his way, but Gunny Bass had said it was all right for him to come along, so they were stuck with him. One thing Ratliff noticed that made him smile inwardly despite the horror all around them was that while Snodgrass looked down his nose at Marines in general, and Gunnery Sergeant Bass in particular, as soon as anything bad happened, what did he do? He called for the Gunny! "Spread out, men," Ratliff ordered, "and search the whole place. Don't touch anything. We don't know what killed these people." The other members of the squad fanned out and began exploring the rooms and corridors radiating off the building's foyer.

Ratliff was thinking ahead already. Someone would have to gather the remains and try to identify them. He shuddered. They'd come to help the people, and now the mission had turned into a graves registration detail.

Snodgrass managed to get control of himself. Gingerly, he reached down and shook a bundle of rags that had once covered a human body. A long white bone rolled out onto the floor. "Yikes!" he exclaimed and recoiled as if it was a poisonous reptile. Lying nearby were the skeletal remains of a human hand. On one finger glittered a ring that had survived whatever killed its owner. Snodgrass reached down to pick it up, and as soon as he touched the bones they disintegrated into a fine powder.

"Lieutenant, I don't think it's safe to touch anything until we know what killed these people," Ratliff said. Snodgrass quickly brushed the powder off his fingers and looked up guiltily. He had the ring.

"I know what I'm doing, Sergeant," Snodgrass replied automatically. Then quickly: "Well, I thought the ring might help identify the body." He felt awkward and embarrassed, being corrected by a mere enlisted man for doing something common sense should have told him was not at all wise. "I thought—"

Ratliff held up a hand for silence. Bass was transmitting on the command net. "Lieutenant, Gunny Bass is headed over here on the double. He says everybody stand fast. The place is secure and . . . and, Jesus, there are hundreds of bodies all over the place!"

Central Station was located in Society 437's subtropical zone. Of the three stations the scientists had established on the planet, Central was the largest, with 846 inhabitants— scientists, technicians, support personnel, and even a few family members. BHHEI normally recruited only single men and women or husband-wife teams without children for its expeditions since the cost of including nonproductive family members was prohibitive. And the separations could be for such long periods that marriages often dissolved before the absent spouse returned. But occasional exceptions were made in the cases of scientists with special qualifications who were willing to subject their families to the dangers of deep-space exploration. Dr. Morgan, for instance, as chief scientist for the Society 437 expedition, had brought along his wife and their children, ages ten to seventeen.

The expedition had been on Society 437 for a full year before communications ceased, and during that time no circumstance, no living thing more than usually inimical to human life, had been detected on the planet. And now it appeared everyone, every man, woman, and child, was dead. That is, they were all dead at Central Station. If there were any survivors, they had not yet made themselves known. But from what the Marines could see, the death visited upon the people at Central had been thorough and horrible.

"Sergeant! Sergeant! Come here, quickly!" Lieutenant Snodgrass shouted. Bass had just arrived and was standing in the foyer of the administration building, wiping the perspiration from his forehead. Staff Sergeant Hyakowa and a navy corpsman came in right behind him. Snodgrass was standing on the second floor balcony that led to the communications control room. Having gotten Bass's attention, he whirled around and ran through a door, out of sight.

Bass looked at Hyakowa and shook his head. Ratliff emerged from one of the downstairs offices and cast an inquiring glance at the platoon commander. Bass shook his head no, and Ratliff returned to searching the downstairs rooms.

"What the hell has Snotty found now?" Hyakowa asked in a low voice.

"Let's go see," Bass answered, and they swiftly mounted the stairs to the second floor. Hyakowa carefully reset the safety on his weapon.

The data control room was surrounded on all sides by windows that looked out over the compound. It was stuffed with banks of computers, scanners, printers, and more esoteric equipment. The skeletal remains of several bodies were scattered about the floor.

"Look!" Snodgrass commanded when the two NCOs came through the door.

"Power's been out a long time, Lieutenant," Hyakowa said. "What's to look at?"

Bass laid a restraining hand on his platoon sergeant's shoulder. "Not so quick, Wang," he said slowly. "The lieutenant's right. Half the equipment that was in this control room is missing."

Hyakowa noticed then the gaping spaces in the console banks where instruments had been removed.

"And what's left has been deliberately destroyed," Snodgrass almost shouted. To prove his point he held up a piece of equipment. It looked to the Marines gathered around as if it had been melted. "Nothing in here works," the lieutenant exclaimed.

"Doc," Bass said to the corpsman, "what do you think?"

Confederation Navy corpsmen were far more than the pill-pushers of old. They had the skills, training, and equipment to perform fairly complicated battlefield surgery and could diagnose and successfully treat the most common diseases and disorders that still plagued mankind. The corpsman, Hospitalman First Class Horner, took the equipment from Snodgrass and examined it closely. He nodded his head at Bass. "I'd say from the very brief postmortems we've run on the bodies so far, someone sprayed those people and this equipment here with a very powerful acid."

"Acid?" Snodgrass shouted in disbelief. "Acid? Who the hell would do that? I've never heard of such foolishness!" He snatched back the piece of communications equipment and held it possessively. "Heat did this, goddamnit! Sabotage!"

"Lieutenant," Horner replied patiently, "acids oxidize material. Same thing as burning. What you've got on that piece of metal is an acid burn. Gunny, it's time to get Commander Bynum in here. That's what I think, anyway." He also thought Snodgrass was losing it—or they didn't teach basic chemistry at the Confederation Naval Academy anymore.

Bass nodded and began speaking into the command net. Snodgrass made as if to protest but Bass silenced him by holding up a hand.

"What the hell do you need the doctor for?" Snodgrass shouted. "Everyone's fucking dead down here! Why don't you get your ass moving, Sergeant, and find out who did this?" Snodgrass's face turned red.

Bass regarded the lieutenant briefly. He realized the communications officer was on the verge of hysteria. "Lieutenant," he replied after a moment, "I am in charge of this landing party, and speaking of 'asses,' you are becoming a big pain in mine." Snodgrass began to bluster but Bass silenced him with a wave of his hand. "Now, Mr. Snodgrass, you stick with the communications matters and I'll command the landing party. Otherwise, sir, I'll have to ask you to return to the *Fairfax*."

Snodgrass just stared silently at Bass for a second or two. "But—But—" He gestured vaguely around the control room. "We need to find out who—what—"

"Lieutenant," Bass answered, "we will, we will. That's why we need the med-sci team, they'll be able to find out. But I'm not putting one foot outside this compound until I know what we're up against down here. And just don't forget one thing, sir. Whoever—or whatever—did this to them," he gestured at the bodies scattered on the floor, "can do the same thing to us."

"Well," Dr. Bynum said as she straightened up and stretched her back, "I really need to get some of these remains back to the ship to do a thorough postmortem, but I've been able to establish one salient fact: First Class Horner's diagnosis that these people were killed by an acid is correct. I deduced that from the nature of the injuries they sustained, as you can see from the condition of the bones and the clothing, and the fact that a great many of these bones have no calcium in them anymore. That explains why they crumble to dust when disturbed."

The Marines gathered around her looked on in silent anticipation. "So what, precisely, does that mean?" Snodgrass asked. Bass glanced over at him sharply. The lieutenant's tone of voice dripped with sarcasm.

"Okay," she replied, ignoring Snodgrass's tone, "take a look at the remains over here." She stepped over to a heap of rags and bones lying undisturbed near the wall. "Now remember, I'm not a forensics expert," she continued, reaching down and picking up a bone fragment, "but anybody can see from these remains what might've happened here." She held out the fragment for the Marines to inspect. "This is the radius, the bone on the thumb side of the victim's right forearm. Note that it is only about four inches long, about a third or a quarter of the normal length of this bone in an adult. The end that connects to the carpus, or wrist, is gone entirely, and that end of the bone"—she rubbed it vigorously with her finger—"disintegrates into a fine power when touched. Note also there is no skull, no cervical vertebrae, the collar bones are missing, and so on. They were not carried away by foraging animals either. This white powder is all that's left of them." She stirred the powder on the floor with a finger. "Observe that there appears to be no right leg from the knee on down. You will also see—" She bent and rummaged among the clothing remnants. "—that the left side is essentially intact." She pulled another bone from among the clothing and held it up. "Left radius. See the difference?"

"So I repeat, Doctor, what happened?" Snodgrass demanded.

Still ignoring his tone, Dr. Bynum held up a clothing fragment. "This is what's left of the shirt the victim was wearing. Note how the right side is entirely gone. See the zipper that ran down the front? The upper half is melted." She tossed the fragment to the floor, where it raised a cloud of fine white dust, the remnants of the dissolved bones. "How many bodies have we examined so far, Gunny?" she asked, turning to Bass. "Maybe twenty? Horner looked at another twenty? They all display similar injuries. To put it simply, so even you can understand, Lieutenant Snodgrass, these people were sprayed with an extremely toxic and volatile substance that literally dissolved the body parts it touched. The reason this particular victim's right radius was not completely destroyed is probably because he threw up his right arm to protect his face and that partially protected the bone on the inside of his arm. Partly."

"Holy shit," someone said softly. Dean glanced nervously at the man standing next to him as all the Marines gripped their weapons more tightly.

"So they were attacked," Bass responded quietly. "This was not some kind of, um, 'environmental' anomaly?"

"No, Gunny," Dr. Bynum said. "These people, all several hundred of them, were deliberately and violently killed. It must have been terrible."

"Oh, Mohammed's big red gonads, Doctor!" Snodgrass exclaimed. "Who? Who would've done it? And how? I've never heard of anything so ridiculous!" Snodgrass's normal arrogance, which was always difficult to endure, had become even more pronounced now that he was frightened. There would be no more daydreams of him saying, "Dr. Morgan, I presume?"

"I know who did it," Dr. Bynum announced. Bass glanced sharply at her. "The people who did this are, quite obviously, Lieutenant, very nasty customers who don't much care about killing whoever gets in their way."

"Amen," Hyakowa said.

"Any idea about the type of weapons used?" Bass asked.

"No, except it was some kind of acid. Judging from the absence of calcium in the affected areas, I'd say specifically some kind of phosphoric acid. Possibly—and I emphasize 'possibly'—white phosphorus. Mixed with organic solvents like carbon disulfide or benzene, it can be very toxic. Judging from what I've seen here, I'd say it was sprayed somehow on the victims."

"Oh, who ever heard of such nonsense?" Snodgrass exclaimed, too loudly.

"Lieutenant, years ago phosphorus was used in military ordnance," Bass said. "I remember reading that it was very effective and very deadly."

"Yes, it caused terrible burns," Bynum added.

"If that stuff was used here," Staff Sergeant Hyakowa said, "how can you defend against it?"

"Good question," Bynum answered. "One thing is to deprive it of oxygen by submerging it in water. Another is to get it off you as quickly as possible. These people were no doubt caught entirely by surprise, so they didn't have a chance."

"It had to have been pirates," Snodgrass blurted, apparently accepting Dr. Bynum's theory.

"How do you get that, Lieutenant?" Hyakowa asked.

"Who else? You know one of my objectives is to check the accuracy of the Project Golem projections, and we know pirates are fully capable of commiting an act like this. Pirates, that's who I say did this."

"Hmm. I don't know," Bass replied. "I admit I don't know much about pirates, Lieutenant, but I do know the use of acid-spraying weapons is not, tactically or practically speaking, the best way to engage an enemy. And then there's the destroyed electronic equipment." He turned to Dr. Bynum. "But absent any other explanation, Commander, I accept yours. If whoever did this, pirates or whatever, is still around, we'd better be ready to deal with them."

Bass looked at the men standing around him. None had

ever seen such slaughter before. Fortunately, it had all happened so long ago that surveying the destruction now was more like exploring old catacombs with ancient skeletons lying around than walking through a butcher shop, which the place must've looked like just after the attack. But each man could imagine what must have happened here. And each also knew that it must have required a lot of manpower to kill all those people. And Bass could tell that the men of first squad, although wary of potential danger, were ready to confront it.

"Okay," he said, "we have two more stations to visit. There may be survivors somewhere. Let's saddle up."

"Charlie," Hyakowa said on the way out of the administration building, "I sure hope whoever did this on Waygone is long gone by now."

Bass did not reply, but he could not get Dr. Bynum's statement out of his mind, that whoever killed all those people were "very nasty customers." And he did not think they had been pirates. But what about those missing electronic components? In the pit of his stomach an unfamiliar and very uncomfortable knot of cold fear was growing.

Absently, Lieutenant Snodgrass fingered the ring he'd put in his pocket. He took it out and examined it. It was beautiful, with a large gem of some sort in the center and an ornate scroll design around the setting. Somebody's class ring, he realized. He looked inside. What he saw there made him catch his breath. And then he began laughing. The laugh rose to an hysterical, gasping, breathless crescendo, and when the lieutenant was able to partially regain control of himself, he started all over again. He held the ring out at the astonished Marines, trying to tell them something, but was laughing and gasping so hard that nobody could understand him. At last he made a supreme effort to get a grip on himself and was able to shout, "Dr. Morgan, I presume?" and convulsed with laughter all over again.

Bass and Hyakowa exchanged troubled glances. "Shit," Bass sighed, "don't we have enough problems? Keep your eye on that boy, Wang. He's going to be big trouble."

CHAPTER
SIXTEEN

Dean crouched in the shade of a building, scanning the sector of the forest he'd been assigned to watch. Owen, suffused a dull pink, indicating he was resting, perched comfortably on Dean's left shoulder. Dean was particularly alert, as were all the Marines, and more than a little nervous after what they'd discovered at Central Station. Corporal Pasquin had been on the squad circuit three times in the past fifteen minutes, asking for reports.

Dean could see nothing bigger than the tube-shaped, flying insects moving out there. It was getting very hot. A tiny drop of perspiration slid slowly down his right temple.

"I hope you aren't sleeping, Lance Corporal," a voice rasped from behind him. Startled, Dean whirled around. It was Pasquin, making a personal check of his fire team's positions. Dean was embarrassed that the corporal had come up on him without being detected and irked that Pasquin would even think he might doze off on guard.

Dean didn't bother to answer. Relations between them had been tense and utterly formal since their run-in at the promotion party. When the corporal did not follow through on his threat to bring him up on charges for insubordination, Dean had been relieved. But, ironically, he had also lost some respect for Pasquin, because it proved he was not a man of his word—and he spoke rashly. Now, Pasquin squatted down beside him. "Hot," he said. Dean nodded. Out of the corner of his eye Dean noticed that Owen had turned from pink to greenish-yellow, which he knew from experience indicated the woo was upset about something but not yet frightened. Ignoring Pasquin, Dean lowered his infra screen and scanned the tree line. Nothing. He blew air out of his lungs—whew!— and raised the screen.

"See something?" Pasquin asked as he tensed and shifted the position of his blaster.

"No. I just noticed Owen here changed colors. I thought he might have sensed something. I think he can tell when danger's nearby."

Pasquin snorted derisively. "I've never heard such crap before, Dean, taking a goddamn pet on a deployment, much less going on alert whenever he shits."

Oh, no, Dean thought, here he goes again! "Well, Top Myer said I could bring him along, and Gunny Bass didn't object, Corporal. Besides, Owen's not just my pet, he's— well—he's third platoon's mascot."

"I know, I know."

"And really, Corporal, the woos can sense danger. When we were down in the caves on Diamunde, Owen—"

"Ah, shit! 'Diamunde,' 'Wanderjahr,' 'Elneal'—that's all I ever hear from you guys! Can't you ever talk about anything else?"

"Well, excuse me all to hell. I'm sorry you weren't with us." Touché for insinuating I'd go to sleep on guard, Dean thought. Instantly, he felt embarrassed by his remark. It was too much like bragging. "Sorry. I was just—" Dean turned his head to look directly at the corporal as he spoke.

"Goddamnit, Dean, keep your eyes to the front! You're responsible for the security of this sector. Don't go dozing off or screwing around with that goofy-looking pet of yours there." Pasquin spoke in a voice loud enough to be heard in the forest.

"Keep it down," Dean said. "Look, Corporal, all I was saying was—"

"Shut up, Lance Corporal Dean! Don't tell me what to do. Goddamnit, one of these days I'm going to strangle that stupid-looking little shit." He thrust a stiff finger out at Owen, who'd begun to turn a light shade of blue.

Dean leaped to his feet so quickly Owen almost lost his balance. "You even breathe on Owen, and so help me I'll—" Dean shouted, forgetting his noise discipline. Pasquin stepped back quickly—and bumped into Staff Sergeant Hyakowa, who'd come from the nearby platoon command post to investigate the shouting.

"What's going on here?" the platoon sergeant asked quietly.

"Uh, nothing, Staff Sergeant," Pasquin muttered, his face reddening. Hyakowa looked inquiringly at Dean, who remained silent.

Hyakowa studied the two for a moment. "All right," he said at last. "Keep it down out here. Pasquin, come with me."

Hyakowa took Pasquin to the nearest building, which turned out to have been a nursery for the station's children. The brightly colored toys lying in disarray all about the small room contrasted vividly with the Marines' chameleons. Hyakowa sat atop what must have been the matron's desk while Pasquin remained standing.

"I know all about what you did to get kicked out of the 25th," Hyakowa said without preamble.

Pasquin felt a rush of embarrassment at the mere mention of his former unit, 25th FIST, "the Fighting 25th," as it was called, a unit with a history almost as illustrious as that of the 34th. Pasquin had felt deeply disgraced that he'd been transferred out. "What happened there was an accident, Staff Sergeant," he muttered defensively. When he heard the whining sound of his own voice in the tiny room, he felt even more embarrassed.

Hyakowa shrugged. "Sure. A very stupid mistake." Privately, Hyakowa thought differently. Pasquin had panicked, it was as simple as that, and men had died. Gunny Bass, for some unfathomable reason, saw it differently, so here Pasquin was. "They sent you to us, Pasquin, because we needed

replacements after Diamunde. Battalion told the Skipper he
didn't have to keep you if he didn't want you. They said they'd
send you to another company or keep you at HQ. Captain
Conorado did not want you, Corporal Pasquin."

Pasquin said nothing at first, just shifted position slightly.
He'd gotten the impression he was less than welcome when
Captain Conorado had given him a cold reception. His first
impulse was to respond, "Well, to hell with you, then!" and
spend the rest of his enlistment on the staff. Now, he asked,
"Well, then why . . . ?"

Hyakowa nodded. "Bass convinced him otherwise. Bass
saw something in you or in your records, Pasquin, that convinced him you were still a Marine. The captain decided to
give you a chance to prove it."

Pasquin's face turned red and he stiffened. "I am still a
Marine," he said, clenching his teeth. "Goddamnit, Staff Sergeant, what happened with 25th FIST was an accident, it
could've happened to anybody! The IG cleared me of
responsibility."

Hyakowa smiled to himself. That's the spirit, he thought.
Maybe Bass had been right. He slid lightly off the desk and
stood in front of Pasquin. "Forget about it. That was then.
This is now. And now," his voice hardened and he extended a
forefinger at Pasquin, "you are riding one of my best men, for
whatever reason, I don't know." He punctuated each word
with a jab of his finger. "Now listen up. This shit must cease.
We are in a very difficult situation here. We may be up against
something—" He searched for the right word. "—well, unusually deadly. Everybody's on edge and everybody's got to
keep his cool. Whatever it is that's bothering you, Pasquin,
you put it behind you and lay off these men."

The two stood facing each other for a moment. It was very
hot and close in the nursery and each man had begun to
perspire.

"You are on trial here, Pasquin," Hyakowa continued, "and
I am the judge. You screw up one more time, like you just
did out there, and your ass is going back to the *Fairfax*

minus those corporal's chevrons. And I'll tell you something else . . . " The platoon sergeant's voice had now turned as hard and cold as ice. "If you get any of these men hurt because of poor judgment or lack of guts, you are finished, goddamned finished with the Corps." Hyakowa was breathing heavily, and for just an instant it wasn't Pasquin standing there before him at all, but the cowardly ensign who'd left one of his men in the enemy's hands back on Elneal. Hyakowa got control of himself again. "Do we have an understanding, Corporal Pasquin?"

"Y-Yes, Staff Sergeant, we do," Pasquin answered immediately.

"Good. Now get back to your position. We still don't know whether anyone's out there."

"All right," Bass said after surveying the carnage and destruction throughout Central Station, "the plans for this station show two alternate data storage locations. Let's find them and see if any of them are intact."

"I've already got my sci people on it," Dr. Bynum said.

Off to the side, Lieutenant Snodgrass grimaced. He should have been the one to think of that. How was he ever going to demonstrate his right to lead the expedition if those two kept thinking of everything before he did?

"I'm going to check my people while we wait," Bass said. "Call me immediately when your people find something."

"Will do, Gunny," the doctor replied, and followed Bass out of the administration building.

Snodgrass was left alone. He looked about the admin building's assembly room. The furniture, much of it overturned, was pitted and sagging. He shuddered as he tried to imagine what had happened. At least the techs from the medsci team had bagged the skeletons and sent them back to the *Fairfax County*.

A sudden clatter made him jump, and he spun toward it, drawing his hand-blaster. He didn't see anyone. That chair, one of the toppled chairs, he was sure it was in a different

position than before. Wasn't it? Had it settled until it overbalanced and come to a new resting position—or did something he couldn't see knock it over? He wasn't sure, nothing
in the room looked the way it should. Was someone in the
room with him, hidden from his view? He couldn't see
anyone no matter how hard he looked or how much he
changed his position to look from all directions.

"Who's there?" he called out, and was glad his voice didn't
crack. No one answered. Was it his imagination? No, he was
sure he'd heard a sound—and no one was there to make a
noise. They didn't have any images of whoever attacked the
station. Could it be the invaders wore chameleons, like the
Marines did, and were still here? He wouldn't see anyone in
chameleons, he didn't have an infra viewer, nor did he know
the cues to look for to see someone wearing the invisibility
uniform.

Tensely, he looked and listened. Nothing moved in his
view. He didn't hear anything in the room other than his own
breathing and the thudding of his heart. He glanced toward
the door and wondered if it was close enough for him to get to
before some invisible assailant shot him, or grappled with
him to bear him down and beat him to a bloody, broken pulp.
He had to try to get out of the room, to escape whoever was
there with murder on his mind. He had to.

At first his feet refused to move, and when they finally did,
they were so awkward he almost tripped himself. But he
made it out of the room and down the corridor to the outside
without falling. He didn't hear any sound of pursuit. He
thought of how silly he'd look if he said he'd heard a noise and
been frightened of it, so he didn't say anything to anyone,
though he did cast frequent, anxious glances toward the entrance to the admin building.

"That's the damnedest thing I ever saw," Data Technician
Second Class Savanajivpahni said, tapping his display. The
science people had set up their computers under a tarp next
to the admin building, and were examining the data crystals

of shuttle activity before communications from the planet ceased.

Gunny Bass was a few meters away, checking the data from the various sensors and the RPV that showed on Dupont's display board. He heard the tech's exclamation and rushed under the cover, getting there just ahead of Dr. Bynum and Lieutenant Snodgrass.

"What is it?" he asked, leaning over Savanajivpahni's shoulder for a closer look. Dr. Bynum and Lieutenant Snodgrass crowded in next to him to watch the display. They saw a blip suddenly appear on the screen, move a short distance, then disappear. An instant later another blip appeared, closer to the center of the display. The two positions were too far apart for the blips to have been the same object. The second blip disappeared and a third, almost on top of the control center, appeared.

Savanajivpahni pointed at the numbers and symbols that scrolled up the side of the display. "These show speed, distance, vector, and mass," he said. "According to them, the blips are shuttles moving faster than shuttles are supposed to go in atmosphere. Each of them came out of nowhere, and neither of the first two returned after it disappeared. The way they act," his voice developed a quiver, "it's like they shifted into Beamspace, and the blips are the same shuttle flicking in and out of Beamspace. But you can't do that in a planet's gravity well."

Bass unbent and stood looking up under the edge of the tarp at the sky for a long moment as he thought about it. The only thing that made sense was that someone had an improved Beam drive that the Confederation Navy didn't know anything about. An improved Beam drive that worked not only in a gravity well, but also in atmosphere, would explain the strange blips and mean that all three were the same shuttle. It didn't seem possible, but that was the only explanation that made sense.

Bass looked back at the display, which was looping

through the strange blipping again. "What's that?" He pointed at the stationary blip.

"That reads as a starship, civilian cargo."

"What's it doing there?" Bass knew where Society 437 was in its supply cycle. As he watched, a smaller blip dropped out of the starship and looped into a spiral toward the planetary surface.

Savanajivpahni shook his head. "I don't know, but it just dropped a shuttle." He glanced at the scrolling data. "If I'm reading the vector right, it's headed toward Aquarius Station."

The intermittent blips of the apparent shuttle flicking in and out of Beamspace reappeared on the loop. Then the blip of the cargo starship flared up. When the flare faded away, the blip wasn't there anymore.

"What happened?"

"Somebody blew up the civilian ship."

"What else have you found?" Bass asked, trying to make sense of it.

"Over here," another tech said.

Bass glanced at the name tag on the woman's shirt: LARISH-NAMOVA. "What do you have?" he asked.

"I've been working on the visuals from the security cameras beginning a few minutes before the unidentified shuttle landed. I've patched them together into a montage." Larishnamova twiddled a dial and flicked a toggle. "I'm afraid it doesn't tell us much." She moved so Bass and Bynum could see her display screen more easily. "This first is outside the control center," she said. An odd-looking shuttle settled into place and a hatch cracked open on its side. A tube of some sort extended a few centimeters out of the hatch and sprayed a stream of greenish fluid at the camera. The image blanked out. "That's all I could get from that one. Whatever that fluid was, it melted the camera."

Bass reflected a moment and remembered seeing various slagged protuberances on some of the buildings.

Another scene appeared on the display screen, the outside

of the admin building. Everything appeared normal until a greenish stream shot out and the visual blanked out. Another scene flickered on. "This is inside the main entrance of the admin center," Larishnamova said. "I have it starting right when the previous one blanked out." The view was of the lobby, as seen from a position high on the wall in a corner. A man, probably a security guard, was lounging behind a short counter in the upper right corner of the picture. The entryway was on the left side, and other doors were visible on both sides of the security counter. The entrance door suddenly flew open and a stream of greenish fluid shot across the lobby at the guard a moment before another stream of fluid flew at the camera and knocked it out.

Those were followed by several more at different places within the settlement. All of them were the same—a stream of greenish fluid obliterated the camera. Sometimes a bit of tubing was visible immediately before the stream came, other times not.

"What was that?" Snodgrass shrilly demanded. "Who did that?" He'd been craning to see over and around Bass and Bynum.

"Have you been able to do any filtering, get a picture of who used those weapons?" Bass asked Larishnamova, ignoring the lieutenant.

Larishnamova shook her head. "I tried. The shooters always seem to be out of the line of sight from the cameras. Either that or in shadows too deep for the cameras to pick up."

Bass looked unfocused into the distance. "That implies they knew the location of the cameras," he said slowly. He turned a puzzled expression to the doctor. "I read all the Waygone reports the *Fairfax* carried, and didn't see any mention of dismissed personnel. Did you?"

Dr. Bynum shook her head. "No. What are you getting at?"

"Someone disgruntled about being fired, someone with a grudge, would know where the cameras were."

"That's not a grudge!" Snodgrass shrilled. "That's . . . " But nobody paid him any attention.

"A scientist or technician joined a pirate band?" Bynum asked.

"Pirates have to come from somewhere."

"Somehow I don't think that's the case here."

"Neither do I." Bass abruptly changed the subject. "The weapons, that green fluid. Have you ever seen anything like that?"

"As I said, my best guess is it's some sort of acid. Otherwise"—she shrugged—"you're the weapons expert here."

Bass shook his head. "I've never heard of weapons that shoot streams of acid."

The two looked at each other, neither willing to be the first to say what both were thinking: The unexplainable blips that approached Central, the improved Beamspace drive, the weapons they couldn't recognize. Something nonhuman did it. The navy and Marine personnel on the mission were prepared to do many things; making first contact with an alien intelligence wasn't one of them.

"Unless you have objections, Doctor, I think we need to get the data from those crystals up to the *Fairfax* immediately. Maybe the shipboard equipment could decipher something we can't planetside."

Bynum nodded. "I'll put it on our next shipment. Better yet, I'll send it immediately." Larishnamova popped the crystal and handed it to her.

Bass looked back at the now blank display while Dr. Bynum headed to the waiting Essay. "A trajectory to Aquarius Station, huh?"

The computers on board the *Fairfax County* were only able to come up with one bit of information the planetside techs hadn't. Spectrographic analysis which, given the quality of the vid on the crystal, was neither thorough nor reliable, tentatively identified the greenish fluid streamed at the cameras as an unknown compound with a dual base of hydrogen chloride and phosphoric acid.

"So what do you want to do now, Lander Six?" Captain

Tuit asked from the communications visual display. At that point his job, his ship's job, was to support the ground forces. He could override any decision the ground forces commander made that, in his opinion, would put his ship in danger. Otherwise he would do everything he could to help the ground commander accomplish his mission.

"I think we've found everything here we can without a more detailed investigation than we can make at the moment," Bass answered. "I think we need to visit Aquarius Station."

Tuit nodded. "That's what I'd want to do in your place. I'll send another Essay down with two more Dragons and a security team under the command of my bosun. They'll be under your command."

"Thank you, Skyhawk." It didn't even cross Bass's mind that the bosun of the *Fairfax County* was a senior chief petty officer, the navy equivalent of a Marine sergeant major. It wouldn't have bothered him if it had. For ground operations he was the senior man on the mission and already had two navy officers under his command. He was in command of the ground forces, and, at least in theory, even an admiral would have to obey his orders. "How soon can I expect the Essay?"

Tuit chuckled. "My sailors would probably mutiny if I made them make planetfall the way you Marines do. It'll take an hour to get the security party ready, and then—" He looked away from the camera for a second. "—another three-quarters of an hour before we're back in the drop window. Say six hours."

"That'll be after nightfall, Skyhawk."

"My coxswains know how to make night landings, Lander Six. Tomorrow's early enough for you to get to Aquarius. Probably be better for you to get there in the morning, after a night's sleep."

"Aye aye, sir." Bass, as anxious as he was to get to Aquarius, knew Tuit was overruling him. A night landing at Aquarius Station, where there was potential danger, could put ship's personnel, shuttles, and Dragons in unnecessary hazard, and the captain was fully within his rights in over-riding the ground commander on this point.

Bass, Hyakowa, Bynum, and Senior Chief Hayes had everyone up and aboard the Essays before dawn. As soon as the sun broke above the horizon, the Essays launched for the two-hour suborbital flight to Aquarius Station. At its end, the Essay carrying third platoon made a combat landing, coming down fast from four thousand meters, while the Essay carrying the navy personnel swung in a wide circle at five thousand meters, ready to come down when the all-clear was given, or to take off for orbital altitude if the landing zone was too hot.

The Essay's coxswain brought the shuttle down fast and smooth to a hover, a meter above the water of the swamp, a kilometer and a half east of Aquarius Station. Its ramp lowered and the three Dragons roared out, splashed into the water, and raced toward the Aquarius Station compound, forming a line three abreast as they went. The Essay launched as soon as the Dragons were safely away.

Bass on Dragon One, and Hyakowa on Dragon Three, were patched into their vehicles' opticals so they could see where they were going. At first all they saw was sluggish, almost stagnant water thickly studded with hummocks of mud bars and small, lushly vegetated islands. The Dragons' air cushions sprayed high screens and higher rooster tails of water that subsided only when they lurched over mud bars—they stayed off the islands, where they couldn't tell what hazards the vegetation hid. Some of the islands were too densely covered with vegetation to see more than a few meters across.

After two and a half minutes of travel at thirty-five kph, the Dragons stopped in the lee of a small island. From there, the large island where Aquarius Station was located was visible across a hundred meters of water. No movement was visible in visual or infrared other than that of the ubiquitous insectoids and foliage that moved dankly in breezes nearly as sluggish as the water. Neither did the high-powered sounders mounted on the Dragons pick up any noises that didn't seem native to the swamp.

"Dupont, launch the RPV," Bass quietly ordered.

"Aye aye," the comm man replied. He already had the recon unit, disguised as one of the tube-bodied insectoids, ready for launch. He hit the button next to the ramp to lower it enough to release his bird, then reclosed the ramp. Bass stood over him, watching the display as Dupont worked the controls to maneuver the RPV in a quartering pattern over the station. Nothing appeared other than the native life.

"Let's go ashore," Bass told Dragon One's commander after watching the display for ten minutes. "Land the navy," he said into his long-range communications unit.

The second Essay landed on the island twenty minutes later.

Aquarius Station was a second-class imitation of Central Station, with only a half-dozen buildings and large bungalows. The admin building was quite small and filled with claustrophobic offices. One building held what was evidently a combination meeting hall and mess hall—"dining room," as Dr. Bynum corrected them. "These people were civilians, they ate in dining rooms, not mess halls"—with an adjacent kitchen. Both the admin and the assembly buildings had apartments that had been used by the top people assigned to Aquarius. Three of the others were laboratory buildings. One of them had a freezer unit for storage of biological specimens. The Marines made a grisly discovery in the freezer— seven bodies. All seven had been killed by projectile or plasma weapons. Everywhere else they found skeletons, some partial, others complete, all with the same markings as those they'd found at Central Station.

They saved the residential block for last.

"Somebody's been here, and recently," Hyakowa reported over the platoon net from the scientists' living quarters.

Bass, with Lieutenant Commander Bynum and Lieutenant Snodgrass in his wake, wasted no time getting over there.

Hyakowa pointed to a dressing table set against one wall of what had been someone's bedroom. The table was covered with a thick coating of vegetable growth accumulated since the tragedy that had killed its occupant. Items of clothing lay scattered on the floor nearby. The surface of the tabletop gleamed dully where patches of the plant growth had been scraped away.

The imprint of a human hand showed clearly in one of the cleared patches.

"Damn!" Bynum exclaimed. "That had to have been made a long time after this place was attacked." She leaned closer to inspect the print. "I think one of them might be a woman." The others gathered around.

"What makes you think that?" Bass asked.

She looked at him, mildly surprised. "The size."

Bass looked more closely at the print. Not much dust lay on it. "How long ago do you think it was made?" he asked.

Bynum shrugged. "Days ago, maybe a couple of weeks?"

"Then there are survivors," Snodgrass whispered. Maybe Morgan had survived. Maybe he could still . . .

"And these clothes, Charlie," Bynum said, bending and picking up a pair of coveralls from the floor. "They're from that closet over there. Whoever was in here was looking for something to wear. And this is a woman's size."

Bass reached over Bynum's shoulder and shook a slender bottle free from the lichens that had covered it.

" 'Persian Kitty,' " he said, reading the label. He removed the glass stopper and smelled the contents. "Whew! Might take some of this back to Camp Ellis for Big Barb." Hyakowa guffawed behind him at the mention of Big Barb. That was the first laugh Bass could remember hearing since they left the *Fairfax*. Somehow it made him feel better.

"Gunny." Sergeant Ratliff's voice broke in over the platoon net. "Better get over to the administration building right away. We've found a message!"

* * *

They stared at the hand-painted message on a piece of metal propped up just inside the main entrance to the administration building.

" 'Grate danger' "? Snodgrass read the words. "Interesting spelling."

"Prob'ly written by an officer—sir," someone snickered. Commander Bynum laughed outright.

Snodgrass whirled around but the several enlisted men standing behind him just looked innocently back at him. But Bass recognized the voice as belonging to MacIlargie. "At ease," the platoon commander said wearily to no one in particular. "I don't want any more of that talk out of you people."

"Well," Snodgrass went on, "obviously written by a pirate."

"How do you get that, Lieutenant?" Hyakowa asked.

"No scientist could be that illiterate," Snodgrass answered in an almost contemptuous tone.

"I don't know," Dr. Bynum said. "I've known some pretty inarticulate scientists. Just because a person has a genius IQ doesn't mean he knows how to spell."

"It was pirates," Snodgrass said firmly. "And they killed these people."

"I don't know, Lieutenant," Hyakowa said. "If it was pirates, what're they doing still hanging around here? And why'd they want us to know where they're at? Looks to me, sir, like some illiterate scientists might've survived."

"Ambush," Snodgrass replied positively. "The pirates want us to go, uh," he glanced back at the message, "thirty kilometers southwest of here to where they're waiting to ambush us."

Everyone looked to Bass for his opinion. He stroked his chin a few times. "Two things, people," he said at last, counting them off on his fingers. "One: there are, or were when this sign was written, survivors. And two: we're going to find them if they're still alive. Let's go climb some mountains." He signaled for Dupont to raise the ship so he could tell Captain Tuit what they'd found and what they were doing next.

CHAPTER
SEVENTEEN

"There it is again," Surface Radar Analyst Third Class, Hummfree muttered. His soft voice was lost in the pings of equipment and the susurration of carefully controlled air that wafted through the comm shack, the analysis center of the *Fairfax County*. None of the other analysts and techs working at other stations looked up at his words. They were as thoroughly immersed in their jobs as Hummfree was in the data that flowed from the string-of-pearls into the monitors he watched. He watched visuals that ranged from infrared to ultraviolet. His monitors showed X ray and radar and could display gamma if he wanted. Graphs—bar, line, scatter, hi-lo, more—jiggled and jaggled before his eyes. But at the moment he was only interested in one thing that appeared in the array of monitors he watched and listened to. An intermittent dot that showed up in the infrared in one small space in the mountains.

His fingers danced over his keyboard, caressed the balls and dials of his controls. His objective was to merge the visual and infrared signals in that space. If he succeeded, he might have a good idea what was generating the intermittent signal in the infrared. Theoretically, what he was attempting was possible. Few navy analysts were willing even to attempt it, though; it was simply too difficult.

SRA3 Hummfree wasn't only willing, he was convinced he could do it. It didn't matter that he'd spent many hours of his own time on that problem over the three days the *Fairfax County* had been in orbit. And it didn't matter that he didn't seem any closer to a resolution. Hummfree had solved problems before in situations where nobody else thought there was a solution, so he was confident of his abilities. Now that Ensign Muhoorn had ordered him to investigate the mountains full-time, he was spending nearly all of his waking hours on the problem, interrupting his work only when the communications chief made him stop for meals or to take a shower. If—no, make that when—he resolved the target, it just might get him that promotion to second class. Hummfree needed a meritorious promotion because he spent too much of his own time working on special projects and too little on studying for the promotion exam.

The red dot showed up again in the infrared. Visual had just a small blur. Quickly, Hummfree zoomed the focus on it. Simultaneously he began to converge the visual and infrared signals on the same spot. For a second they didn't quite merge; theoretically, at geosynchronous orbit distance, the string-of-pearls' infrared sensors couldn't resolve anything much smaller than a one-meter radius, and the visual couldn't see details smaller than fifteen centimeters, even when seeing conditions were optimal. But Hummfree had reprogrammed the string-of-pearls software to allow him to use long baseline interferometry from four satellites. By having the computer average the best of the scans in the visual and infrared, then overlapping them, he gave form to what he tried to focus on. He transferred the data to storage, slapped the toggle labeled SFFT, and called out, "Chief, Mr. Muhoorn, take a look at this."

"What?" Chief Petty Officer Kranston asked through teeth clenched as though they gripped a cigar. He got up ponderously from the station where he oversaw the work of his men and took the one step that put him behind Hummfree's left shoulder. He plugged his headset into the console.

"What do you have, Hummfree?" Ensign Muhoorn asked when he reached Hummfree's right shoulder.

Hummfree pointed at the wavering image, only a few pixels high, on his main screen. "That's a man."

"Is it one of the Marines?" Muhoorn asked, trying to understand what he was looking at. "Or one of our med-sci team?" It might have been a man. If he read the scale right, it was the about the size of a man, and it did appear to be vertical like a biped, rather than horizontal like most animals. But the young navy officer couldn't make out enough detail to tell who it might be, or even if it really was a man.

"The Marines are wearing chameleons, we wouldn't get one in the visual," Chief Kranston said. "And none of our med-sci people would be alone." He pressed the earpiece of his headset closer and listened as he studied the flickering, overlapping, different resolution images that didn't quite coalesce into something his eyes could be sure they saw. "Doesn't seem to be saying anything, but I hear sounds that might be from him. Sounds like he's taking a piss." Then to Hummfree, "Where is it?"

Hummfree's fingers danced and the image changed to show an area large enough to include Aquarius Station. A red arrow pointed at the spot where the indistinct image was. Thirty kilometers to the northeast, an orange circle showed the location of Aquarius Station, where the Marines were awaiting Captain Tuit's approval for what they wanted to do next.

"Bring him back," Kranston ordered. When Hummfree changed the screen back to the image that might have been a man, the figure was moving up the side of the mountain until it vanished.

"I think they're staying in caves and only come out once in a while, maybe only one or two at a time," Hummfree said. "That's why the string-of-pearls has so much trouble picking them up."

"You're really sure that was a man?" Muhoorn asked.

Hummfree hesitated before answering. "Sir, I'm not positive, but I'll bet on it and lay odds. It has the right kind of heat signature, and there's no record of this planet having indigenous surface-dwelling life-forms with that degree of body heat."

The communications officer looked at the chief, who was still studying the display.

Chief Kranston clapped Hummfree on the shoulder. "If you're willing to lay odds, I'm willing to back your bet."

"I'll notify the Skipper," Muhoorn said. He went to his station and reported to Captain Tuit.

"Get precise coordinates," Kranston growled, "Longe, lat, and altitude. Them mud-sloggers down there're gonna need them."

"Roger, Skyhawk. Lander out." Bass returned the handset of the comm unit to Dupont and chewed on his lip for a few seconds while he digested what he'd just been told. Then he said, "Round everybody up. We're moving out."

In a few minutes the entire platoon plus the med-sci team and the navy security team were assembled in the main assembly room of Aquarius Station. The Marines, except for a few Hyakowa assigned to keep watch on the outside through the windows, looked at Bass attentively. Most members of the med-sci team looked either mildly curious or somewhat annoyed at being called from whatever they'd been doing. The navy security team tried to look as tough and blasé as the Marines and almost succeeded. The difference was, the Marines didn't try to look tough and blasé.

"I have news," Bass said as soon as they were assembled. "The *Fairfax* has found people." He held up his hands and patted the air to fend off a barrage of questions. "If everybody will hold on, I'll tell you everything I know. It won't take long, because I don't know much. A surface radar analyst aboard ship pinpointed the location of what he believes is a human being in the mountains thirty kilometers southwest of here, just like the message we found said. I have the coordinates." He shook his head. "I'd rather send a drone to investigate without endangering any of us, but we don't have an RPV with legs long enough to travel that far and be able to loiter." He nodded toward Dr. Bynum. "And any people we find will probably need medical attention, so we have to take medical personnel with us. I think, if Lieutenant Commander Bynum concurs, that the tech people will be better used by staying here. Senior Chief Hayes and his people will provide security for them. The rest of us will leave as soon as we can get our gear stowed aboard the Dragons.

"Most of the land between here and the foot of the mountains is swamp. There's no way around the swamps. The ride won't be comfortable. The place where this possible person was seen is on the side of the mountain. It's too steep and rugged there for the Dragons, so we'll have to go the last part of the way on foot. That is all. Pack up and let's go."

The Marines immediately began exiting the assembly room. They didn't have much packing to do, but knew they'd have to help the others. Besides, they had their orders and obeyed immediately.

"But you haven't told us who it was that was seen," Lieutenant Snodgrass called out.

Bass shrugged. "I don't know who it was. Like I said, the SRA *believes* he found a human being. No identification beyond 'probable human' is available."

"Was it Dr. Morgan?" Snodgrass shouted.

"Mr. Snodgrass . . ." Bass's voice clearly showed his annoyance. "If the analysts couldn't identify it as any more than 'probable human,' they certainly couldn't give a name to it. Now get ready to board the Dragons."

"Why do we have to go on the surface, why not fly in the Essays?" a corpsman asked.

"Because the Essays can't land in a swamp, and the ground is too rugged where the swamps end for an Essay to put down. Now move out."

"Do you think the person who was seen is one of the pirates who did this?" Snodgrass demanded. "Is that why you want all the Marines to go? If it's the pirates, you're unnecessarily putting everybody in danger if you don't leave most of the Marines here to protect us. Once the Marines go, there's nothing to stop the pirates from attacking us." He ignored the glare Chief Hayes shot at him.

"I told you why the entire platoon is going and taking the medical people. The survivors will need immediate medical attention. Anyway, it's unlikely any pirates are still around here, if there were any pirates to begin with."

"It's pirates. Pirates slaughtered these people."

"We don't know that," Bass snapped. "And even if the people on the mountain are pirates," he raised his voice to speak over Snodgrass's continued objections, "they're stranded here and will be deliriously happy to see us. I don't think we have anything to fear from pirates—they won't be interested in crossing thirty klicks of swamp to attack you. Now get ready to move out."

"Nobody move!" Snodgrass shouted. "I'm going to get clearance from Captain Tuit. It's too dangerous for all of the Marines to go. Captain Tuit will agree with me that a squad of Marines should go to investigate before anybody else goes."

"Mr. Snodgrass!" Bass bellowed. Everyone still in the room looked at him—the Marines, Dr. Bynum, and Senior Chief Hayes with amusement, the other members of the med-sci team nervously, not knowing what to expect. "May I remind you that I am the commander of the ground force. I issue the orders here, not you. I am taking the entire platoon with the full agreement and blessings of Commander Tuit. Now, Snotty, wipe your nose and get your ass in gear." With that he stormed out of the room.

Snodgrass turned bright red. It was the first time anyone had used the name to his face. He had to pump his chest to loosen it enough to scream, "I'm an officer, you're only an enlisted man! I'm taking command and pressing charges! You're under arrest!" He flinched as though struck when a hand lightly touched his shoulder. He jerked toward it and saw Dr. Bynum's gently smiling face peering at him.

"Lieutenant," she said softly, "this is an amphibious operation under hostile conditions. It is under the command of the ground forces commander, who happens to be Gunnery Sergeant Bass. I'm here because I have a job to do in the ground force. You're here just for the ride, not because you have a function. But if you want to play rank games, I outrank you. *I* order you to get ready to move out. In the future remember that all of us obey the orders of the ground commander. That way you won't get embarrassed again by speaking out of line."

"You—You can't give me orders!" he sputtered. "You're medical corps, I'm a line officer."

Bynum nodded. "That's right. And you're a communications officer, you can't give orders to the ground forces commander either." She reached into a pocket and pulled out a tissue. "Take this, blow your nose. You'll feel better." Leaving the astonished Lieutenant Snodgrass holding the tissue, Dr. Bynum left to get the med-sci team ready to leave.

Before Snodgrass could recover, an arm draped across his shoulders. He jerked his head around and saw Senior Chief Hayes's face smiling softly from too close for comfort.

"It's time to be calm, sir," Hayes said in a gentling tone. "You're an officer, Mr. Snodgrass. It's important you appear cool and collected."

"But—"

Hayes squeezed Snodgrass's shoulders tightly enough to force the wind out of him. "There's no 'buts' here, sir. I know your sense of propriety is offended by being under the command of an enlisted man. Hell, I'm a senior chief, I outrank him too. But he's an honest-to-God mud-Marine. When it comes to ground operations, he's forgotten more about it than the two of us combined will ever learn—and he's forgotten damn little of what he's learned. So for the ground operations, I follow him. But I'll tell you one thing, sir. When it comes to securing an installation, I know more than he does. My sailors and I are securing this station. You'll be safe with us.

"Now be a good officer, Mr. Snodgrass. Buck yourself up, straighten your uniform, look the role of an officer." Hayes gave a final squeeze and walked away, leaving Snodgrass too dumbfounded to even sputter.

Hyakowa joined Bass just outside the door. "That's telling

him, boss." The platoon sergeant glanced over his shoulder to make sure no one was listening. "Most officers are pretty good. How come we keep getting stuck with the assholes?"

Bass merely grunted.

Snodgrass had one final objection to Bass's orders.

"You can't take all the medical personnel. Most of them are hospital corpsmen, only a couple of them have any field experience or training. They're liable to get injured because they aren't up to going cross-country with Marines."

And you are? Bass swallowed the words before he said them. Instead he said, "We don't know how many survivors there are. All of them will need medical attention. I'd be derelict if I didn't take as many medical personnel and equipment as I can."

"I'm going with you. I'll see to it that you don't mistreat those medical people."

Bass blinked in astonishment at Snodgrass's arrogance. "I think that's one of *Lieutenant Commander* Bynum's functions," he said.

Snodgrass flinched, but repeated his demand. "I'm going with you."

Bass shrugged. "Suit yourself." He waved him toward the Dragons.

Four Dragons went in a column. The fifth remained behind to bolster the security of Aquarius Station. Bass rode in the lead Dragon with first squad. Lieutenant Snodgrass rode in the second Dragon with the assault squad. The medical team rode in the third. And Hyakowa and second squad brought up the rear.

From her vantage point low among the root columns of a tree at the edge of a nearby island, showing only her head from her eyes up as she breathed through her gills, the watcher saw and heard the Earth barbarians leave the smaller station in four of their vehicles. She carefully memorized the time and direction of their departure to report to the Master when time came for her to give her report. Then she turned her attention to the vehicle that remained behind.

Vaguely, she wondered why it was left, but hers wasn't a curiosity that needed to be satisfied. She had been bred for work and obedience; curiosity that needed satisfaction served neither of those functions, so she had it in very small store. It was the hope and expectation of the Masters that in a very few more generations, her descendants would have no curiosity left whatsoever. Patiently, as she had also been bred, she watched the smaller station and the vehicle that was left behind. Even though she wasn't particularly curious about it herself, she knew the Master and the leaders would want to know about it, so she watched in order to be able to report.

After a time she saw a barbarian carry a parcel from one of the buildings and walk to the vehicle. He left the vehicle after a few moments without the parcel. Later, he made the round-trip again, and returned the parcel, much smaller now, to the building. If pressed for an opinion, she would conclude the parcel was likely food for Earth barbarians who were in the vehicle.

Food. Hunger. She realized she had been in the hide position for longer than a day without eating. Twice during that long stretch she had briefly left her hiding place to void her body wastes where they would not pollute her body, which must always be kept clean. Now that she had thought of food, she realized she was hungry. Void. Hunger. Two halves of a whole. The one implied the other. The other demanded the one. The transparent membrane tucked under the outer corner of her eyes slid across them and she dipped her head fully beneath the surface. Things, strange things, swam in those waters. All of them could be eaten, even the one that could eat the People, though none of them tasted like the food she ate at Home. The Master and the leaders insisted they eat the things that swam in the waters, so she and the others ate them. The Master insisted that they also swallow the droplets that gave them the necessary nutrients the things that swam did not. She did not have a droplet with her, but her hunger was suddenly great and she must eat.

She watched the things that swam past. Most of them were small and she would need many of them to quell her hunger. A few of the things she saw were bigger, so much bigger that catching them could cause turmoil in the water, turmoil the barbarians or their instruments might notice. She could not catch one of the larger things that swam; the leaders would not approve of her attracting the attention of the Earth barbarians or their instruments, even if she moved to another position and was not found. Cautiously, she raised her head to look at the smaller station again. Nothing had changed during the moment her gaze was fixed on the things that swam. She submerged once more. There, that one. She had no name for it, but she'd eaten it before with pleasure. It was the shape of a rope, as long as her forearm and as thick as three of her fingers together. She moved a hand, slowly, like a leaf drifting in the water, to the level where it was swimming and waited patiently as it undulated closer. When it was a hand's length away, she snatched it up.

The swimmer twisted and writhed in her grip and tried to bring its tooth-rimmed, circular mouth around to gouge her hand, but her other hand was faster and grabbed the head. She brought both hands toward her face and bit down hard on the neck of the swimmer. Holding it in her grinding teeth, she twisted it forward and back, her hands operating in opposition to each other. The head came off and she dropped it. She eased back into her watching position and contentedly chewed on the body of the swimmer. It did not taste as good as the similar swimmers at Home, but it tasted better than most of the other swimmers in the strange swamp. The People cooked, they had always known how to cook, but they had been eating swimmers raw for thousands of years. Eating the strange swimmer raw while hunkered down with only her eyes and the crown of her head above the water seemed not in the least strange to her.

At length, the Master and the fighters asked for her report.

* * *

"Uncomfortable" wasn't the word Lieutenant Snodgrass would have used to describe the trip across the swamp. There weren't clear channels of water for the amphibious, air-cushioned Dragons to travel for any distance. They constantly swerved around obstacles in the water, or humped up and rolled over tussocks, some vegetated, others barren. Unseen objects below the surface of the murky water disrupted the uniformity of the air cushion on which the Dragons rode, and sometimes knocked a skirt flap aside. The drivers seemed unable to go even a hundred meters without slamming into something hard and sending vibrations thudding through the vehicles. All in all, Lieutenant Snodgrass would have called the ride "gut-wrenching," "torturous" and, yes, even "terrifying." But not "uncomfortable."

"We're out of the swamp, mountain ahead," the driver of the second Dragon in the column announced nearly five hours after leaving Aquarius Station.

Snodgrass's sigh of relief came out as a groan. Then he yelped as the Dragon clanked over an uneven bed of boulders.

The bouncing, jouncing, and banging were worse on the lower slopes of the mountain than they had been in the swamps—everything was harder there. It was another half hour before the terrain became so steep and rugged the Dragons couldn't continue. Everyone was rubbing at least one sore spot as they dismounted. They looked around in dismay. They were in the path of a recent landslide. A swath several hundred meters wide had been gouged from the forest that blanketed the mountainside. Boulders, ranging from gravel to house-size, littered the pathway. Broken tree ferns lay between, shattered stumps stuck up here and there. Insectoids of all sizes fluttered about the edges of the forest.

Hyakowa began putting out security even before Bass assembled the rest of the platoon and the med-sci team. In a moment second squad's second fire team, which Hyakowa had sent to the edge of the forest, reported back. The forest floor was covered with thick underbrush—they wouldn't be able to get through it without making a lot of noise.

Bass left his helmet on so the Marines in the security posts could hear him on their radios, but raised all helmet shields and rolled up his sleeves so the med-sci team members, none of whom had infras, could see him. He looked at his locator to determine their exact position before speaking.

"We have to go five kilometers that way." He pointed uphill and to the right. "We'll go up this slide for about a kilometer and a half, then we have to find a way through the forest."

"Why don't we go the same way those people went?" a member of the medical team asked. "Surely they followed some sort of path."

"Fine. Show me the path and we'll follow it." Bass looked directly at the corpsman who asked the question. Abashed, she looked at him and feebly lifted her hands in a gesture that said she didn't know where the path might be.

"That's right," Bass said. "We don't know how they got up there, so we have to find our own way." He saw worried expressions on some faces. Not on the Marines, though. Unknown landscapes were a natural environment for the men who went to strange places to fight the Confederation's battles. "Don't worry about getting lost." Bass directed his words to the medical team. "I've got our destination logged on my map, and I'm in constant touch with the string-of-pearls, so we'll always know where we are. If anybody does get separated after we get off this slide, don't worry about being lost. All you have to do is go downhill until you reach the swamp, turn right until you reach the slide, then go uphill until you reach the Dragons. We won't leave anybody behind. We're Marines.

"Any other questions?"

When there weren't any, he said to Hyakowa, "Leave one gun team with the Dragons for security. Send out one fire team on each flank, then let's move."

CHAPTER
EIGHTEEN

Lance Corporal Schultz took point, that went without saying. Almost every time third platoon was on the move, Schultz put himself in the position most likely to run into danger first. He didn't consider himself expendable, not by any means. He believed he was better at spotting an enemy or other dangers than anyone else in the platoon. Or the company. The truth be known, Hammer Schultz thought he was the best pointman in the entire Confederation Marine Corps, perhaps the universe. No troop formation he had ever led in a hostile situation was surprised by walking into an ambush. Not that Marines walked into ambushes very often—they were exceedingly good at what they did, and often carried top-of-the-line equipment that allowed them to do their jobs even better. But Schultz was so much better at spotting danger than most Marines that he simply didn't trust anyone else to do the job right. Besides, having someone not as good as he on the point would needlessly endanger him. And when the shooting started, Schultz wanted to fire the first shot. He firmly believed that the man who shoots first is most likely to live to talk about it—not that Schultz talked about the fire fights he'd been in, or much of anything else. Schultz wanted that hot spot.

So Schultz led third platoon and the medical team up through the skree left in the wake of the landslide. He carefully picked his way around boulders and found paths where the footing was most stable across the gravelly areas. The route he followed and the care he took in finding it resulted in a slow pace for the column that followed him. For once, Lieutenant Snodgrass had been right, the members of the medical team weren't accustomed to covering any distance over rugged terrain. Quickly they were in danger of exhaustion. Fortunately, the slow pace allowed them to keep up. But Schultz wasn't looking for stable footing for the benefit of the medical team; he wanted stable footing in case the Marines had to move fast and fight. The route angled this way and that, but averaged more than a hundred meters from the torn edge of the forest.

A hundred meters short of the klick and a half Bass had given for the climb up the slide, Schultz started looking for sign of a route through the forest. He made a face, but didn't comment, when somebody else spotted a way first.

"Hey," Claypoole's voice crackled over the platoon net, "I see something." His position on the right flank had him closer to the forest than anybody else.

"Everybody, hold your places," Bass ordered over the platoon net. "Three-two, check it out."

"What do you have, Rock?" Corporal Kerr asked. He angled his own climb to his right to join Claypoole.

Claypoole raised an arm to let his sleeve slide up and expose it, then pointed under the fern trees. "Looks like a game trail."

Kerr looked where Claypoole pointed and saw it—a line, maybe half a meter wide, where the moist dirt was packed down and slick-looking. "Could be," he said, and wondered what kind of animal made a slick trail. Nearly every game trail he'd ever seen looked trodden or scraped. The one before him was smoothly rippled, as if something heavy and uneven had rolled it out.

"What do we have?" Sergeant Bladon asked.

Kerr pointed.

"Cover me." Bladon slipped between the nearest tree ferns and squatted next to the slick. After studying it for a moment, he touched it and rubbed his fingers together. Standing, he wiped his fingers and returned to Kerr and Claypoole.

"Three-six, three-two," he said into his comm unit. "Those local amphibians—do they live this high on the mountain? The slick is damp with water. It's wet, but not slimy. I get the impression soft-bodied things use that trail."

"Is it clear enough for us to follow?" Bass asked.

"That's an affirmative. As far as I can see it's going in the right direction, and once we get in from the edge, there isn't very much in the way of underbrush. Not like down below."

"All right, we'll follow it. Hammer, get to it. See if you can parallel it without walking on it." Walking on a trail is seldom a good idea in a hostile situation—people tend to set ambushes and booby traps along trails. "Flankers out fifty meters."

Bladon heard MacIlargie groan over the squad net. "Don't worry, Mac," he said. "It's clear enough in there you won't be struggling through too much crap." Chuckling, he added, "And Corporal Kerr and I will both be able to keep an eye on you. You won't get into any trouble." Then he had to step aside to let Schultz pass under the trees. "Second fire team, take your flank. Stay clear of the trail," he ordered as soon as Corporal Dornhofer followed Schultz. He glanced toward MacIlargie in time to see the PFC glare at him before sliding his light-amplifier screen into place. He held off a grin until his own light screen was in place.

The fernlike trees towered to ten meters and more. Their fanned fronds blocked most of the direct sunlight. The light that penetrated to the ground mostly filtered through the nearly translucent foliage. Under them it was dim, almost like early dusk except for the greenish tinge to the light. Schultz led the way thirty meters uphill from the glistening trail. Kerr and his men flanked the platoon an equal distance downhill from it. The platoon's main body was probably far enough off the trail to be outside the killing zone of an ambush, yet close enough for the right-side flankers to keep it in view. Any farther and the density of the fern trees would completely block the view of the game trail—it wasn't really as clear as Bladon had told MacIlargie.

Kerr shivered when he lost sight of the rest of the platoon. His universe suddenly closed down to himself and the two Marines with him. The silence amid the fern trees was broken only by the quiet *squelch* of their footsteps on the damp ground, the occasional *scrunch* as one of them stepped on a treelet and broke its stem. Even those few sounds were muted by the proliferation of fronds, making the sounds seem eerily distant. The silence stood in sharp contrast to the din of the battle at Turlak Yar where he'd nearly been killed. The dim, greenish light was nothing like the desert brilliance that had drenched the village on Elneal. There, he'd been in a fighting position with one other Marine as the battle raged around them; here, he was in close contact with just two Marines. The mountainside forest was not a place where horsemen could mount a charge. And there was no detected threat. Still, being out of sight of the rest of the platoon in a potentially hostile situation brought back the memories of his last fire-fight, a tsunami that threatened to overwhelm him and curl him into a fetal ball from which he might never emerge—something had horribly killed the members of the scientific mission here, and that something might still be present. The surge of confidence Kerr had felt on the initial recon at Central Station abandoned him and he struggled to keep himself under control, to maintain vigilance, to prevent his men or anyone else from seeing the terror welling up in him. The recon at Central had been dangerous only in his mind; no enemy was there, no one had shot at him.

Something made a *plop* up ahead and he almost lost it. Almost, but not quite—the reflexes that had been drilled into him during his time in the Marines, and honed on many operations, took over. He dove to the ground and rolled, pointing his blaster in the direction of the sound. "Down!" he ordered on his fire team net, then immediately switched to the command circuit and reported, "Right flank has something up ahead." He dropped his infra screen into place. If there were warm bodies up ahead, he might be able to spot their heat signatures through the foliage.

"What is it?" Bass's voice came back.

"Don't know. I heard something." He flipped back to the fire team circuit. "Rock, Mac, do you see anything?"

"I can't see anything," Claypoole replied.

"I heard it," MacIlargie answered.

"We all heard it, but none of us see anything," Kerr reported.

"Where was it relative to you?"

"Sounded almost dead ahead."

"All right, I'm deploying the platoon on line, angled to your front. Go downhill, then swing back up, try to get behind it to check it out. Stay low in case we have to fire."

"Roger." Yes, stay low, stay very low. It wouldn't do at all to get fried by Marine fire. Kerr raised one arm at the elbow to expose his forearm and signaled Claypoole and MacIlargie to follow him, then slithered downhill on his belly. Turning up the amplifiers on his earpieces, he was able to hear them slithering behind him. He hesitated at the game trail, afraid to expose himself for the second or two it would take to slide across. Then he remembered his chameleons rendered him effectively invisible in the visual; he let his training and reflexes take over and slithered across. Fifty meters downhill he stopped and waited for the other two to reach him.

"How far ahead do you think it was?" he asked when they reached him.

Claypoole had his shields up, and Kerr saw him shake his head. MacIlargie simply said, "Dunno."

Kerr thought sound wouldn't travel far through the fern trees, the noise couldn't have been even fifty meters away, possibly half that or less. He rose to a crouch. "We'll go forty meters, then back up," he whispered. If there was an ambush waiting along the trail, they'd come at it from behind. He hoped they would. They had been uphill from the game trail. The ambush would be facing it unless the ambushers had heard the Marines behind them and turned around.

After going thirty-five meters Kerr stopped. "Mac, wait here for my signal," he said.

MacIlargie murmured "Will do" and lowered his infra screen so he could see Kerr's hand signal.

Five meters farther Kerr stopped again and ordered Claypoole, "Go five more meters, wait for my command."

"Right." Claypoole dropped his infra screen and went five more meters, stopped and looked back. He could just make Kerr out through the fern trees.

Kerr looked to his left and right, saw both of his men waiting for his command. He heard another *plop* and inwardly shivered. He still hadn't had his test of fire, still didn't know if he could fight again or if he'd panic. When they arrived at Central and his fire team scouted, they didn't meet anyone. This time he knew someone or some*thing* was up ahead. He took a deep breath to control a shudder. It was time for him to find out whether he still had it in him to be a Marine corporal or any kind of fighting Marine. He raised his left hand to shoulder level, then thrust it forward. The three Marines began moving uphill.

Fifteen meters up, before the game trail came back into sight, scattered hints of red began to appear on Kerr's infra screen, and his anal sphincter clenched. The hints of red didn't resemble human heat signatures. But whatever had killed those people at Central or in Aquarius Station didn't have to be human, or even warm blooded. It didn't even have to be intelligent.

After twenty-five meters the trees abruptly ended at the edge of a small clearing in a flat spot on the mountainside. The game trail led into the clearing. Another led away from the opposite side. A pool filled most of the clearing, probably runoff from a recent rainfall. Many animals were in the pool or gathered around it. Several of them, with tails as thick as their torsos, were nearly a meter long, with shiny, red-speckled bodies that slinked from side to side as they slithered about on legs so short they didn't quite hold the bodies above the ground. A few others were bulkier, perhaps weighing twenty kilos, pale green bodies spotted with brown or blue. Those had massive hind legs folded alongside their abdomens, and neckless heads that seemed to be nearly all mouth. Most of the animals were smaller and skittered about between the larger few. Some of the animals were tussling, perhaps mating or in mating competition. Most of them carried their heads pointed up into the air as though they were looking for something above them.

As the Marines watched, a half-meter-long, tube-bodied insect ventured into the air of the clearing. The legs of one of the large, pale green animals straightened like coiled springs suddenly released and it flew into the air. An impossibly long tongue shot out of its mouth almost faster than it could be seen and snagged the large insectoid. The green animal *plopped* when it landed. As large as the flying animal was, only the tip of its tail and a few outer edges of its many wings were visible outside the amphibian's mouth. The amphibian swallowed and all of the creature disappeared.

Kerr sagged, the tension suddenly drained out of his body. An animal that captured prey with its tongue probably didn't spit acid to eat away a human body.

"All clear," he said into the command frequency. "It's local fauna."

"You sure there's nobody else around?" Bass asked.

Kerr rotated through his screens. "Nothing visible in visual or infra," he replied.

"Rabbit, verify," Bass ordered.

"Roger," Sergeant Ratliff acknowledged. Bass listened as Ratliff ordered his point fire team to move at an angle downhill to approach Kerr's fire team from the side, and his second fire team to move forward to a position directly uphill from it. He told Dornhofer he'd be right behind first fire team.

In less than two minutes Ratliff and his point fire team reached the side of the clearing to the left of Kerr and his men.

"Kerr, by the numbers, make a move so I can verify who I see in infra," Ratliff said. He saw a pseudopod of red lift from the central of the three human-sized heat signals his infra screen showed and wave in a circle.

"Rock, make a move," Kerr ordered.

Ratliff saw Claypoole's movement.

"Mac, do it."

Ratliff watched MacIlargie's verifying arm wave.

"Confirmed," Ratliff said. "I don't see anything else that looks like a warm-body heat signal. Pasquin, do you see anything?"

"Negative," came the reply.

"There's a clearing downhill from you. Approach with caution."

"Roger."

In another moment the second fire team reached the uphill side of the clearing.

"Great Buddha's balls," someone murmured.

Ratliff checked his motion detector. It didn't show any movement beyond the pool clearing and the Marines who ringed it. "All clear," he reported.

One of the massive amphibians sprang into the air to catch a broad-winged insect.

"Hey, that's Leslie!" Dobervich exclaimed.

"What?"

"Yeah," Dobervich said. "When I was a kid my family had a dog about that size. She was off-white and loved to eat, always hopping up to catch treats, just like that."

"Your dog caught insects with her tongue?"

"Your dog had a mouth that big?"

"No, she didn't have a mouth that big, and she didn't catch her food with her tongue. But she should have had a mouth that big the way she was always begging for food." Dobervich stood and stepped into the clearing.

The amphibians stopped what they were doing and looked around for danger. They hadn't heard any of the radio transmissions the Marines made, and the Marines had moved quietly enough that the animals hadn't heard their approach. But they did hear the sound of Dobervich stepping into the clearing.

"Freeze," Ratliff ordered. None of the Marines moved; they barely breathed.

After a moment without seeing or hearing anything else threatening, the amphibians began to return to their mating and feeding. One of the big hoppers saw Dobervich's unscreened face hovering in midair and read it as some sort of insect. It hopped up and shot out its tongue.

Dobervich yelped and swatted at the tongue, but as fast as he moved, the tongue was faster. It hit and withdrew before he made contact. The amphibians scattered out of the clearing at Dobervich's yelp.

"Yep, just like a dog," Schultz said. "Licked your face." He hawked onto the ground.

"Quite a display there," Bass said dryly. "Your leslie is gone. Let's get back on the move; we've got some survivors to find."

In less than a minute third platoon and the medical team were back on the move.

Again Schultz led the platoon uphill and to the right. He didn't attempt to travel in a beeline, but constantly looked at the lay of the mountainside, picking a route that even the medical team members could negotiate without undue difficulty. At the same time, Schultz led them past as few potential ambush sites as possible, while always moving in the general direction of the sighting.

His senses registered the sounds and sights of normal activity among the animals that lived in the mountain's forest, and filtered them out. He'd notice any unusual behavior, which would alert him to danger. He couldn't write a paper on the activities of the indigenous life-forms of Waygone, but he'd studied the scientists' reports on those life-forms during the voyage from Thorsfinni's World and made his own observations during the time he'd been planetside. He strongly suspected he'd notice anything out of the ordinary. He was generally very good at that kind of observation. Nobody survived as pointman on as many different worlds as he had without being very good at observing native fauna.

It wasn't anything in particular that caught his attention.

The leslies and other amphibians Schultz saw or heard were going about their usual hopping, slithering, plopping, splashing movements. The insectoids buzzed and flitted about without a seeming care until some were snagged by flicking tongues and swallowed whole by an amphibian—and those that weren't snagged and swallowed ignored the fates of their late cousins.

Nothing that met Schultz's senses changed. But he felt something. Men in combat, maybe not all of them but certainly some, develop a sixth sense that tells them when they aren't alone. Sometimes it can even tell them in what direction the danger is in, even when they can't identify anything in particular that alerted them.

Schultz stopped and eased down to one knee, his head swiveling slowly, eyes burning into every shadow. "Hold up," he murmured into his helmet radio.

"What do you have?" Ratliff asked.

"Nothing." But he kept looking. The feeling he had wasn't distinct, it didn't tell him which side the danger he felt came from or whether it was ahead of him or behind. "Someone's watching us," he murmured. "Don't know where."

"Are you sure?"

Schultz didn't bother to answer. He put out his motion detector and started alternating between his infra and light-gatherer screens. He heard Ratliff order the rest of the squad to do the same. He waited and watched. Nothing showed up on any of his sensors.

"Who's watching us, Hammer?" Gunny Bass asked over the radio.

"Don't know. I feel them." The other Marines thought Schultz had no nerves, that he was always calm. But just then he was almost jittering. It was unnatural to him that he could feel someone watching without knowing in what direction to look for the watcher.

"They can't see us, Hammer," Bass said. "We don't have any evidence they can see in infrared."

"If they know how to look they can."

"Not many people know how to look."

"Are they people?"

It was Bass's turn to not answer.

After ten minutes with none of the Marines seeing or hearing anything that seemed out of the ordinary, and none of their sensors picking up sign of anything that wasn't native fauna, Bass ordered Schultz to move out.

He didn't move; not even his eyes swiveled. He repressed a shiver. The shiver was a combination of blood lust and uncertainty. He was primed to fight and kill and die. He wasn't a watcher, he was a fighter. The Earth barbarians were his prey, it was his duty to close with them and kill as many of them as possible before they killed him. Every fiber of his being ached to do that. He couldn't close and kill now, though. His orders were clear: find them, track them, find out how many there were, report back when they joined with the others. The watchers were females, quiet unaggressive creatures, who could sit quiescent for long periods of time and observe. He was male, a fighter, an aggressive creature bred and trained to fight and kill. But this time the Master decided a female sitting quietly wasn't the right one to watch. They didn't know where the Earth barbarians were, how they moved, what formations they used. To gain that information, the Master decided to use a fighter. He was chosen. It pained him almost to death to know the enemy was nearby and yet not attack. But he must do as the Master said; obedience was as much a part of his makeup as aggressiveness and the need to kill the enemy. To make sure he obeyed, he was sent naked and unarmed.

He felt uncertainty because he couldn't see them. Only the electric receptors that ran from his gill slits to his hips had told him that he neared them. And almost as soon as he realized they were only ten large one's lengths away and he had settled into a hiding place to watch, they stopped as though they knew he was there. Now they were on the move again. Why did they stop? Why did they resume climbing the mountain? He did not know, he could see only a few, far back in their column, and could hear nothing that they said.

The invisible ones, those he sensed were most dangerous, moved silently as well as invisibly. The few he could see, near the end of the column, made noise as they moved through the forest. He waited until they passed him, then rose and followed the sounds of the visible ones.

They were close, only a few hundred more meters to the spot where the *Fairfax* had detected what appeared to be a man. Schultz, still the first man in the column, was rounding an upthrusting of rock when he stopped. His nose crinkled as he sniffed the air. The pungent aroma of an unbathed body wafted to him. He slid his infra screen into place and carefully examined the mountainside to his front. All that showed in infra were tiny, fleeting specks that were probably small amphibians going about their business.

"Someone's near."

"Can you tell where?" Dornhofer asked.

Schultz raised his infra and sniffed again. The light breeze was coming from his front. The way the air seemed to eddy, he guessed the smell came from somewhere on the other side of the upcropping, where he couldn't see. "Wait, I'll check." He carefully picked his way downhill until the woodier trees that grew that high on the mountain blocked his view of the rocks. He sidled along until he was sure he was well beyond the end of the outcrop, then began climbing. Soon he smelled the pungent aroma again, mixed in with another, more fetid odor. He guessed whoever it was must be facing uphill and began circling to approach him from the side. In his right hand he carefully kept his blaster aimed where he looked. He used his left to flip his infra screen up and down as he examined the area in the visual and the infrared.

There! He saw the signature in infrared. He flipped his infra up and saw an emaciated man rising from a squat and adjusting trousers that were almost too ragged to bother with. A long knife hung from a scabbard on his belt. A mass of brown slopped down the mountainside behind him, soiled leaves scattered in and around the brown mass. Clearly he'd just found a survivor. He dropped the infra back into place and carefully looked around. No other signatures. The man picked up a hand weapon, looked around nervously, then began to climb the mountainside.

"Freeze right there," Schultz ordered.

The man froze, his weather-beaten face blanched at the words.

"Wh-Who, where are you?" He didn't move except for his head and panicky eyes as he searched for the source of Schultz's voice. The pistol dangled from his limp hand.

"I've got you in my blaster sights. Anyone else nearby?"

"N-No. I-I'm alone." The man was visibly quivering.

A wet stain that spread suddenly on the seat of his pants convinced Schultz the man was telling the truth.

"Put your weapon down by your feet, then lay on your face."

While the man complied, Schultz reported his discovery on the command net.

"Rabbit, join him," Bass ordered. "I'll be right there."

Ratliff left Schultz guarding the man as soon as he arrived and set his other men in positions uphill from him.

"Wh-Who are you?" the man asked in a quaking voice. "What's going on here? Why can't I see anybody?"

"Confederation Marines," Bass said—he arrived in time to hear the man's question. "Nobody sees us until we want them to. Who're you?"

"Th-They call me Sharpedge."

"Are you one of the scientists from Aquarius?"

"No—y-yes! I'm from Aquarius! I'm one of the scientists. Yes!"

"A scientist called 'Sharpedge'? Why don't I believe that?" Bass said, eyeing the scabbard on the man's belt. He softly padded to Sharpedge, swiftly drew the knife, and stepped back out of reach before the man could move. "Nice blade, Sharpedge. What's a scientist doing with a knife like this? You don't look like a field biologist. Or a geologist." He tested the edge of the blade with his thumb; it was very sharp.

"Th-There are things out here, a man needs to defend himself." Sharpedge raised his head and looked about maniacally.

Bass grunted.

"Wh-Where are you? If I can't see you, how do I know you aren't one of those things?"

"Do 'those things' speak Confederation English?"

"I—I don't know."

"Well," Bass said walking around to the front of the prone man, "do 'those things' look like this?" He squatted and raised his screens to show his face.

"People! We're saved!" Sharpedge scrabbled forward until his groping hands touched invisible clothing, and hugged Bass's knees. "You're really Marines! We're saved, we're saved," he burbled, before breaking down in tears.

CHAPTER
NINETEEN

Whatever it was that had scared Sharpedge so badly, once he began trying to describe it to the Marines, he broke down into wild screaming and clutched Bass's legs even more tightly. Bass shook his head and gently disengaged Sharpedge's arms from around his legs. They weren't going to find out much about "those things" until the man calmed down. "Are there any other survivors?" he asked.

"Yes, yes," the emaciated man gasped. "Yes, about a dozen, there's George, Rhys, Lowboy, Minerva—"

" 'About' a dozen? Don't you know?" Schultz muttered.

"Yes, a dozen, a dozen," Sharpedge answered quickly, wiping tears from his cheeks.

"Where? How far?" Bass needed to know.

"Not far, no, not far! Just back up the slope! Not far! Georgie makes us come down here to shit 'cause he don't like us doin' it back in the cave."

"You're living in a cave?" Hyakowa asked.

"Yes, a big one. Just up the mountain."

Bass spoke into the command net. "Dr. Bynum, would you come up here with one of the corpsmen?" He turned back to Sharpedge. "Okay, so there's a dozen of you, you're living in a cave just up the mountain from here. And you're scientists?"

The prostrate man nodded vigorously.

"Just what kind of 'science' do you practice?" Bass asked.

"I'm a chemical, er, a chemicarist, like, you know?"

Dr. Bynum, accompanied by a corpsman and the unbidden

Lieutenant Snodgrass, who'd been trying all day for an excuse to get to the head of the column, came up and stood beside Bass. Briefly Bass explained what he knew about Sharpedge. "Can you check him out real quick, Doctor? He looks half dead. I'd like to know if he's capable of leading us to the rest of the survivors."

Sharpedge shied away when Bynum tried to touch him. Then he noticed Owen, perched precariously on the corpsman's medkit. The woo glowed a pinkish red and its huge eyes stared unblinking at Sharpedge, indicating intense curiosity. "What the hell is that?" Sharpedge shouted.

"That's Owen," Dr. Bynum replied. "Don't worry, he eats rocks. Now relax, I'm a doctor. How do you feel?" Sharpedge nodded that he was all right. Bynum produced her field diagnostic kit and began checking the man's vital signs, asking him questions while she read his pulse, temperature, respiration, blood pressure. "When's the last time you had a bath?" she asked, wrinkling her nose. Sharpedge just grinned, revealing yellowed, broken teeth. "That's what I thought," she said grimly.

Finished, she stood up and faced Bass. "He's a little malnourished, low on trace minerals, but good blood pressure, suffering from a mild bacterial diarrhea but otherwise in pretty good shape. What have you been eating?" she asked Sharpedge.

Sharpedge shrugged. "We got some food from Aquarius a couple of weeks ago, but until then we ate the slimies, whenever we could catch 'em, and there's fungus and stuff that grows back in the cave we kin eat, and little things like worms back in the pools, and some of them bugs with wings too—"

"This man is no scientist," Snodgrass interrupted. Bass silenced him with a nasty look.

"What are 'slimies'?" Dr. Bynum asked.

"Oh, those big frogs like, with the long tongues. The tongues are really good."

"He means the 'leslies.' " Dean grimaced.

"Probably a good source of protein," Dr. Bynum said.

"Well, Mr. Sharpedge, do you feel like taking us to see your friends?" Bass asked.

"Yessir!"

"Hammer, you and Mr. Sharpedge here take the point."

Prodding Sharpedge forward with his foot, Schultz muttered, "Let's go." He'd try to stay upwind of the captive along the way.

In a salvaged jumpsuit that had belonged to a proctologist named Morgan, Rhys Apbac scrambled over the barricade, and once outside the cave, stretched luxuriously in the bright sunlight. The rations Cameron and the others had brought back from Aquarius Station, not to mention the clothing Rhys was wearing, had done wonders for the survivors' morale.

Far down the slope Rhys spotted movement. That pisspot, Sharpedge, he thought. He watched the figure scrambling up the rocky slope. As he got closer Rhys could see Sharpedge was carrying on a conversation with someone—but he was alone. "Finally lost it," he muttered and shook his head. Then he saw something out of the corner of his eye, a shadow maybe, but it looked as though a portion of one of the boulders just behind Sharpedge had moved.

Now Sharpedge stopped and waved his arms vigorously. He shouted something but the wind carried the words away. Undaunted, Sharpedge continued the climb.

That movement again! There it was! Something had moved over the ground, Rhys was sure of it. His blood ran cold. Could the things camouflage themselves like that? Were they following that little shit directly to the hideout? Yes! He'd heard stories of animals on Old Earth that could change color to blend with their surroundings. He turned to shout out a warning when he spotted something else. About fifty meters behind Sharpedge a man walked out from behind a boulder. He was followed immediately by several others, walking in a staggered line with intervals between them; they were definitely human. As Rhys watched, three more emerged and continued walking up the slope behind Sharpedge.

"We're saved! We're saved!" Sharpedge was shouting, his voice thin and reedy on the wind, but the message was unmistakable. Rhys yelled for the others to come out of the cave. Cameron was the first to emerge. He stood silently beside Rhys as Sharpedge drew near.

Breathing heavily, Sharpedge covered the remaining distance in a few bounds. An idiotic grin on his face, he stood before Rhys, his chest heaving so hard he couldn't speak for a few moments so he gestured to his right. Schultz raised his infra screen, and his face eerily appeared beside Sharpedge. "Hi," he said. Cameron caught his breath when he saw the face. "Confederation Marines," he whispered, "they're wearing chameleons."

"Marines! The Marines have landed! We're saved!" Sharpedge gasped. The other Marines in the point element established a perimeter around the cave mouth, and in a few moments Bass and Staff Sergeant Hyakowa arrived, followed immediately by Dr. Bynum and Lieutenant Snodgrass, who had refused to return to his position near the rear of the column as Bass had told him to. Bass told the rest of the platoon to wait where they were and remain alert.

Snodgrass shouldered his way to where Bass and Hyakowa were standing. Suddenly he caught his breath and his heart skipped a beat. Shoving Bass rudely aside and grinning stupidly, he extended his hand to the pirate and said in a loud voice, "Dr. Morgan I presume?" This was the triumphant culmination of the lieutenant's plans and the herald of a bright future. This moment would go down in history! Snodgrass was on top of the universe at that instant and king of all he surveyed.

Snodgrass couldn't explain the ring he'd found back at the station—maybe Morgan had a brother along, Morgan was a common enough name—but he'd seen enough stills and vids to know that the man standing before him was the famous scientist. Most convincing was the fact that he was wearing a jumpsuit with the BHHEI logo over the right breast pocket and a name tape over the left that read in big black letters, MORGAN. Cameron had brought it back from Aquarius Station and given it to Rhys.

"Is that true? Are you Dr. Henry Morgan?" Bass asked.

Rhys looked at the lieutenant's outstretched hand and then at Bass. "Hell no," he replied, a touch of annoyance in his voice. "My name is Rhys and I'm a goddamn pirate. I demand to be arrested."

Bass reached out with one hand, seized Lieutenant Snodgrass by the collar and physically jerked him back, spun him around, and shoved him toward the rear of the column. "And stay out of my way—sir!" he said.

Rhys began jumping up and down and dancing with Lowboy, who had just come out of the cave. They were joined by the rest of the survivors. Minerva stood quietly beside Cameron, and he took her hand and held it in his own, as the others screamed and shouted with joy. Sharpedge laughed and nodded, smiling idiotically, and grinned at the Marines standing beside him.

"Quiet!" Bass shouted several times. "This man here tells us you were attacked by some kind of monsters. What kind—" This started another round of hysteria.

"Horrible . . ."

"Big like a man and slimy . . ."

"Snouts full of teeth . . ."

"They breathe fire!"

"No! No! They have sticks that shoot fire! I saw Johnny burned alive!"

"No! No! Some kind of liquid they spray from their noses and . . ."

"Shut up!" Cameron shouted. He shouted several more times and gradually the hubbub died away. "I'm George Cameron, Gunny, and I'm in charge here."

Bass cocked a curious eyebrow at being addressed as "Gunny," but kept quiet to let the man talk. It didn't necessarily mean anything that Cameron knew what to call him.

After all, some people outside the military were familiar with the Marine Corps rank structure and forms of address.

Lowboy snorted at Cameron's statement, but declined to say anything.

"We're all that's left of the Red 35 Crew pirate company," Cameron continued. "Over a hundred of us came here to raid this place, but somebody else came too and we were ambushed. We've been stranded about a year. The things that attacked us and killed the scientists before we arrived are intelligent, though they aren't human. I think they're amphibians. They have weapons that spray some sort of corrosive substance that dissolves human flesh and bone. They can be killed. I shot two of them. We don't know how many there are or where they come from. I think they know where we are, but for some reason they've left us alone. And now, Gunny, I formally request you arrest us and transport us to the nearest magistrate to stand trial for our crimes. But first, would you kindly get us the hell off this planet?"

During the short speech Hyakowa stared intently at Cameron. There was something, he couldn't quite put his finger on it, but the platoon sergeant had the uncanny feeling he'd seen this man somewhere before.

"You recognized my rank," Bass said matter-of-factly. He too felt there was something familiar about this man.

"Ol' Georgie knows a lot about military stuff," Rhys said. Since Cameron had returned from Aquarius with supplies, he'd come to respect their putative leader more and was no longer so quick to criticize him.

"We only ask that you get us off this stinking world as quickly as it's convenient, Sergeant," Cameron said, hoping he could change the subject.

"In time Mister . . . Cameron, did you say?" Bass replied. "First I want my medical team to examine your men—and women." Some of the pirates definitely were females, and the one clinging to Cameron's arm might not be too bad-looking if she was cleaned and fattened up a bit. "I think as the ground commander here I must have some legal authority to put you under restraint, but ultimately it's the captain of the CNSS *Fairfax County*, which is in orbit, who'll have to take responsibility for you." He turned to Dr. Bynum. "Lieutenant Commander, would you examine the, uh, survivors? Meanwhile, Mr. Rhys and Mr. Cameron, I want you two to tell Staff Sergeant Hyakowa and me everything you know about the, uh, 'things' that attacked you."

Bass led the pair to a large boulder and they squatted in its shade. He would have been glad to move inside the cave mouth for the damp breeze that was coming out from the interior, but it stank so badly that he decided to stay in the open air. After checking the platoon's perimeter security, Hyakowa joined them.

"This is Staff Sergeant Wang Hyakowa, third platoon's platoon sergeant," Bass said.

"Does that mean you're the platoon commander, Gunny? No officer?" Cameron asked. He cursed himself for opening his mouth.

Bass looked at Cameron a moment before replying. "Our officer was killed on another deployment," he answered. "Now, tell me what you know about the things that attacked you."

"Well," Cameron began, "they look like—I don't know," he shuddered, "like—"

"Like salamanders or somethin'," Rhys answered. "Only bigger, and their arms and legs are bigger too, but they don't have hands exactly. And they stand like men."

"They are a vicious and intelligent life-form," Cameron added. "They attack with neither warning nor provocation. They have weapons that spray their targets with some kind of acid that acts almost immediately. Dissolves flesh and bone. I think it dissipates quickly, though. And when they're shot with a blaster, they go up in a flash, burn themselves to a vapor."

"How many of them are there?" Hyakowa asked.

Cameron shook his head. "Lots, is all I can say."

"Where are they now?" Bass asked.

Again Cameron shrugged. "They're down in the swamp. I think they're some kind of amphibious life-form and they prefer to spend most of their time in damp, dark places. I figure we're high and dry here so that's one reason they haven't come for us, but I just don't know."

"Like the leslies?" Bass asked. "That is, those large, frog-like amphibians, the things you've been feeding off of?"

Rhys laughed. "Hell no! Nothing like them."

"Are they indigenous?"

Cameron was surprised by the question, but on reflection it made sense. If those things were native to Society 437, surely they would have made their presence known sooner than they had. But if they weren't . . . Just then he didn't want to think about what that implied. "I don't know."

"Are you sure they're still here? When was the last time you saw any?"

Cameron looked at Rhys and Lowboy. "How long's it been, a few months, right?"

Rhys grimaced. "That's too recent. Better if we never saw them."

"Okay," Bass said after a pause. "Go back and have our medical people check you out, then we'll talk about what we're going to do with you."

After they were gone, Bass and Hyakowa stayed in the shadow of the rock for a while. "I have the strangest feeling, boss, that I know that Cameron guy from somewhere."

Bass nodded. "But right now, Wang, you get a couple of men together and start gathering personal details on these pirates. I need to talk to Captain Tuit."

"And then what, Charlie?"

Bass clapped his platoon sergeant firmly on the shoulder. "And then we get out of here, Wang. We get out of here."

Staff Sergeant Hyakowa picked Corporal Pasquin and Lance Corporal Dean to assist him in interviewing the pirate survivors. Most of them gave their real names, but the Marines recorded whatever names and personal histories the pirates offered. When Hyakowa told them cooperation would hasten their departure from Society 437, they were more than forthcoming. Everyone but Cameron.

"George Cameron is my real name, Sergeant." He rolled down his right sleeve as he spoke. One of the corpsmen had just given him a badly needed shot of vitamins.

"Mr. Cameron, I know you from somewhere," Hyakowa said.

Cameron looked away abruptly. "No, I don't think so, Sergeant. We've never met before."

"But you were a Marine, weren't you?"

"N-No. Of course not."

Dean and Pasquin looked on as the two talked. Cameron did seem familiar to Dean, but he couldn't place him. Maybe if he could see the man's face without the beard he could remember where he'd met him. The voice was naggingly familiar.

" 'Cameron'? 'Cameron'?" Dean mused. "What nationality is that?" Cameron, caught unawares, did not answer. "You know, in college I read a book called *The Decameron*, by a fourteenth century Italian, Giovanni Boccacio. It reminds me a little of you guys here. It's about a bunch of people who flee the plague—"

"Who did you say wrote that book?" Hyakowa asked sharply.

Dean was startled by the platoon sergeant's tone. Cameron went white. "Uh, that was Giovanni Boccacio, Staff Sergeant."

With a wild shout Hyakowa jumped on Cameron and threw him to the ground, knocking the wind out of his lungs. He began strangling the pirate with both hands. Pasquin and Dean were so startled by the attack that for a few seconds they could only gape in astonishment at their platoon sergeant. Minerva acted first, leaping onto Hyakowa's back and trying to pull his head off. She screamed furiously; Hyakowa shouted curses; and Cameron gasped and gagged as his face began to turn blue.

Pasquin stepped forward and grabbed Hyakowa's right arm, levering it back with all his strength. "No! No, Staff Sergeant!" he shouted. "Stop! Let him up, for chrissakes." Dean shook off his surprise and stepped up to wrench Minerva off Hyakowa's back. Everyone else stopped what they were doing and stared at the group. Dean grabbed the platoon sergeant's other arm and, together with Pasquin, pulled him off the gasping pirate and dragged him backward.

"What the hell's going on here!" Bass asked as he ran up to the trio.

"That sonofabitch is *Baccacio*! Ensign Baccacio!" Hyakowa gasped, spittle flying from his lips, his face purple with the intense hatred that possessed him. He sucked air into his lungs. "He's back, Charlie, a goddamn criminal now, and I'm going to break his neck!" He tried to break the hold Pasquin and Dean had on him but they held fast.

"He's right, he's right, Gunny!" Dean said. "I recognize his voice now! It's Baccacio! It really is!"

Bass knelt beside the prostrate man. "Are you really my former platoon commander?"

"Yes, yes, Gunny, it's me," Baccacio gasped.

"You sonofabitch," Bass sighed. Baccacio was the man who'd abandoned him in the Martac Waste on Elneal and left a man behind after the Siad warriors attacked the platoon at the village of Turlak Yar, the most disgraceful conduct on the part of a Marine officer Charlie Bass had ever heard of. And there he was, leading a band of pirates on this godforsaken world. Bass stroked the butt of his hand-blaster speculatively. No, no time for revenge now. "You weren't worth a shit as an officer and now look at what you've become." He turned to Hyakowa. "Let him loose." They stepped back, ready to grab him again if he sprang back to the attack. But Hyakowa just stood still, breathing heavily. "Wang, this man is our prisoner. Don't touch him again," Bass said.

Minerva helped Baccacio to his feet. Tentatively, he massaged his throat where red welts were beginning to appear. "I guess I should've picked an alias like 'Smith,' huh?" he said, a wry smile on his face. Only Pasquin thought the remark worth a laugh. "Yeah, Gunny, it's me all right," he continued in a rasping voice. "I screwed up back on Elneal and I screwed up even worse when I became a pirate. I don't blame Hyakowa for trying to kill me. I've had that coming for a long time now. And I'm your prisoner, no argument about that. The only thing I want to ask you—not for me, but for my friends here—is to get us the hell off this place. What happens to me after that I deserve, several times over."

Bass spoke into the platoon net and called up his squad leaders. Dr. Bynum and Lieutenant Snodgrass, attracted by the commotion, also joined the small command group.

"Okay," Bass informed everyone, "nobody's going anywhere for a while." That elicited a shout of angry dismay from all the pirates except Baccacio, who just stood silently in front of Bass. "I've talked this over with Captain Tuit and he agrees. Our mission now is to find out what happened here, and to do that we've got to find those 'things.' " He turned to address Baccacio directly. "You people have seen them and you know what they're capable of. I can't send you back to the *Fairfax County* until we've eliminated them, and I'll need you for that. Your women can go up as soon as we can get them to a landing zone for an Essay to come in, but you men will stay with me."

"I ain't staying here!" Lowboy shouted. "I ain't staying!" Several other pirates muttered their agreement.

"Let me tell you men something. Listen carefully." Bass looked in turn at each of the bedraggled pirates now gathered around in a loose semicircle. "You will do what I tell you to do or I will shoot you all. You men are going with me and no more discussion."

"Gunny, how about some weapons, then?" Baccacio asked.

Bass stared at the former ensign in astonishment. "Really, Mr. Baccacio, what kind of fool are you anyway?" He turned to his squad leaders. "Saddle the men up. We're—"

"Sergeant," Lieutenant Snodgrass interrupted, "I think you

should send these pirates back to the *Fairfax County*. They're unreliable criminals—"

"Yeah," Rhys interjected, " 'unreliable,' that's us. And we're dangerous too!"

"—untrustworthy men, and you can't count on them not to betray you. I think you'd be far better off going without them. I'll escort them back to the ship, if you'd like."

"No, Lieutenant," Bass replied.

Snodgrass's face reddened. "Sergeant, I am the ranking line officer in this party," he replied, emphasizing "line officer," which clearly excluded Lieutenant Commander Bynum, who outranked him, but as a medical officer could exercise no command authority in an operational situation. "I think I should talk to Captain Tuit myself and transmit my observations before you do anything further."

"Lieutenant, the line to the bridge is open," Bass replied calmly, folding his arms.

Snodgrass hesitated briefly, surprised that Bass had acquiesced so easily. Then he asked the watch officer on the bridge to patch him through to Captain Tuit. "Put Gunnery Sergeant Bass on with you, Lieutenant," Captain Tuit ordered as soon as he came into the net. "Now, Lieutenant, what do you want to tell me?" he asked as soon as Bass acknowledged he was on. Snodgrass explained the situation.

"And what do you recommend, Lieutenant?" the captain asked, his voice deceptively mild.

"Send the prisoners back right now, sir, and put me in command of the rest of this operation. Sergeant Bass can take care of tactical matters, but I should be the one to make the strategic decisions."

" 'Strategic decisions'?" Tuit mused. "Gunnery Sergeant Bass?"

"Sir, if the lieutenant gets in my way again, I'll send him back on the next Essay along with the women."

"Well, Lieutenant, I guess that's that."

"But, sir!"

"Lieutenant, you came along on this operation as a special

communications officer. Well, to communicate effectively you have to listen. You aren't listening. Now, Lieutenant, wipe your nose, stick your hands in your pockets where they won't get you into any trouble, and stay out of Gunny Bass's way. Skyhawk out."

Snodgrass stood with his mouth open. He had just been reprimanded by a senior officer—who knowingly did it within the hearing of enlisted men!

"All right!" Bass turned to his squad leaders. "We move out at first light. Our objective is an island about halfway to Aquarius Station." He pointed northwest, toward where the maps showed an island, a direction far from the route they'd taken to reach the mountain. "That island can probably serve as a landing zone for an Essay. Once we've got it secured, the women go out."

Minerva spoke up. "Sergeant, I want to stay here with Georgie."

Bass regarded her for a moment. All the pirates knew what they were up against, they had seen the creatures and knew what they could do. Yet, unlike the men, Baccacio's woman was willing to stay on Society 437 if her man did. What the hell did she see in him? "We'll see," he replied. He turned back to his squad leaders: "Set secure night positions, one-third alert." While the Marines were organizing the night perimeter, he had Dupont notify the waiting Dragons when and where to meet them.

After an uneventful night, they moved out at daybreak. On the way to the island, Bass got a message from the *Fairfax* that made him wish he'd decided to meet the Dragons somewhere on the mountain and ride them through the swamp. Those things were still around and dangerous.

CHAPTER
TWENTY

"Ralston, everything up?" Senior Chief Hayes asked his number one, Boatswain's Mate First Class Ralston.

"Infra, motion, sounders, the works," Ralston replied. "Even got two RPVs up there quartering the area for a couple klicks in every direction."

"Good. Let me know if anything shows up on them."

"Aye aye, Chief."

"I mean that. Anything on any sensor."

Ralston looked up at the chief. He'd seen the remains in Aquarius and some of the remains the med-sci team sent up to the *Fairfax* from Central Station. He knew that what they might be up against was worse than anything he'd ever heard of. "I mean it too, Chief. Gonna be a snowy day on Alhambra before me or any of the boys slips up on this assignment."

Chief Hayes looked around the room, *his* control room, buried as deep as it could get in the Aquarius admin center, which wasn't as deep as he would have liked. Four sailors, all armed, were at consoles, senses glued to the data coming in at them. None of them were technicians, they were all boatswain's mates and deckhands. He'd picked the toughest men in the *Fairfax County*'s crew for this job. The men he knew were the best bar fighters, the best shots, and the coolest under physical pressure. They might not be the best and brightest among the crew, but in a fight, they were the ones he wanted covering his back. They and the four escorting the techs, who were investigating whatever it was they were investigating throughout the station. Ten men, including himself and Ralston, and a lone Dragon. That's all he had to defend the place if those things, whoever or whatever they were, came calling.

He looked back at Ralston. "You give me warning if someone's coming, we can beat off an army."

"You give me the army, I'll give you the warning."

Hayes squeezed Ralston's shoulder appreciatively and left to check on the techs and their escorts. He hefted his blaster into a more comfortable position for carrying. Idly, he wondered how those Marines managed to carry the damn weapons all the time without pulling something out of joint.

The Master sat cross-legged in the squared-off cave, a room in one of many such formations his fighters and watchers had located during the past year. Small lights set in the corners near the ceiling provided adequate illumination. The watcher who had sat so quietly for three days, watching Aquarius Station, knelt in front of him, bowed over so her forehead touched the mat-covered floor. For the occasion, since watchers were seldom called to give reports to the Master themselves, her scale-hair had been untangled and a flowing robe draped over her so she more resembled a female of the leader class. The Master found her almost presentable, almost a person. He stifled a snicker at the thought. That would be undignified. He brushed away the idea of keeping her for that night's bed almost before the thought formed.

"Give me your report," he growled. "Raise your head so I can properly hear you," he added when she began speaking into the mat at her face.

The watcher placed her hands flat on the floor and raised her face; her eyes stayed properly down.

"Master, the Earth barbarians came as you said they would. They were in five of their water-dancing vehicles. They stayed less than one full day, then they left in four of their water-dancers. Most of them—" She faltered. "This— This one thinks most of them—" Her face twisted with the pain she expected her next statement to bring to her. "This one could not tell for sure. Most of them were invisible."

The Master restrained himself from lashing out at the watcher. Invisible? "If they were invisible, how do you know they were there to begin with?" he asked gruffly.

"Master, this one could feel their presence." She twisted her arms, drawing her elbows away from her sides to indicate she felt their electric emanations through the sensors on her sides.

The Master grunted.

She gave the time and direction of the departure then continued, "This one watched very carefully, Master. This one came to recognize differences between the barbarians so this one could tell them apart. There are eleven who this one saw and can recognize. There might be more who this one did not see often enough to distinguish. Four that this one saw and can recognize carry instruments of some sort, but do not seem to have weapons. The others all carry the forever guns."

"Where are their positions?"

"This one thinks there are some that stay in the water-dancer. At least this one saw barbarians carry in things that were smaller when they came out. This one never saw any come out without first going in. The others, everyone this one knows of, stay in the building with small rooms and files. The ones with instruments are always accompanied by one with a forever gun. They go into the other buildings but always come out again."

"Do they have a routine?"

"No, Master. They come and go at odd hours, except for three times a day when one of them carries a package to the water-dancer."

The Master thought for a moment before deciding the watcher had told him all she knew. He wondered why she said some of them were invisible. Was it possible? That watcher was the first who was in a position actually to see the newly arrived barbarians. No, it couldn't be, the barbarians from

Earth were not sophisticated enough to even think of making themselves invisible.

"Take her away and beat her for lying," he said to one of the leaders. Even if truthful, watchers needed to be beaten occasionally to keep them alert.

The watcher went quiet and docile after one small cry when the leader grasped her arm.

The half hour before dawn is one of those times when people, no matter how awake, are least alert. Alertness at that hour requires a special effort. Perhaps it is because back in the primordial murk of the ancestors of modern man, that was the hour when protopeople began to awaken for the new day, and the night predators were returning to their lairs. Hardly anyone is alert while waking up, and when the predators are in their lairs, there is no need for alertness.

The half hour before dawn was when a force of forty fighters closed their noose. Earlier, they had slithered out of the water onto the island and began crawling toward the admin building. They didn't come onto land in one group; except for an arc in front of the Dragon, they were scattered around the island's perimeter. Neither did they all come ashore at the same moment. Their times were staggered so they would all be at the same distance from the admin center at the half hour before dawn. They moved in short rushes, now in one direction, now in another, mimicking the movement of the local amphibians. A technician would have to have been very alert to notice the pattern reported by the motion detectors—as alert as someone would be a half hour after dawn. They were within seventy-five meters of the admin center before Seaman First Class Broward noticed the pattern.

"They're coming!" he shrieked when he realized the random movement he was watching on the motion display wasn't random. His hand slapped the panic button, sounding an alarm throughout the admin building. The alarm was loud enough for the attackers to hear. Simultaneously, the panic button sent an alarm to the Dragon and beamed an alert to the *Fairfax*.

"Up!" a leader barked. *"Charge!"*

The leaders and fighters leaped to their feet and raced toward the admin building. The six nearest the Dragon ran to it. The doors to the admin building were locked, and the ground floor windows shuttered or barricaded. The Dragon was buttoned down for the night. The six reached the Dragon just as its engine roared and it lifted on its air cushion. That didn't phase the fighters; they knew what their weapons could do.

They had never before come against a water-dancer, but they had faced ground-effect vehicles at Central Station and were confident their weapons could destroy it. They pointed their nozzles and sprayed. Patterns were etched on the armor of the Dragon's sides and small holes appeared on its thinner skirts. Air jetted out through the holes, and the Dragon sagged on its reduced cushion.

Frantically, the driver shot forward to get out of range of the weapons, but one leader was close enough to jump and grab a tie-down near the rear of the Dragon. He scrambled onto its top. Groping in the predawn dark, his hands and feet found additional tie-downs, wires, spokes, and knobs to hold onto and he used them to pull and push himself forward. As he crawled he broke every hold fragile enough to snap or bend under the pressure of his hands or feet. He knew some of those things allowed the Dragon to communicate. Others were probably sensors that showed the crew the outside world. With luck, he was isolating and blinding the water-dancer.

In the crew compartment monitors and displays blanked out.

"Shit!" swore Mechanic's Mate Third Class Agropolis, the Dragon commander. "One of them's on top of us. Spin it, try to throw him off," he ordered Seaman Second Class Omega, the driver.

Omega stomped on his pedals and slammed his control stick left and right, and the Dragon slewed and jerked so violently it would have tossed the crew around if they hadn't been strapped in.

More monitors and displays went blind.

"Shit," Agropolis swore again. "Turn around, see if you can get the gun on any of them. I'm going topside." He drew his hand-blaster, waited a second for the Dragon to reverse its facing, then opened the commander's hatch and stood up. He twisted around to face the top of the Dragon and struggled to bring his hand-blaster to bear. He couldn't see enough of the top from where he was. He reached out with his free hand for a hold and pulled himself higher. The gun next to him cracked and shook him when it fired. He had to brace the hand that held his weapon on the face of the Dragon to keep from losing his grip and falling back into the crew compartment. He lurched upward, one hand on the hold, the other braced on the slope, and saw a shape that didn't belong on top of his vehicle. He fought against the jerking and shuddering of the violently maneuvering vehicle to get a firmer grip on the hold and raised his hand-blaster. He took too long.

The leader had both feet and one hand on solid holds when he heard the commander's hatch clank open. Instantly, he pointed his weapon to the front. When a head rose over the forward edge of the water-dancer, he brought the nozzle of his gun to bear and fired. The barbarian took the full stream in the face and fell back, unable to even scream in the agony of his death.

The water-dancer's gun cracked again, and a ball of fire struck two fighters, who flared up and went into forever. Keeping his weapon at the ready, the leader scrabbled forward and looked over the edge at the front slope of the water-dancer. The barbarian he'd just shot hung backward over the lip of his hatch, his torso and hips bouncing and rolling with the violent movement of the vehicle. Holding as tightly as he could, the leader lowered himself far enough to jam the nozzle of his gun through the hatch past the legs of the dead barbarian. He angled it toward where he thought the driver was and sprayed.

Seaman Second Class Omega screamed when the acid flow hit his side and began eating away his flesh. His agonized, dying thrashing struck the controls and made the Dragon buck more violently than when he'd made it buck deliberately.

The bucking broke the leader's hold and he slid down the front of the Dragon. He let go of his weapon and grasped for holds with both hands, but the bucking and slewing were too violent and things slipped past his fingers before he could close on them. He hit the ground and the Dragon rolled, twisting and turning, over him. The jets of air the huge vehicle rode on slammed him from one direction, battered him from another, stomped on him from a third. He was mangled and dead before Omega's feet slid off the pedals and the Dragon settled its fifteen tons on him.

An assault team of two leaders and a dozen fighters hit the rear of the admin building at the same time the six attacked the Dragon. They didn't waste any effort attempting to break in through the ground doors or windows. One fighter, a large one, stood facing the building, his feet spread, hands braced against the wall. A small one clambered onto his shoulders and gripped the windowsill just above his head. A third fighter, carrying a heavy hammer, climbed up until he was able to fling one leg over the small one's shoulder. He slammed the hammer against the window frame until it burst in, then dropped the hammer as he clambered in through the opening. Before he could grasp his weapon, a barbarian threw open the door of the room and sprayed rapid fire bolts into it from his blaster. One hit the fighter and sent him into forever. But by then a leader was through the window and sprayed a stream of acid at the barbarian. The barbarian dropped his weapon and stumbled back into the hallway, screaming and tearing at his melting, eroding flesh.

In a moment both leaders and all of the fighters except the large one who was the base of their ladder were in the room. One leader gave hand signals and the fighters raced out of the room then split into two groups to run in both directions. A moment later they were followed by another assault team of two leaders and ten fighters. There were doors on both sides of the hallway, many of them closed. The fighters slammed open the doors that were closed, firing into the rooms, and sprayed into the open doors before entering. Sometimes fire came out of the doorways, and one or several fighters flashed into oblivion before others were able to shoot into the rooms and kill their occupants. But whether the barbarians died alone or took fighters with them, the barbarians always died.

Three minutes after Seaman First Class Broward sounded the alarm, Senior Chief Hayes, Boatswain's Mate First Class Ralston, their eight sailors, and the four techs were as dead as the crew of the crippled Dragon.

The Master looked upon the scene. "Seventeen of them dead and only twenty of our fighters gone to forever." He grunted in satisfaction. He looked to the south, toward where the Earth barbarian fighters had joined up with the ones who ran in disgrace rather than stand and die honorably. "We will destroy them." He looked with restrained glee at the two for-ever guns that had survived the fighting. They will try to take prisoners, he thought. They will not have a prisoner, not even for a moment of the short time they have left alive.

CHAPTER
TWENTY-ONE

The watcher lay well-concealed in a marshy spot where she could observe the island the Earth barbarians now occupied in force. She had been there for a long time—long enough for even her to notice the time was long—since before the invisible ones arrived. Her sole mission was to watch in the direction of the mountain where the smelly ones dwelt. But it was the noisy ones she had been sent there to wait for, and to warn of their arrival. The Master in his wisdom knew they would come for the smelly ones, and then return through the swamp.

The receptors on her sides sensed the movement of the barbarians as they neared the island and climbed its far side, then she began to hear their voices. That was very strange because when she looked toward the voices she saw no one. With some slight agitation, she observed the electronic impulses that impacted her sensors, which told her the barbarians were where she heard the voices, a place barely a hundred meters away. Were the Earth barbarians invisible? Those she had seen dead in their settlement had been visible. She wondered idly why the new ones were invisible. After a short time she saw some barbarians with her eyes and was satisfied; they looked like the dead ones.

Later the earth trembled with the arrival of water-dancers. The watcher noted the time of their arrival.

The visible barbarians stood taller than the fighters and leaders, though not as tall as the large ones. Even mostly submerged and a hundred meters downwind of the barbarians, the watcher could still smell the presence of sodium chloride and other elements in the fluids that the barbarians' pale skin exuded.

Silent, alert, the watcher closely regarded Lance Corporal Hammer Schultz, whom she couldn't see with her eyes.

It took the platoon nearly all day to cross the swamp to the island. The trip could have taken half the time, but after receiving word from the *Fairfax* about the attack on the navy security team at Aquarius Station, Bass slowed the pace and put everyone on sharper alert. This time the things hadn't attacked a bunch of scientists and technicians with no combat training, nor a pirate band that wasn't expecting a fight; they'd wiped out a trained security team. They were every bit as dangerous as Baccacio and the pirates had said.

The trek was especially hard on the pirates and Dr. Bynum and her medical team, but none dared complain, and Bynum was not about to advise Gunny Bass on his tactics, especially not in view of the renewed danger. Lieutenant Snodgrass, knee-deep in mud and perspiring heavily while fighting off the flying pests, was tempted to say something, but he'd learned his lesson—for the time being. Besides, the tension remained high, so everyone concentrated on staying alert. During the frequent breaks, people remained mostly silent. When they did talk, it was only in whispers.

The sun was low on the horizon by the time Schultz reported reaching the island. The ground rose steadily where he came out of the swamp. Although it was surrounded by water and deep mud, and covered by a layer of springy vegetation a few centimeters thick, the island was relatively dry and firm. Schultz declared the area solid enough to bring in an Essay. "But Gunny, I don't know. There's something about this place—be very careful." Schultz warily eyed the vegetation that sprouted in the swamp, aware of how easily it could conceal large numbers of people—or things—until they got very close.

Bass was instantly alert. Schultz's sixth sense for danger

was well-known and very reliable. He ordered the rest of the point element to proceed with extreme caution as they established a defensive perimeter for the night. As dangerous as it was for the people planetside, Captain Tuit wasn't willing to send an Essay down for a night landing. He felt there was a possibility—and Bass agreed with him—that the things didn't know where the Marines were. Landing an Essay would surely tell them.

"Okay, ladies," Bass said to the four pirate women after the Essay landed in the morning, "let's go. Get on board the Essay and you're out of here." Three of the women did not have to be told twice and bolted for the boarding ramp without so much as a backward glance at their men. They were criminals too, and they'd made very bad choices in the men they'd picked as companions, but they weren't stupid. But the woman called Minerva hesitated.

"Sergeant, I want to stay with Georgie. I already said so." She glanced at Baccacio as she spoke.

"Minnie, go with the others," Baccacio said quietly.

" 'Georgie' is not his name," Bass said.

"I don't care if his name is Joe Shit, Sergeant," Minerva snapped, "I stay with him." She grabbed Baccacio's sleeve.

Bass considered. Two things Charlie Bass admired were loyalty to friends and guts. The woman had both in Marine-like quantity, even if the quality was weak since the man she admired so much was Baccacio, of all people. Ah, yes, Baccacio. There was something different about him. Bass gave a mental shrug. The woman might be a good influence on the former ensign, and it might turn out that Baccacio could be of some real help to them. "What did you say your name was?" he asked her.

"Minerva, but Georgie calls me Minnie. You can call me Minnie, Sergeant."

"Okay, Minnie, you can stay."

"You're fucking nuts!" Rhys Apbac hollered. "Dumb bitch! Get on the ship," he added.

"That's no way to talk to a woman, you dukshit," Bass said mildly.

Lieutenant Snodgrass, who had recovered somewhat from the long trek through the swamp, felt compelled to reassert himself. "Gunny, I think you should send the females back to the *Fairfax*. It is not proper to expose them to danger."

Bass raised an eyebrow. "Lieutenant, why don't we discuss this in private." He walked a few paces away from the others and put his arm around Snodgrass's shoulder. The lieutenant winced at the familiarity but was too tired to protest.

Speaking in a low voice so he would not be overheard, Bass said, "Lieutenant, you are positively the sorriest example of an officer I've ever seen, bar none." Snodgrass stiffened and sucked in his breath preparatory to an outburst, but Bass silenced him by continuing, "You have done nothing but screw things up since you joined this operation. Great Buddha's balls, man, did you really think that big pirate was Dr. Morgan? Do you know how silly you looked? You've become a laughingstock, Lieutenant." Bass couldn't help but laugh at the memory of Snodgrass with his hand stretched toward Rhys. " 'Dr. Morgan, I presume?' " Bass said, recalling the lieutenant's words. He shook his head but couldn't keep himself from laughing.

Snodgrass, astonished and taken aback, could only work his mouth silently.

Bass stopped laughing. "I'm sending the women back, all but Minerva, and she wants to stay. Now, Lieutenant, you've been flaunting your status as a line officer ever since we started on this mission, but as of right now you can take that Academy commission of yours and stick it straight up your ass. You are a mere communicator, and from what I've seen so far, not a very good one. You swung a spot on this operation for your own selfish reasons, Lieutenant. I know that and so does everyone else."

Snodgrass was shaking now, he was so angry, but Bass would not let him speak.

"Now, we might need a communicator, so that's why I'm

keeping you here, despite the fact that you are a worthless little twit. But Lieutenant, if you mess up anymore, I'm not sending you back to the *Fairfax*. Oh, no! I'm going to take you behind that fern tree over there and beat the living shit out of you." He took his arm off Snodgrass's shoulders and walked back to the command group without another word, leaving the lieutenant fixed to the spot, gaping stupidly at Bass's rapidly retreating back.

"You and Snotty had a little kissy-kissy session?" Hyakowa asked.

"Yeah, we're good buddies now, Wang," Bass replied brightly. "Now let's get everybody out of the way so the Essay can take off."

While Bass conferred with his command group, the remaining pirates sat in the shade of a large fern tree, a disconsolate group of frightened and hostile men. Baccacio and Minnie sat by themselves while the rest whispered in their own little group. Baccacio noted that Lowboy cast several suspicious glances his way. Labaya stared sullenly at the ground, as if he did not like what Lowboy was saying. It was evident to Baccacio that Labaya felt dejected because Maya had deserted him, and he'd never been that fond of Lowboy or Rhys.

"That lieutenant, whatsisname?" Lowboy whispered to the others.

"Shotglass, Snotgrass, something like that," Rhys whispered back.

"Yeah, Snodgrass. Keep your eye on him, boys. He's our ticket out of here."

"Look at the lovebirds." Rhys nodded at Baccacio and Minerva.

"Ex-Marine." Lowboy spit the words out. "Keep *both* eyes on him."

Baccacio decided to ignore the other men. "Honey, thanks for sticking by me, but you should have gone with the other women."

"I know, Georgie, but to hell with it. I want to stay with you."

Good old Minnie, straight to the point, Baccacio thought. "There'll be another opportunity, probably very soon," he said. "I want you to go when it comes up."

"No."

He decided to change the subject. "Minnie, you know, I've got to stay with the Marines. There's something I got to do."

"What did you do to piss them off at you?" Minerva asked.

Baccacio told her briefly about his cowardice on Elneal, how he'd lost his nerve and, worse, left men behind in enemy territory when he ordered his platoon to run away. He told her how Hyakowa had reacted then. "He was right, Minnie. And now I'm at the end of my rope. I've got nowhere to go but up."

Minerva shook her head. "Whatever you did back then, love, it doesn't make any difference to me. I seen what you're made of and I'm sticking with you." Those words were the finest compliment the onetime Marine ensign had ever received. He leaned over and kissed Minnie full on the lips. Rhys blew a long raspberry but the two ignored him.

"I thought about this, Minnie, even when I was doing my worst to forget. See, that's why I joined the Red 35 Crew. I figured if I couldn't be a brave man, I'd be a bad one. I figured it was the Confederation that screwed me up, not me. I wanted to get back at them all." He grimaced. "Guess I found out that I could be a pretty good bad man, huh, Minnie?"

She responded by punching him lightly on the shoulder.

"Well," he continued, "sooner or later these Marines are going to run up against those things, and when they do, they'll need every hand they can get. Besides, we owe those bastard things a killing, a lot of killing." He paused and took a breath. "I'm not going to let these men down a second time, Minnie." He shook his head vigorously. "No. I just regret you might be there with me. I don't think Charlie Bass really understands what he's up against this time."

* * *

Bass called Staff Sergeant Hyakowa and Dr. Bynum to where he had established a temporary command post in the shade of a Dragon. "Wang, I want you to send a reinforced fire team east and another one west. Have them go two kilometers. Schultz is antsy and Owen's been wearing his alarm colors and quivering all over the place."

"Owen's like the canaries miners used to take underground in the old days," Dr. Bynum said. "When they stopped singing, the miners knew they were in the presence of dangerous gases."

"Yeah," Hyakowa added, "and that meant the canaries were already dead."

Bass snorted. A dead Owen did not appeal to him. "Do either of you have any idea what we might be up against?"

Dr. Bynum shrugged. "Whatever they are, they're deadly. I talked to the pirates extensively about those things while I was examining them. Nobody could agree on precisely what they looked like or how they killed their victims. Hell, the pirates were scared to death. You saw how panicked they became when we mentioned the things, and it's been a year since their only encounter with them." She wanted to add what they'd done to the security team at Aquarius, but she'd known Chief Hayes and most of the other sailors who died there. She knew they were good men, brave men, and even thinking about their being killed by those things was too painful.

"Yeah," Hyakowa added, "they all say the things shout something when they attack but nobody can agree on whether it's words or animal noises. But one detail's consistent. The things killed with weapons or organs that spray a deadly acid. And how do you explain the missing electronic equipment?"

"Gunny, we might be up against a very intelligent alien life-form here, something more than felinoids with an overwhelming desire for a good grooming," Dr. Bynum said.

"Or a warm meal," Bass added. He had already concluded that. "I wonder how all those scientists could live here for so long, exploring and testing everything like they did, without running into those things. Are they native here or—"

Hyakowa shuffled his feet. "Intelligent aliens? If they aren't from here, then . . . ?" The three of them silently contemplated the implications.

"Well, we'll find out," Bass said. "Now, Wang, get your patrols moving. Have them both turn around an hour and a half after starting out even if they haven't made a klick and a half. Tomorrow we'll call for a hopper from the *Fairfax* and do a full-scale reconnaissance."

Hyakowa nodded and left to organize the recons.

"Doctor, I'm real glad you volunteered to stay behind with us, but please, for tonight anyway, I want you and your medical team to fort up in one of the Dragons."

Dr. Bynum's mouth twitched up in a tiny smile, a grimace to anyone who didn't know her. "Sure, Gunny."

"Can you use that blaster?" Bass nodded at the hand-blaster Bynum had procured from somewhere and was now wearing slung from her equipment belt.

"Yes, and I will use it if I have to." She was smiling broadly.

"Well, Doc, good to have you along," Bass said, standing up. He needed to talk to Sergeant Kelly about the platoon's night dispositions. Actually, he would have enjoyed just conversing with Dr. Bynum for a while. Her ebullient personality and sound common sense appealed to him. He also knew she was steady under fire, and he respected that in anyone, man or woman.

"Take two aspirins and call me in the morning," Dr. Bynum replied.

After Bass departed, Bynum sat in the shade for a while, sipping coffee one of the corpsmen had prepared. She liked Bass for the same reasons he respected her. *I'll bet that bastard is good in bed,* she thought, and her smile widened.

"May I talk to you for a moment, Doctor?" Lieutenant Snodgrass asked. Bynum started. He'd come upon her unnoticed, and she was not in a mood to deal with him just then. But her professional ethic overrode her instinct.

"Sure."

Snodgrass squatted down and drew circles in the sand between his feet before saying anything more. "Doctor, I can't help noticing you get along well with Sergeant Bass," he began. He said it in a way that implied there might be something more than professional interest between them. Hot anger flashed through her, but she said nothing. "Well," Snodgrass continued, "I just don't understand him. I'm going to prefer charges against him once we're back at base."

"For what, Lieutenant?" Bynum was frankly astonished.

"Disrespect. Insubordination," Snodgrass said, waving a hand casually. "Whatever."

"Lieutenant Snodgrass, you're lucky he doesn't have you up on charges."

"Me? Don't be ridiculous! He threatened me!"

"Well, I'm a doctor, not a lawyer, Lieutenant, but the only threat I ever heard Charlie Bass make to you was to send you back to the *Fairfax*, and he had good reason to do that. And if you press charges against him, I'll be only too happy to testify to that effect. So consider carefully."

Snodgrass shook his head and smiled deprecatingly, as if his suspicions had been confirmed. He said, "I should've guessed. Yeah. It's 'Charlie' Bass to you, 'Sergeant' or 'Gunny' to the rest of us. I should've guessed."

Dr. Bynum got to her feet. Hesitantly, Snodgrass also stood. He was much taller than the doctor, but she seemed to loom over him. "Lieutenant, kindly explain what you meant by that remark," she said, her voice carefully under control.

"You heard what I said, I said what I meant," Snodgrass answered, somewhat defensively.

"If you ever question my professional competence again, my competence as a medical officer or as a navy officer, it's I who will have your miserable ass up on charges, Lieutenant. And if you have anything further to say about Gunnery

Sergeant Bass, keep it to yourself. He knows what he's doing, he's in charge down here, and our lives depend on him."

The two stood glaring at one another, Bynum regretting she'd lost control, Snodgrass trying to think of a comeback.

"She's right, you know." Both were startled to see Baccacio standing nearby. Neither had seen him approach. He'd come over to ask the doctor for a cup of coffee for Minnie and had overheard part of the conversation.

"You! You? You're a goddamned criminal!" Snodgrass blurted. "You're also a coward!" he shouted. "You're a—a—an unfrocked Marine!"

"Yes, I am. All of the above," Baccacio answered mildly. Staff Sergeant Hyakowa had just come down the ramp from the Dragon and now he stood silently to one side, listening. "I was once as fouled up as you are now, Lieutenant, except I had even less justification because I was an enlisted man before I was commissioned. You, with your Academy background, have only an imperfect military education. So you'd better listen to the doctor, because when the shooting starts, Charlie Bass is the man you want on your side, if you want to live through it."

Snodgrass snorted, whirled about and stomped away.

"Could I bum a cup of coffee from you, Doctor?" Baccacio asked. Bynum smiled and poured him one.

As Baccacio walked away from the Dragon he looked up and only then realized Hyakowa had been listening. Their eyes met briefly. Baccacio looked away quickly, but not before he saw Hyakowa give him an almost friendly nod.

About an hour into his leg of the reconnaissance, Sergeant Ratliff reported a very strange discovery: hollowed-out man-sized spots in the soft ground of a mud bar. Most interesting of all, the wallows—for that's what they reminded Ratliff of—were filled with some kind of organic material. "It looks like, uh, well, something's been laying eggs in there. Gunny, I think we've found a breeding ground."

But the most startling discovery was made by Sergeant

Bladon. He was so excited he forgot to use proper radio procedure making his report. "Gunny! We found artifacts! We know what they look like!"

"Calm down, Tam," Bass said. "What do they look like?"

"Gunny, they look like—they look like—well, they look like, uh, skinks!"

CHAPTER
TWENTY-TWO

First squad's patrol made it back before the other patrol, and Sergeant Ratliff displayed the material they brought from the wallows—curved, leathery objects that could well have been eggshell fragments.

Dr. Bynum was the first to examine them. She peered, poked, prodded, and twisted the fragments. "I'd need to run a full analysis," she said to Bass when her examination was finished, "spectrum, culture, molecular, the whole works. But, yes, they certainly resemble reptilian eggshells."

Bass looked around. A few of the Marines, some of the medical team, and Lieutenant Snodgrass were gathered around the doctor. But the pirates kept their distance and were casting apprehensive glances toward them.

"Mr. Baccacio," Bass called out, "would you come here please."

Almost reluctantly, Baccacio joined them.

"Ever see these things before?" Bass asked, and handed him an egg fragment.

Baccacio nodded. "Yeah. This looks like a slimy egg. The big ones that jump, they lay eggs like this. You call them leslies. When we first discovered slimy eggs, we tried to eat some." Baccacio made a face. "They're too runny to cook right, and they taste awful. The grown animals are edible, though even thoroughly cooked, their meat is slimy, like okra or the stuff in scotch broth." Baccacio began to hand the shell back, then looked at it again. "I don't know," he said after a moment in which he calculated the size of the whole egg.

"This seems a lot bigger than the eggs we tried to eat." Indeed, the curvature of the shell fragment suggested the whole egg might have been the length of a man's hand, maybe bigger.

"Could it be from a bigger animal?" Bass asked.

Baccacio shrugged. "Maybe. We only took eggs from a couple of nests. After we found out how awful they were to eat, we stopped bothering with them. Maybe different slimies lay different-sized eggs, maybe they grow after they're laid . . . No, the eggs wouldn't grow. Would they?"

"These animals don't lay their eggs in water?" Dr. Bynum asked, ignoring Baccacio's question about eggs growing.

He shook his head. "They may look like frogs, but they don't seem to have a tadpole stage. They make nests on mud bars where water can seep through the soil and keep them moist."

Bass and the other Marines were disappointed. They'd hoped the eggs were laid by the aliens that wiped out the scientific settlements. Knowing they were egg-layers and where one of their breeding grounds was could be an important step in finding them and possibly capturing one, but Baccacio had dashed that hope—unless the tool-users laid eggs too. Only theirs would probably be larger.

Just then second squad's patrol returned. Everyone was eager to see the "artifact" they brought back—everyone but the pirates. The Marines were sure, even before they saw it, that the artifact was something made by the intelligent aliens; the pirates were afraid it was.

Sergeant Bladon held out his hand, fingers spread, and let the artifact dangle. It was a locket hanging from a chain. He handed it to Bass.

Bass took it gingerly, almost reverently, and peered at the artifact in his cupped palms. Several of the Marines from first squad and the gun squad crowded close to look. They shifted to allow Dr. Bynum to squeeze in for a look. Lieutenant Snodgrass jostled his way through the knot of Marines and reached for the artifact.

"Pull that hand back or lose it," Bass said softly, without looking up.

Flushing, Snodgrass snatched his hand back.

It was a locket, no doubt of that. The casing looked to be some kind of bivalve shell, though none like Bass had ever seen. Its front was delicately carved into a shallow relief that could have been a stylized sun with a planet orbiting it. Bass made no guess about what a curved line that led from a dot far off to one side might mean. He turned the locket over to look at the back side. It wasn't carved; instead it held the lines and whorls that had grown on the shell when it held a live animal. The chain from which the locket hung was made up of tiny shells of a different type, and Bass couldn't see what held them together, though he knew there had to be some kind of strong thread running through them. The only metal he saw was the edge of a hinge along one side. Gently, he held the locket on the edge away from the hinge and pried. It made a light *pop* when it opened. Two images were engraved on the inner surfaces of the shell halfs, portrait heads.

The faces were distinctly, disturbingly, humanoid. They had two front-facing eyes that slanted downward from their outer corners so they formed shallow Vs above short noses. Lines that could have indicated very flat ears snuggled against the sides of the skulls. The features of one, oval, face were much finer than the other, which was more square and roughly featured. The finer face had a small, soft-looking mouth, where the other looked as though it would bare rending teeth if its lips peeled back. Bass couldn't tell skin texture, but the images gave the impression that the skin was slick, or moist. Neither head seemed to have hair; instead they had what looked like a scaly covering. The covering was caplike on one head, and hung to somewhere below the bottom of the engraving on the finer head. The most disturbing thing about the faces, though, could have been a mere trick of the lighting. As low as the relief was, the faces seemed to be sharply convex, snubby and reptilian.

"Mr. Baccacio," Bass called out. "What do you make of

this?" He looked around for the pirate leader, his onetime commanding officer.

Reluctantly, Baccacio joined him, the Marines parting to let him through. He looked at the images and nodded. "Yeah, that's the things." He leaned in to examine the images more closely. "The one on the left is, anyway. I didn't see any that looked like the one on the right." The one on the right was the one with finer features.

"I can't tell for sure," Dr. Bynum said, "there's no way of telling relative size from these engravings, but the one on the left gives the impression of greater mass, that it's much larger than the one on the right." She took a deep breath, then continued, "The one on the left is a male. The other's a female. Males are the fighters," she said to Baccacio. "You've only seen fighters, that's why the other doesn't look familiar."

"Just because, among us, men are fighters and women aren't doesn't mean that's true for an alien species," Bass said.

Bynum shrugged. "We've colonized more than two hundred planets," she said, "and explored a couple of thousand more. With almost all animal species we've encountered, on Earth or elsewhere, females might hunt, but males are the fighters. When you consider the fundamental biological reason for that, you have to conclude that it's likely a fairly universal rule."

Bass grunted. Bynum was probably right, but he wasn't going to say so. "Am I seeing this wrong, or do their faces actually protrude?" he asked Baccacio.

Baccacio nodded. "A bit. Their faces are pretty sharply convex. What did one of your men call them? Skinks? Yeah, they stick out just like that, almost like their bodies should be horizontal rather than vertical. A lot like the crawling red amphibians around here."

"So you think they're indigenous?" Bass asked again. He kept hoping someone would tell him yes.

Baccacio merely shook his head. He had no idea.

"What about the strange track of the shuttle that landed at

Central Station?" Hyakowa asked. He looked at Baccacio. "You didn't land at Central, isn't that right?"

Baccacio shook his head again. "We made one landing, at Aquarius Station."

"Offworld," Hyakowa said. That was the only answer that made sense, no matter how awful it was.

A hostile, space-faring, alien species wasn't something Bass wanted to think about, not in the situation he and his Marines were in. But they had to find these skinks and capture one of them to find out what they were. "Do we have security out?" he asked the platoon sergeant.

Hyakowa nodded.

The new watcher marveled. What she had been told was true, some of the Earth barbarians were invisible. Not that she would ever doubt the word of a leader. It was just . . . She'd never heard of an invisible person. Gods and spirits, yes, but not a person. She knew the invisible barbarians were not gods, and they were not spirits. The Master had sent the leaders and fighters to fight and kill the barbarians, and the barbarians died. Gods and spirits do not die when shot by the weapons of the People.

She listened more closely from her position hidden in the roots of a tree at the edge of the island. Yes, her ears agreed with the receptors on her sides, there were far more barbarians on the ridge than she could see—and not all of them were in hiding positions. Sometimes she could see a face or an arm hanging in midair where her other senses told her someone stood. Somehow, these Earth barbarians wrapped themselves in cloaks that concealed them from vision. That would not save them, though. The People had senses the barbarians from Earth did not have. Those senses would tell the leaders and the fighters where the barbarians were so they could find them and kill them even when they couldn't see them.

Without removing any of her senses from the ridge she was watching, she caressed the forever gun the Master gave her with his own hands. She wondered if she would have the honor of using it.

Two hundred meters from the command post, on a knob that poked up near the western end of the island, PFC Clarke idly gazed toward the swamp from where the gun team manned an observation post. "What do you think the other squads brought back?" he asked.

"Dunno," PFC Kindrachuck, the gunner, replied. He was supposed to be keeping watch with Clarke while Corporal Stevenson slept, but was leaning back against a boulder that had managed to make it that far from the mountain during an old landslide. His chin rested on his chest and his eyes were closed. "First squad found eggshells, I heard that."

"Yeah, but what did second squad find?"

"Something." Kindrachuck was having trouble staying awake and almost wished Clarke would shut up and let him doze off. The only thing that kept him from telling his assistant gunner to shut up and let him sleep was the fact that he was supposed to be on watch.

Clarke didn't say anything for a few minutes. The sun was low on the horizon, not far above sunset, and casting long shadows. Some of the shadows were moving. Clarke slid down his helmet's magnifier and light-gathering shields for a better look. "Damn," he murmured, "some of those things sure get big."

"What?" Kindrachuck mumbled.

"The leslies. I see some of them that look almost as big as people. And a few that are a lot bigger."

"What, where?" Kindrachuck said, annoyed.

"Take a look." Clarke peered at the animals he saw emerging from the swamp. "Some of them seem to be carrying things," he said quizzically.

"No, the leslies can't carry things. No hands." Kindrachuck sat up and slid his infra screen into place. The land and vegetation hadn't cooled enough for him to make out anything more than the faintest smudges of red against it. "How can you see anything?"

"Magnifier and light gatherer."

"Shit," Kindrachuck snorted. How come Clarke thought of that and he hadn't? He changed shields and looked at what Clarke saw. "Oh, hell, wake Stevenson." He moved into position behind the gun. "We've got company coming," he said as soon as he heard Stevenson was awake.

Stevenson automatically flipped down the right shields and saw about twenty upright bipedal forms moving in their direction. They seemed to be carrying short lengths of something flexible. He toggled on the command circuit of his radio. "Three-six, Oscar Papa Two. Company's coming," he murmured.

"Give me a description," Bass's voice came back.

This is very strange, the leader thought. He involuntarily flicked the nictitating membranes in, out across his eyes, to clear away any residual water that might be occluding his vision, but still couldn't see the Earth barbarians his other senses told him were on the slope ahead of his platoon. Maybe the watcher at Aquarius Station who said she couldn't see all of the Earth barbarians hadn't been lying after all.

Not being able to see the Earth barbarians meant he didn't know how many there were, but that didn't really matter. The barbarians from Earth were weak when his kind last saw them. The ease with which their small force had killed the thousand in the scientific stations proved that they had grown weaker during the intervening centuries. Even the ones that had stood and fought were easily defeated before their survivors fled high onto the mountain.

The leader flicked his nictitating membranes across his eyes again to moisten them, and glanced to his sides. His fighters were disciplined and ready. Even the large ones were keeping good order rather than rushing ahead. He saw that they were closing toward the middle of the formation. That meant there were very few of the Earth barbarians, just as he thought. Either few, or they were very tightly bunched up. Either way they would be easy to kill. His fighters would close on them and pour death on them. It was good that the leader had ordered the platoon to go naked; by the time they were close enough for the Earth barbarians to see their weapons in this dim light, they would be well within range. Until then the stupid Earth barbarians would think they were simply larger amphibians. He and his fighters were amphibian, but they weren't amphibians. He doubted the Earth barbarians could appreciate the subtlety; they'd never been subtle.

He looked to his sides again. His fighters were beginning to cast glances in his direction. They knew they were almost within range, and were waiting for his instructions to commence washing the Earth barbarians with their weapons. Just a few more paces and he would give the signal.

"Their faces, do their faces protrude forward?" Bass demanded.

"Yes," Stevenson answered. "Like a snake's."

Bass looked at Baccacio, who had listened to the brief radio report. Baccacio shivered as he said, "That's the things. They're coming." His hands clenched; he wished they held a blaster.

It wasn't something Bass had to think about. He had three Marines facing twenty or more aliens who he knew murdered without warning, mercy, or provocation. If his entire platoon was there, maybe he could try to communicate with the aliens—but three men . . . "Flame them," he ordered.

"You can't do that!" Snodgrass yelped. "They're an alien intelligence. You can't just order the destruction of the greatest scientific discovery of all time! We have to talk to them."

Ignoring him, Bass looked around to see who was available. Second squad and the other gun team were already in defensive positions. "First squad, on me," he ordered. He heard the staccato of a gun firing on the knob, punctuated by the cracks of a single blaster. "Hyakowa's in command here."

Snodgrass grabbed Bass's arm. "You can't do this!"

Bass didn't even look at him. His eyes were fixed on the knob. He saw brilliant flashes of light from beyond it. "Platoon Sergeant, this man is under arrest. Put him with the other prisoners."

"Aye aye, Gunny," Hyakowa replied as he grabbed Lieutenant Snodgrass and flung him toward the knot of pirates.

"Let's go, first squad."

Bass and the ten Marines of first squad sprinted toward the observation post, where the sound of firing was already ebbing. At a signal from Dr. Bynum, a corpsman grabbed a medkit and raced after the Marines.

The firefight was over by the time Bass and first squad reached the knob. Corporal Stevenson was prone behind his blaster, shaking his head and repeating again and again, "I saw it but I don't believe it." Kindrachuck still had his shoulder to his gun, sighting downslope as though looking for more targets. Clarke stared slack-jawed down the slope in the direction the things had come from, so shocked by what he'd seen he didn't seem to be aware of the steam that rose from a gaping wound that bubbled on his hip. The corpsman saw the wound and immediately knelt next to him and cut away his trousers to examine it.

"What happened?" Bass demanded as he scanned the landscape. There weren't any of the skink-things in evidence. "Where'd they go?" He was aware of Ratliff positioning his squad to defend the position.

"They flashed," Stevenson said, not looking away from where the skinks had been. "I saw it but I don't believe it."

"What did you see, damnit?" A ragged swath of ground about sixty meters away was seared, most of the springy growth burned away. It looked like more damage than could be accounted for by the firing he'd heard.

Stevenson rolled onto his side and looked up at Bass. "Every time we hit one, it flared up—I mean, it totally went up in flames. *Any* kind of hit. We could feel the heat of them burning from here." He slowly shook his head.

Kindrachuck started talking softly. "If you hit a man with a short burst from a gun, you'll flame him. He'll burn. When he's done burning, you're left with a crispy critter; those things just flared up even with one hit. And they didn't leave any corpse behind. They just vaporized."

Bass looked at Stevenson and Kindrachuck. In his experience, bodies didn't simply vaporize, not even when they were hit by a short burst from a gun. Then he remembered what Baccacio had said, that he shot two with his blaster and they vaporized. Bass hadn't believed him. He looked downslope and still didn't see anything other than the scorched area. He glanced at the corpsman, who was using a scalpel to dig something out of Clarke's hip. "How is he?"

"I sedated him," the corpsman replied without looking up from his work. "This is an acid burn. I think there's some still active acid in there. He should heal all right after I get the rest of it out."

Bass grunted. It was another point on which the pirates seemed to have told a garbled truth, and a confirmation of the security camera vid tapes at Central. He'd never heard of acid weapons. "Cover me," he ordered, and trotted to take a closer look at the scorched area.

"Watch where you step," Stevenson called after him. "Some of their weapons blew up, some of that acid might be laying around."

Bass stopped at the edge of the scorched area. What he saw defied belief. He hadn't counted, not on a conscious level, but he was sure there hadn't been many more than a dozen blaster shots and the gun had shot less than a quarter load. Sure, concentrated fire could slag solid rock. Concentrate enough fire and it could melt armor plate. But the small amount of fire the gun team put out couldn't account for the condition of the ground. A swath about fifty meters wide was scorched, more thoroughly in some places than in others. Where it was more scorched, the dirt had melted and now glistened, mirrorlike. Great heat still radiated from the patches of burned ground, sending Bass back from it. Small bits of ground cover remained between the melts. He ignored the heat long enough to approach the edge of the scorched area, where he squatted and picked at one piece of vegetation. It was brittle and dissolved into powder between his fingers. Sweat pouring off him forced him back again. He stood and looked beyond the scorched area. Stevenson had said some of the weapons blew up; maybe he could find some fragments that could be analyzed and tell them something about these things.

He spotted a curved piece of metal about the size of his hand and that looked like a chunk from the wall of a cylinder. Bass dropped to one knee to look at it, but didn't touch it right away. A strip of something flexible lay alongside the chunk of metal, partly drooping over it. A patch of ground cover on its other side was eaten away, and thin smoke drifted up from the hole. Bass leaned over the hole and peered into it. The smoke came from glistening spots of a milky green liquid on the dirt at its bottom. He had to pull his head away because the fumes stung his eyes. He drew his knife and thought of using it to get some of the liquid out of the hole, but didn't have anything to put it in. He looked back uphill, but the corpsman was still working on Clarke. Well, maybe the corpsman had put the acid in a specimen jar. He used his knife to pick up the piece of metal. The flexible strip came with it. He started back toward the observation post, holding his knife off to the side so nothing corrosive on the artifact could drip onto him.

Blaster fire suddenly erupted from the platoon position.

"We're under attack!" Hyakowa shouted over the radio.

"Details," Bass said coolly into the command circuit. He dropped the artifact.

"Unknown numbers," Hyakowa replied more calmly. "They came from the north, we're inside a horseshoe."

"There're some between us?"

"I believe so. I can't spot anyone in my infras. I hear their voices."

Stevenson was listening and broke in, "Use light amplifiers, they don't show on infras."

"Roger." Hyakowa broke off long enough to pass the word to the platoon, "Raise your infras, use light gatherers." Then back to Bass, "There's at least fifty, maybe more."

"Casualties?"

"None that I know of."

"We'll maneuver," Bass told the platoon sergeant, "and try to hit the ones on your right flank from the rear. Get reports from all teams. Don't forget the navy and the prisoners."

"Roger." Hyakowa turned his attention to checking on the half platoon he was with and fighting off the unexpected attackers.

"Third fire team, stay here," Bass ordered. "Everybody else, come with me."

CHAPTER
TWENTY-THREE

Rhys Apbac's eyes lit up when he saw Staff Sergeant Hyakowa, hand firmly on Lieutenant Snodgrass's arm, bringing the navy officer to join them.

"Well, well, Sarge, what's this? You invisible boys think we need ourselves a real officer now that we know our fearless leader is a disgraced coward?"

Hyakowa ignored him and pressed down on Snodgrass's shoulder until the lieutenant sat on the ground. Infuriated and humiliated, Snodgrass didn't hear the pirate. He glared up at Hyakowa. "I'll have your stripes for this, Sergeant," he said through gritted teeth.

"Maybe we can combine our court-martials, sir," Hyakowa retorted. "In the meantime, stay here where you won't get into any more trouble." He turned abruptly and went to check the defensive positions. He had more important things to do than deal with a communications officer who thought he was the second coming of Admiral Nimitz.

Lowboy reached over and nudged Snodgrass. "Hey, sailor-boy. That Marine thinks he's hot shit, don't he?"

Snodgrass glared at the pirate. Lowboy laughed in his face.

A hundred meters to the east of the landing zone and not far below the highest point of the island, second squad's second fire team was in another outpost where the ground dimpled behind a slight ripple of earth when the skinks hit the gun team to the west.

Corporal Kerr's guts fluxed when he heard the first shots.

This is it, he thought. This is real, there's fighting for sure now. He struggled to keep tremors from shaking him apart, fought to hold in the terror-beast trying to break out of the place where he'd locked it. Then MacIlargie jumped to his feet to run toward the firefight, and Kerr grabbed him and pulled him back down with a thump.

"What do you think you're doing?" he rasped, the terror-beast held at bay.

"There's a firefight, we've gotta go help them."

"This is our position, we stay here until ordered to move."

"But—"

Claypoole slapped the back of MacIlargie's helmet. "But nothing," Claypoole snapped. "You've been in combat before. You know that they can come from more than one direction."

Kerr nodded at Claypoole approvingly. "Rock is right," he said to MacIlargie. "Never run toward fire until you know something, or have orders to head toward it. That's a good way to get yourself flamed by the wrong people."

"But . . . " MacIlargie shut up when he saw the look Kerr was giving him. He turned to Claypoole for support but Claypoole was looking at him the same way.

"Whoever it is, if they've got any smarts, they're coming this way too." Kerr looked to the swamp a short distance east of the observation post. The sun was low, but it hadn't yet dropped below the top of the knob, and their shadows were stretching long below them, pinpointing their positions for anyone in the wetness. "Get as low as you can." Their shadows shortened dramatically as they got flat behind the ground ripple. Kerr lowered his infra screen. So did Claypoole and MacIlargie. They began to hear things below them, but nothing showed up in the infrared.

Kerr still quivered, but fear allowed a truce within him.

Lance Corporal Chan looked nervously to his right. From his fire team's position he'd have to stand up to see the knob where the gun team had its observation post. He'd been on combat operations; he knew better than to stand up during a firefight just to satisfy his curiosity. The fight sounded one-sided; he only heard the gun and one blaster firing. That didn't mean the gun team was firing at shadows, though. He knew Corporal Stevenson was too level-headed to open up when there weren't real targets. Besides, there were brilliant flashes of light that didn't come from plasma bolts. Was somebody using silent energy weapons of some sort? His infra showed him Gunny Bass was leading first squad, heading for the observation post. Then the firing stopped. What happened? He turned his attention to his men. PFC Nolet was all right, he'd been on operations with the platoon before—more than Chan had. The only question was PFC Rowe, but even he had a couple of operations under his belt before joining 34th FIST. They should be all right.

Chan scanned the slope through his infra. Then he raised the screen to use his naked eyes. Sometimes normal vision showed things infra couldn't pick out—especially if a warm body was in front of or next to something that had been heated up by the sun. And there were other ways to disguise a heat signature.

Sergeant Kelly called Hyakowa to him. "I already checked the positions," he said. "Everybody's on edge, but all approaches are covered. Anyone coming at us is going to meet a wall of flame."

Hyakowa grunted. Nervously, he glanced toward the west. He wished Gunny Bass would tell him what happened down there, but knew that as soon as the platoon commander had enough information to pass on, he would. The firefight was over and nobody had called for the doctor, so maybe there weren't any casualties, at least none the corpsman with first squad couldn't handle.

"The Dragons are in position to give covering fire to everyone but the west OP," Kelly continued. "My gun team can go wherever it's needed most." He looked at Hyakowa and saw the concern in the platoon sergeant's face. "We're ready, we'll be okay."

"What if there's too many of them?" Hyakowa asked in a voice almost too soft for Kelly to hear.

"There isn't any such thing as too many."

Corporal "Rat" Linsman was growling low in his throat. The firefight at the west OP had been over for a few minutes, but he didn't believe the action was done with. He couldn't tell what it was, but something was making noise in the swamp at the water's edge. Nothing showed up in his infra, and he couldn't see anything but water, mud, and vegetation with his bare eyes or even his light amplifier. That didn't make any difference, something was down there. And if that something was the same thing that wiped out the scientific stations, fought the pirates, and killed the navy security at Aquarius, it was very nasty. He wanted to have his fire team light it up, burn whoever—or whatever—was there. He'd seen that locket and its images. The one that looked like its lips hid sharp teeth, he didn't want to wait for it to come to him, he wanted to fry it before it had a chance to get those teeth anywhere near him.

"Watson," he ordered, "use your infra. I want to know the instant any red shows up on them."

PFC Watson already had his infra screen in place. "Roger."

"Hruska, use your light gatherer." He thought for a second. "And your magnifier." This was Hruska's first action, and he needed every edge he could get.

"Okay, Corporal," Hruska said, nervousness making his voice quiver.

Linsman clapped him on the shoulder. "You'll be all right, you'll see." Linsman kept switching among infra, light gatherer, and naked eye. They were going to see who—what— was coming as soon as they made a move.

The Masters snickered about the slight resemblance they had to the indigenous life-forms of Society 437. The foolish barbarians they faced had no experience of intelligence that didn't live on their own worlds, and would fix on those superficial similarities and see them as just another kind of local amphibian. They wouldn't make that mistake for long, but it would prove fatal. The leaders ordered their fighters to strip naked, then stripped naked themselves. The leaders ordered their fighters to cover themselves with mud, and slavered mud over themselves. They paid particular attention to the shoulder straps, so they wouldn't be detected by a casual glance. The barbarians from Earth had devices that allowed them to see in the infrared; the leaders knew that and laughed among themselves. Their body temperatures were lower than the barbarians', so they wouldn't register on infrared scanners the same way an Earth barbarian would. And the mud they smeared on themselves would further reduce their infrared signatures. Their bodies were the color of mud. They were smeared with mud. They would be crossing mud until they reached the springy ground cover, but by then their weapons would almost be within range. It was dusk, light was dimming and shadows lengthening. The barbarians' attention was fixed to the west, to the diversion. The Earth barbarians would not see the leaders and their fighters approaching until it was too late. The barbarians were stupid that way—they had never had any subtlety.

The leaders signaled and the advance up the slope began.

"A skink is coming," PFC Hruska said. He wiggled, trying to get lower behind his blaster, and sighted in on the body he saw through his light amplifier.

"Where?" Linsman looked where Hruska's blaster was pointing. He lifted his infra screen and dimly saw a form advancing up from the swamp bank. He dropped the light gatherer and magnifier shields into place and saw several bipeds that could have been skinks. None of them appeared to be carrying a weapon, but each seemed to have a hand tucked behind its body. Did they have hands? They must have hands if they made that locket.

"Flame it," he ordered. That was the problem with boots—new Marines—they didn't know when to fire without waiting for orders. "Use your light gatherer and magnifier," he told Watson, and picked a target of his own. He pressed the firing lever and saw the plasma bolt hit the skink he aimed at. Then his jaw dropped. The skink flared up in an almost blinding flash of light, leaving behind just a blackened spot of steaming mud.

"What's going on?" MacIlargie twisted around to look back toward the landing zone. He saw the flashes of blasters firing along the side of the island, and brighter flashes downslope from the blasters. He lifted his infra and saw the silhouettes of shapes he hadn't seen before. "Oh, shit." He spun back to his front and saw what he hadn't seen through his infra screen. *"Fire!"* he screeched, and put his words into action. Thirty meters away a skink flared. "They don't show in infra," he shouted as he picked another target and fired on it.

Kerr and Claypoole each fired a blind shot before lifting their infras to see what they were shooting at. The skinks were close enough to shoot back. Green fluid spurted out from their weapons and spattered a wide area around the three Marines.

Bass and the Marines with him were halfway back to the landing zone when PFC Dobervich let out a bloodcurdling scream and fell, doubled over in agony. Corporal Dornhofer, the closest to Dobervich, saw the green fluid smoking as it ate through the wounded Marine's chameleons and into the flesh of his right side. Beyond Dobervich, Dornhofer saw several forms wielding what looked like hose nozzles. Short streams of green fluid spurted from the nozzles, one stream just missing him. He twisted to point his blaster and flamed the nearest enemy. The shock of the skink flaring up staggered him backward a couple of steps, and that stagger saved his life as another stream of green fluid squirted through the space he'd just occupied.

"Rotate right!" Bass bellowed. "They're on our right," he added unnecessarily. He thought he saw more than a dozen skinks, some running about, others down in kneeling positions, all spraying green fluid indiscriminately. He flamed one before dropping his infra and looking to see that his Marines were reforming to face the threat. Corporal Pasquin already had his fire team down and returning fire, and Sergeant Ratliff was positioning Stevenson and Kindrachuck where the gun could do the most damage. Dornhofer and Schultz were coolly picking off the skinks nearest them, and the corpsman was shielding Dobervich with his own body as he tried to tend his horrific wounds. In seconds half of the skinks were vaporized, and Dobervich was still the Marines' only casualty.

Bass looked down the slope beyond the attackers and saw more skinks rushing up to reinforce them.

Corporal Goudanis looked up the slope and saw the Marines caught in the open by the attacking skinks. It looked like there were too many skinks, they could easily overrun Gunny Bass and the eight Marines with him. With a glance he took in his own situation. Clarke was heavily sedated and couldn't do anything. Despite his years in the Corps, Quick had no infantry experience beyond the training exercises on Thorsfinni's World. The only man he knew he could rely on was Van Impe. No, there was one thing he could rely on Quick for—to keep watch. After four years of embassy duty, Quick knew how to keep watch and guard things.

"Quick," he ordered, "watch the swamp, let me know immediately if you see anything. Van Impe, come with me." He got up and ran.

They didn't go far, only fifteen meters, but it was far enough to give them enfilading fire to support first squad. They dropped into prone positions and began pouring fire into the flank of the skinks.

* * *

"What's going on?" Lieutenant Snodgrass cried when the attacks broke out all around the perimeter.

"We're under attack by those things, you dumb shit," Rhys shouted as he tried to crawl under the skirts of a Dragon.

Lowboy hadn't moved from his place yet, he was shaking too hard from terror to find a hiding place. The navy officer's question got through to him, though, and he lashed out with an open hand to smack the side of his head. "They're gonna kill us, and you called them 'the greatest scientific discovery of all time.' " He balled his fist to hit Snodgrass again, who dove away from him and looked at him wild-eyed.

"But—But—" Tears washed down Snodgrass's face. He hadn't done anything wrong to get hit for, but everything was going wrong, very wrong, all around him. Then he knew what he had to do. The pirates needed a leader. Somehow, he had to get them armed and organized. They could fight the aliens and win. Then he'd be recognized for the great officer he was. The idea that he might be thinking irrationally didn't occur to him.

MacIlargie's first shot was rushed and he missed. So did the blind shots from Kerr and Claypoole. One of the skinks yelled something in a voice halfway between a liquid gargle and a harsh bark. The other skinks, about twenty of them, screamed out in similar voices and began running toward the three Marines.

"Roll!" Kerr shouted, too busy to notice his fear. "Change position." He dove to the side and rolled over twice. When he stopped rolling his blaster was in his shoulder and he flamed the nearest skink. Two other bright flashes showed that Claypoole and MacIlargie also had hits.

"Keep moving!" Kerr shouted. The ripple of ground the Marines were behind stretched across most of the width of the island. He knew the skinks couldn't see them unless they could see in the infrared, but they'd be able to see where the Marine fire came from and would concentrate their own fire on those places. There were too many skinks coming for the

Marines to dare allow them any stationary target. A stream of green fluid struck where Kerr had just moved from and spattered. He didn't notice, he was too busy picking a new target. All his earlier fears about how he'd react to danger and combat were forgotten as the instincts and reactions he'd honed during his years in the Corps took over and he directed his men in fighting this strange foe.

"Enemy right!" Corporal Pasquin shouted as soon as he heard Dobervich scream. He dove to the side and found a skink to flame. There were so many of them it was almost too hard to pick one to shoot at. He looked for his men. Claypoole was prone on his right, firing steadily. MacIlargie was on his left, firing more maniacally, but his aim seemed true. The darkening sky was strobe-lit by dying skinks. He picked another target and had the satisfaction of seeing another brilliant flash.

"Shit-*shit-SHIT!*" Claypoole shrilled. A spray of green struck the ground a meter to his front and a globule hit the back of his hand on the forestock of his blaster. Instinctively he slapped the hand onto the mud. The burning eased and he grabbed the forestock again and flamed the skink that had just shot him. The flash the skink made when it flared up was all the anesthetic Claypoole needed. He laughed out loud as he flamed another skink. This was his second wound. He figured he'd be a laughingstock for having two "dumb stripes" on the sleeve of his dress scarlets.

MacIlargie's eyes were wide and his mouth gaped as he shot skink after skink. The fluid they sprayed came close, but the mud that most of the acid streams hit dampened the splashing. Smoke rose from spots on his chameleons where drops landed, but he wasn't hit himself—at least he didn't think he was, he didn't feel pain anywhere. But there were so damn many skinks.

George Cameron—ex-Marine ensign Baccacio—ignored the byplay between the navy lieutenant and the pirates. He was busy trying to find a weapon. None were laying about and there weren't any wounded Marines nearby for him to take a blaster from. He searched out Hyakowa.

"Staff Sergeant," Baccacio said when he dropped next to Hyakowa where the platoon sergeant was trying to direct the defense of the landing zone. "I know you hate me, but I can use a blaster. Give me one, I'll add to our firepower."

Hyakowa gave him a quick but hard look. Baccacio was right on both points: he knew how to use a blaster, and Hyakowa hated him for a coward. But the Marines could certainly use all the extra firepower they could get.

Hyakowa pointed at one of the Dragons. "I put your weapons with the medical team. I'll tell Dr. Bynum to give you a blaster. Better yet, I'll give all of you your weapons; before this is over we may need every hand that can pull a trigger. I guess I'll have to put Snotty in charge."

"Thanks. Then where do you want me?"

Hyakowa listened for a few seconds to the flood of reports coming to him from the fire team and squad leaders, then pointed to the east. "Two-two's in danger of being overrun. Go there."

Two-two. "That's Corporal Kerr, isn't it?"

Hyakowa nodded.

Baccacio jumped up and bolted for the Dragon with the medical team. He'd refused to call in a medevac hopper for Corporal Kerr when the man was nearly killed on Elneal—he'd insisted there wasn't enough time to wait for one to come. And he had abandoned one of Kerr's men. Baccacio wasn't wearing chameleons. Not only did he have to run across a hundred meters of open ground to reach Kerr's position—a hundred meters in which any nearby skink could see and shoot him—but if Kerr saw him coming, the Marine might shoot him, and Baccacio wouldn't blame him if he did.

Baccacio couldn't let worries about what might happen slow him down. They were in a fight for their lives and needed every possible man fighting.

* * *

Chan stopped firing and looked with dazzled eyes for more targets. He didn't see any, though he heard continuing fire from other positions and could see the flashes of more skinks vaporizing.

"Report," he said, suddenly remembering his new responsibility as a fire team leader.

"I'm okay," Nolet replied. "I think. Got enough ammo."

"I'm all right," Rowe said. "Three spare batteries."

"What do you mean, 'I think,' Nolet?"

"Some of that stuff splashed on me. Burns like hell, but I think I'll be all right. It doesn't burn as much as it did a few minutes ago."

Chan scrambled the few meters to Nolet to check out his wound. His stomach churned when he saw it. A large globule of acid had hit Nolet's upper right arm and eaten away a chunk of flesh all the way to the bone. The raw sides of the wound were congealed; it was effectively cauterized. Most likely the pain was ebbing because the nerve endings were deadened by the tissue damage. At the bottom of the hole Chan saw a glimmer of green. The acid was still there, still eating at flesh surrounding the bone. "Corpsman up," he said into his helmet radio's squad circuit, "Two-three." Then to Nolet, "Hang on, this might hurt." He got out his knife and started digging out the remaining acid before it could eat all the way through the arm.

Nolet screamed.

"No!" Bass bellowed. He aimed at a skink pointing its weapon nozzle at the corpsman working on Dobervich and pressed the firing lever. The skink flared just as it fired and its shot went wild. Another skink was running toward the corpsman and Bass shot it as well. He saw the fire coming in at the skinks from the side and knew who it had to be from. He toggled his radio switch.

"Goudanis, protect the doc," he said. "Who's watching your front?" He grunted at the reply; he understood why Goudanis left that job to the former embassy Marine. Then he returned his attention to the skinks in front of him and the Marines to his sides.

Schultz was as cool as Bass had ever seen him under fire. The career lance corporal was in a kneeling position, calmly switching his aim from one skink to another, picking them off like targets on a range. Schultz had noticed the same thing Bass saw about the skinks—they held their fire until they were close, about thirty meters from their targets. Did everyone else notice that? He hoped so, but it didn't matter now because most of the skinks were within range of their weapons and beginning to fire at the flashes of the Marines' weapons.

Bass saw the corpsman sharply shake his head, then grab his medkit and scramble away from Dobervich.

Baccacio stopped before he reached the east outpost; the skinks were almost on top of it. He deliberately put his blaster to his shoulder, just like on the range, and flamed a skink. He wasn't distracted by the alien flaring up, he'd seen that a year earlier when he first fought them. He picked off another skink, then tried to see where the Marines he was reinforcing were. He couldn't see them because he wasn't using infras, but he could see the flashes from the muzzles of their weapons. The flashes came from too many places for only three Marines. He smiled tightly. Yes, that Corporal Kerr was a fine Marine, he had his men moving between shots to keep the skinks from zeroing in on them. He picked another target and flamed it.

Hyakowa spun toward the medical team's Dragon when he heard a scream from inside it. He saw two skinks charging toward the amphibious vehicle. Neither was firing its weapon, but both were aiming odd nozzles at the open back of the Dragon. The platoon sergeant threw his blaster into his shoulder and flamed one. He shifted his aim toward the second but didn't get his shot off—he didn't need to. A bolt of plasma shot out of the inside of the Dragon and the second skink flared. Hyakowa raced to the Dragon, shouting to identify himself to the people inside.

Dr. Bynum stepped outside just as Hyakowa reached the rear of the Dragon. She held a hand-blaster at the ready.

"As a doctor, I'm supposed to save lives," she said. "This is the first time I ever saved lives by taking one." She began trembling and looked like she was about to fall. Hyakowa caught her and held her to his chest.

"Yeah, the first time's really hard," he said soothingly. But when he thought about it, he couldn't remember the first time he'd flamed a man. He guessed that was the kind of memory he didn't want to keep. "Everybody okay in there?"

Dr. Bynum pushed away from him. "It's not hard, Staff Sergeant," she said. "This wasn't. I killed that one and I'm glad. I'll kill any more that come toward me or my people. Now, you Marines take care of us, and the medical corps will back you up." She hefted her hand-blaster. "With bandages or blasters, we'll back you up."

"You got it, Doctor." He looked around for more skinks that might have broken through the defenses.

Corporal Linsman looked for more targets. There weren't any on his part of the ridge, though the sky was still filled with the lights of skinks flaring up elsewhere around the perimeter.

"Report," he automatically ordered.

"Present and accounted for," Watson immediately replied. "Ammo's fine."

"Hruska?" Linsman said when his new man didn't speak up.

"Where'd they go?" Hruska asked. "I don't see any."

"Are you all right?" Linsman asked harshly.

"What? Yeah, I'm okay. Where'd they go?"

"We killed them, that's where they went. When I say 'report,' you're supposed to tell me if you're all right or if you're hit, and how your batteries are holding out."

"But the skinks, they were just right here."

"They aren't here now. This is when you tell me if you're okay and if your blaster has enough power."

"Huh? Oh, right. I forgot," Hruska said in a rushed voice. There was a moment's pause, then he added, "I'm not hurt and I have two spare batteries for my blaster."

Linsman shook his head, then made his own report to Sergeant Bladon.

Bladon told him about Nolet getting hit. "The corpsman says he might lose that arm," he finished.

Linsman swore. He looked around. Fewer flashes of light were brightening the evening sky.

Goudanis and Van Impe fired repeatedly into the flank of the skinks attacking the rest of their squad. Strangely, the skinks didn't seem to notice the fire coming from their side. It was as though they had been told to attack straight ahead and keep going forward no matter what. Goudanis kept glancing to his right, down the side of the knob, looking for skinks coming at him and Van Impe. None came that way. He checked with Quick a couple of times, but Quick reported no activity from the swamp at the end of the island until the very end.

"I see some going back into the swamp," Quick reported. "They're headed northeast." He suddenly realized he hadn't seen the skinks come from anywhere else. They must have been in hiding along the edge of the swamp below him, waiting to exploit any opening along this portion of the island when other skinks broke through the Marines' lines. If they had, he might have been the only one in their way. He listened and heard their voices and splashing move away.

"They're headed north," he reported.

The fight was over.

"Squad leaders report," Bass ordered as soon as the firing stopped. There was a pause while the squad leaders checked with their fire team leaders and the fire team leaders checked their men. The reports came in. He already knew about Clarke and Dobervich. Dornhofer, Nolet, and Claypoole were also wounded. Staff Sergeant Hyakowa reported no casualties among the medical team or the pirates.

"Snotty's doing his best to make a major nuisance of himself, though," Hyakowa said. "You listen to him, you'd think we just precipitated a major intergalactic incident, or destroyed the greatest scientific discovery of all time."

"Asshole," Bass muttered. "I should have sent him back to the *Fairfax*." There was another question he needed an answer to: "How many of them got away?"

It took a moment for the answers to get back to him—an unknown number of skinks was heading to the north. Either they were regrouping prior to making another attack or they were fleeing.

"Everybody, to the perimeter," Bass ordered over the all-hands channel. "Including the OPs. I don't want anybody in an exposed position."

CHAPTER
TWENTY-FOUR

"Sir, it's your call," Bass said to Captain Tuit, who was sitting on the bridge of the *Fairfax County* in orbit far above Society 437, "but they're on the run and we can't waste any time following up, before they regroup or reinforce. The tactical momentum is with us now, sir, and I don't want to waste the advantage. We can run them down and kill them."

"Don't you want to talk to them, Gunny, find out who they are and what they're doing on this planet? This is a tremendous discovery, an alien intelligence, and all you want to do is stomp these things out like bugs?"

"Sir, I'll talk to anything that doesn't have a weapon in its tentacles. But if they're armed and want to fight, I'll shoot first. Besides, for all we know, they might still be holding some of our people prisoner. At least I've got to find out where their base is and search it. If they resist, I'll kill them; if not, I'll sit down and have a beer with them. But it's your call, Captain."

Captain Tuit considered. There was one possibility that really frightened him about the situation down on Society 437, but he hesitated to mention it. It was his call, all right—let Bass continue to pursue the aliens or withdraw the landing party and the surviving pirates and head home. Well, the skinks had killed more than a thousand people on 437, and whatever their purpose in committing that slaughter, Hank Tuit was not going to sit down and talk it over with them.

"Go get 'em, Charlie," he said.

"Thank you, sir. Here's my plan: Dr. Bynum says the casualties are too badly wounded to move overland with us. They've got to get back to the sickbay, where more definitive medical care is available, so I want an Essay to evacuate them."

"Combat landing?" the captain asked. A normal landing would require three degrading orbits and take five hours or more.

"No, sir. They need to be stabilized first, and Dr. Bynum will need time to be sure they can stand the liftoff. I'll leave them with a couple corpsmen with two Dragons and move out at first light tomorrow. We'll go on foot with the other two Dragons as support. We'll follow the skinks by the trail they left. When the casualties are evacuated, the third Dragon will join us. It's going to be slow work, Captain, because the string-of-pearls is having difficulty tracking the things. We'll have to proceed cautiously."

"Gunny, I have just the man for running an electronic surveillance. Hummfree. You may remember him. He's a surveillance specialist of the first order. And he's the one who pinpointed the pirates' location for you."

"Yes, sir, I do remember that lad. Many thanks."

"Good plan then, Gunny. I'll launch the Essay on your call. Skyhawk out."

Bass switched to the platoon net and called the NCOs and Dr. Bynum to his position. Let the scientists and philosophers contemplate the skinks and try to figure out the whys and wherefores of their origin and purpose, Bass told himself. "But for me," Gunnery Sergeant Bass whispered, "it's time to rock and roll." Grinning fiercely, he bit off the end of a Clinton and stuck it between his teeth.

"Ma'am, I ain't going, and that's it! Court-martial me if you want to, but I am a walking wounded and I'm gonna walk out of here and do some wounding of my own," Claypoole told Dr. Bynum. He shook his head stubbornly.

"Lance Corporal, that wound could get infected and then

you could be in very serious trouble. You need time in the sickbay for it to heal properly."

"No, ma'am," the Marine answered. He shook his head again.

Dr. Bynum sighed. "Lance Corporal, try to keep the dressing in place, and keep it dry if you can. As soon as this is over and you're aboard the *Fairfax*, report directly to sickbay. Now go back to your squad." As a doctor, she thought Claypoole was being incredibly stupid. At the same time, she couldn't help but admire his determination and courage.

"Aye aye, ma'am!" Claypoole said. He picked up his weapon and charged down the ramp.

Bynum went to examine the stasis pods where Clarke and Dornhofer were sedated.

"All signs stable," HM1 Horner, who was monitoring the casualties, whispered.

"Larry, the Essay'll be here soon. Nothing's going to happen until then."

"Don't worry. If it does, we'll be ready." He nodded toward the crew compartment and patted the side arm he carried. "But Commander, begging your pardon, why don't we switch places? A ship's doctor is a hell of a lot more important than old Tom and me." He nodded to Hospitalman Second Class Hardesty, who was adjusting settings on Clarke's pod. Hardesty grinned at them, revealing gaps where he'd lost front teeth in a brawl years before that he'd refused to have replaced. He'd thought the missing teeth gave him a rakish air, made him look like a pirate. But after seeing real pirates up close, he was seriously considering dental implants.

"What? And miss the excitement?" Dr. Bynum replied. "No, no, Larry, 'rank hath its privileges,' and I'm pulling it on you two this time. Besides, you've got Owen to keep you company." The woo sat contentedly on a ration box, twiddling its appendages as he consumed a box of dirt. The soil on Society 437 seemed to contain good nourishment for the woo, which had gained weight since their landing. Dean had given him over to the corpsmen for safekeeping. "Okay, boys, be good." She clapped Horner on the shoulder, gave Hardesty a thumbs up, and walked down the ramp.

"Lieutenant," Lowboy said softly, sidling up to where Lieutenant Snodgrass was standing, watching the Marines prepare to move out. "Can I say something?"

Snodgrass looked down his nose at the disagreeable little man. Lowboy grinned back at him, his deferential smile revealing the rotten yellow teeth behind his cracked lips. But Snodgrass liked the man's deference. He'd gotten very little proper respect in the recent past. In fact, he had even begun questioning his own judgment, a rare event for Argal Snodgrass. Years before, one of his uncles had told him, "Argal, if one person says you've got a tail behind you, well, you'd just ignore him, wouldn't you? If two people say you've grown a tail, you might begin to wonder a bit. But if a third person says you've got one, you'd better turn around and take a look." He'd never followed that advice—until now.

"Well, sir, I was jist thinking, why ain't you in charge of this operation here? You're an officer, ain't cha?" Lowboy smiled even more broadly.

"I'm a navy officer," Snodgrass replied haughtily. "This is a *ground* operation and the Marine's in charge, even if he is only an enlisted man."

"Well, I was jist wondering, is all. I mean, you got education, right, Lieutenant? You know starship navigation and all that stuff, don't cha?"

"Yes, Mister, uh . . ."

"It's Lowboy, sir, at your service." Lowboy made a slight bow.

". . . Mr. Lowboy. Starship navigation is a big part of an officer's education at the Naval Academy. I was number two in that subject in my graduating class. Engineering was my best subject, though. One day I'll command a starship, Mr. Lowboy. I am a navy line officer, you know."

"So I figured, Lieutenant, so I figured," Lowboy said, reflectively working a forefinger in his ear as he spoke. "Say,

Lieutenant, why don't cha do us all a favor and speak to the sergeant. Hell, we're no good to anybody down here. Let us go back to the *Fairfax* with the wounded. We just want outta here, Lieutenant, that's all. We've been refugees on this stinkin' planet nearabouts a fucking year now, sir, and we want off this place." Lowboy's voice had taken on a whining tone and he'd screwed up his face to make it look as if he were about to cry. "It ain't fair that goddamn sergeant of yours wants to keep us down here, nossir. We ain't no damn good to him or anybody else, and that's the Buddha's truth, Lieutenant."

"Well . . ."

"You can volunteer to stay behind, kind of supervise us, Lieutenant?" Lowboy added hopefully. "You can get along with people, Lieutenant; that damned sergeant can't get along with nobody. But if that Sergeant Bass knew you was looking after us, I bet he'd agree. Please, Lieutenant. Please?"

Snodgrass considered. He was tired of being made a fool of. At least back on board the *Fairfax* he'd have the respect due a navy line officer from navy men.

"Gunny, may I talk to you?" Lieutenant Snodgrass asked.

"Sure, Mr. Snodgrass, but make it fast. I've got to check the night defense dispositions."

"Gunny, I suggest you send the pirates back to the *Fairfax* with the wounded. You won't need them anymore, and I'll volunteer to stay behind and see they get on the Essay. They'll only be in your way otherwise. Then I'll join you when the last Dragon comes forward."

"Mr. Snodgrass, I may need every man we've got before this is over, and the pirates can fire a weapon. If we run into more of the skinks or if they've got prepared positions to ambush us from out in the boonies, I'll need every trigger-puller I can get."

"Gunny, you know they're worthless. Look at them. They're undernourished and scared permanently out of their wits. They won't be worth a damn to you in a firefight. I'll volunteer to stay behind and get them aboard the Essay. Then maybe I should go back to the *Fairfax*. I've been no good to you down here."

The tone of resignation in Snodgrass's voice was something new. Bass considered. Snodgrass was right, he conceded. "Okay, Lieutenant, you get the pirates together and keep them together until you get them into the brig on board the *Fairfax*. You've got the responsibility. First thing you do, Mr. Snodgrass, is take their weapons back."

Best of all, Bass reflected, he'd be getting rid of Lieutenant Snodgrass.

"Gunny, can I talk to you for a second?" The voice came from behind Bass while he was making his rounds.

Bass whirled around and glared at Baccacio standing behind him. "What is this, talk Charlie Bass to death day?" He sighed. "Make it real quick, Mr. Baccacio, it's almost dark and I want to check the perimeter by daylight."

"Minerva and I don't want to go back to the *Fairfax* right now, Gunny."

"Of course not. The *Fairfax* means the brig for the both of you until we can dump you into the hands of a Confederation magistrate."

"I know. You have to do that. But I want to stay with you for another reason. Afterward, sure, I'll gladly face the music."

"Get to the point, will you?" Bass said. He had no time for the coward-turned-criminal.

"I was a lousy Marine officer, Gunny, and I'm even worse now," Baccacio said with great feeling. "This is the last chance I'll have to undo some of that for a long, long time, maybe forever. I want a spot on one of your fire teams. Goddamnit, I want a chance to be a Marine again."

Bass stared at the former ensign. Baccacio's face had turned red and there were tears in his eyes. Weeping men, although he'd seen them often enough, embarrassed Charlie Bass, but there was something more to Baccacio than a worthless failure crying in self-pity; Baccacio had handled himself during the skink attack. And apparently he'd held the survivors of the pirate crew together for nearly a year, despite the fact that they seemed to hate his guts. And they hated him because he was braver and smarter than they were.

"All right," Bass answered softly. "Go over to the Dragon and pick up some gear. But you and Minerva stick close to me while we're out there." Bass did not even try to persuade Baccacio to send Minerva back to the *Fairfax*. "Get a weapon for her too," he called after Baccacio.

Baccacio hardly heard him. He'd given up the most precious thing in his life, and now he had a chance to get it back again.

"Sergeant Hyakowa?" Corporal Pasquin said respectfully as Hyakowa finished reviewing the platoon's night dispositions with Gunny Bass. "May I have a word with you, please?"

"I want one with *you* first, Corporal," Hyakowa said. He stood looking at Pasquin thoughtfully for a moment. "Thanks for stepping in and stopping me when I jumped on Baccacio. I lost control there. He just isn't worth bruising my knuckles over."

Pasquin's faced turned a deep red.

"Another thing, Corporal, you performed well under fire. You deployed your fire team expertly for a man who's never been in combat before. Good work."

"Uh, thanks. Staff Sergeant . . . ?" Pasquin's face turned a darker shade of red and he stumbled over his words, but finally got them out: "You were right to chew me out back at Aquarius Station. I—I was acting pretty dumb. I was feeling sorry for myself. I was not acting like a Marine corporal." Pasquin drew himself up stiffly to the position of attention as he spoke.

"So you were, so you were. But Corporal, that's behind us now. Go back and get your men ready for the night. Oh, one more thing. You have some unfinished business to attend to. Do you know what I mean?"

At first Pasquin looked bewildered. Then it dawned on him

what his platoon sergeant meant. "Yes, Staff Sergeant, I do. I'll take care of it right now."

A few minutes later Pasquin called Lance Corporal Dean aside. "Can I speak to you?" he asked. Dean was surprised at his deferent tone. He'd also been surprised when Pasquin jumped in to separate Hyakowa and Baccacio, and at how he'd reacted under fire. He respected Pasquin for that, but was suspicious of the new tone in his voice. Still, he'd come to realize there was more to the man than his being a pain in the ass.

"Lance Corporal Dean," Pasquin began formally, then took a breath and paused. "No." He started over. "Look, I—I—well, I've been unfair to you. I—I acted like an, um, well, like an asshole, Dean, and I realize that now. I'm sorry." He stuck out his hand.

Dean hesitated for only an instant before taking the corporal's outstretched hand. They shook.

"Dean, you did well. You've been under fire before, a lot, and I'll tell you this honestly: I knew all along I could rely on you and the other men when the shooting started. I wasn't so sure about myself, though. But man, you didn't hesitate. We were a team, Dean, and we kicked some skink ass." Pasquin hesitated for a moment. "Dean, I've got to tell you something. You got a minute?"

"Sure, Corporal Pasquin."

"Call me Raoul. Hell, you'll be a corporal yourself soon enough."

"My name's Joe, if you care to use it."

"Joe, I came here from the 25th FIST. They're based on Adak Tanaga. Ever heard of it? Tanaga's got the worst climate in all of Human Space. Most violent storms of any planet known, especially near the polar regions, and that's where the 25th is based. You know the Corps," he laughed nervously, "it picks the worst sites on a planet and plops a FIST down there. Anyway, Joe, I gotta tell you what happened to me there, so you'll understand—so you'll know what was eating me. Will you give me a few minutes?"

Dean nodded.

"Well, I was an acting recon team leader." Dean showed surprise, and Pasquin smiled self-consciously. "Yeah, I was a Force Recon Marine, Joe. A good one too. Straight four-o on all my fitness reports, tip-top physical shape, all that." Dean was startled as he remembered threatening the corporal the night of the party back in Bronnoysund. Force Recon Marines were experts in hand-to-hand combat.

"I had another corporal, two lance corporals, and a communications man with me, and we were out humping the boonies, keeping in shape and practicing land navigation, living on the edge. Patrols had been out trying to find us but they didn't have a chance, not with my team. We were good, Joe, damn good.

"We'd been out a week. What you've got to know is that back on Tanaga the weather changes real quick. It can be mild and sunny, and then in ten minutes a Willie can blow up on you, winds of a hundred kilometers an hour, and the temperature drops to way below freezing. 'Willie' is what the settlers call those storms. You get caught in the open in one of those things . . . " He left the sentence unfinished. "It wasn't the season for Willies just then, but on Tanaga seasons are a laugh anyway and you've got to be prepared for bizarre weather the whole year.

"We were having trouble with communications that whole week, so we were keeping alert to any sudden changes in air pressure and temperature drops that'd indicate the approach of severe weather. Normally we'd have been getting regular meteorological reports, but we'd been out of touch for two days at that point, so we were kind of thrown back on our instincts and what we knew of the weather signs. When a Willie blows up on you, you gotta just go to ground, find what cover you can, and try to wait it out. If it catches you out in the open, you're up shit creek.

"I'd been keeping us under cover the whole time, moving mostly at night but practicing concealment in open country during the day, planning a route that'd leave us plenty of terrain features to cover our movement. But, well, we were all getting tired by then and I decided to hell with it, we'd just hump across this flat space, maybe two or three kilometers broad, and head back to the base. If a patrol got us, so what, we'd already run circles around them. Hell, we'd proved we were good. All I wanted was a cold beer and a good night's sleep."

Dean nodded. How many times had he wished for the same thing?

"The other corporal, Taff—well, forget his full name. He was against taking the exposed route. He said we wouldn't do it under combat conditions and what if a storm blew up on us before we got to the hilly terrain on the other side? I was team leader and I overrode him." Pasquin was silent for a few seconds, staring at the ground, the muscles in his jaw working. "I overrode him. We were halfway across when the comm man noticed it'd suddenly turned cold. You've never seen a Willie, Joe. The whole sky turns dark as night and the clouds blow up on you like time-lapse vid. You can see the wind roaring along the surface of the ground, throwing shit up in the air, a big cloud of dust rolling in on you. In five minutes the temperature dropped twenty-five degrees. The only thing we could do was go to ground and huddle together. We got into a slight depression and managed to throw on some protective gear."

Pasquin paused again. "Well." He sighed. "I was lucky. I lost all the fingers on my left hand, all my toes, my ears, and my nose to frostbite. Yeah," he laughed, touching a finger to his nose, "wonderful how the doctors can graft shit back on you. Feels like the old one." He wiggled his nose between two fingers. The nose and fingers looked perfectly normal to Dean. "It must have plummeted to thirty, forty degrees below zero in just minutes. The comm man and one of the lance corporals froze to death on the spot. That storm lasted only ten minutes, Joe, and two of my guys froze to death before it passed over us." Abruptly, Pasquin stopped talking; his vision seemed to focus somewhere inside.

"So what happened then?" Dean asked.

"So Taff, the remaining lance corporal, and I dragged our two dead buddies twenty kilometers before we could establish contact with base, and they sent a hopper for us. The lance corporal died before we got back. Because I wanted to get home a day early, I killed three good men, Joe.

"There was an inquiry, after Taff and I got out of sickbay. Taff blamed me straight out. He was right. The only reason they didn't bust me is because, despite the frostbite injuries, I got the three of us and the two dead Marines back to safety. But Joe, I didn't panic. That's what everyone thought happened, but I didn't. I just got careless and tired and made a bad decision. Ever since I've been of two minds, blaming myself and rationalizing. You know, 'Anybody could've made the same mistake,' and so on. Getting kicked out of recon was the hardest thing. Taff, who was my best friend, he was hard over what happened. You know, we're pretty tight in recon. Those guys who died were his friends too. Threatened to kick my ass. So the CO put me into the supply depot until he could arrange a transfer out of the 25th. And here I am. Only Captain Conorado, Gunny Bass, and Staff Sergeant Hyakowa know what happened. Now you. I've been leaning on you, Joe, because you're the kind of Marine I once thought I was. It's that damn simple. Well, I don't care if you tell any of the other guys. Not now. I ain't making any more stupid decisions. But I've got a ways to go to make up for the one I did make back there."

"Well, you came a long way today, Raoul," Dean said.

Pasquin smiled. "Well, maybe. We sure kicked some ass, didn't we, Joe?"

"We sure did." Dean smiled now. "But one thing, Corporal? You have to apologize to Owen too."

Pasquin started and then laughed. "Hell, apologize? Sure I'll apologize! I'll even kiss the little shit!" He put his arm around Dean's shoulder and together they walked back to where the rest of the squad was having coffee.

* * *

The remnants of the Red 35 Crew hunkered in the shade of a fern tree, talking quietly.

"Jesus's double-headed dick!" Lowboy crowed. "It worked, it fuckin' worked!" He slapped Rhys on the shoulder and punched Labaya lightly in the chest. "I got that stupid sailor to get the sergeant to let us go back to the *Fairfax* with the wounded! And best of all, that navy jerk agreed to let us keep our weapons!" Lowboy doubled over with laughter.

"That's good," Rhys said, "even if we go to jail. Anything's better than this stinking place with those goddamn *things* crawling all over."

"Great Buddha's balls, you idiot!" Lowboy snarled. "What the hell we been talking about all day? You dumb shit! We ain't going to jail." Sometimes Lowboy didn't know if Rhys was as stupid as he let on or if looking stupid was just his way of making a joke. He hoped it was the latter. "Now listen. Labaya, think you can fly one of them Essays?"

Labaya, an ex-navy bosun, nodded. "Yeah, why?"

"Because," Lowboy said, speaking slowly and distinctly, "once we lift off, we overpower the crew and use the Essay to get us back to the *Anacreon*. Then we're out of here free!"

"You sure this can work, Lowboy?" asked a burly pirate whose name was Dufus.

"Christ's bleeding hemorrhoids, no wonder they call you Dufus," Lowboy said. "Sure it'll work. Callendar?" He turned to a small black man with prominent cheekbones. Callendar seldom spoke, but he liked killing.

"I'm with you, Lowboy. I don't want to go back to jail, and I sure don't want to stay here on this planet."

"How do we find the *Anacreon*?" Rhys asked. "And once we do, how do we get her out of here?"

"That's where Snotglass comes in. He's got training as a starship navigator and an engineer. See, Rhys? Education does count for something." Lowboy laughed raucously.

"Lowboy, how do we even know the *Anacreon* is still out there?" Sharpedge asked.

Lowboy thought for a moment. "We don't, but we do know

who Scanlon left in charge of her, don't we?" He looked at each of the other pirates and nodded.

"Killer Kalb," Rhys whispered in sudden understanding.

"Right," Lowboy said, "and he would never have left Scanlon down here." He snickered. "If the bastard had been a woman, they'd have had a dozen kids by now."

"Then why didn't he come for us before this?" Labaya asked. He seemed to be the only one among the surviving pirates who realized what an insane idea Lowboy's getaway was, but he was not about to go against Lowboy.

Lowboy shrugged. "I think they're all dead up there's what I think. I think the *Anacreon* is just orbiting around up there, a dead ship."

"What killed them?" Callendar asked.

"How far can one of those Essays go on its own?" Lowboy asked Labaya, ignoring Callendar.

"I don't know. Once it reaches orbital altitude it doesn't take much fuel to change altitude and speed. If it's in a stable orbit, it can keep going after the crew dies because the air ran out."

Lowboy laughed. "That's enough to find the *Anacreon*. Can the *Fairfax* spot us?"

"You know it can, Lowboy. And they'll take us out, once they find out what we done."

"No, they won't. We'll have hostages, remember?"

"But we're going to kill the Essay's crew, aren't we?" Rhys asked.

Lowboy struck the big man lightly on the side of his head. "God's dripping dick, you big genius, they won't know that on the *Fairfax*. And we ain't killing their lieutenant. He'll do the talking for us, if it comes to negotiating. And once we're back on the *Anacreon*, we'll have him put her into Beamspace and we're out of here. Nobody'll ever come after us. We make one short jump, then change directions. Nobody'll have any idea where to look." Lowboy laughed and the others joined in. All except Labaya.

* * *

Lieutenant Snodgrass watched the Marines disappear into the swamp. He stood for a long time in the clearing, ankle deep in mud and dead vegetation, and listened as the sounds of the advancing Marines slowly diminished. In time it grew very quiet. Dimly, he could hear the Dragon commander talking to Bass on the command net. The pirates, crouching in the shade of a fern tree, laughed among themselves. One of the corpsmen walked out onto the Dragon's ramp and urinated into the mud. Plash, plash, plash, went the golden stream. Snodgrass could hear it clearly from where he was standing.

Lieutenant Snodgrass looked at the dense foliage that grew all about the clearing. He shuddered. No, he told himself, no problem. The Marines had chased off all the skinks.

The Dragon commander called Snodgrass on his helmet unit. "Lieutenant," he said, "the Essay is twenty minutes out. Better get your, er, troops into the bay and strapped down."

"Roger that," Snodgrass answered. He turned and swaggered back toward the pirates, scratching his behind with one hand. "Not yet, Uncle Bob," he whispered, "not yet."

Ten meters behind the lieutenant's back a sharply convex face projected slowly out from behind some fernlike growth, its eyes nictitating as it watched the foolish young man walk away.

CHAPTER
TWENTY-FIVE

It was the mid-watch, and Commander Hank Tuit sat on the bridge of the *Fairfax County*, sipping from a mug of galley coffee and smoking a Clinton. The bass duet, "The Lord Is a Man of War," from Handel's *Israel in Egypt*, played on his private sound system. Of all Handel's oratorios, he liked that one best. The vigor and masculinity of the music and the unequivocal righteousness of its hero, the biblical Moses, appealed to him. Just then he figured they needed someone like Moses, to pull off a miracle.

Commander Tuit frequently came to the bridge on the mid-watch. That was always a quiet time for a vessel in space, and he would take his chair then, to sit and work out problems. But often he would just sit and relax. The watch officers knew not to bother him when he was on the bridge during those hours, and he did not bother them. He found the underway bridge of a naval vessel an enormously comforting place. It was restful up there, listening to the muted sounds of the duty watch monitoring the ship's systems, the officers and ratings talking in muted voices throughout the quiet night.

After the last report from Bass down on Society 437, Tuit had left word with the watch to contact him if there were any further developments. Back in his cabin, he worked on the dispatch he would soon send to Fleet in a drone. But something was bothering him about the situation on Society 437 and he couldn't quite put his finger on it. So he grabbed a Clinton and made his way back to the bridge. He knew that until the mission was over he'd be living out of his captain's

273

chair anyway, and that night Commander Hank Tuit, captain of the CNSS *Fairfax County*, had some real problems to resolve.

Things on Society 437 couldn't have been worse. First, during the last few days the Marines had found everyone there dead, apparently deliberately and horribly murdered. It was a civil and scientific disaster of totally unprecedented proportions. Dr. Nikholas Morgan was known and respected throughout the Confederation, and his death would come as a terrible shock to billions of people.

And Hank Tuit was going to be the bearer of those tidings. He had come to rescue those people, not cart their desiccated remains home in body boxes.

But worse, far, far worse than the deaths of all those scientists, was that Dr. Morgan's expedition had been ruthlessly wiped out by *aliens*. *Sentient* and evidently malevolent starfaring aliens. That was what Gunnery Sergeant Bass and Dr. Bynum were coming to believe, and that caused a terrible sinking sensation in his gut because he trusted their judgment. Humanity had spread out over a volume of thousands of cubic light-years during the last three centuries of interstellar travel, and, with the exception of the felinoids, nothing even approaching intelligent alien life-forms had ever been encountered. Well, the woos on Diamunde also seemed to have a degree of intelligence, if the Marines were to be believed. The woos, at least, were friendly.

Sitting on what could be the most momentous discovery in human history, Commander Hank Tuit knew very well that he might go down in the books not as the first man to make contact with an intelligent alien species, but as the first man to be wiped out by them. Tuit realized he was no Horatio Nelson, and he could accept that; so long as he commanded the bridge of a naval vessel, any vessel, he would be happy. Yes, he was a superannuated navy officer in command of a fourth-rate vessel on a routine rescue mission. That was just fine with him. But fate or blind chance or plain bad luck had set him right smack dab on the razor blade of history, and he would just have to slide down it. No matter how things turned out on Society 437, nothing would be the same for him after the mission was over.

The latest report from the string-of-pearls had the aliens retreating from Bass's position, so apparently they'd had enough of Marine firepower. That was very good. It was even better if the skinks were indigenous to Society 437. *But were they?* That was the big question. If not, that was bad, *very* bad, because they would have had some way of getting there, and if they had starships, where were they? More to the point, how many skinks were there, and could they call in reinforcements? Bass had inflicted heavy casualties on them during the attacks his men had repelled, and it appeared that Chief Hayes and his men had killed a lot of skinks before being overrun. Had they just been probing, to determine the Marines' strength and weapons? Or had they been all-out attacks that depleted the skinks' strength? If they had a fleet lurking somewhere beyond the *Fairfax*'s sensors, his little scow wouldn't stand a chance.

Well, Captain Tuit reflected grimly, the *only* responsibility I have right now is to this ship and my crew, and if saving them means fighting whomever or whatever, no matter the odds, then fight it will be. His second responsibility was to warn the Fleet and request reinforcements.

Should he recall the Marines and get the hell out of there? *No.* He would not run. Turning away from danger was not in Captain Tuit's nature. Besides, he was duty bound to find out what was going on down there. And Bass was confident he could hold his own. That would have to do.

The thought of running reminded him of Lieutenant Snodgrass. As if he didn't have enough problems to deal with, Snodgrass had initiated what amounted to a goddamned mutiny planetside. Well, he would deal with Snodgrass in good time. The kid was bright, graduated in the top five percent of his class at the academy or something like that. And he had connections. But his judgment was zero. Tuit had seen young officers like him before. Either they learned their business and went on to become admirals, or they wound up like that ex-ensign, Baccacio.

Baccacio. Tuit shook his head. He felt the pirates' presence on Society 437 was just an example of being in the wrong place at the wrong time. He would turn them over to the first Confederation magistrate after the mission was over. They were not his worry. In fact Bass had kept the men down on Waygone because he thought they might be of some help. It seemed now, however, with the possible exception of that ex-ensign of Marines, maybe that had been a mistake. But Snodgrass was the one who had screwed that up. Snodgrass. Well, if he survived and Bass was able to pull things together despite the lieutenant's stupidity, there were ways of handling the young officer without the trouble of a court-martial. A goddamned court-martial was the one thing Tuit didn't need on top of everything else he had to deal with. Tearing a wide strip of hide off that young man's ass would be more effective and Captain Hank Tuit was an expert at *that*.

"Victoria," he said to his computer console.

"Yes, Captain Tuit?" a pleasant female voice answered.

"Victoria, let's see my report to Fleet."

"Aye aye, Captain." The report flashed on his screen immediately. "Captain, I took the liberty of correcting an egregious grammatical error," Victoria said, just the right note of humble apology in her voice. Several paragraphs into the report a line flashed yellow as the computer zoomed in on it. "You needed the subjunctive mood there, Captain. It should read 'If it *weren't* . . .' instead of 'If it *wasn't*.' As you may recall, the subjunctive mood is required when writing of an event or an act not as fact but as contingent or possibly viewed emotionally, as with doubt or desire. I hope you don't mind, sir."

Jesus H. Christ! Captain Tuit thought. Well, I should've used the dictating mode instead of trying to write the goddamn thing myself. First chance, he told himself, he would change the computer's name from Victoria to something else. "Thank you very much, Victoria."

"You are entirely welcome, Captain. I might add, sir, there were no spelling errors," Victoria added, almost as if the computer were apologizing for its automatically correcting the captain's grammar. "How may I assist you?"

"I want to dictate the rest of the report, Victoria. Are you ready?"

"Indeed, Captain, I am." Stupid question; Victoria was *always* ready, but Victoria had been programmed always to be friendly toward her users. And Captain Tuit knew that very well.

Briefly, Captain Tuit expressed his misgivings about the aliens and warned of the possibility of a hostile fleet lurking somewhere in the quadrant. He deliberately omitted any reference to the pirates. Wary of bureaucrats, military or otherwise, he felt it would be better to leave out mention of them. For now. Some second-guesser back at Fleet might jump to the conclusion that somehow the pirates *were* behind the slaughter, and the "aliens" were some sort of diversion. That would definitely lower the priority of Fleet's response. And when the reinforcements arrived, if the *Fairfax* was no longer there, headquarters had to know what they might be up against.

Finished dictating, he said, "Victoria, knock all that into shape for me."

"It's done, sir."

"Good. Get me the comm shack." The image of Chief of Communications Kranston flashed onto his screen.

"Chief, Victoria has a dispatch for Fleet. I want it sent pronto. Use more than one drone. Send at least six," he added, "and program them to make the jump as soon after release as possible." If more than one of the drones made it, there'd be no doubt back at Fleet HQ that the *Fairfax* was in big trouble.

"Aye aye, Skipper." Captain Tuit's screen reverted to his report. Within thirty seconds the drones would be on their way. That made him feel a little better. Tuit took a long drag on his Clinton. He drew the smoke down deep into his lungs and expelled it slowly through his nose and mouth, savoring the rich flavor of the tobacco. He sucked his teeth reflectively. "Lieutenant . . ." He turned his chair about to face the watch officer.

"Sir?" Lieutenant Tom Light responded at once.

"Sound General Quarters."

"Sir?"

"No drill, Lieutenant, sound GQ." From now on the crew of the *Fairfax* would be on full combat alert. Captain Tuit refocused his attention on the Handel, which had now reached the tenor aria, "The Enemy Said." He listened carefully. "I shall pursue, I shall overcome, I shall destroy them." He loved the unbridled ferocity of that aria, even if it belonged to the bad guy. Well, he thought, old Moses really screwed up *his* day. Nope, he thought, we don't have a Moses, but we've got the next best goddamn thing—Gunnery Sergeant Charlie Bass and a platoon of Marines. He headed for the comm shack.

"Third Class Hummfree, I have a job for you, if you think you can do it," Commander Tuit said. He'd caught everyone by surprise when he walked into the surveillance department without warning, and everybody not glued to instruments stood gaping at him.

None gaped more than SRA3 Hummfree, who never expected to be addressed by the ship's captain without the Skipper first speaking to the watch commander, or at least the chief. "Y-Yes sir," Hummfree stammered.

"Don't be so fast to agree," Tuit said. His lips quirked in a half smile. "Or are you asking what the job is?" He shook his head and held up a hand to stop Hummfree from trying to answer. "This is a job that maybe even you can't do. If you can't, no one will think any the less of you. It might be impossible. Understand?"

Hummfree didn't trust his voice, so he nodded.

"Those things the Marines are fighting down there, do you think you can track them?"

Abruptly, Hummfree's nervousness went away. "I believe so, sir," he said confidently, his eyes glowing above a wide grin.

Tuit cocked an eyebrow and Hummfree's grin wavered.

"Well, I can try, sir."

"All right, here's what we know about where they went. See if you can find them."

Tuit spent two minutes telling Hummfree and Kranston everything Bass had relayed to him about the skinks' movement. Before the captain was through talking, Hummfree was bent over his controls, diddling dials and tickling toggles. The ship's captain and the chief nodded at each other; if anyone could track the skinks, it was Hummfree. Tuit motioned the chief to accompany him out of the compartment into the passageway.

"That boy bothers me, Chief," Tuit said in a voice pitched low enough it couldn't be heard in the compartment. "I've never seen a third class so deserving of promotion to second class, even if he doesn't study for the test. But he's so good at what he does, I really won't want to put him in a supervisory position and lose him for what he does so well."

"I know what you mean, sir. Been thinking exactly the same myself."

"Maybe between us we can figure out how to promote him and keep him in the same job."

CHAPTER
TWENTY-SIX

"Try to take one alive," Dr. Bynum said as the sun rose.

Gunnery Sergeant Charlie Bass's gaze was fixed on the swamp he and his Marines were about to enter as though, if only he looked hard enough, he'd be able to see where the skinks had gone and what nasty surprises they might have left in their trail. "Sure," he replied absently. He was thinking of how he and his Marines would kill the skinks when they found them, how they could kill them without losing any Marines.

The doctor saw his expression and realized her words hadn't gotten through to him. She groped for his invisible sleeve and tugged on it to get his attention. He turned his gaze to her.

"I'm serious, Charlie," she said, her eyes boring into his. "This is important. This might be the first-ever human contact with an alien intelligence. We can't just meet them and kill them all, we have to try to establish communications of some sort with them."

" 'Might be'? I've never heard of another contact."

She shrugged. "There have been rumors of alien contacts for centuries. And I'm only a navy doctor. For all I know, the Confederation knows about alien species elsewhere, maybe even has established contact with some."

Bass cocked an almost disinterested eyebrow.

"One hears things. Rumors, innuendo." She shook her head. "I don't know. But I do know it's important that we at least make the attempt to talk to these aliens."

"Right," Bass said dryly. "Try to talk to them. Maybe we can keep them from shooting first." Yes, the Marines would do their best to keep the skinks from shooting first. The Marines would do their best to get in the first shots.

"Charlie, I mean it."

He nodded. "I know you do, Lidi. But you also have to understand that my primary responsibility isn't to make friendly contact with aliens. My responsibility is to keep us all alive, and deliver a report on what we found here. At this point, the fact that there is a hostile presence in this area is more important than bringing a live alien back." He held up a hand to stop her from the sharp reply she was about to make. "I know getting one of them alive is important. But preserving the lives of all of us is more important to me."

"Charlie, if all you want to do is bring us all back alive, we can leave the surface of this planet right now, as soon as a couple of Essays can get down here."

"Right. And leave a hostile group of aliens to attack the next human expedition that makes planetfall here."

"We don't know that the ones who attacked us are the only ones here."

"We don't know they aren't." He thought back to the stored data that showed the landing of the pirates and what appeared to be the aliens' landing as well, showed the destruction of the pirate ship and the departure of what he believed must have been the alien vessel. "There isn't evidence for more than one landing," he said. "I think we have to assume these are the only ones. We're going to wipe them out. We'll try to get one to take back with us." He said the last sentence fast to keep her from arguing.

"Try, Charlie."

"All right, Lidi. We'll try," he said, knowing that the only trying they would do was to find and kill the skinks. Bass signaled to Hyakowa and the platoon moved out.

The comm shack on the *Fairfax* was quiet, save for the ever-present whispers of the climate control system and the muted beepings and tings of the surveillance monitors, phones, and other human/machine interface devices. None of the three surface radar analysts or the other technicians hunched over their equipment said anything aloud. They would speak only when they had something to report. Ensign Muhoorn sat in his chair, barely visible in the comm shack's dim lumination, motionless except for the times he raised the mug of strong navy coffee to his lips for a sip. Chief of Communications Kranston blended into the shadows half a meter from the communications officer. Kranston didn't bother drinking coffee, but some of the sailors in the comm department claimed that he had an intravenous setup under his uniform and mainlined his caffeine. Kranston's attention was fixed on the back of SRA3 Hummfree, where the young sailor seemed to grow out of his task chair. Kranston suspected that Hummfree had somehow managed to grow an umbilical that connected him directly to the galley and the head. Kranston could think of no other way that would allow a man to spend as many uninterrupted hours at his station as Hummfree spent at his.

Hummfree caressed his keyboard, diddled his dials, tickled his toggles, brushed his buttons. He began with a small-scale, multispectral view of a many-kilometer-long area directly to the north of the island where the Marines had fought off the skinks. He'd watched the fight in visual. The image wasn't good, the light was poor, and their clothing—or body color, he hadn't been able to tell—was almost the same hue as the mud and dirt that spotted the ground. Still, what little he was able to make out, the appearance of the aliens struck him on some primordial level, raised an atavistic fear and revulsion in him. Intellectually, he knew they—the Marines on the surface, the medical team with them, the ship's officers—should be doing their best to make contact with the aliens, to talk to them, to make peace. Emotionally—the incomplete image he had of them made him want to kill the aliens, to fight and kill until not a single one was left alive anywhere in the universe. He didn't know it and wouldn't have cared if he did, but his reaction was similar to that of any other species in Earth's history when it came face-to-face with another species that occupied the same ecological niche. It didn't matter that the skinks had gills on their sides and were aquatic; their niche was the human niche. Besides, they had struck first, without warning or provocation, and before any of the humans they attacked were even aware of their presence.

Hummfree wanted to find those skinks for the Marines and do his part to help kill them.

The large area he examined at first held too many unidentifiable, transient signals for him to identify. He narrowed his viewing area to include only the kilometer north of the knob where the fighting took place. A few moments' examination identified every trace he saw as one or another of the indigenous amphibians or insectoids. He shifted his focus north less than a kilometer to allow for overlap between the area he'd just searched and the next one. What was that, just disappearing off the north edge of the new area?

Swiftly he switched focus north again. He saw the bright red infrared signatures of Dragons near the bottom edge of the new display. Yes, to the sides and ahead of the Dragons were the Marines, stretching in a double line almost two hundred meters long from the back of the Dragons to the point. A couple of hundred meters ahead of the Marines, a tiny dot swept back and forth ahead of the axis of their advance. That must be the UAV, scouting ahead. He wondered briefly how the Marines were controlling it, and decided the controller was set up inside one of the Dragons. Ingenious, those Marines. Even though they weren't a tool he normally used, Hummfree knew enough about the disguised aerial observers to know that they weren't designed to be guided from inside a moving vehicle. He decided not to tap into the UAV because his focus and its wouldn't be in the same area and the extra detail might only confuse him.

He shifted focus back to the area he'd just entered and left. Again, after a few moments' search there were no traces he could not identify as benign. He returned to the area with the

Marines. They had advanced, but he could see he would finish searching that area before the lead Marine reached the northern edge, and he'd be leading them. Soon he'd have to extend his search to cover the areas to the sides of the Marines' route. How soon? He had no way of guessing how long the skinks would continue in a straight line before they turned east or west. Maybe he should already be extending his search to the sides. Maybe he should have extended it right from the edge of the knob. Maybe the skinks had gone only a couple of hundred meters before they changed direction. Maybe the skinks were moving in the areas he wasn't looking at. Maybe they were passing through the interstices between his observation areas. Maybe. Maybe and maybe and maybe. A man could go crazy thinking about the maybes. Hummfree decided to quit worrying about the maybes and continue to search north for a few more kilometers before broadening his search track to the sides. Damn, too bad neither of the other analysts on the *Fairfax* was good enough to be reliable in his search. It didn't cross his mind that he was nearly the only Surface Radar Analyst rating in the entire Confederation Navy who was that good.

The susurration of sounds in the comm shack continued uninterrupted.

"Can you see anything, Hammer?" Bass murmured into his helmet radio.

"Enough," Schultz replied. A moment earlier the platoon's pointman had seen a footprint in the surface of a mud bar. It seemed to be pointing in the direction they were heading. The print was splayed, much wider across its front than a human footprint, and it was unshod. The leslies and some of the other amphibians had footprints as long as a human print and splayed wider at the front, but this one had a distinct heel, much like the mark left by a human foot. The amphibians that they didn't have to worry about didn't have heels. He had no doubt the print was left by a skink. Schultz shifted his pack

and pressed on. Until he stopped seeing signs, he was going
to assume the retreating skinks were still ahead of them.

The swampland had uncounted, uncountable channels.
Mostly, the water moved so sluggishly a casual observer
would think its motion was either simple eddies caused by
wind or by animal movement, or tidal movement. In only a
few places did the water slip and slide across its bed in the
manner of a stream, and even then it never built up enough
speed even to ripple. The contours of the swamp bed were
smooth, and outside the faster moving streams they gently
undulated, sometimes rising as much as a half meter above
the water, never receding more than chest deep to an average
man, not even where the water ran most true. Some of the
areas above water were just transient bars of mud. Some were
more permanent land colonized by vegetation that rooted and
held the mud together.

The swamp was filled with a cacophony of sounds. Schultz
cataloged them, fixed the sounds in his mind so he'd recognize them, then lost them to his consciousness so they
wouldn't distract him. He'd heard the skinks yelling during
the firefight and knew their guttural, barking voices weren't
like the booming or hissing of the native amphibians. He
heard the plopping of the bodies of the native amphibians in
the water and on the mud when they jumped, the splashing
when they scampered from a mud bar or islet into the water.
The skinks were bigger than the native amphibians, and their
sounds would be different. And the skinks were skilled, if fa-
natic, fighters—they'd generally move too quietly to plop and
splash. Those sounds could also safely be ignored. Once
those normal animal sounds were eliminated, the only sounds
left to Schultz's ears were the whispering of the breeze, the
small noises made by the Marines behind him, and the thrumming of the Dragons to the rear.

Schultz eyeballed everything. He switched back and forth
between his infra and light amplifier, necessary in the gloom
under the swamp's canopy. Every few minutes he stopped
to use his light-gatherer and magnifier screens together.

Although he found the occasional mark of the skinks' passage, he never saw or heard anything that told him how far ahead they were or where they were going. That was all right; he was in no hurry. Sooner or later the Marines would run them down. Then he, the Marines, would kill the skinks. No one attacks Marines and gets away with it, no one wipes out a human research station on an otherwise uninhabited world and lives to boast about it. Those were messages Schultz was determined to broadcast to the universe.

"What do you have, Hammer?" Bass asked when the double column stopped three and a half hours and several kilometers from where they'd begun.

"A bivouac," Schultz said. "Nobody's home."

"Wait one, I'm coming up." Then Bass added to Hyakowa, "Lander Five, establish a defensive perimeter." He toggled on his HUD to pinpoint the dot that showed Schultz's position and headed for him. He saw another dot also approaching the pointman.

Bass found Schultz and Sergeant Ratliff prone under a fringe of small, flimsy swamp trees at the edge of an islet. He lowered himself and bellied his way in between them. He immediately saw Schultz was right. Someone—or something—had bivuoacked there. The islet had a narrow fringe of growth at each end, but the fringes were new growth. More vegetation had been there, but over the surface of most of the islet it was beaten down to form a mat. None of the growth had yet had time to spring back up, if any of it still could, and no new growth was visible. He widened the area he scanned. The surrounding water was quiet. It looked like Schultz was right about nobody being at home. He glanced to his sides and saw that Schultz had deployed a motion detector.

"Lander Five," he said into the command circuit.

"Five, go, Six."

"Contact Skyhawk, I want a complete scan of this area." Hyakowa was closer to the Dragons and clear communications with the *Fairfax* than he was. He wasn't going to send anyone into the bivouac until he knew more; it could be a trap.

"Roger, Six." A few moments later Hyakowa came back on the command circuit. "Six, Skyhawk is scanning. Do you want verbal or data pack?"

"Data pack." Then he could go to one of the Dragons and see the situation while one of the analysts walked him through what he was looking at. It would give him far more information than a verbal report. "I'll be back," he said to Ratliff and Schultz, then slid back and headed for a Dragon. "See if you can spot any sign beyond here."

By the time he reached the Dragon, the data pack was being downloaded to its computer. He brought up the display. Bright dots showed the disposition of the Marines and the Dragons, a moving dot was the UAV. Fainter spots of red, some moving, some stationary, were scattered about.

"Talk to me," Bass said as soon as he put on the radio headset.

"You know which ones are you?"

"I know which dots are my people."

"Good. Wait a second, let me try this. I'm not used to talking to planetside troops." A slight smile quirked Bass's lips. He recognized the voice of SRA3 Hummfree and thought that evidently the sailor wasn't used to radio communications either—he didn't bother with proper procedures. There was a few seconds pause, then a circle appeared around some of the faint marks. "See that?"

"Northwest."

"Right. That's local amphibians, the big insect eaters. I've seen enough of them I can recognize their signatures. Same with these." The circle vanished and another appeared just west of the Marines. "This here," a different circle enclosed a vaguely visible pink smudge, "is a colony of smaller amphibians. Everything I can see is one or the other of them."

"Wait a minute! What's this?" A tiny red line, undulating near one of the Marines, was circled.

"I haven't seen it before. It's not one of them skinks, though. It's too big, and the heat signature's wrong."

Bass flicked on his HUD to see which Marine that line was near.

Goudanis. "One-three," Bass snapped into the all hands circuit, "heads up. Something big is approaching you from your right front." He glanced back at the data display. "It's less than thirty meters away."

"Six," Goudanis said, "it's got to be underwater. We're on land and I don't see anything."

"Keep an eye out for it. I'll let you know if it goes away."

"Roger, Six."

"Skyhawk, do you see anything else?" Bass asked into the satellite radio.

"Nope, that's everything. That big thing is the only thing I can't identify. Listen, if you find out what it is, would you let me know?"

Bass heard sudden shouting over the platoon radio, and the simultaneous crackle of blasters.

"Stand by," he told Hummfree. "We're about to find out." While he was speaking on the radio he signaled the Dragon commander to head for the fire, fast. The Dragon nearly hit its top speed covering the hundred meters to where first squad's third fire team was firing at something.

The Dragon roared onto the spit of mud Goudanis and Quick were on. The firing had stopped and Bass scrambled out of the Dragon before its rear ramp finished dropping.

"What happened?" he demanded, racing toward his men. Then, "My God," as he saw what they had killed.

A large, tubular creature lay part way out of the water, its rear half floating on the surface. Its body, banded like an earthworm, was nearly eight meters long, more than a meter across, and half that much high. A great maw with rows of spiked teeth filled its front end. Bristlelike whiskers ringed the maw. It had no eyes or visible hearing organs. Muscular contractions continued to ripple its rubbery hide. Great pocks were burned out of its front portion, where Goudanis and

Quick had shot it. The insides of the holes were seered black. Bass slowly stepped toward it and looked where one hole was bigger than the others. He guessed two blaster bolts had struck there. Deep inside the rear portion of the hole he saw the stump of a cord the color of milk turned bad. He took a couple more steps and looked at the forward edge of the hole, where he saw a corresponding cord stump. He looked back at the Marines who'd just faced this monster. Their faces were drawn. He was sure that if he could see their bodies they'd be quaking.

"When did it die?" he asked.

Goudanis nodded toward the hole Bass had just examined. "When we hit it there."

"Looks like it's got a notochord. You were lucky to hit it deep enough to sever it. That's probably what stopped it."

The second Dragon arrived and Dr. Bynum climbed out. *"Mon Dieu,"* she whispered when she saw the beast. In a second she was over her shock and ordering her people to take measurements and samples. While they rushed to do her bidding, she turned to Bass.

"Did we have any warning about this, Charlie? I don't remember anything about a creature like this in the reports we read."

Bass shook his head. "I didn't see anything either. Maybe the exploratory mission didn't get into the right parts of the swamp to find it. Big predators aren't common anywhere, and this is certainly a big predator."

Bynum looked at the corpse and blinked a few times. "Well, we'll get enough samples to fit it into Waygone's biota, if not its ecology."

Bass snorted. "I'd say its place in the ecology is top of the food chain."

She nodded. "I imagine you're right. Look at those teeth! They could shred a man with one bite."

The immediate danger past, Bass turned his attention back to the platoon and their current mission. "Listen up," he said into his all-hands circuit. "If there are any skinks in the area who didn't know we're here, they know now. Be alert for them. Also watch for really big, ah, worms." He switched to the squad leaders circuit. "String-of-pearls didn't see anything else it couldn't identify. No point in waiting any longer, we're going to check out the bivouac area. Rabbit, don't move until I get to you." He reboarded the Dragon and gave Humm-free information on what the odd signal was while he rode to the islet with the beaten down vegetation.

"Find anything?" he asked when he rejoined Ratliff and Schultz.

"Found a footprint on the next island," Schultz said. "Goes north."

"All right, we'll follow it. But first let's check this bivouac, see if we can find anything."

"How are we going to check for booby traps?" Ratliff asked.

"The skinks don't seem to use explosives or large vehicles. I'll run a Dragon over it. Its weight will either set off any antipersonnel traps or disable them."

"I like it," Ratliff said.

Bass flicked to the Dragon circuit to give the order. Before he could tell the Dragon commander what he wanted, he received a message.

"Skyhawk wants to talk to the Actual. Sounds important."

Bass reboarded the vehicle. "Lander Six Actual. Go, Skyhawk."

"Lander Six, Lima Zulu is under attack," said the voice of the starship's communications officer. "Return to Lima Zulu with all possible speed. Over."

"Roger that, Skyhawk. Any details? Over."

"Negative details, Lander. Are you on the move yet? Over."

"Third platoon, mount up," Bass ordered into the all-hands circuit. He was no longer paying attention to the *Fairfax*'s communications officer; he had a platoon to gather together and move out. If the ship was passing on any useful information, Dupont or the Dragon commander would let him know.

He was disappointed about not being able to examine the bivouac; it might have information they'd need. But getting back to the knob was more immediately important.

It took the platoon about four minutes to regroup and get aboard the two Dragons. What they didn't have was much time for Bass to make plans for what to do when they got back to the landing zone. Hell, he thought, I have no idea of what's going on, so what kind of plans can I make? Bass wasn't concerned that they'd run into an ambush along the way. As far as he knew, the skinks didn't have any explosive weapons that could damage the Dragons. The most dangerous time would be when they stopped to dismount the Marines. If any skinks were in the right place, they could do serious damage. They'd have to dismount outside the LZ and approach it on foot. But from what direction? He needed information badly.

"Raise the Dragons at the LZ," he ordered the Dragon commander.

It took a moment, but finally the commander said, "Got 'em." He handed the mike to Bass.

"Dragon Three, what's your situation?" Bass asked.

"I have you on my monitor and will link up in less than thirty seconds."

"Say again? You aren't at the Lima Zulu?"

"Negative. We were ordered to find you and link up."

"What's going on?" Just then Dragons Three and Four came into view in the Dragon's artificial light monitor. Gunny Bass's jaw clenched at the sight. Parts of the Dragons' armor plating were slagged and he saw a gaping hole in its flank. Suddenly he was glad he hadn't had the time to run one of his Dragons across the bivouac.

"I have the casualties and the medical team aboard," the Dragon Three commander said. "The pirates are fighting the skinks."

"How many?"

"I'm not sure. I think Lieutenant Snodgrass and three or

four pirates were still alive and fighting when the lieutenant ordered us to find you."

"Skinks?" Bass shouted. "I mean, how many skinks?"

"I don't know. Too many."

Bass swore under his breath. For the first time on this mission he wished they had Marine Dragons, or at least Marine crews. A Marine could tell him how many skinks were attacking. Maybe he was asking too much to expect a sailor to know that.

"What direction are they attacking from?"

"They're all over the place."

Again Bass swore. That sailor wasn't giving him anything he could use. They were going in blind.

"Keep moving," he ordered the driver of his Dragon.

CHAPTER
TWENTY-SEVEN

Lieutenant Argal Snodgrass spent the hours waiting for the arrival of the Essay strutting about with an air of importance and self-confidence he did not really feel. At first light, when the third platoon had pulled out to follow the trail of the retreating skinks, he'd watched their progress with what was, for him, an unusual degree of trepidation. He did not feel the soaring sense of independence he thought he would as he watched the Marines disappear into the fern trees, because it had slowly dawned on him that truly he was on his own.

The Dragon in which the corpsmen tended the casualties sat with its ramp down, and another Dragon sat not far away. The pirates had found a clump of ferns nearby that gave enough shade to protect them from the intense sunlight, and they spent the hours there, talking among themselves in low voices.

Snodgrass whiled away the morning slogging around the clearing, pretending to watch the surrounding forest. The two corpsmen and the crewmen in the closer Dragon offered him only cold and begrudging awareness when he climbed the ramp and attempted to converse with them. And whenever he approached the pirate group, they suddenly stopped talking, and resumed only when he was out of earshot. And he did not like it at all, the way that man, Lowboy, leered at him. He thought the ridiculous little man was probably homosexual.

Thinking of ridiculous little men made Snodgrass reflect momentarily on some of the things he'd done since they'd been on Waygone, especially when he mistook the pirate

Rhys for Dr. Morgan. His face still burned at the thought. That Bass had later openly laughed in his face over the incident did nothing for his self-confidence.

His unusually self-critical train of thought was interrupted by the Dragon commander's announcement that the Essay was at last inbound.

Hospitalman First Class Larry Horner checked Clarke's stasis pod for the umpteenth time. Respiration, blood pressure, pulse, all were normal. The stasis devices would keep the wounded men in a state of deep suspended animation until they could be transported to the *Fairfax*'s sickbay, or until they reached port, if Dr. Bynum couldn't repair the damage. He laughed, remembering the story, possibly apocryphal, of the corpsman who'd slept in a stasis pod when off duty. Over the years, his buddies noticed he wasn't aging as quickly as they were. In the end he was court-martialed for "misuse of government property," but the ten years he'd added to his life made the fine and loss of rank worth it.

He glanced at the ramp and thought about raising it. It was getting hot in the passenger compartment, but since the Essay was on its way, he decided not to. Lieutenant Snodgrass and his pirates would have to come aboard, and that would only mean lowering the thing again in a few minutes anyway.

On the opposite side of the bay, HM2 Tom Hardesty fiddled with the settings on Dornhofer's pod. "Prettiest girl I ever seen, was smoking thule in my latrine," he chanted softly. His mind was light-years away, where cold beer and warm lips waited for him in a cozy bar in Duma City on Bulon, the *Fairfax*'s home port. "When we get back to home port, Larry, I'm gonna—"

"Danger! Danger!" a tiny voice shrilled.

Automatically, Horner drew his side arm and whirled toward the ramp, just as a skink charged up and into the compartment. Horner fired from the hip without aiming. The bolt struck the skink directly on its snout. The creature screamed and then flashed into vapor.

Owen hopped up and down on his ration box shrieking "Woooo! Woooo!" his appendages flapping and his eye stalks bobbing up and down. In the space of ten seconds he flashed through the entire spectrum of visible colors, but neither man saw it. Nor did either man realize at the time that Owen had shouted the warning.

"Close the ramp! Close the fucking ramp!" Horner screamed before realizing the crew couldn't hear him. "Tom, cover me!" he shouted as he lunged for the emergency control that would raise it. Tom was already down on one knee, the muzzle of his hand-blaster aimed over the ramp. Horner hesitated to mash the button. No, gotta get the lieutenant on board, his mind screamed. He punched into the onboard intercom system instead. "Get the lieutenant aboard!" he screamed at the Dragon commander. The gunner began acquiring targets and firing at them. The Dragon shook with the crackling of the cannon.

Hardesty fired his handgun.

Lieutenant Snodgrass didn't know what made him turn around, but when he did he screamed in terror. Dozens of skinks had crept out of the fernlike forest and they all seemed to be charging directly at him! They were running upright, their bodies slick with mud, some with long metal tubes clutched in their forearms and others holding nozzles attached to devices strapped to their backs. He could clearly see their slender fingers clutching the tubes and nozzles he guessed were the acid-throwing devices that dissolved human flesh. It seemed every one of them was pointed directly at him.

The farther Dragon didn't appear to be in danger, for now. But some of the skinks had managed to creep up to the nearest Dragon unnoticed and were directing streams of acid on its armor plate. The liquid sizzled on and through the outer plating, and Snodgrass realized that if the machine did not pull out of range quickly, the corrosive acid would eventually eat through. Fortunately, the lowered ramp faced away from the direction of attack.

Without thinking about it, Snodgrass thumbed his throat mike and screamed, "Dragon! Close the ramp!"

"Lieutenant, get on board!" the Dragon commander screamed back. The petty officer's voice was so loud in Snodgrass's helmet it hurt his ears.

"No time! Close the ramp and get out of here!" the lieutenant said nervously. "They're eating through your armor plate! Get out. Get out!" For the first time in his life Argal Snodgrass was thinking of someone else first. He knew he could never reach the temporary safety of the Dragon, and if it did not get away immediately, the eight men inside would be lost.

"We'll cover you!" the Dragon commander said as his gunners directed enfilading fire into the mass of advancing skinks. Bright flashes marked hits all along their line, but there were too many of them. And the skinks attacking both Dragons now were so close, the gunners couldn't depress the barrels of their cannons fast enough. The second Dragon was fully alert now, but could not fire without hitting the other Dragon. "Essay's ten minutes out!" the commander said.

Snodgrass fingered his throat mike again, changing channels. "Essay pilot, this is Lieutenant Snodgrass. Abort the landing. I say again, abort the landing. This LZ is hot. We are under attack. Do you hear me?"

Later the Essay pilot swore he didn't believe the Lieutenant at first because his voice was so calm. "Ah, please say again your message," the pilot responded laconically.

"Abort the landing!" Snodgrass screamed.

"Ah, roger that, Lieutenant, we are aborting the landing," the pilot replied.

Snodgrass switched back to the Dragons' channel. "Both of you, get out of here. Go after the gunny. We will draw the skinks off. Move, move, *move*!" With that he fired at one of the skinks spraying the closer Dragon, and was gratified to see it flare up into vapor. It was the first time the lieutenant had ever fired a weapon in combat.

Meanwhile, Snodgrass had quickly been backing toward a deep depression in the earth about thirty meters from the nearer Dragon. His intention was to take cover there and hold off the skinks from that position. He had no idea where he'd gotten that idea from or what made him act on it.

"The Dragons are leaving! They're leaving us!" a pirate screamed hysterically.

From just over Snodgrass's shoulder someone fired a blaster. The shooter was taking careful aim. *Crack, crack, crack!* Three more skinks evaporated. It was Rhys. He really was too stupid to feel fear.

"Come back," Lowboy screamed at the Dragons. "Come back, the Essay is coming! The Essay is coming!"

"No, it isn't," Snodgrass said as he joined the small group of desperate and quivering men. "I canceled the landing. The Dragons are going after Bass. We had to get the wounded—"

With a sickening *crack!* Lowboy smashed his blaster's butt on the bridge of the lieutenant's nose. Blood flew everywhere as Snodgrass collapsed to the ground, his helmet flying off his head and bouncing out of reach; now they were without any way to call for help. The skinks, momentarily disorganized by the departing Dragons' cannons and Rhys's accurate marksmanship, milled about. Screaming incoherently, Lowboy grabbed Snodgrass by the collar and started dragging him toward where the Dragons had been—and toward the skinks. "Run! Run!" he screamed, dragging Snodgrass through the mud facedown.

A stream of acid arced out and hit the pirate they called Dufus directly in the groin, splashing onto his legs and torso. He twisted about wildly, screaming hysterically as the substance instantly ate through his clothes and began dissolving his flesh. Momentarily distracted, Lowboy dropped Snodgrass.

The cold slime had revived the lieutenant somewhat. He rolled over on his back, drew his hand-blaster and pulled the trigger. The little pirate exploded in a bright flash, blood, bone fragments, and guts spraying everywhere. Snodgrass staggered to his feet, a foot of Lowboy's intestines dangling obscenely over one shoulder. He brushed the filthy innards away and waved his gun at the remaining pirates. "Back! Back to the hollow! Now, goddamnit, do it now!" he croaked through his broken nose. Rhys was the first to turn and run for the hollow, and the others followed. Snodgrass stumbled along behind them.

They piled into the depression, gasping and choking. It was about a meter deep, filled with slimy mud and water. Nobody objected. They wallowed gratefully in the muck and struck their heads cautiously up over the edge.

"Check your weapons," Snodgrass said firmly. The whole front of his face throbbed with pain and the exertion of the run for cover. He daubed a handful of cool mud over his broken nose and the pain subsided a bit.

"Four against twenty." Rhys grinned. "I've got maybe twenty bolts left in my piece."

"Six for me," Labaya gasped.

"I'm out," Callendar said, tossing his weapon into the mud. He reached down into a boot and took out a knife. Its long steel blade glinted in the sunlight.

"I have a dozen left," Snodgrass said. "That's thirty-eight shots against twenty, twenty-five skinks. We've got to make every shot count. We can't let them get close enough to douse us with those acid guns."

"Here they come!" Rhys shouted. He braced himself on the edge of the swale and, holding the butt of his old blaster firmly into his shoulder, began squeezing off shots. The others took careful aim and fired slowly and methodically. Callendar, crouched in the muddy bottom of the depression, took out a whetstone and began honing his knife.

The skinks twisted and dodged as they rushed forward, and only four flashed into oblivion. But when their ragged line came within range of the humans and some stopped to discharge their own weapons, their aim was bad. Apparently, charging across the open space while taking fire from the Dragons and the men in the swale had unnerved them. But some of the acid splashed into the swale. Several drops spattered the left side of Snodgrass's face, one tiny globule burning off his earlobe and another sizzling into his cheek. The pain was almost unbearable, but he reached down and smeared mud onto the wounds.

The four men crouched in their hole, breathing heavily, clutching their weapons. Rhys examined his left hand, where a drop of acid had burned all the way through—he could actually see through it. He screamed and plunged the hand into the mud and held it there. "That's better," he sighed. He held up the mud-caked hand and flexed his fingers. "Look, it still works!"

The surviving skinks dropped into a prone position and tried to drop their shots into the depression. "Jesus, they fight like men!" Rhys cursed. He popped up and flashed a skink who had managed to crawl within a few meters of their position. "They're closing in on us!" he screamed, his voice a falsetto.

"On three we stand up and give them a volley," Snodgrass shouted. "Try for the nearest ones."

The three desperate men stood as one and squeezed off several shots. Some skinks flashed, but a stream of acid sprayed directly into Labaya's eyes. He screamed horribly and staggered backward. The others watched as the whole front of his face began to dissolve. His screams rose to a piercing high-pitched wail.

"I've seen this once too often," Callendar said, and calmly buried his knife in Labaya's heart. He reached down and picked up the dead man's pistol. "Two bolts left," he said matter-of-factly.

"You've got two shots, Rhys?" Snodgrass asked.

"Three," he answered disgustedly.

"And I've got—one." Snodgrass couldn't believe the reading on his power pack. "I've got one shot left! How'd that happen? Jesus, we've got six bolts left among the three of us."

"Shit happens, Lieutenant. When I was in the infantry—"

"You were in the infantry, Callendar?" Snodgrass said incredulously.

"Yeah. I was a sergeant squad leader. Anyway, green troops always lay down too much fire. No use crying about it now."

"Hey! They're moving back!" Rhys announced. Sure enough, the nine remaining skinks were crawling rapidly. When they reached a spot about fifty meters away, they stood up.

"I could hit one from here with this hand-blaster," Callendar said.

"We can't afford to waste the shot," Rhys reminded him.

"Yeah, and they know it," Snodgrass observed. "They're just standing there. What's up?"

"Lieutenant, I think they're waiting for someone," Callendar answered.

"Who?"

Callendar shrugged. "Their officer."

Snodgrass sighed and laid his head down on the lip of the depression. "The longer they wait to finish us off, the better chance we've got that Bass'll come for us or maybe the Dragons will come back and fry them. Jesus, if I ever see that Gunny again I'll kiss him."

Callendar snorted. "I'll kiss his ass and give you twenty minutes to draw a crowd."

"You know, I can see your teeth through that hole in your cheek, Lieutenant," Rhys observed. Gingerly, Snodgrass placed a forefinger in the hole. Sure enough, he could feel his gums through the hole.

"I wonder why it doesn't hurt," he said.

"I don't know," Rhys answered. "But I had this professor once—"

"What? You went to *college*?" Snodgrass exclaimed.

"Yeah. I got a master of arts in English lit," he said offhandedly.

"It was never obvious," Snodgrass said.

"If you're going to be a pirate, you don't get far running around quoting Shakespeare."

The skinks were still milling around. The sun beat down mercilessly, and Snodgrass was suddenly aware of how thirsty he'd become. But the conversation was steadying his nerves. All thought of fame and promotion had evaporated from the lieutenant's mind now. In a few moments the skinks would advance again and he would die. He reached down to remove the knife from Labaya's boot and placed it on the rim of the hollow, where he could reach it easily. He realized then that he wasn't afraid of the skinks anymore.

"Where the hell did they all come from?" Rhys asked no one in particular. "I thought the Marines greased almost the whole bunch the other night, and they're chasing the only survivors." Snodgrass could only shrug.

"Probably left over from the attacking force, and now the Marines are between them and home base," Callendar said. The minutes dragged by slowly. The skinks continued to mill around just within pistol range, but the men held their precious fire.

"So why did you guys become pirates?" Snodgrass asked.

"Same reason you become a navy officer: I was stupid, needed money, and love guns," Callendar said with a chuckle.

Snodgrass grinned back at him. "I become—became a navy officer because I wanted to see the universe and be famous." The other two laughed. "How about you, Rhys?"

"Me? Oh, I just sort of fell into the trade, you might say. Took a job with a school system on one of the newer worlds—doesn't matter which one—I was gonna prey on my girl students while writing my dissertation."

"Dissertation? On what topic," Snodgrass asked.

" 'The Sunshine Motif in the Lieder of John Denver.' *Very* hot topic."

"The classics!" Snodgrass cried.

"I even had some interest from a publisher. But on the way in-system our ship was taken. I got friendly with my captors and opted to stay with them when the exchange was made. Then I just drifted around several systems for a while, earning a reputation, you might say, and wound up with Scanlon.

"How about you, Lieutenant? I had you figured for a prize navy asshole, a real prima donna. You sure acted the part convincingly enough there for a while. Now you pull this Medal of Heroism shit. And you fried that bastard Lowboy." Briefly he told Snodgrass what Lowboy had planned.

"Would you have gone along with that plan?" Snodgrass asked.

Rhys shrugged. "Yeah. I *am* a pirate, you know."

"Well, it never would've worked. Your ship wasn't in orbit when we got here. If you'd taken the Essay, you'd only have cruised around the planet a few times before the *Fairfax* would've taken you."

"How?" Callendar asked.

"I'd have told them to," Snodgrass answered firmly. "Gunny Bass would've figured out a way to get a boarding party onto the Essay." There would be no more criticism of Gunnery Sergeant Bass from him.

"Yeah, I guess that's the new you, huh?" Rhys replied. "What gives with you? How'd you grow up so suddenly?"

"I really don't know," Snodgrass answered, surprised, now that he considered it. "I—I just figured the wounded had to be protected. I don't know." He shrugged.

"Hamlet," Rhys answered with conviction. "You're just like Hamlet. When he stopped to think things through, he always screwed them up, but when the chips were down he—"

"Uh-oh, college boys, somebody's coming," Callendar warned.

"—was a man of action," Rhys finished. "Just stop thinking, Lieutenant, and you'll be okay. Thinking never did anybody any—Jesu, what in hell is *that*?" They all stared at the spectacle in front of them.

From out of the tree ferns on the far side of the clearing an extraordinary figure emerged, a skink, but it walked erect and purposefully, just like a man. In one hand he carried a long rod, obviously an acid gun of some kind, but he swung it rapidly back and forth as he walked, as if he were a swordsman testing the balance of his blade.

The other skinks, who had been grunting and hissing among themselves, now fell silent. The officer skink gestured with his weapon, and the nine surviving attackers fell into a straight line. The men could clearly hear his sibilant hissing and grunting as he addressed his troops.

"Ten skinks, and we got six shots among us," Callendar whispered. "Better make every shot count, and then . . ." he patted the knife at his belt. "Hey!" he said suddenly, "look at that officer. He's just waving his acid gun around. You know what? I bet they're as low on ammo as we are! Sure! They used up most of their basic load and they can't resupply because Bass has cut them off from their base. Hey, maybe we've got a chance after all."

"What if it comes down to hand-to-hand?" Snodgrass asked. "Some of those skinks are pretty big."

"Fight dirty, then," Callendar responded.

"Go for their eyes," Rhys advised. He turned to Snodgrass and put out his hand. "You got my vote, Lieutenant. We sure have put up one hell of a fight. Been nice knowin' ya." They shook.

"Let them get almost up to us, and then get out of this hole and in among them," Callendar advised. "That way they won't be able to use their guns without hitting another skink."

The officer skink shouted something. It sounded to the men like *"Bungee!"* He repeated the word three times, and the nine skinks shouted, *"Bungee! Bungee! Bungee!"* The officer took his place in front of the line, raised his gun over his head, and they charged.

"He's mine," Rhys whispered.

"You take the right of the line, Lieutenant, and I'll take the left," Callendar shouted.

The skinks came at them quickly, covering half the distance in only a few seconds. The three held their fire to be absolutely sure of their shots. At thirty meters they fired their last bolts. The officer skink disappeared in a flash. So did five others. The remaining four came on. They did not fire their weapons but held them like spears.

"They *are* out of ammo!" Snodgrass said in amazement.

"Knives!" Callendar shouted, throwing his blaster down. With a scream of triumph he drew his wicked blade and jumped out of the hole. *"Aarrggh!"* he screamed and ran at the nearest skink. Two skinks jumped on him, and the three fell into the mud in a tangle of arms and legs, the skinks grunting and hissing and Callendar screaming and cursing. He sliced open one skink with a vicious slash of his blade, but the other pinned the pirate under its powerful legs and began smashing its empty weapon into his face.

Rhys thrust with his knife at a huge advancing skink. Though twice his size and grunting with the effort of running, the skink seemed light and agile on its feet. It parried Rhys's knife thrust and rammed the point of its spear deep into the center of Rhys's chest. Rhys staggered back, taking the embedded weapon with him. He stared down at it in surprise. The skink closed in, its arms held open to grab the dying man in one final deadly embrace. Rhys lurched forward, his knife thrust out in his right hand as he tried to pull the spear out of his chest with the other. They collided with an audible *thud*, and the knife buried itself in the skink's midsection. The heavier skink impelled Rhys backward. Rhys thrust desperately with his legs to stay upright and with all his remaining strength drove the knife downward, slicing the skink's belly wide open. Reeking tendrils spilled out in heaps. The skink gurgled and hissed and thrashed about wildly before dying.

Rhys crawled out from under the mess and staggered to his feet, swaying drunkenly, just managing to keep his balance. With his left hand he continued trying to pull the weapon out of his chest. No good. He was too weak. He dropped his left hand to his side and staggered over to where the other skink was pounding Callendar's head into mush. With one last supreme burst of effort, Rhys plunged his own knife to the hilt into the thing's back and fell heavily to the ground. Hissing and snorting violently, the skink rose to its feet to reach around and pull out the knife, but a dark brown fluid gushed out of its mouth, it gave up a snorelike groan, then fell on its side.

Breathing heavily, completely oblivious to the fight going on around him, Snodgrass had dropped his blaster and drawn his knife. Now he concentrated on the skink weaving and bobbing just out of his reach. It too breathed in gasps, and the lieutenant could smell its fetid breath. They circled one another warily. Snodgrass was finding it difficult to keep his footing in the slick mud as the skink danced back and forth lightly on its splayed toes. Clearly, mud was its element.

Suddenly, it dashed forward and rammed at the lieutenant with its weapon. Snodgrass sidestepped and sliced at the thing's neck. His blade struck flesh, and blood, surprisingly-red, spurted from one side. The skink staggered and dropped its weapon, clasping both hands to the wound in the side of its neck. Seizing the advantage, Snodgrass stepped in and plunged his knife into the creature's side, once, twice, a third time. But the knife stuck in the skink as it tried to whirl away from the attack, leaving Snodgrass unarmed. He jumped out of its way as the thing staggered about in the bloodstained mud, hissing and gurgling. Finally it collapsed and lay still.

For years—his whole life till then—Argal Snodgrass had been an arrogant, snot-nosed punk, and he had just taken it all out on this alien. In those brief moments of desperation, the old Snodgrass had evaporated like a blasted skink.

He stood, panting heavily, perspiration streaming off of him, and looked down on his vanquished attacker. Wearily, he stumbled over and checked Rhys and Callendar. They were both dead, as were the four skinks.

Out of the corner of his eye Snodgrass caught a glimpse of movement. A skink appeared from among the ferns on the opposite side of the clearing, from the same spot the attack had been mounted. Snodgrass gasped—the skink was carrying a blaster.

Purposefully, the skink walked toward Snodgrass, who backed off, wondering if there was a way he could charge the skink, dodging the bolts it was sure to fire at him any second. The skink stopped ten meters from the site of the hand-to-hand fighting and deliberately pointed the blaster at one of the skink corpses. The corpse flared up. Methodically, ignoring the human, the skink switched aim and flamed another of the corpses.

Snodgrass watched in disbelief as the skink flamed all of the dead skinks, then turned the blaster on itself and vaporized.

The adrenaline that had held him keyed up throughout the fight suddenly drained out of him and, totally exhausted, he collapsed unconscious.

Argal Snodgrass floated up, up, up. He felt no pain. He was wrapped in a wonderful white cloud of cotton. He wanted to stay there forever, forever. No more goddamn fitness reports to worry about, no more smirking subordinates, no more supercilious superior officers, no more of the chickenshit he once thought was so important. If this is death, he thought, where have you been all my life?

Suddenly, consciousness came back to him like a huge fist in the face. He was back on Society 437 and he hurt everywhere, everywhere. He gasped and groaned. He was being held up by two Marines. A voice said, "He's coming to." Another said, "It's about time; he's not hurt." The voices hurt his head. In front of him stood a blurry figure. He blinked. It was Bass, the remnant of a Clinton stuck in one corner of his mouth.

Hands on his hips, Bass leaned close to the lieutenant's smashed nose and grinned. "Horatio, I don't know how the hell you did it, but sure looks to me like you held this bridge."

CHAPTER
TWENTY-EIGHT

"No friendly casualties except the pirates—all of them are dead," Bass reported to Commander Tuit a few minutes later, thinking only of the pirates who'd fought alongside Snodgrass. "The medical team is okay." He glanced at Dr. Bynum for confirmation and she nodded. "The previous casualties are stable. No friendly casualties other than the pirates. I think it's safe to land the Essay now and get the wounded and the med people up to you."

"What about you, Lander?" Tuit wanted to know. He thought the Marines should lift off as well and they should all get out of there. Leave the string-of-pearls in place so it could gather information during the time it would take the Confederation to mount a full-scale expedition to Society 437. He thought one platoon of Marines simply wasn't enough to properly handle the situation. The Marines were tough, but they already had one dead and four wounded, and three of the casualties were seriously injured.

"We've got to find those things and deal with them," Bass said.

"They can wait, Gunnery Sergeant. They're probably stranded here. The Confederation Navy can mount another operation to come and capture them."

"Sir, I don't think they're stranded. I think they were left behind deliberately to attack and kill whoever came to investigate what happened to the science mission."

There was a pause. Tuit had spent more time than Bass studying the satellite data that showed the landing of the alien ship, or shuttle, whatever it was, and then its return to whatever nebulous place it had come from. Damn those scientists! Why hadn't they had anything looking outward? There was no information on where the alien ship had come from or where it went. The little information they had told Tuit that Bass was probably right. The skinks were a defense garrison, left to kill whoever came after the BHHEI mission. Eventually, he suspected, more of the murderous aliens would come to Waygone and reinforce the garrison. If the Marines found and destroyed the garrison, it might discourage the aliens in the future, convince them that perhaps it would be better to talk.

"All right, Commander Ground Force, you have my go-ahead to find the aliens' base of operations and destroy it. Try to take prisoners."

"Aye aye, sir." Bass almost smiled.

They waited long enough for the Essay to complete its orbit and touch down. Once the casualties were safely off-world and the Marines had a chance to snatch an hour's worth of badly needed sleep, they set out again. Bass had tried to send Dr. Bynum and her medical team back to the *Fairfax*, but she wasn't having any of that.

"Gunnery Sergeant," she said levelly and with a stern face, "don't make me pull rank on you."

"Doctor," Bass said just as levelly, "you can't. As ground forces commander, I outrank you no matter what our rank insignia say." But he smiled as he said it.

"Charlie," Dr. Bynum said, returning his smile, "I somehow don't think you're the kind of man who'd manhandle a woman to make her do something she didn't want to do."

Bass dropped his smile. "Lidi, you might be surprised what I'd do to a woman if it meant saving her life."

They stared at each other for a long moment.

"Charlie, you or your Marines might—probably will—need me when you find the skinks. And speaking as a scientist, if I can get my hands on one, we can learn a lot about them. If I'm not with you, I don't believe I'll get that chance."

"I appreciate your position, Lidi. Everything you just said is true. But today will probably be too dangerous for a woman. Besides, I'm keeping two of your corpsmen, they can take care of any casualties. And if they can save one of the skinks from getting slaughtered, well, they can keep him."

"Not good enough, Charlie Bass. Besides, you're letting that Minnie come with you."

Bass shrugged. "She's a civilian, I don't have any jurisdiction over her."

"Bullshit, Charlie. You have jurisdiction over anybody on this planet you want to. And she's a pirate, you already put her under arrest. She belongs to you just the same as that Baccacio, or Cameron, or whatever name you want to call him."

"Well, yeah, but—"

"No 'Well, yeah, but,' Charlie Bass. I'm going with you and that's final."

After that the argument petered out.

Bass had everybody mount up on the Dragons and they headed into the swamp. They rode as far as the day before, then the Marines dismounted and resumed wading. They didn't take time to check the bivouac.

Schultz led the platoon ever deeper into the swamp. When he could, he trod across dry ground covered with Waygone's ubiquitous springy ground cover or along the firm mud bars that stood above the water. When there wasn't ground above water, he led them through shallows that were ankle, knee, thigh, sometimes chest deep. Part of his attention was divided between visual scouting of where to go next and feeling with his feet to make sure he had firm footing. The rest of his attention was focused on seeking signs of skink passage and watching for danger. He ignored the recognized signs of native fauna. His pathfinding usually worked. He saw enough sign of skinks to be confident the Marines were on the right trail, and he never saw danger, including any more of the big worms. The occasional surveillance reports from the *Fairfax* agreed with Schultz's decisions.

The swamp was redolent with odors emitted by rotting vegetation. The Marines coughed from time to time because of the irritation the gases caused in their noses and throats. The members of the medical team, most of whom were still unused to the exertion, coughed more. Everywhere they stepped, their feet squelched, sloshed, or splashed. The mating and territorial croaks of swamp amphibians sent shivers up many spines and helped keep everyone alert.

"Maybe the swamp critters know there are things too tough for even them," Claypoole replied when MacIlargie wondered aloud why they never ran into more of the large carnivores.

Kerr gave no sign of having overheard the byplay, but he approved of MacIlargie's caution and Claypoole's confidence.

In early afternoon Bass decided to rest the platoon and told Schultz to find a defendable elevated spot. Nearly a half hour later, still looking for and occasionally finding skink spoor, Schultz stopped on one of two adjacent hummocks.

"I need to set up an oxygen tent," Dr. Bynum gasped when the platoon stopped near dusk. "These gases, it's too hard to breathe, everyone's respiratory system is getting too irritated." She paused frequently, since talking was hard in the miasma of the swamp. "They need, we all need, some relief."

Bass grunted. There were twenty-six Marines left in the platoon. The medical team was another four, including the doctor. "How much relief can we get?" he asked. Baccacio and Minnie made thirty-two people in the group.

She shrugged. "Set the tent up now. Make it big enough to accommodate four people at a time. Everybody can get an hour inside overnight. It'll help a little."

Bass nodded. "Set it up." He heard coughing from the area the medical team was in. "Your people use it first." He went to check the defensive positions Hyakowa and the squad leaders had established.

"Put out motion detectors," he ordered once he was satisfied with the positions his Marines were in. "If anything we can't see comes by, flame it." Then he called for an NCO meeting. "Schultz too," he added.

While Staff Sergeant Hyakowa was gathering the squad and fire team leaders toward the platoon command post, Bass updated his tactical map and prepared it for transmission to the NCOs' HUD displays.

"Here's the latest report from the *Fairfax County*," he said when the NCOs joined him. He didn't acknowledge Baccacio, who had joined the meeting without invitation. He transmitted the map to his NCOs. It showed their position at the bottom and continued for a couple of kilometers to the north. "All trace of the skinks disappears from the string-of-pearls' sensors about three and a half klicks from where we are." An area a bit more than an acre in size near the north edge of the map was suddenly rimmed in red. "That surveillance tech they've got up there, Hummfree, thinks the skinks went to ground."

The men ate their rations while they talked and studied the HUD. "What's the terrain like there?" Ratliff asked.

"Thought you'd never ask," Bass said. He made an adjustment and the red-rimmed area enlarged to fill the entire display. A pond took up about half its area, and the rest appeared to be tiny islands, or peninsulas separating channels of sluggishly moving water. Large vegetation, some resembling mangroves, grew along the edge of the pond. "That pond isn't deeper than two meters anywhere. Hummfree checked the filed reports of the mission's xenogeologists. He says there should be caves along the bank."

"They're in caves?" Bladon asked.

Bass shrugged. "Maybe. Maybe they got under those trees and managed to disappear so completely not even Hummfree could spot them; Hummfree doesn't think so."

"That means we try to find the caves and go in them," Hyakowa said.

Corporal Linsman grimaced. Goudanis shook his head but

didn't say anything. Pasquin shivered. Kerr kept his face blank. Chan simply nodded—he was claustrophobic and had fought inside a cave before, but wasn't going to show how much the prospect frightened him.

"We all need a bath," Schultz grumbled.

"If I hear anything new on detected movement," Bass said, "I'll tell you. In the meanwhile, you all know about the oxygen tent?" The squad and fire team leaders nodded. "Set up your rotations for that, along with a twenty-five percent watch. If there are no questions, do it."

The NCOs glanced at each other, but no one raised a question. They returned to their men. Hyakowa took Baccacio aside and drew a map in the mud for him.

Everyone was still coughing at daybreak, but not quite as much as before.

"I guess your oxygen tent did some good, Lidi," Bass said.

Dr. Bynum's smile was a bit strained. "It seems to have, yes. Or maybe we're simply adjusting to the stench."

Bass chuckled. "That happens. People can get used to anything that doesn't kill them right away."

She curled a lip at him.

"How soon will your people be ready to move out?"

She looked about at the preparations. "About ten more minutes. Assuming everybody already ate when they were supposed to instead of waiting."

"Anybody who didn't eat will have to eat on the way or go hungry." He looked at the sky through the treetops, cloudless patches brightening with the dawn. "We should already be on the move."

"Now, now, Charlie, these are sailors, not Marines. They aren't used to this."

"Not being used to it won't keep them from getting killed."

A quick glance told her he was being neither sarcastic nor facetious, but deadly—an appropriate word choice, she thought—serious.

"They'll be ready to move out in less than ten minutes."

"Good." He walked away to check on the Marines.

Schultz could have led the platoon to the pond quickly, but he moved as slowly as he had before the break. He knew this was exactly the kind of situation where they were in danger of being ambushed—if he were leading the skinks, he'd set up an ambush on their back trail, at the approach to their encampment. So it was nearly an hour before he stopped, hidden in foliage, at the edge of the pond. He used all of his visual screens and a motion detector to probe the area while he waited for Bass to come to him. The pond, more than half an acre in size, was longer east-west than it was north-south. Part of the north and most of the east sides were rimmed with the mangrovelike trees, and most of the rest had lower growth. Several waterways led into it.

"Anything?" Bass whispered when he eased into position next to Schultz.

Schultz shook his head.

"The string-of-pearls hasn't detected any movement leading from here," Bass said. "If they went to ground, this is where they must be."

Schultz spat into the pond. The plop sounded just like one of the small amphibians jumping into the water. "We don't have echo locators," he said.

Bass nodded. Nobody had anticipated they'd have to search for caves, so the echo locators used to detect underground cavities weren't included in the *Fairfax*'s equipment.

"We do it the old-fashioned way," Bass said.

Schutlz spat again and began stripping off his equipment.

"Don't go in the water until I tell you to."

Schultz grunted assent.

Bass and Hyakowa positioned the platoon. Sergeant Bladon with one fire team and one gun team was sent to the northeast, beyond the mangrove islands, to block a possible skink withdrawal. Most of the rest of the platoon went to the west and southwest, where they could fire across and into the front of the mangrovelike trees. Hyakowa took Sergeant Ratliff and Corporal Pasquin to the islet on the north to provide close cover for the divers.

The water was murky, and filled with slowly drifting leaves, twigs, and other organic detritus. Schultz realized immediately that even with goggles he was going to have to find the caves by feel because he wouldn't be able to see an opening. He regretted not being able to use a light to help his search—they didn't know what frequencies the skinks saw in, and so didn't know what frequencies they couldn't detect either. At least he only had to search where the bigger vegetation, the mangrove-things, grew to the water's edge, he thought. The ground sloped too smoothly everywhere else for cave mouths to form and hold. And he wasn't doing it all alone. Claypoole and MacIlargie were in the water with him. In Schultz's opinion, neither one was yet a great Marine, but they were both good and they both tried hard. The only problem with having them in the water with him was that Corporal Pasquin was the closest man covering them on the surface. Schultz didn't trust Pasquin. But then, Schultz didn't trust anyone who hadn't proven himself on at least a couple of operations with him.

The three Marines in the water were armed only with knives. Even though their blasters could fire underwater, the heat from the plasma bolt would instantly turn the water into steam and vapor along its path, and in a confined space might parboil the man firing it. Knives were the only weapons they had they could use underwater.

What if the skinks are in water-filled caves? Claypoole wondered. They have gills, they can breathe underwater. We won't be able to fight them. It didn't register on him that the acid from the skinks' weapons would not be as effective underwater. If it had, he would have worried that they had other weapons that did work submerged.

It was difficult work, even though the breathing apparatus the medical team jury-rigged for them from oxygen bottles and surgical tubing allowed them to stay below without worrying about coming up for air every couple of minutes. The roots of the trees were gnarled, forming a three-dimensional web that might have been constructed by a battalion of maddened spiders.

"If a space is too small for you to fit through easily," Bass had said, "don't worry about it. Most of the skinks are smaller than us, but they've got some giants. The openings to their caves have to be big enough to let their big ones get through."

So they didn't worry about the tight spots, just searched as methodically as they blindly could through the mad spider's castle for spaces between the roots that would easily admit their bodies. For nearly an hour, every time they found an opening between the roots, it led to a gushy, slimy wall of mud held in place by rootlets. Then Claypoole felt a current of water. He backed out of the space he was in and floundered to the surface.

"I think I found something," he gasped as soon as he spit out his mouthpiece.

Schultz checked out the tunnel. There was a sinkhole several meters in diameter that angled downward under the bank, beneath the roots. Its oval quickly narrowed until it was less than a meter on its long axis and not quite as wide in the other direction. Schultz felt the walls of the tunnel and knew it had been made or improved—it had a lining of some woven material. The tunnel went down at a forty-five-degree angle for several meters, then leveled out for several more before angling up. He stopped as soon as he realized he was almost able to see in the water. He stopped breathing when the bubbles of his breathing apparatus popped on the surface; anyone watching the water's surface would see them. Schultz eased back into the level part of the tunnel, where his bubbles rose to the ceiling. When no one had come into the tunnel to investigate the bubbles after five minutes, he took a deep breath, held it, and swam forward once more. Still underwater, craning his neck, he saw the surface ripple. The tunnel widened as it neared its top. No shadows appeared on the surface. He rose until his face was barely submerged, and slowly turned around. He was in an apparently empty room with what looked like a glowball mounted high in one corner, but he was too low to be able to see the lower half of the room. Still holding his breath, he let himself drift up the last few inches and soundlessly broke the surface. As quietly as he could, he breathed deeply.

He made no attempt to climb out; he slowly turned around again and realized he was right to stay in the water. The room wasn't large, only three or four meters in diameter, nothing more than a vestibule, with a tunnel about a meter and a half high and wide leading from it. A skink guard sat next to that one exit. Schultz wanted to spit in disgust; the guard wasn't watching, he was doing something with what might have been a personal computer. *Dummy,* Schultz thought. With one surge he could be out of the water and kill the skink before it reacted or gave any warning. Schultz's fingers flexed on his knife, but he decided against action. He could hear low growling from beyond the tunnel exit. It would take the platoon time to prepare its assault on the cave, and the dead guard might be found before then.

Satisfied he'd learned as much as he could, Schultz lowered himself below the surface, doubled over and aimed himself downward. He checked the time and took hold of the sides of the tunnel to propel himself along. He didn't use his breathing apparatus, not because he thought his bubbles would alert the unalert guard, but to see how hard it would be to traverse the tunnel without breathing. There were only three breathers, and if more than three Marines would be going in, they would have to hold their breath. Schultz determined that it was a short swim, half a minute. Nobody should have a problem.

The watcher fretted. Her instructions had been clear: notify the fighter inside the cave entrance as soon as the Earth barbarians passed the pond, then return to her position and watch for any others that might follow. But the barbarians didn't pass the pond, they stopped. While she considered whether she should notify the waiting fighter that the barbarians weren't moving on, they got between her and the cave entrance. So she couldn't notify the fighter. All she could do was follow her original instructions and wait for the barbarians to move on so she could do her duty. But what if the Earth barbarians didn't move on? If they went back, she could notify the fighter of that, that was within the scope of her instructions. If they found the cave entrance, they could go in without those inside having any warning. And then what? Except for a few watchers, all of the People were in the caves. She would not have done her duty. But no one had told her to notify the fighter if the Earth barbarians entered the caves.

She pondered the problem for a long time before she realized the fallacy in her thinking. The Earth barbarians did not have gills; they could not enter the caves because the cave entrance was through a water-filled tunnel. Her gills fluttered gently with relief. Everything was fine. She would wait until the barbarians moved on, and then notify the fighter inside the entrance.

"That's what we're going to do," Bass said, concluding his briefing. "Any questions?"

The only questions anyone had concerned the layout inside the caves and how many skinks were in there. But realizing that nobody had the answers, no one asked.

"So who's going first?" Bass said. He knew that being the first in could be suicide, and he didn't want to make that assignment.

Schultz gave Bass a look that said he'd asked a stupid question. He, of course, would be the first one in.

"I'll go," Baccacio said.

Bass gave him a searching look.

Baccacio smiled crookedly. "If I get killed, it won't be any loss to you, and it'll warn you that someone's waiting."

Out of the corner of his eye Bass saw Schultz nod slowly one time. "You follow Schultz," he said. "Once everybody's in, stay out of the way. You aren't in chameleons."

"My fire team next," Corporal Kerr said.

Bass looked at Claypoole and MacIlargie, who appeared grimly ready. "You got it," he said. "Me next. The rest of second squad in the middle, then Staff Sergeant Hyakowa. First squad brings up the rear." Bass had already told them the gun squad and medical team would remain outside.

"You have to have a corpsman along," Doc Horner said. "Do you want me with you or with the platoon sergeant?"

Schultz went first. He carried a breathing unit but didn't use it. At the bottom of the tunnel he set it down and made sure it was securely fastened to its rock anchor. It was there in case anyone behind him had a problem. Ten seconds behind him, Baccacio followed. He trailed a rope that they would secure to something in the entry chamber, and each man behind the lead team would pull himself along the rope instead of free swimming. The ex-Marine carried his own blaster; Kerr, behind Baccacio, carried his own and Schultz's. Claypoole and MacIlargie followed Kerr at close intervals. Then Bass waited anxiously for the tug on the rope that would tell him the chamber was secure and he should bring the rest of the platoon through.

Schultz approached the end of the tunnel the same way he had the first time, and took the same precautions. Again he saw nothing from a few inches below the surface, so he slowly drifted upward. Before he reached the surface he saw the shadow of Baccacio rise almost level with him and put a hand on Baccacio's shoulder to stop him. Schultz's face eased out of the water and he slowly turned in a circle. The same guard sat looking at the same something in his hands. Hardly raising a ripple, Schultz moved toward the edge of the tunnel mouth closest to the guard and lifted his hands out of the water. As soon as they touched the floor inside the chamber, he surged out of the pool and lunged at the startled guard.

The guard opened his mouth to cry out, but Schultz was on him too fast and knocked him hard against the wall. One hand held the skink in place while the other slashed his knife across the base of the skink's throat. The skink's arms flailed about and his feet pounded on the floor while his torso twisted under the pressure of Schultz's hand. His gill slits opened wide as his gills struggled to draw oxygen from the air. Schultz pulled his knife hand back and plunged the blade chest-high into the skink and twisted. The skink suddenly went rigid, then slumped. Schultz lowered it to the floor, and it lay motionless save for the blood that flowed out of it.

Baccacio looked at him oddly. "You knew he had gills, why'd you cut his throat?"

"He had a voice. Keep him from yelling." He looked through the opening of the lone tunnel leading from the chamber. "The doctor's got her specimen."

"Yeah." For lack of anything else, Baccacio tied the rope to the skink corpse. He yanked on it. In two more minutes both squads had crowded inside the chamber.

CHAPTER
TWENTY-NINE

The short tunnel ended in a T a few meters in. It had the same kind of woven covering as the underwater tunnel and the entry chamber. Light came from both branches of the T. Bass thought the skink voices did too. "Here goes," he murmured, and lowered himself full length along the tunnel. He pulled himself forward on his elbows until his head was at the far end and cautiously looked in both directions. To the right, the tunnel turned or ended in the corner of a room; he couldn't tell which. Voices came from that direction. To the left, the tunnel widened into a room where skinks were sitting cross-legged around a low table, talking and eating what looked like raw fish and something grainy and white. He counted seven skinks, one more elaborately dressed than the others. Then he noticed that all seven carried swords tucked inside sashes around their waists.

Swords? None of the skinks that attacked them on the ridge had carried swords. And the pirates hadn't said anything about seeing skinks with swords, though Snodgrass had said something about the skink officer handling a stick like it was a sword. The swords must be ceremonial, Bass decided. Perhaps the meal was as well. Two other skinks came into view, females, if they were right about the images in the locket. They carried bowls and wore gowns that fell to their feet. They kneeled next to the table and ladled more food into the serving dishes on it. The elaborately dressed skink growled several words. The two females bowed low then stood, still holding the bowls, and backed away, out of Bass's view.

Suddenly, one of the skinks looked in his direction. Before Bass could pull his head back from the tunnel intersection, the others jerked their eyes toward him.

What's going on? he asked himself. Can they see in the infrared? There was a barked shout, then a sharp *whisp*. Hearing it, Bass had a vision of the skinks drawing their swords.

"Shields up, there's going to be fire," he said rapidly into the platoon circuit.

Nineteen Marines and the corpsman, plus Baccacio and Minerva, were crowded into the tiny chamber. They had no room to move. If the skinks managed to fire an acid thrower into it, they'd have mass casualties. If the Marines fired, plasma would be bouncing everywhere, flashing the skinks and frying some Marines as well.

There was no room for Bass to back up. Marines were crowded even at his feet, waiting for him to move on so they could leave the entry chamber. But he couldn't leave, and footsteps were coming toward him. He heard a few growled words—whoever was coming was calling to the dead guard.

He had no time, he had no choice. If he waited for the skink to come closer, he was dead and so were his Marines. Bringing his blaster to bear, Bass braced his feet against the sides of the tunnel and pushed forward until his head and shoulders were in the connecting tunnel.

A skink, bent slightly under the low roof of the tunnel and holding a sword, was scuttling toward him. Bass pressed the firing lever, and a wave of heat from the skink-flash washed over him. In the glare he glimpsed skinks pulling back, trying to get away from the fire.

Footsteps raced at him from the other direction and a guttural voice cried, *"Bungee!"* Bass started to twist around, but knew the charging skink was too close and he was about to be sprayed by an acid gun or chopped by a sword.

A body thudded into his side and he heard the sharp

crackle of a hand-blaster next to his head, followed by a wave of heat washing over him from the right. When he twisted around, he saw Baccacio laying next to him in the tunnel intersection.

"You told me to stick close to you," Baccacio said, then looked back down the right-side tunnel as Bass looked to the left.

"Tunnel's clear," Baccacio said.

"So's mine," Bass said. Where the skink had vaporized, the walls were singed and small flames licked at the matting. He switched back to the platoon circuit. "No one's in sight now. Squad leaders, each of you assign one man to stay with the doc. First squad, follow me, we're going down the left tunnel. Staff Sergeant Hyakowa, take second squad down the right tunnel. Everybody keep your shields up, when we fire, there'll be plasma bouncing all over the place, and we don't need any casualties from friendly fire."

"What about the dead skink?" Hyakowa asked.

"Leave it with Doc Horner. We'll get it out later. Now let's do it!"

He scrambled the rest of the way out of the tunnel then ducked low and darted into the room with the low table. As he raced through the room he saw a small skink huddled against a side wall. He flamed the skink before he noticed it was one of the females. He came up against the far wall and flattened himself against it, taking in everything in the room. Baccacio flattened himself against the wall a couple of meters away.

The room was bigger than the entry chamber, about five meters deep and a bit wider. Pillars shored up the ceiling. Woven mats covered the floor. The walls and ceiling had the same covering as the tunnels and were springy to the touch. Bass guessed the covering kept the walls from crumbling, and maybe provided structural support to the tunnels and chambers as well. The room's furnishings were spare. Low cushions surrounded the table. Four smaller, flimsy-looking tables with vegetation displays on them flanked dark tunnel mouths on the side walls. He briefly lowered his infra screen and saw first squad still in the tunnel.

He looked at the tunnels leading from the room. Did he dare split the squad and go both ways? He raised a hand and let his sleeve slide down so his men could see his hand signal. Stay put, he signaled, then dropped his sleeve back into place. He padded to one exit and listened. He heard a slow, echoing drip, as if the exit opened into a great, empty cavern. Staying close to the wall, he padded to the other end of the room. There the sound was tight, as though the tunnel squeezed shut just where the light ended. Still, he heard intermittent whispers, rustles of cloth, a barely audible metallic *clink*. He bared his arm, signaled "This way," then stepped into the dark tunnel and slid the light amplifier screen into place.

Immediately he could see that the tunnel continued for ten meters or more. Two other tunnels branched from each side before the main tunnel opened into another room. There was no one in that room. The branching tunnels would be tricky; they faced each other across the main one. He stopped just short of the first pair and looked back. Baccacio was right behind him and signaled that he'd check one while Bass checked the other. Bass shook him off. Baccacio was visible, since he wasn't wearing chameleons. "Schultz up," he said into the squad circuit, then looked at a blank place on the wall so he could spot Schultz's movement in his peripheral vision. Using touches, he told Schultz to check one side while he checked the other. He felt Schultz's tap acknowledging the instructions.

The two Marines lowered themselves to the matted floor and peered around the corners. The two "tunnels" were just entryways only a meter long, shorter than they were high or wide, which opened into empty rooms. Bass lifted into a crouch and bolted into his room, spinning around as he entered it so he could command the whole space quickly. Low platforms lined the room; probably beds, he thought. A chest-high shelf that ran around the walls above the platforms held what looked like personal objects. It was an unoccupied barracks room. Without disturbing anything, he returned to the tunnel. Schultz had found the same in his chamber. The two eased along the tunnel and checked the next two side tunnels the same way, with the same discoveries. The room at the end of the tunnel had a higher ceiling than the others they'd seen, nearly two meters. Its furnishings were larger versions of the platforms in the smaller barracks rooms.

Bass was deciding what to do next when Schultz hit him hard enough to send him flying back into the tunnel. A stream of acid splatted against the wall near where he'd been standing. Almost simultaneously, Schultz fired his blaster and the other tunnel flashed with the brilliance of a skink vaporizing.

Schultz raced across the chamber, dove onto the oversize platform next to the tunnel and angled his blaster to fire into it. He sprayed several bolts into the tunnel and was rewarded by an answering flash as another skink flared into oblivion. The rest of the squad ran in behind him and took up positions that would allow them to fire at the tunnel without hitting each other.

Second fire team formed the squad's rear point. Corporal Pasquin stationed Godenov in one of the barracks room entrances and himself opposite it to watch the rear. He put Dean just inside the main tunnel to link between them and the rest of the squad.

Godenov's position let him see a moving shadow in the room with the table. "Heads up, someone's coming," he said into the fire team circuit. He took aim down the tunnel; so did Pasquin. Dean ducked into the larger barracks room and took cover behind a corner before edging far enough out to look back where they'd come from. More shadows shifted in Godenov's vision.

"Are you sure?" Pasquin asked over the fire team net; he couldn't see anything from where he was.

"Moving shadows," Godenov answered.

"Izzy sees shadows behind us," Pasquin reported on the squad circuit.

"Keep everybody in place," Bass ordered Sergeant Ratliff, then ran to the other corner of the main entrance, opposite Dean.

"Who sees anything?" he asked.

"I saw a shadow move," Dean said. "Can't swear it's a skink, but the lights in that room were steady when we were there."

Bass grunted. Dean was right about the steady light. It was very possible someone had come out of the other exit from that room. Or someone might be coming from the tunnel Hyakowa had taken second squad down. He decided to check with them.

"Lander Five, this is Six," he said into the command circuit. He wasn't surprised when only static answered him; the radios couldn't transmit very far underground. He had no way of knowing how second squad was doing, or of calling them for assistance.

He thought a shadow humped briefly along the floor and asked Godenov, "Did you see that?"

"Yeah. Someone's getting closer."

"Recon," Pasquin murmured as he slipped out of his niche. "Silent, invisible, deadly." It was the motto of Force Recon. Pasquin crawled along the tunnel to the next barracks room.

Bass wanted to call him back, but he didn't; they needed to know what was making the shadows move.

"I see three skinks," Pasquin reported. "Two of them are carrying acid guns. They look like they're getting ready to make a rush."

Before Bass could tell him to stay low and not fire unless he was discovered, Pasquin said, "Oh, shit," and flamed one of the skinks. It flared up. The three of them were so close together it ignited the other two. Their combined heat was great enough to explode the acid canister of the one he shot. Globules and droplets of greenish fluid sprayed all around the room and into the tunnel.

"I think they knew I was here," Pasquin reported, his voice shaky. "One of them pointed its weapon at me."

"Anybody else in there?"

Pasquin gave a nervous laugh. "I don't think so. That acid sprayed around too much when the tank went off. Anyone else in there had to be hit by it." As he spoke he was drawing his knife to dig out a globule of acid that was eating its way to the bone of his left arm. He glanced quickly into the tabled room. His nose was assailed by a sharp odor, and the floor was coated with a film of green. He didn't think he'd be able to safely cross the room to get back to the entry chamber for Doc Horner to see to his injury.

"Unless they've got some way of protecting themselves, nobody's following us from that direction until the acid neutralizes." Smoke was beginning to waft from the walls near the vaporized skinks.

Bass, unaware that he had a casualty, rolled over to look the other way. The only threat he saw was his own Marines.

"Hammer?"

"Let's go get 'em," Schultz snarled. He'd heard Pasquin's report. If they didn't have to worry about their rear, they could move faster. He assumed the skinks had a bolt hole and were headed for it, so the Marines had to move fast.

"Move it out," Bass said. He hurried into position behind Schultz, in front of third fire team.

Second fire team continued to bring up the rear. Pasquin was the last man in the column. He was walking backward, watching the rear—he didn't want anyone to see him working on his wound, didn't want anyone to know he'd been hit. He grimaced when he looked at the wound, where flesh was bubbling and fizzing into a viscous liquid. It drained when he tipped his arm to let it run and there was almost no blood; the acid effectively cauterized the walls of the wound. The pain was decreasing; he figured the acid was destroying nerve endings. He wondered if cutting away the flesh at the sides of the wound would get rid of the acid more effectively than simply digging out the green fluid.

The tunnel beyond the room with the high ceiling had no openings off it. It quickly turned left, then right again after a few meters, then right again, then sloped sharply down. From the top it looked like it leveled off when it reached a depth below the floor of the tunnel they were in. Bass wondered why it wasn't filled with water; it had to be far below the water table. He touched the side of the tunnel. The woven covering resisted the pressure of his fingers. He guessed it had an impermeable layer under it to keep out water. He wondered if that tunnel began as a natural formation like the rest of the complex or if the skinks had dug it, then he discarded the thought as immaterial.

The tunnel leveled out for several meters and began to rise. Second squad was coming down the other slope.

"You're positive you didn't overlook a passageway they could have gone down?" Bass asked Hyakowa after getting his report. They had their screens up so they could see each other's faces.

"Damn right I'm positive. Are you sure *you* didn't miss any?" There was a touch of heat in Hyakowa's voice. "Besides, they were in front of us the whole time."

"Only the one going in the opposite direction." Bass knew Hyakowa wouldn't miss anything. He hunkered back on his heels, wondering where the skinks could have gone. He had climbed the other slope and held a squad leaders' meeting to bring all four leaders up to date on everything. Both squads had followed skinks, both squads had been shot at, and both had killed skinks. No casualties—Bass still didn't know about Pasquin. The complex was roughly circular, with a continuous tunnel cutting through some rooms, and other rooms branching off it. The only place they hadn't checked was the tunnel off the tabled room, and that was in the opposite direction from where the skinks had gone. So where were the skinks they'd both followed?

"Teleportation?" Bladon asked.

"What?"

"They seem to have something superior to a Beam drive. They seem to be able to detect us even in our chameleons.

They've got guns that fire an acid our med-sci team says can't exist. They've got both lungs and gills. Why *not* teleportation?"

Bass looked at Ratliff. "When this is over I want you and Sergeant Kelly to straighten him out. Teleportation smacks too much of the occult." Still, he wondered if Bladon could be right. Teleportation, no matter how wild the idea was, sounded like the only explanation.

"Nah," Bladon said. "Forget about teleportation. None of us saw anything that could be a transponder station."

Bass glared at Bladon, wondering if he could get away with slugging him.

A shout from the bottom of the tunnel snapped him back. "What is it?" he called back, already on his feet and heading down.

Goudanis was at the bottom of the tunnel looking at a spot low on the wall. Bass looked at it and didn't see anything to catch his attention; it was simply the same weaving that covered the rest of the interior of the complex.

"Listen," Goudanis said, and smacked the palm of his hand against the wall near the top. Then he hit the wall near the floor. The top of the wall sounded solid, the bottom gave a dull thump—it sounded hollow.

"How . . . ?"

Goudanis shrugged. "When I was a kid, I was fascinated by medieval history. I remembered reading stories with castles that had secret passageways—with doors so cleverly hidden you couldn't see them even when you knew where they were. We should have caught the skinks in a pincer, but they weren't here. They had to go somewhere. Why not a hidden passage?"

Bass looked at him with admiration. "I knew promoting you was a good idea." He squatted down and used his magnifier screen to look at the wall. After a moment he noticed a faint break in the weave. He traced it around. It made a near-perfect circle that began more than half a meter above the floor and overlapped the floor. Even though he probed, he couldn't find a latch or hinge.

"It's just big enough to let one of the big skinks through," he said.

Bass called Hyakowa and the squad leaders down to see what Goudanis had discovered. He marked the circle with a stylus so it was clearly visible, then told them, "Everybody on the upper level. I want one man from each squad in a position to see this. On my signal they're to flame it, then back off. We don't know what's on the other side, so it's important for them to get out of the way as soon as they fire. Got it?"

They all nodded.

"Do it."

A couple of minutes later everyone was on the upper level. Schultz was halfway down on one side, Kerr on the other. Both were far enough upslope that they couldn't see each other. It was Kerr's responsibility to tell Schultz when to fire.

"Ready, Hammer?" Kerr asked.

"Always," Schultz growled.

"On three. One, two, three!" They fired simultaneously and leaped up the tunnel, out of the way of whatever might happen next.

At first there were just a few crackles as the weaving around the hidden doorway burned.

"Take a look," Bass ordered.

Schultz went headfirst, down far enough to see the hidden doorway. "It's gone," he reported. He stayed in place, blaster to his shoulder, ready to flame anything that emerged. "I see smoke."

They heard a snapping and crackling and tensed, ready for action.

"It's burning," Schultz said after they listened to the sounds for a moment.

"What?" Bass asked.

"Where we blasted it. The matting's burning." He paused. "So's the dirt behind it."

Bass dropped to his belly and slid down to see for himself. Small flames flickered around the edges of the burnt matting. Tendrils of smoke drifted up from the flames and began easing up the ceiling of the tunnel.

Bass swore. The smoke would rise and drive the Marines out of the underground complex, but would leave the skinks untouched, wherever they were. Then something about the burning dirt caught his eye and he used his magnifier and light amplifier. He'd been right about the walls of the lower tunnel being permeated with a waterproofer. Water was beginning to seep through the walls where they were scorched by the plasma bolts. He saw something else as well—a dense smoke was dribbling from around the charred area where tiny flames flickered, smoke dense enough to sink rather than rise. The waterproofer was volatile and could burn.

"You see what I see inside?"

Schultz grunted.

"Come on." Bass slithered down to the opening. Schultz passed him on the way down and already had his blaster aimed into the hidden passageway when Bass reached it. This tunnel led down at an acute angle and seemed to widen at the bottom. Is there a room down there? Bass wondered. Is that where they are? The heavy smoke was spreading and thinning along the widened area. He heard a muffled cough.

"Let's scorch the walls," he whispered. "Don't hit them directly, I don't want to go far enough into the walls to start the water coming through, just get the waterproofer burning."

"Good," Schultz said. He readied his blaster to give the wall a grazing shot and waited for Bass's command.

"Now," Bass said, and pressed his blaster's firing lever.

Two bolts of plasma skittered along the mid-line of the downward tunnel walls. The matting flamed up along the path of the bolts and burned with tiny flames at the scorched edges. At the bottom more matting sparked into tiny flames. The exposed dirt began to steam and more smoke dribbled from the walls.

"Do it again," Bass ordered. Both of them raised up slightly and burned swathes just above the first. "Again." They dropped and fired bolts along the bottom of the walls. In seconds thick smoke was flowing slowly from the entire length of both walls.

They heard more coughing. A skink voice rose in demand. Another voice snapped back. More coughing. Many voices shouted. Great coughing. A scream that might have been an order. Then the sound of movement and shadows swiftly grew at the bottom of the tunnel.

Bass and Schultz each fired one bolt, then scrabbled back up to where first squad waited. Light and heat blasted up the hidden tunnel. More smoke flowed up from below, and soon the overhead was covered with a drifting cloud. The Marines waited.

Bass knew he'd have to send someone down there to make sure the skinks were all dead, and to find out if they had another exit from whatever space was down there. That was going to be dangerous. Not only because of any skinks that might lay in wait, but because of the dense smoke that had to be filling the lower chamber. He had no idea what effects that smoke could have on a man. The chameleon uniform would provide some protection from it, unless it was acidic enough to eat through the fabric. He'd have to send someone back into the entry tunnel to retrieve a breathing unit because the smoke might damage lungs. Better do that now, he decided.

"Wang," he said into the command circuit, "send someone back to retrieve a breather from the water."

"Roger," Hyakowa replied.

Bass waited with growing apprehension for the breathing unit to arrive. Smoke was filling the tunnels, and the light in the connecting tunnel wavered as the flames ate at the weaving. He wondered whether the man Hyakowa had sent would get back before the smoke filled the tunnels and they had to withdraw.

His thoughts were yanked away from the breathing unit and the growing smoke by jabbering from below. Live skinks *were* still down there. He heard the thud of feet, then a giant skink burst out of the hidden tunnel and turned left, crawling very fast toward Hyakowa and second squad. Bass fired at it, but the skink was out of his sight almost before he pressed the lever. But his bolt did hit a second giant skink that was just pulling itself out of the tunnel and turning toward him. The wave of heat from the flaring giant took away his breath and almost knocked him back. More of the matting flamed up. Then there was a chain-reaction of flashes from the tunnel to the lower chamber, and a few screams were sharply cut off. The tunnel must have been filled with skinks, he thought, all of whom flashed. He clearly heard the crackle of fire, then flames leaped out of the lower tunnel followed by a dark plume of acrid smoke.

"Out!" Bass roared. "Everybody get out!" Instantly, all the Marines turned and raced back the way they'd come. Behind them flames shot along the tunnels, hungrily eating at the walls and giving off billows of smoke.

"What's happening?" Doc Horner asked when MacIlargie reached the entry chamber.

"We had them trapped, maybe all killed," MacIlargie gasped. "The Gunny wants the breather." He barely noticed the dead skink laid out next to the entry pool, where it could be easily pulled into the water and out and given to Dr. Bynum.

"I'll get it," said Quick. He removed his helmet and stepped into the water. He was back in a moment, tossing the jury-rigged breathing unit out of the water, when his eyes popped wide and, still in the water, he shouted a warning.

The servant huddled in the service room. She had gone demurely when dismissed and waited patiently to be ordered to bring more food or drink. The drip of water soothed her during her wait. Then the Master had shouted and she heard the leaders prepare to fight. She heard a blast that could only come from one of the Earth barbarian's forever guns, and she heard feet running away from her. She cowered with fear as feet thudded into the Master's quarters. Her side receptors told her one of the barbarians looked into the serving room, but she was in a corner and he didn't see her in the darkness. Then the feet thudded away, following the Master and the leaders who had been dining with him. They went in the direction of the leaders' quarters. Forever guns shot and shot again. Soon after, she heard the three fighters in the hidden chamber move into the Master's quarters to follow the barbarians, then the horrid, horrid, sound of a forever gun. She saw the brilliant flash as the three fighters went into oblivion. Then the barbarians thudded farther away and she heard no more.

What was she to do? She was a servant, not even a watcher. All she knew was to wait patiently and do the bidding of whomever she served. But somewhere deep inside her was an atavistic need to do something. If only she knew what was happening elsewhere.

After what seemed a long time, it slowly dawned on her that the Earth barbarians must have come in through the entry tunnel. How they might have done that, she did not know, since the barbarians could not breathe underwater. Still, she had heard no digging. She had not heard a forever gun before the Master realized the barbarians were there and shouted orders. The Earth barbarians must have somehow taken the guard prisoner. Oh, the shame of it! She must do something to free him. But what could she do? She was a servant and knew nothing of fighting; she didn't even have a weapon.

Then her eyes lit on something a leader had forgotten in the serving room: a forever gun taken from the smaller barbarian settlement. Yes, she could take that and use it to free the fighter from his shame.

She stood, lifted the blaster from the pegs it rested on, and softly padded toward the entry chamber. She ignored the agony in her feet where she stepped in acid; her pain had to be less than that of the captured fighter. She stepped into the chamber. No barbarians were there, but the fighter who guarded the entry lay dead next to the water. Then a face appeared above the water.

* * *

MacIllargie spun toward the tunnel and dodged to the side when Quick shouted. A small skink stood there holding a blaster. He fired and it flared up, but not before firing the blaster it held. Its bolt hit the dead skink guard and its corpse flared up.

"Anybody hurt?" Doc Horner cried.

"I'm okay," MacIlargie said.

"I wasn't anywhere near it," Rowe said.

"Shit!" Quick swore.

Doc Horner saw that the side of his face was scorched from the blast that had flared the skink corpse. He pulled Quick out of the water, then grabbed his medkit and began working on the burns.

MacIlargie ran out with the breathing unit, back to where the rest of the squad waited. A moment later he came stumbling back in with Corporal Linsman behind him.

"Get out," Linsman shouted. "The whole damn place is on fire."

CHAPTER
THIRTY

Gunnery Sergeant Bass called the *Fairfax County* and asked for digging equipment. Captain Tuit sent down a digger in a combat landing and the Marines had it in less than an hour. While waiting for it, the Marines watched for smoke seeping through the ground. The digger operator immediately set to work on the most promising smoke holes, and in a couple of hours had enough of them fully opened to allow the smoke to rise as quickly as the fire-heated air would lift. After a time no more smoke came out of the underground complex.

Unwilling to go below so late in the day, and until he was sure the air was clear, Bass set the platoon up in a double security perimeter, some facing the island to watch for any skinks that might still be alive and try to escape, the others watching outward. Tomorrow would be soon enough to go back down.

"Where's my prisoner, Charlie?" Dr. Bynum demanded as soon as she was able to corner him.

He shook his head. "I'm sorry, Lidi. We had a corpse for you, but one of them had a blaster and flamed it before we could bring it out." He shook his head again. "I was glad we got the corpse, even if we couldn't capture one alive. It would have given us a lot of information—including why they vaporize when they're hit by a blaster bolt."

She stared at him searchingly and decided he really had wanted to bring one of them out for her.

After a long silence, Bass asked, "Do you have any idea why they flare up like that when they're hit by a blaster bolt?"

She shrugged and shook her head.

"Could their body chemistry be radically different from ours, based on something more volatile than carbon?"

"Charlie, be serious. Can you think of an element more volatile than oxygen? Oxygen's not the base of our chemistry, but it's so thoroughly integrated into it that we can't live more than a few minutes without it."

He grunted. After another moment he asked, "Can you think of anything?"

She considered it, then said, "Their body temperatures are a bit lower than ours, yet they don't seem any more bothered by the tropical heat than we are. They live at least part of the time in water, and water leeches out warmth. Maybe they have a much higher level of body oil than we do. I don't know."

She lost herself in thought again, then sighed. It was the first time people had met an alien intelligence, and they killed it. Well, the first time that she knew of.

"Will we see them again?" she asked, knowing the answer.

"Yes."

"What will happen then?"

"They'll try to kill us."

"What will we do?"

"We'll kill them."

"Will we shoot first?"

"Maybe. I don't know." He paused in thought. "Maybe," he finally continued, "this group had a rogue commander. Maybe the next time they'll try to talk before they start killing."

"Will you Marines allow them to talk?"

"Lidi, Marines fight and kill, that's our job. But Marines aren't usually sent in until there is violence, or until violence seems inevitable. They probably won't run into Marines first."

Dr. Bynum shook her head and slowly walked away. Something told her the skinks hadn't had a rogue commander. She felt that when people met the skinks again, there would be more killing, more unnecessary death.

In the morning Bass led second squad back down into the complex. This time they rappeled down a rope through a digger hole. They took lights with them.

The place was hardly recognizable. All of the weaving on the walls had burned, as had the floor matting and most of the spartan furnishings. In the lowest area, the waterproofing had burned away and partially collapsed the walls. Bass didn't dare send anyone down to investigate the chamber where the skinks had briefly secreted themselves before Corporal Goudanis discovered the hidden door. They came upon quite a few small rooms behind concealed doors. Several of them gave evidence that skinks had been there when the fire swept through. Bass wondered in passing if those had been females, and if any of them had been juveniles. He was disturbed at the fanaticism of the skinks, that they all died rather than surrender or try to escape, when staying meant death was inevitable.

The Marines poked and prodded the ashes in each of the rooms, looking for artifacts. But there was nothing to find; everything had been reduced to ash. Bass wondered why a species that vaporized when burned would build and decorate with materials that burned so thoroughly. Maybe they had used only local materials, and the only available, or easily available, materials were flammable. If that was the case, what did they use on their home world? He suspected he'd never know unless he was sent there to fight and kill them.

Finally, satisfied they weren't going to learn anything in the underground complex they didn't already know, he ordered second squad to return to the surface. He was the last one to leave. He stood for a long moment in the room where he'd seen the sword-bedecked skinks eating and let his eyes unfocus into nowhere.

Who were the skinks? Where were they from? What had been their purpose in landing on Society 437, and why had they attacked the scientific mission with no warning? Why hadn't they attempted to open communications? Had they perceived some sort of provocation?

Or had the skinks tried to communicate, perhaps using some form of transmission of which humanity had no knowledge? Had the lack of response convinced them that human beings were hostile and that they needed to make the first strike? Did they think that would convince human beings to reply to their communications?

If that was it, there would be fighting every time humanity and the skinks encountered each other, until someone stumbled across a means of common communication. But what could that be?

The universe is a larger and stranger place than you know, Gunnery Sergeant Charlie Bass, Confederation Marine Corps, he told himself.

Finally, Bass climbed back up the rope into the air.

"Skyhawk, this is Lander Six," he said into Dupont's radio. "Beam us up, Scotty."

EPILOGUE

Bass leaned heavily against the bulkhead of the Dragon, his feet propped up on a ration box. He was tired to the bone. He bit the end off a Clinton, his last until he could get to the supply he'd left on the *Fairfax*, and stuck the unlighted cigar into a corner of his mouth. I really am getting too old for this stuff, he thought. But he always thought that after a mission. Society 437 had been a hard one, but it was over. Did they get all the skinks on Waygone? Would someone run into others again somewhere else in Human Space? He didn't know the answers and, just then, he didn't give a damn.

Dr. Bynum came over and took a seat next to him. She was tired too. "We should think about retiring, Charlie," she said. "What is it you wanted to see me about?"

Bass thought for a moment about retirement with Dr. Bynum. "Both of us? Same time, same place?" He smiled.

Dr. Bynum smiled back but did not answer.

"Doc, I want you to do me a favor, a big one."

"You name it, Gunny." He leaned across the aisle and spoke quietly for a full two minutes.

"Risky, Charlie," she replied. She thought a moment. "But can do. For you I can do it. Sure. Why not?"

"The Essay that's going to take you back to the *Fairfax* will be here in ten minutes," Bass told Baccacio and Minnie. "I don't have much time, so listen up. You're both going on a very long trip."

Baccacio gave a lopsided grin. "I know, Gunny. The only

thing I ask is that you put in a good word for us. I—We tried our best to make up—"

Bass waved the former ensign into silence. "No time for all of that, Mr. Baccacio. Back on Elneal, well, I could've killed you for what you did then. But you aren't the same guy anymore. I don't know what you are, but you aren't a coward. Here's the situation. Both of you were severely wounded—"

"What . . . ?"

Bass nodded. "You were both seriously wounded. Dr. Bynum does not expect you to recover, but we're sending you back to the *Fairfax*, where she can try to stabilize you in the sickbay."

They stared at Bass with mouths open. Unnoticed by either, HM2 Hardesty stepped up behind them, an injector poised in one hand.

"We will have to put you both into stasis," Bass announced. Hardesty leaned forward, a huge grin on his face, and with two swift movements injected the pair. "When you awake," Bass continued as they crumpled to the floor, "you will be far away from here, but not in jail." But neither heard the rest of the sentence that had just been passed upon them.

Bass sighed. If his plan didn't work, his ass would be in a sling for sure. What the hell, he thought, they'd earned the favor.

"And I'm telling you," HM1 Horner insisted, "that thing of yours there, that woo, can talk, Dean." HM2 Hardesty, standing behind Horner in the troop bay, nodded vigorously in agreement.

Dean looked at the other Marines gathered around and shrugged. They all nodded. Everyone looked at Owen, which was perched happily on the edge of Dean's bunk. Its huge eyes stared merrily up at the men and he glowed a soft, contented pink. "Doc," Dean replied, "he's never said anything to me in all the time he's been my companion. The people on Diamunde, who've had woos for hundreds of years, they never heard them talk. Now you tell me Owen said something. What?"

" 'Danger,' " Hardesty replied firmly. "He warned us when a skink tried to come over the ramp of our Dragon, Dean. He hollered 'Danger!' and that's the God's honest truth."

"Owen," Dean said, turning to the woo, "say something. Go on, say something." Owen stared silently back at Dean. The men waited patiently.

"Say something, Owen," Hardesty begged the woo. "Say what you said on the Dragon, Owen. Come on, c'*mon*!" Owen swiveled his head and just stared placidly back at the two corpsmen.

Horner sighed disgustedly. "I give up. But Dean, he did talk, he did."

"Yeah," Dean replied. "Sure. Next you'll tell me you caught him reading a field manual." The other Marines burst into laughter.

The pirates who had stayed behind on Society 437 were transported to the *Fairfax County* in five body bags and two stasis units. The remains of Rhys Apbac, Labaya, Callendar, Sharpedge, and Lowboy were consigned to the morgue for burial in space, following the usual ritual aboard naval vessels. Baccacio and Minerva went into the far corner of a remote medical storage compartment.

"Always liked Marines," Captain Tuit was saying as he and Gunnery Sergeant Bass sipped hot, strong galley coffee on the bridge. "Always liked having you aboard my vessels."

"Always liked navy men myself, sir, especially old salts like you."

"Gunny, you and your men, you did good back on Waygone. You did damn good. So, as commander of this vessel I am taking it upon my own authority to reward you. I had my navigator plot a somewhat different inbound course for us. We're going to come out of our jump in the vicinity of St. Brendan's. Your men and my crew are going to enjoy seventy-two hours of liberty in New Cobh before we head back to home."

Bass's jaw dropped. New Cobh, settled by Irish immigrants two and a half centuries before, was an infamous liberty port beloved by the crews of Confederation Navy and commercial vessels. In New Cobh there'd be plenty of beer and plenty of buxom colleens willing to help the Marines drink it. "Sir, I can't tell you how much—well, thank you, Captain! Thank you very much!"

Tuit laughed and sipped his coffee. "This is my last voyage, Gunny. I've decided to hang it up when we get back. Just as well. They'll have my ass in a sling for delaying our return. The drones will have reached Old Earth by now, and the government's going to be in a real turmoil over what happened on Society 437. They'll want to court-martial me for letting you kill all those nasty skinks instead of negotiating a treaty of friendship with them. And when they find out I took this side trip to reward your men instead of heading straight back, well, there'll be hell to pay." He shrugged. "And to make it even worse, we've got the remains of the exploratory party on board."

"Thank you for excusing my Marines from that graves registration detail, sir," Bass said with feeling. Once the skinks had been dealt with, the crew of the *Fairfax* had formed shore parties to gather the remains of as many of the scientific party as could be found. The remains would be taken back to Old Earth, identified through DNA samples, then returned to their families.

"Somebody's going to accuse me of desecration for not moping all the way back to port playing funeral dirges. Fuck 'em if they can't take a joke. I must be the prize of all the navy screw-ups, Gunny."

"No, sir, you are not. You may be a bit careless of your status on the promotion list, but you, sir, are definitely not a sc—er, you know." He felt a very strong surge of affection for the grizzled old captain. It had been officers like Tuit who'd kept him in the Marines all his adult life, officers who thought first of their men and second of their careers.

"That former ensign of yours, Baccacio, is he going to make it, Gunny?"

"No, sir. Dr. Bynum says no way. She'll keep him and his woman on ice if they don't die before we reach port. Maybe they can do something for them once we're back. But I doubt they'll last that long."

"Damn shame. Baccacio came through in the end, though, didn't he?"

"He did, sir. So did Lieutenant Snodgrass."

Captain Tuit nodded firmly. "Always knew that boy had it in him. All he needed was a swift kick in the ass to get him started in the right direction. Will you go to bat for Baccacio, put a word in for him, if he lives long enough to be turned over to the authorities?"

"You bet, Captain. I owe him that much."

"Well, okay, Gunny, we've got one day standard before we make the jump. We'll get rid of those dead pirates before we go, and if your two are still alive, we'll take them along with us. I'll keep the female pirates in the brig the whole voyage. That's about the only jail they'll see, and it serves them right for hanging out with such bad company."

An hour later Dr. Bynum informed Captain Tuit she'd taken Baccacio and Minerva off life support. He had been listening to Handel and half resented the interruption. He turned to the watch officer. "Notify the padre. Assemble a burial detail. Get it done right away. You preside. Damned if I will, not for a bunch of goddamn pirates. I want the whole shebang over in an hour. Make the standard burial-in-space entry in the log afterward."

"Aye aye, sir," the watch officer answered. "Uh, Captain, do you have the names of the deceased handy?"

"No, Lieutenant," he answered, annoyed the officer would bother him with such a question, "you'll have to get them from the sickbay. Who cares? Good riddance. Don't waste any time on them. Oh, hell, just say 'Deceased pirates consigned,' words to that effect. I don't see any reason to waste any verbiage on a bunch of criminals." Humpf, he thought, junior officers these days can't think for themselves.

After the *Fairfax* made planetfall on St. Brendan's, a group of Marines emerged from the port district to slake their thirst and passion among the bars and bordellos of New Cobh. Two, a man and a woman, shook hands with their comrades and disappeared into the fogbound night. They were not missed when the *Fairfax* resumed its voyage three days later.

Some years after these events, three young men, all brothers, walked into the Confederation Marine Corps recruiting office in New Cobh. They were determined to follow proudly in the footsteps of their deceased father, who had once been an officer of Marines. Their family name was Cameron.

Visit www.delreybooks.com— the portal to all the information and resources available from Del Rey Online.

• Read sample chapters of every new book, special features on selected authors and books, news and announcements, readers' reviews, browse Del Rey's complete online catalog and more.

• Sign up for the Del Rey Internet Newsletter (DRIN), a free monthly publication e-mailed to subscribers, featuring descriptions of new and upcoming books, essays and interviews with authors and editors, announcements and news, special promotional offers, signing/convention calendar for our authors and editors, and much more.

To subscribe to the DRIN: send a blank e-mail to sub_Drin-dist@info.randomhouse.com or you can sign up at www.delreybooks.com

Questions? E-mail us at delrey@randomhouse.com

 www.delreybooks.com